T0323054

SLEEPING DOGS

Also by Russ Thomas

DS ADAM TYLER SERIES

Firewatching
Nighthawking
Cold Reckoning

SLEEPING DOGS

RUSS THOMAS

**SIMON &
SCHUSTER**

London · New York · Sydney · Toronto · New Delhi

First published in Great Britain by Simon & Schuster UK Ltd, 2024

1 3 5 7 9 10 8 6 4 2

Simon & Schuster UK Ltd
1st Floor
222 Gray's Inn Road
London WC1X 8HB

Simon & Schuster: Celebrating 100 Years of Publishing in 2024

Simon & Schuster Australia, Sydney
Simon & Schuster India, New Delhi

www.simonandschuster.co.uk
www.simonandschuster.com.au
www.simonandschuster.co.in

A CIP catalogue record for this book
is available from the British Library

Hardback ISBN: 978-1-3985-0755-5
eBook ISBN: 978-1-3985-0757-9
Audio ISBN: 978-1-3985-0759-3

Typeset in Bembo by M Rules
Printed and Bound in the UK using 100% Renewable
Electricity at CPI Group (UK) Ltd

For Lisa,
And for George,
Together again, somewhere.

24 years ago

Except for the dog, the girl is all alone in the dark.

She lies in an enormous bed, under a blanket, clutching the animal's thick, shaggy hair between her fingers. She can feel his heart beating under his warm skin, his chest rising and falling in rhythm with his breathing. She can hear the soft wheeze of air flowing in and out of his mouth and smell the yucky scent of meat on his breath.

She doesn't really know if it's a boy dog – the men who brought her here didn't tell her its name – but she has decided it is.

He's a big dog, but then, all dogs are big to her. She isn't scared though. She likes dogs.

She doesn't like the men.

Time passes in the dark. The girl doesn't know how long. She has a pink plastic Minnie Mouse watch on her arm, but even if she could see it she isn't very good at telling the time yet. She has no toys to play with. She has nothing but her own thoughts in the dark, and the warmth of the blanket, and the gentle breathing of the dog beneath her hand.

The door opens, and for a moment she thinks it's her mummy she can see in the doorway as she squints against the light. But it isn't her mummy. It isn't one of the men either. It's the scary thin lady who doesn't talk to her.

The thin lady comes straight towards her, leaving the door open. The light from the hallway is blindingly bright, and all the girl can see is a tall, skinny shadow standing over her. A hand reaches down and grabs her arm, pulls her upright. The dog growls and shuffles away as the girl's hand presses down on its stomach.

The woman pushes something wet and sticky against the girl's mouth. She tries to say 'No!', but as her lips part, the cold metal spoon forces its way inside. Without her thinking about it, her tongue scoops up the lump of jam. Then the spoon is gone again, and the woman places a hand over her mouth.

'Swallow it!'

The jam tastes all dirty and bitty, but the girl swallows, and then a nasty taste makes her screw up her face. She doesn't cry though. Her mummy's always telling her not to cry and she wants to be a good girl so that her mummy comes to get her.

The thin lady walks away, and the girl collapses back onto the bed next to the dog. The door closes and the light is swallowed up. The darkness comes back even thicker than before.

Next time the door opens it will be her mummy coming for her and she'll have some proper food with her, pastries and breads and all the lovely foods her mummy makes. Not the strange nasty-tasting jam the thin lady brings. After that, everything will be all right. She yawns.

They might let her keep the dog if she asks nicely. She'll probably get a special treat after this. Because none of this is her fault. She didn't run away. She didn't talk to strangers. She wasn't bad. She won't be punished. She'll be rewarded, for being a good girl. When her mummy comes.

Sleeping Dogs

The girl drifts slowly into sleep. The dog growls and flops a paw across the girl's forearm, its claws pressing deeply into her skin.

sunday

1

Detective Sergeant Adam Tyler slams the car door and presses the lock button on the key fob. He glances up and down the road, scratching absently at the scar on his cheek. It's busy with traffic, even though the afternoon sun is still fighting its way through the treeline and the daily evening commute has barely begun. Whatever the time of day, buses, taxis and cars rattle constantly in both directions along Abbeydale Road, one of the main arteries that connects the centre of Sheffield with the more prosperous suburbs to the south-west. In another hour or so, this artery will be clogged. Tyler intends to be long gone by then.

He turns and looks up at an impressive, if slightly run-down building. The Abbeydale Picture House is awkward in its grandeur, shabby with decades of neglect, perhaps a little ashamed of its glorious past and its uncertain future. It's a peculiar building that he's never paid much attention to before: a tile-clad 1920s cinema that was once the most luxurious 'Picture Palace' in the city but which fell into disuse in the 70s. Since the millennium, restoration plans have changed as often as the organisations attempting to save it, but the building refuses to die. Even now, the late afternoon sun bathes one façade in golden glory while the rest squats in shadow, a fitting tribute to its divided history.

He's always been aware of it, of course. The impressive open dome tower over the corner entrance, the white faïence tiles that clad the exterior. It sits on the brow of a slight hill that causes the road to swerve and drop away from it, at the epicentre of an area that was hipster-chic long before hipster-chic was a thing. Nestled among a variety of international restaurants, antique curio shops and micro-breweries with unlikely names, it stands out, a landmark to which any local would be able to direct you.

But, Tyler thinks, the building's distinctiveness is also part of its anonymity: everyone *knows* it, but does anyone *see* it? Much of it is still in a state of disrepair. Does anyone pay that much attention to who's coming and going? He certainly never has. Among the crowds of commuters and social drinkers, it might not be easy to sneak in here completely unnoticed, but it would be easy to go un-noted.

A sudden vivid image comes to him: craning his neck to get a better look at the tower above while he walks hand-in-hand with his mother, dragging his feet and stumbling over the uneven paving even as she hurries him on, blaming him for a tardiness that only now does he surmise can't have been all his fault. Tyler doesn't remember any family or friends living around this area back then. He wonders idly where they would have been heading in such a hurry. It can't have been long afterwards that his mother walked out on them. Perhaps she'd had a lover nearby.

He shakes off the memory and rounds the building. The main entrance on the corner is boarded up with a contractor's logo and a 'Considerate Constructors' guarantee, but there's a side door off the car park that once led down into the back area of the old underground ballroom. It still has a vintage sign above it, advertising the snooker hall that more recently became a multi-lane shuffleboard venue. This entrance, too, appears to be locked, but Tyler notices the fire door is slightly buckled. He reaches out and hooks a finger behind the metal plate. Glancing around once to see if anyone is going to challenge him, he pulls sharply, and the door swings open with a click.

He hesitates now, knowing he shouldn't be doing this. But the whole place appears closed for renovations, so finding the owner and gaining the relevant permissions might take days, or even weeks. And he has to remind himself – none of this is official yet.

The door opens into a stairwell that was once clearly impressive. The wooden bannister is still largely intact, and the space is decorated expansively with ornate panels of coving. But the effect is spoiled by the lack of any wallpaper or other adornment; the walls are whitewashed, the only colour that of the pitted brickwork visible where the plaster has flaked and fallen away. Hanging heavy over all of this is the smell of damp and mould, and the air has a thick, wet feel to it. The door swings gently closed behind him and, after a few moments waiting for his eyes to adjust to the dark, Tyler gives up and pulls out his mobile, switching on the torch.

He takes the stairs and soon finds himself lost in a labyrinthine network of corridors, doors and anterooms. He had no

idea the building was so big. At one point, on what he hypothe-
sises is probably the third floor, he finds the projection room and
manages to orientate himself. There are two enormous vintage
projectors pointing down through porthole windows that give
him his first partial views of the auditorium. But shortly after
that he's hopelessly adrift again.

Many of the rooms are locked or boarded up, but he tries
each one in case someone could be hiding inside. Most contain
an assortment of junk: pots of paint, boxes, buckets, cleaning
equipment, scaffolding, plywood, ladders ... the list is endless.
But there are many more esoteric items as well. A giant sign that
reads 'Stricly No Entry' in foot-high lettering, abandoned in
the corner of a stairwell, presumably after the spelling mistake
was noticed. A leather three-piece suite in remarkably good
condition, the sole occupant of a room bearing the most beautiful panelling, but painted in the sort of oranges and yellows not
seen this side of the 1970s. Another room filled entirely with
three-foot-long balustrades made of polystyrene. Tyler finds
at least five separate toilets, some seemingly in working order
but others clearly not – one is filled with soil and the brittle,
stick-like corpse of a pot plant. And then, two rooms that are,
apparently, still in use. Dressing rooms, he guesses, for the bands
that play here occasionally. A whiteboard sports the most recent
set list for a band named KornAtak who played a few months
ago. There's a microwave with a half-eaten Pot Noodle next
to it. He checks it for mould and finds none. Recent then. It
would be easy enough for someone to live here, even if it wasn't
very comfortable. The only thing he hasn't seen so far is a bed.

The more he searches, however, the more it dawns on him

how nonsensical the search is. He tries to move quietly, but if there is someone here, they would almost certainly be able to hear him moving about, and more than likely would be able to see his torch. Although many of the areas are lit well enough by external windows, he has to keep it switched on as he frequently turns corners and finds himself suddenly plunged back into darkness.

On his descent from the dressing rooms, Tyler finds himself in what he supposes once passed for backstage. It's an enormous area that stretches the entire width of the building, open all the way to the wooden timbers of the roof a good hundred feet or more overhead. The entire back wall is one enormous expanse of red brick, its sole feature a black metallic ladder leading up into the rafters. Hanging at various levels between the roof and the ground are several gantries made of scaffolding and wooden planks, which seem able to be raised and lowered, providing access to various lights and pieces of equipment.

The opposite wall consists of some sort of temporary panelling that must be the back side of the cinema screen Tyler had seen from the projection room. A door set into the side allows him to step through into the auditorium itself.

It's incredibly impressive, even in its decaying grandeur. A curtain still hangs on either side of the screen, though it's frayed and rotting, and he doubts it will hang much longer. He steps around it carefully, emerging onto the sagging wooden stage. Above him are more of the complicated gantries. He hesitates for a moment, then picks his way forwards tentatively, the ancient boards groaning under his feet. A small flight of steps leads down into the seating, which seems to have fared a bit better over the years. Some of the seats look damp and rimed with mould, but still serviceable. Making his way up the centre aisle, Tyler notices a number of small pools of water. The roof, though largely intact, has been less than efficient at keeping out the most recent storms. He suddenly remembers reading somewhere that all productions have been suspended for the time being while it's checked and repaired, and wonders again if he should even be in here. The whole ceiling could fall in on him at any moment.

The back of the auditorium leads into a bar that's unstocked but otherwise ready for action, and from there he follows a corridor round past some more toilets to the front corner entrance which he'd found locked from the outside. He checks it again from this side, but there's definitely no way to open it without a key. He must have been over most of the place by now and there's no sign of anyone, unless the Pot Noodle counts. But that could just as easily have been left by one of the contractors.

Retracing his steps back to the auditorium, Tyler's mind wanders to Scott and the way they'd left things. He shouldn't have let Scott walk out of the pub like that. If he'd stopped him, they could be curled up together on the sofa right now, jumping at some ridiculous horror film. Tyler has no idea why Scott, an otherwise highly intelligent man, insists on watching these low budget, poorly acted schlock-fests. When he's called out on it, he just smiles, in that slightly infuriating way he has, as though he knows the great secret of life and happiness.

As Tyler circles the expansive hall again, looking into every recess and trying every locked door, he wonders if he should have paid more attention. To the films, to Scott himself. Their relationship has been strained lately and Tyler knows it's his fault. He's never going to win any Best Boyfriend awards but this time things had seemed to be going pretty well, at least for a while. Even the evening TV thing. Before Scott had appeared in his life, all calm, knowing smiles and absolute acceptance, Tyler couldn't remember the last time he'd even switched on his television, let alone made it three seasons through a box set. But Scott was all for wind-down time, and on those evenings that weren't what he called 'Proper Dates', when Tyler inevitably finished work an hour and a half later than he said he would, Scott would grin and let him in and settle back in front of the telly, expecting Tyler to join him. Even the fact that Tyler often brought his laptop with him and tapped away throughout the movie never seemed to upset him. At least, Tyler didn't think it did. Is that what he'd got wrong?

Picking his way back to the stage, he has to admit to himself, he didn't hate those evenings in front of the telly. He was getting used to the warmth of another human being pressed up against him while he worked, Scott's hand snaked around his middle, his right leg tossed casually over Tyler's left, his face burying its way into Tyler's side every time the dramatic strings screeched from the speakers.

But then this case had come along and he'd got predictably obsessed with it. They hadn't argued or fallen out, as such; Tyler had needed space and Scott had given it to him. But how much space was too much?

Their conversation in the pub earlier gives him hope that it isn't too late. When this is over, Tyler promises himself, he'll make things up to Scott. But even as he thinks it, a stark truth hits him. It's never over, is it? There's always something else.

15

A grating sound echoes down from somewhere above the stage and he flicks his torch upward. One of the wooden-planked gantries is swaying slightly.

'Hello?' he shouts up at the ceiling. The light from his phone doesn't reach anywhere near far enough, and all he can make out are banks of shadows. It could be one of the city's homeless who's snuck in here to keep warm for the night. Or it could be someone else. 'I'm Detective Sergeant Adam Tyler of South Yorkshire Police,' he announces into the room, his words echoing back to embarrass him. 'If there's someone else here, you need to make yourself known. You're not in any trouble.' Tyler's voice fades away into the darkness and there's no further sound, other than the faint tolling of bells from the Catholic church up the road. No more sign of movement either, but he can't shake the feeling he's not alone.

Feeling his way over to the side of the stage, he finds another metallic ladder attached to the wall. He puts his foot on the first rung and pulls. The ladder seems solid enough but the anchor points in the mortar shift a little. Tyler's less worried it won't hold his weight than that the whole thing might come away from the wall. Still, he heads up.

The ceiling is much lower on this side of the screen, perhaps only half or less than the distance backstage. At the top, he strains his eyes but it's far darker here with only the torch of his mobile and the odd gap in the roof letting in the faint evening light. He senses more than sees a movement of some sort, and pans the phone across, trying to illuminate the hidden corners on the far side of the gantry.

He inches his way along, testing the wooden planks beneath

his feet with each step before moving on. Looking down at the stage far below, the angle allows him to see a number of holes that hadn't been obvious when he'd crossed it. A thought creeps up to trouble him: no one knows he's here.

Why *is* he here? A suggestion, born of a half-hearted investigation, itself born of an anonymous tip. He likes to believe that's why no one knows; because all of it's so flimsy he hasn't felt the need to tell anyone. But truthfully, he accepts that it's more than that. It's an old pattern of behaviour, one he'd thought – hoped, perhaps – he'd put behind him. The need to play his cards close to his chest, to not include others, to work alone. Things had been different lately: he and Mina had reached an understanding and, though he was unlikely to ever be accused of being an over-sharer, they'd found a way of working together that he thought suited them both. She relentlessly questioned him about everything, and he did his best to supply her with full and frank answers.

But this case is different. He *couldn't* include her, not once he realised what it could mean, and he knows she wouldn't have appreciated him letting anyone else in. So here he is again, falling back into old habits, relying on the tried and tested behaviour of his past. He thought he'd put that man behind him.

There's that movement again. Tyler steps forward, raising the torch. 'Police!' he shouts into the darkness on the far side of the stage. 'Come out.' As he inches forward, the gantry sways under his weight.

He's almost at the end when something launches itself at him from the dark, accompanied by a furious flapping sound. Tyler falls backwards, letting go of the phone as he comes down hard on his behind. The pigeon flutters past his face and settles on a metal lighting rig a few metres above. He hears his mobile hit the stage below with a dull thud and a cracking sound. The light goes out.

'Shit!' he says, the pigeon cooing its derision from above.

He climbs slowly back to his feet, the gantry creaking alarmingly as it swings. He needs to find his way back down before ...

He doesn't see what hits him, just feels the massive blow to the back of his head. His vision clouds, even in the darkness, and suddenly he's shooting forward, the metal scaffolding falling away before him with only the slightest resistance. There's a moment when Tyler is suspended by nothing, tipped forward, arms windmilling, trying to arrest his forward momentum. But then the planks beneath his feet begin to slide backwards and he knows he's lost. There's no way left for him to save himself.

They say your life flashes before your eyes at the end. Tyler isn't sure he's ever believed that, but the tumble into nothingness feels far longer than it should. He sees his father hanging from the bannister in their house all those years ago. He sees Mina shaking her head at him for his stupidity. He sees Doggett raising an eyebrow with characteristic contempt. And he sees Scott, smiling his secret smile, analysing him in ways he never shares. Scott. He's sorry about Scott most of all.

Then he hits the stage.

2

Mina hesitates a moment and then presses the doorbell. She clutches the neck of the wine bottle in her left fist while her right hand fiddles with the top she's wearing, trying to inch it further down her midriff. Why the bloody thing keeps riding up is anyone's guess. She'd spent far longer agonising over choosing an outfit than was warranted, considering the occasion. She'd even briefly considered asking her cousin's opinion. Priti considers herself something of a fashionista and recently started a YouTube channel dedicated to her latest purchases, much to the dismay of a large part of the family. But in the end Mina had decided that any enquiry would have provoked unwanted questions as to the nature of the event. Questions that would lead to answers Priti would most certainly tease her about. Then she'd be fielding enquiries left, right and centre, some of them well-meaning; her Aunties would want to know every painful, excruciating detail. And some of them less so; she could certainly do without Uncle Nazir getting wind of any of this. At least, until *this* was actually a thing. Truth be told, she wasn't entirely sure how any of them would react but she knew they'd all have something to say on the matter. She also knew that telling Priti about it was a sure-fire way of ensuring the rest of the family would know in minutes.

As she shuffles on the doorstep, wondering if she should press the bell again, Mina glances back down the road. The sun has long dropped below the horizon but it's still light enough for her to pick out the taxi that dropped her off, pulling out of the estate back onto the main road. Too late to go back now.

Why am I here?

She hates things like this. *Dinner parties!* It's Mina's idea of hell. Well, maybe not quite that bad, but it certainly isn't her idea of a good time. She doesn't do dinner parties. Any more than she does clubbing or football matches or . . . blind dates! What had she been thinking?

She hasn't been on a date, blind or otherwise, for months. The last guy had been an accountant she'd met through the Salaams app. He'd taken her to a Turkish restaurant on London Road and it hadn't been too bad to begin with. He'd actually been better looking than his profile picture suggested, and although he'd been a little nonplussed when he found out she was police – not only police, but a detective – this hadn't appeared to put him off in any serious way. It usually did.

But then they'd come to ordering. She'd hoped she was going to get away with a simple saksuka, but after several minutes of cajoling, followed by an attempt to recruit the waiter into persuading her to try the lamb kofte, she'd had to make the ultimate confession – that she was vegan. His reaction might have been comical had it not been so utterly mortifying. After a good half an hour focused entirely on why she was wrong, during which time she watched him put away his own weight in meat and cheese, his sheer disbelief that anyone would choose this 'alternative lifestyle' irritated her to such an extent that she'd faked a stomach ache and left. She hadn't heard from him again, thankfully, although she was annoyed he might be thinking it was her delicate sensibilities toward meat-eating that had put her off, rather than his pathetic behaviour. Why couldn't she just have been honest?

After that, and because of work, dating had inevitably fallen by the wayside, and she'd been okay with that. Until now. Emma Ridgeway and her bright ideas. Emma's a very hard person to say no to, even when you have a good reason, and 'I'm not dating at the moment' is not the sort of comment that Emma considers a good reason.

There's the sound of a gate catch clicking somewhere off to the right and Mina backtracks to look around the side of the house.

'It *is* her!' shouts a loud voice, and a relatively small woman – it isn't as though Mina is all that big herself – emerges with a frown on her face. 'I told her that was the bell but she never bloody listens to a word I say.'

Mina's only met Leigh Radden a couple of times in passing, usually when she's been picking Emma up after a night out. But on all those occasions she was little more than a figure behind a darkened windscreen. This is the first time she's seen the woman up close, although her face is familiar enough from the TV.

'Mina,' Leigh says, smiling now and reaching for her hand. 'We meet properly at last!'

Mina expects a handshake, but in fact Leigh clasps Mina's hands in her own and grips them fondly. At least, Mina thinks it's meant to be fond, but there's something about the woman's smile that looks false. There's no warmth in her eyes at all. Then Leigh has her arm around Mina's shoulders and is ushering her towards the garden gate. 'We're round the back,' she explains. 'Taking advantage of the weather. Em's been desperate to try out the new barbecue. It's been such a shocking summer.' Leigh speaks in staccato sentences. Statements that somehow don't leave room for returned comment; Mina's yet to get a word in.

'Is that for us?'

'Oh, yes, sorry.' Mina passes her the bottle and Leigh makes a show of admiring the label.

'Mmmm,' she sounds out with pursed lips. 'I honestly had no idea Brazil produced wine.'

Mina feels her cheeks flush.

'Mina's here,' Leigh announces, and strolls ahead of her into the garden.

The space opens up before them and it's quite something, not that Mina expected anything different. A lush green lawn, bordered by well-weeded beds of brightly coloured flowers and trees, and carved irregularly in two by a path of paving stones leading down to the bottom end of the garden. Here sits a patio dotted with an assortment of plushly cushioned garden furniture; the sort of expensive stuff Mina always thinks looks too good to be outside. Lanterns hung on fence posts and strings of fairy lights lend a festive air in the gathering dusk. But all this is only a backdrop canvas for the true stars of the show. Dotted around the garden on plinths and pedestals that wouldn't look

22

out of place in the grounds of a stately home are Leigh's sculptures – great hunks of marble and metal that give the scene a weight and gravitas almost at odds with the ephemeral flora that surrounds them.

'Wow!' Mina says, and she means it. The effect is breathtaking.

'Oh, I'm so glad you like it,' Leigh says, with all the false modesty of the minor celebrity. She probably insisted on answering the door via the back gate for this very reason, to lead her guest through her work and give it maximum impact. Mina chides herself for being uncharitable; it was probably just that Emma was busy in the kitchen.

The party, such as it is, is gathered under the twinkling lights of the patio. Dusk is swiftly settling into night, but a chiminea is giving out a warming glow and a group of seven or eight women are standing around it with generous glasses of white wine. No sign of any men, Mina thinks with a palpable sense of relief. Her date isn't here yet then. She wonders if he might have cancelled and is surprised to feel a slight sinking regret in her stomach.

Leigh isn't at all what Mina would have expected her to be. Emma's so loud and brash and full of life. So ... American. Mina had thought her wife would be, well, if not the opposite, then at least complementary in some way. But in fact, the two women are very much alike, in that respect, at least. The difference is that Emma's gregariousness seems natural, whereas Leigh's feels fake.

Mina shouldn't really be surprised. She'd seen Leigh talk once on a BBC Four documentary a few years ago, about some artist or other who'd recently died, and she'd behaved then very much as she is now. Mina had assumed she was turning it on for the cameras, but apparently not. To find out the sculptor is exactly the same in real life as her celebrity persona is disappointing. She doesn't like the woman, she realises.

As Leigh introduces her to the group, each of the women eyes Mina almost like a curiosity, reminiscent of the queen being introduced to yet another commoner she has to make small talk with. They are all, to a one, middle-class white women of a certain age. Mina's met their kind often enough – the interactions always go the same way, and usually end with them reminding her that their taxes pay her salary.

She wonders if she's being unfair, letting her prejudices seep out. But she also notices that once the introductions are over, they withdraw back into their cliques, closing shoulders and continuing their conversations almost mid-sentence, effectively cutting off any chance of her engaging with them. Leigh floats back up the garden towards the house and Mina finds herself pushed back almost to the fence.

It's at this point that the heels she'd been so unsure about wearing finally decide to live up to expectations and betray her, the right one slipping off the patio and burying itself in the soft soil of the border. As her knees buckle and she begins to go down, she has a brief moment to be thankful that at least no one has brought her a drink yet, as she'd be throwing it down herself right now, before a hand reaches out and grabs her arm. 'Whoa!' says a soft voice in her ear.

One of the middle-class ladies has come to her rescue.

'Thanks,' she says, clutching at the proffered hand and

scraping the remaining mud from her stiletto onto the edge of the patio.

'They take some getting used to, eh?'

At first Mina rankles at the assumption. How dare this woman assume she doesn't know how to wear heels! But then it occurs to her that it's meant in a comradely way, as though she too is a little out of her comfort zone. The comment makes her reassess the woman, and there's certainly something a bit different about her. Her hair has flecks of grey in it, which somehow makes her seem younger than the others, who all have uniform dye jobs. The summer dress she's wearing looks off-the-rack as well, compared to their expensive bright floral outfits, and she isn't sporting any of their giant metallic accessories, just a thin gold necklace that she plays with nervously as she talks. She's wearing a lot less makeup too, and her cheeks are bright red, flushed.

'You look about as comfortable here as I am,' the woman says, echoing Mina's thoughts. And then, as she realises what she's said, 'Sorry, I just meant, you look like you'd rather be somewhere else.'

Mina laughs as the woman apologises all over again.

'No, it's okay,' Mina says. 'I know what you mean. You're right, this isn't really my thing.'

The woman smiles and whispers, 'Me neither. I'm Ruth,' she adds, sticking out her arm.

'Mina.'

As she takes Ruth's hand, Mina notices her fingernails are a rich burgundy, but they're cut unusually short. The colour bleeds into the cuticles.

'How do you know Leigh Raddon?' Ruth asks, as though the celebrity in their midst deserves her full name.

'Oh, I work with her wife. With the police.'

Ruth's eyes widen a little. 'Ooh, I bet that's interesting.'

This is the other way people tend to respond when they find out what she does. If they don't run a mile, they fixate on the grisly details. It's why Mina doesn't do parties. But Ruth surprises her by moving the conversation on without asking any further questions about her job.

'What do you think?' she asks, her voice dropping to such a low register that Mina struggles to hear her. She gestures with her glass at the statues dotted through the garden.

'It's . . . lovely,' Mina manages, a bit lamely. She has to admit, she personally doesn't really get fine art, and certainly not the kind of abstract sculpture Leigh produces, all lumps of concrete and metal with rounded curves and sharp corners. This was another reason for not wanting to come tonight, the chance she might be made to feel humiliated for not knowing the right things about the right subjects.

Ruth grins a little conspiratorially. 'I have to admit,' she whispers again, her voice apologetic, 'it's all a bit beyond me.'

Mina smiles back. 'Me too. It *is* pretty though.'

'It is,' Ruth agrees.

Mina finds herself warming to the woman. Perhaps she really is as out of her depth as Mina is. She's about to ask what Ruth does for a living when a movement at the house catches her eye and Emma emerges from the patio doors with a man in tow. She moves down the path virtually hopping from slab to slab, a drink in either hand, excitement oozing from every pore. And then Mina's eyes settle on the man properly for the first time. 'Oh, no,' she groans, and Ruth shoots her a concerned look.

'Hey!' Emma virtually shouts, and grabs Mina in as warm an embrace as she can manage with her hands full. When she pulls back, she passes one of the glasses to Mina. 'Mocktail,' she says, sipping from her own glass. 'I'm on call so I've got the same. You'll love it. You look amazing! Thanks for coming.' She adds the last sotto voce, as though it's all some grand conspiracy they've cooked up between them, rather than the result of the relentless browbeating Emma has been engaged in for the past few weeks.

'Thanks for inviting me,' Mina whispers back, playing her part.

Emma grabs hold of the man's hand, pulling him forward from where he has been waiting patiently. 'There's someone I'd like you to meet,' she says, her face unable to contain her delight.

But before she can go on Mina interrupts, 'Actually, we already know each other.'

'How's it going, Mina?' Danny smiles at her, and Mina has to admit to herself, he looks good, a little more grown up than he did the last time she saw him.

'Oh,' Emma exclaims, and it's difficult to tell whether she's dismayed or just factoring this new information into her plan. 'I guess you guys worked together?'

'Me and Mina were cadets together.'

Mina can feel her cheeks burning. Why on earth did it have to be him? But then she wonders why she's so put out. Surely it's better this way. At least she knows Danny, so she won't have all the awkwardness of trying to make small talk with some bloke who's only trying to get in her pants. Why then does a small part of her feel disappointed? Had she actually been looking forward to this?

She becomes aware she hasn't spoken. 'I thought you moved away,' she says, and the statement comes out as more of an accusation than she intends.

Danny just grins at her. She can almost hear what he's thinking. *Same old Min!* He always called her Min. It used to annoy the hell out of her, which, she suspects, is why he did it.

'Yeah,' he says. 'I was in London but I just got transferred back.' There's a hint of something, a hesitation in his voice that says there's more to the story. Knowing Danny, he probably messed something up and got transferred away from whatever carnage he created. She wonders if that's fair though. It's been a few years now, and he really does look . . . Mina's not sure what exactly. More confident somehow. More solid.

He certainly seems more serious. The old Danny would have been chattering away about something inane by now, or have wandered off to talk to someone else. Instead, he says nothing, merely holds her gaze as he lifts his beer bottle to his lips and takes a sip. He's been working out too, that much is obvious. Yes, definitely more solid.

'You look . . . well,' she says, and finds herself blushing again.

'Thanks.' He grins. 'So do you.'

A circle of space has opened up around them. Emma has somehow managed to corral the others away and is gently parting the long, tall necks of some lupins to expose a hidden statue. Mina's suddenly aware they're on their own. She needs to nip this in the bud before it goes any further. Not that Danny ever seemed to think of her that way in the past but . . .

'Listen,' she says. 'I don't know what Emma's told you, but I'm really not looking for . . . Well, I mean, you and me . . . You know? It's ridiculous. Isn't it?' She shouldn't have added that last bit.

'Mina,' Danny says, still smiling. 'I think maybe you've got the wrong end of the stick.' He nods at Emma. 'I met Emma the other day and she mentioned you in passing, and I thought this would be a great way to catch up. Especially since we're going to be working together. Wait!' The grin widens. 'Was this . . . Was this supposed to be a date?'

'Oh. I . . .' Her face feels like it's on fire. Then his words register properly. 'What do you mean working together?'

Danny frowns. 'I thought you knew. In fact, I wondered if maybe you'd suggested it.' He looks down at the ground. 'I guess that was me getting the wrong end of the stick.'

'Danny, what are you talking about?'

'I'm your new Uniform liaison. I mean, CCRU's, not *yours*. Specifically.' He pronounces it 'sea-crew', as everybody does nowadays. 'As I understand it, now you've got civilians working with you, the higher-ups thought you'd need someone on hand to do the grunt work. You know, reading people their rights, handling arrests, all that jazz. I'm your new gopher!' He grins at his self-deprecation, then pauses and studies her for a moment. 'I figured when DS Tyler spoke to me that maybe you'd put him up to it. For old times' sake.' The grin dissolves. 'But I guess you didn't know anything about it.'

No, she didn't. *Bloody Adam Tyler! Now what's he up to?*

She's thankfully saved from any further embarrassment by Leigh, who begins tapping a pen against the side of her glass and then launches into a lengthy speech about how her 'vision for the landscape was realised'. It seems a bit grand for what is essentially a suburban garden in Sheffield, but Emma stares at her with adoration. Again, Mina feels guilty. She loves Emma; the least she can do is learn to get on with her wife.

Danny's listening to the talk with more interest than she remembers him showing in anything in the past. He used to have the attention span of a five-year-old. Perhaps he really has grown up at last. She remembers once having to steer him away from a particularly grisly crime scene before he vomited all over the evidence. He'd never exactly been a stickler for the details back then. She wonders idly if that's changed as well. If not, he'll probably end up causing them more problems than anything else. Why didn't Tyler talk to her about this? She hopes he knows what he's doing. Having said that, people do change, don't they? Perhaps it won't be as bad as she thinks.

Emma manages to sidle up to her and whispers in her ear, 'He *is* kinda hot, isn't he?'

Mina reddens again. 'Stop this,' she says firmly. 'I'm not interested in him, and anyway, it sounds like we're going to be working together.'

Emma sighs. 'Shame. You two would have made such a cute couple.'

'Even if we weren't, he's ... well, he's such a boy!'

'He looks like a man to me. If I wasn't happily married, I'd definitely ask him out!'

'Will you just stop?'

'Fine, fine.' Emma holds up her hands in mock surrender. 'Just . . . think about it. If not him, someone else. Mina, you need to get a life.'

'Thanks!'

'You know what I mean.'

Perhaps aware someone's talking about him, Danny glances across and catches Mina's eye. He smiles and she looks away, trying to pretend her eyes were just passing over him, not lingering. She notices Ruth, hanging back from the crowd, standing awkwardly with her arms wrapped across her tummy. She recalls that their conversation was interrupted a bit abruptly and makes the decision to go back over after the Leigh-show finishes to try to pick up where they left off. It's too early to leave yet and she isn't about to spend the whole evening talking to Danny.

Just then Mina's phone trills loudly, and Leigh stops mid-sentence and glares at her. Mina mouths an apology and rushes up the garden towards the house, extracting her phone as she goes, aware that every eye in the garden is on her. Still, it's a welcome reprieve.

She doesn't recognise the number, but she answers it anyway. She's technically not on duty but with a bit of luck it'll be something serious that gives her an excuse to leave. 'Mina Rabbani.'

'DC Rabbani? It's PC Andrews. Rob.'

'Hey, Rob.' For a moment she wonders why he's ringing her and where he got her number from, but before she can come up with anything he gets straight to the point.

31

'DI Doggett asked me to ring you . . .' He trails off.

'Uh-huh?'

'It's . . . It's DS Tyler, Mina. It's bad.'

3

The first thing Detective Inspector Jim Doggett notices about the scene is the smell; a rank, sweet scent of mould and decay. He looks around the dilapidated cinema and sighs heavily.

'Jesus Christ, Tyler! What a shithole.'

Doggett doesn't expect to die on the job. He expects to go out at a ripe old age – ninety-two or ninety-three – after a short but painless illness. In his own bed preferably, in the arms of his fifth wife. He's actually only two wives down at this point, but he hopes he has time to squeeze at least a couple more in before then. Yeah, that would be the way to go. *On the job* perhaps, but definitely not at work.

But he's a police officer, and he's known enough colleagues who've cashed in their chips early to be aware that it's always a risk and worth having a plan for, just in case. If he does have to go out sooner rather than later, then in his mind it'll be in a hail of bullets, defending a busload of schoolchildren. An unlikely scenario, granted, even if he suddenly decides to retrain as a firearms officer – and they certainly wouldn't want him now – but still, it's good for a man to have a dream.

The one way he doesn't want to go is quietly, or without explanation; the perpetrator slipping away into the night before anyone can know who they are. The blade in the dark, the unexpected car crash, something meaningless. He doesn't suppose any of these thoughts would have crossed Tyler's mind, but if they had then he'd bet his last Jaffa cake the lad would have agreed with him.

Doggett looks down into the great gaping hole in the stage where the boards had given way under Tyler's weight. It was a drop of about eight to ten feet, he reckoned, onto a bed of cardboard boxes by the look of it. Enough to do you a mischief, but you'd be hard pressed not to walk away from it with a bit of assistance. *What the bloody hell happened, lad?* He glances up to the gantry suspended above, and notes that one of the scaffold railings is swinging loose. *Jesus Christ! If he fell that far . . .* Returning his gaze back to the hole, Doggett sees one of his officers traipsing through the assorted wreckage in the storeroom below. He must say something out loud, probably what his old French teacher would have called 'a swear', because DS Vaughan starts and looks up at him.

'Oh!' she exclaims, and the fact that she exclaims is one of the reasons he can't bloody stick the woman. 'I didn't know you were here yet, sir.'

'Where the bloody hell is the Crime Scene Officer?' he shouts, the planks under his feet creaking ominously and sending a cloud of dust billowing down around Vaughan.

'We're not sure this *is* a crime scene as such . . .'

'No, Jenny.' He tries to keep his voice level. 'We're not *sure* of anything, that's why we *assume* it is. Now get your bloody size eights out of there. Sharp!'

For a moment he thinks Vaughan is going to salute him, but then she merely nods and backs out of the room. Doggett inches his way to the edge of the stage. He really should make more of an effort with the girl. She's green as Kermit's cock, but they all are when they arrive, aren't they? Mina used to jump three feet in the air whenever he so much as looked at her, but at least she always had the gumption to mutter something under her breath while she did it. That's the difference, he thinks. He likes to push people, to see what they're made of and just how much they'll put up with before they bite back. But Jenny Vaughan never bites back. She's a bloody machine! One of these days, soon, he's going to have to do something about her.

As though his thoughts have summoned her, Mina comes tearing into the building and down the aisle. Doggett walks up to meet her.

'Where is he?' she asks. No, demands. That's the difference – Vaughan exclaims, Mina demands.

Why couldn't he have a Mina instead of a bloody Vaughan? Mina was wasted on that Cold Case unit with Tyler. The thought feels like a betrayal, especially given the circumstances, but he pushes his emotions away. Time for that later.

'On his way to the Northern General,' he tells Mina, taking hold of her arms gently. 'Hopefully, he'll be there by now.'

'What happened? Is he . . . ?' She obviously can't finish the thought, let alone the sentence.

'He was hanging on when they left,' Doggett tells her. 'But I'll be honest, it's touch and go.'

There's a moment of silence while they both take in what he's said. She tries to hide her feelings but her face betrays her, flicking between relief that the news isn't worse and dread at the realisation that it still could be.

'What happened?' she asks again.

Doggett looks up at the ceiling. '*That* is the sixty-four-billion-dollar question.'

'You think he fell? From up there?'

'Tyler's a lot of things, but he's never been clumsy.'

'Pushed then.'

It isn't a question, but he answers it anyway.

'Nothing to suggest that yet, but we're only just getting started. Assuming I can keep DS Vaughan from trampling on any evidence.' He adds the last just as Vaughan appears from the short corridor that leads behind the stage. She looks sheepish but avoids apologising for once. Maybe she's learning. 'Well?' he asks her.

Vaughan frowns. 'Sir?'

'Did you find anything while you were down there poking through my crime scene?'

Vaughan shuffles nervously. *Bite back, woman!*

'It looks as though he landed on some boxes. Flyers, mostly, for a fundraising gig they're doing in a few weeks. The manager was planning on handing them out at a few bars tonight. That's the only reason he went in there. Otherwise, they might not have found Tyler for days. Those flyers probably saved his life. In more ways than one!'

He glares at her flippancy. 'Assuming he is still alive.'

Mina shoots him a look which he does his best to ignore.

Vaughan shuffles again. 'The manager wants to know when he can get the flyers. The bars round here do a good trade on a Sunday and he's worried if they don't advertise soon—'

'I don't give a toss what he's worried about. I want this place locked down – the whole building. No one in or out until we go over everything. And I want to know who's been here. Today, yesterday, all bloody week if necessary.'

'That's just it, boss. The manager reckons no one's been in here for at least a couple of weeks. The work's stalled while they come up with some more money so the whole place has been kept locked and—'

'Tyler got in, didn't he?'

Vaughan shuts her mouth.

'What was he even doing here?' Mina asks.

'I was sort of hoping you could tell us that. You do work together, don't you?'

Mina glares at his sarcasm and then shakes her head, her disquiet outweighing her irritation with him. 'He's been quiet lately,' she says, the hesitation betraying her thoughts. She might as well have said, 'He's been up to something again.'

He holds up his hand to her and turns back to Vaughan. 'Well?'

She blinks at him in confusion.

'Get on with it then!'

'Sir.' Vaughan scuttles off to give the bad news to her manager friend.

Doggett turns and heads back down the aisle to the front of the cinema. Mina follows. 'What's he been working on?' he asks her. 'Any particular cold cases you've been looking at?'

'I don't know,' she says. 'You know Tyler. He's not exactly forthcoming at the best of times.'

'And these aren't the best of times?'

She hesitates again before answering. 'He has been working

on something, I know that much. But like I said, the last few weeks he's been quiet. As you know, CCRU's changed a bit since Diane and Suzanne joined us, and we all pretty much look into separate stuff now. We meet every week to discuss progress. But I've noticed over the past few weeks, Tyler's not said much.'

Doggett considers this as they reach the front of the building and emerge into the night air. The lad's not lazy, which means he was working on something but chose not to share it. He takes a deep breath, clearing his lungs of the fusty mould from the cinema. 'Okay,' he says. 'Maybe you should go to the hospital. See what's happening. With any luck he's sitting up and telling Diane what a clod he's been for losing his footing.'

'She's at the hospital?'

Doggett nods. 'I rang her first. She'll be with him by now.'

'You sure you don't need me here? What about his car?' She points across the road.

'I'll handle that. No, you get off. I've got enough trouble keeping Vaughan from messing up the scene, I don't need your bloody great boots trampling over everything as well.'

Mina smiles but it's half-hearted, he can tell.

'Trust me, Mina,' he says to take the sting out of his words. 'If there's anything to find here, I'll find it. You need to be with him. Just let me know if anything changes.'

'Of course.'

'Then, in the morning – and I mean that, get yourself some sleep – you need to talk to the others, see if they know anything. Go through his files, work out why he was here. In the meantime, I'll go over this place with a fine-toothed comb. If there was someone else here, we'll find out.'

For a moment she looks as though she's going to argue, but then she just nods and marches away, ready to take down whatever obstacles stand in her way.

God help you, Tyler!

If the lad isn't dead already, there's a good chance Mina might kill him.

4

Sheffield's Northern General Hospital is about three miles from the city, a sprawling patchwork of interconnected buildings, large and small, new and old, scattered across a 100-acre campus. Its enormous number of corridors form a network of veins and arteries across several storeys, and by now Mina's pretty sure she's walked all of them. Her search isn't helped by the fact the place is built on the side of a hill, meaning you can go in on the ground floor of one building and come out on the second floor of another. Also, there's pretty much no phone signal.

She must have been here hundreds of times over the years, mostly when she was in Uniform, and usually handcuffed to some idiot with a cracked head from a pub fight, but she still struggles to navigate her way around. In the end, she visits A&E three times as well as four different wards of the Huntsman building before she finally finds someone who seems to know where Tyler is. She's directed to the Critical Care Unit, but when she gets to what she thinks is the right door, the intercom goes unanswered. After a few minutes an orderly emerges with a huge cage of folded sheets and she slips through behind him.

Diane Jordan looks up from a seat in the waiting room and the expression on her face turns Mina's stomach.

'Is he . . . ?' Mina starts, but then rationalises that if Tyler were already dead, Jordan wouldn't still be sitting there. Probably.

'They're operating on him now,' Diane says, reaching out to put her arms around Mina.

They hug tightly, for far longer than Mina finds comfortable. It wasn't all that long ago this woman was her boss and physical contact of any kind would have been unthinkable. But their relationship has changed dramatically over the past few months they've been working together again. And Diane has changed too, since her month-long incarceration at the hands of a killer. The hugging is part of it, as though she's reminding herself to cherish human contact while it's available. She laughs more freely too. Her retirement on the grounds of ill health may have been for physical reasons on paper, but Mina suspects that in reality it was just as much about her mental health.

Diane finally pulls away. She limps slightly as she moves, her leg still not fully healed from the trauma it suffered. 'I haven't managed to speak to anyone yet. All I know is they rushed him into surgery as soon as they got here. Oh, God, Mina, he was such a mess.' Her face crumples, and to Mina she's never looked more vulnerable. The woman is Tyler's godmother, as well as his closest confidante and the person who pretty much raised him after his father died when he was a teenager. If Mina thought her own grief was bad, it must be nothing compared to what Diane is going through. She has no idea what she can possibly say to her.

'I'll see if I can find someone,' she says, more for something to do than anything else. But a cursory search up and down the corridor finds only closed doors and an empty reception desk. It's late, and she guesses the hospital is more lightly staffed than it would be if it were daytime. Anyone who *is* here is no doubt doing a very important job somewhere. Saving Tyler's life, she hopes.

She finds a shuttered window with an old-fashioned doorbell fixed to a shelf and a sign that says, 'Ring for attention.' She presses it a couple of times, but nobody responds. After a few minutes she tries again, but this time immediately turns on her heel and walks back to the waiting room.

Diane's standing at the window now, not particularly looking at anything since the glass is frosted, staring at it rather than through it. She looks older than she did this morning, but then, this accelerated ageing is also nothing new. Since she was rescued from her own near death experience Diane has . . . *withered* is the word that springs to mind. Mina supposes that's hardly surprising, given what the other woman went through, but it saddens her, nonetheless.

Not all the changes are negative though. Diane's cut back massively on the booze, a task that couldn't have been easy even under normal circumstances. Tyler's never mentioned her newfound sobriety, but Mina knows he's relieved about it. As far as Mina knows, Diane's given up smoking as well; when they'd first met, DCI Jordan was well known for sneaking out of the office to inhale a tab-end as rapidly as possible. It had been something of a running joke.

But despite the positive changes, and the brave face she puts on things, Mina can't help thinking of her former boss as somewhat reduced, a shadow of the force of nature she used to be. They never talk about it – Tyler never talks about anything – but Mina gets the impression he thinks it's retirement that disagrees with her. It was one of the reasons he'd asked Diane to come back in a civilian capacity. But Mina is less sure; the woman carries demons neither of them are privy to. Still, when Tyler got the okay to expand the unit and went to Jordan to ask her to come back, Mina was pleased, albeit a little surprised, when she said yes.

So, over the past few months DCI Jordan has become Diane. No longer 'ma'am', although sometimes Mina still forgets. Her former boss has adapted to her new role pretty well, only occasionally forgetting herself and telling Mina what to do, and always apologising for it afterwards. Are they friends yet? Mina isn't sure. But colleagues, certainly, often sharing a glance and a smile over Tyler's head whenever he misses some nuance to the conversation. Despite this tentative, budding friendship between them, if that's what it is, Mina knows Diane's holding something back. Perhaps it's just the whole ex-boss thing, but she doesn't think so. It's something more. Something in Diane. Something broken.

The door swings open behind them and a ridiculously handsome man in a tight white shirt walks in. Mina's first thought is that it's the doctor come to tell them what's happening, and she can suddenly hear her mother's voice in her head.

Ay, Mina, a doctor!

It's an old voice though: her mother has long since stopped trying to set her up with people. A relief. But then, why does some small part of her feel disappointed about that?

'Scott!' Diane says, limping her way across the room to him.

Mina recognises her mistake. Scott is Tyler's boyfriend. At least, she thinks he is; Tyler rarely mentions him. She only knows he's seeing someone because Diane let it slip a few weeks ago.

While Diane catches Scott up on the information they have so far, Mina examines him. He's extremely good-looking, in a boyish sort of way. She feels herself colouring at the thoughts she'd had when he came in. But then, she'd had similar thoughts about Tyler when they'd first met. It hadn't taken long for him to disabuse her of any notions. Not that she'd had any.

'And you must be Mina,' Scott says, stepping forward and embracing her in her second uncomfortable hug of the evening. *Why is everyone so quick to throw their arms around each other all the time?*

'Tyler's told me all about you,' he continues as they finally break apart. She has a sense he might have noticed her reticence. Perhaps she'd stiffened more than she thought.

'Really?'

Scott tips his head to one side. 'Well, no, obviously not. But I managed to drag a few things out of him.' He smiles.

'You call him Tyler?' she asks.

'Doesn't everybody?' The smile widens. 'I tried Adam for a bit, but it didn't stick.'

She finds herself warming to him. He has a way about him that's disarming, she supposes, rather than charming. She finds that refreshing – in her experience most good-looking guys know that they are and play up to it every chance they get. For some reason Danny pops into her mind, but not because she's ever thought of him that way. He definitely *did* seem as though he'd grown into himself though.

What's wrong with me? Now, of all times! She tries to stay focused on the here and now.

'Do either of you have any idea what he was doing there?' Diane asks, and the question's very similar to the one Mina had been about to ask the two of them.

She shakes her head. 'He's been . . .' She doesn't know quite how to say it.

'More like the old Tyler?' Diane suggests.

Mina nods. 'I'll admit, it's been worrying me. I started to wonder if he'd fallen back into old habits.' With Scott here she doesn't want to say anything explicit, but she doesn't need to. It's clear they both know what she's talking about. The Circle.

The same set of circumstances that had led to Diane's incarceration and injury had revealed the man responsible for the death of Tyler's father, and the intangible organisation lurking behind him. The Circle, as far as they could tell, were a shadowy organisation made up of local entrepreneurs who had their own vision for Sheffield, and who were prepared to go to any lengths to see it realised. Although their operative within the force had been uncovered and the hired killer who did their dirty work was safely behind bars, there were still too many unanswered questions. Since then, Diane, Mina and even Doggett had all voiced their concern to each other that Tyler's crusade to find his father's killer would morph into a new quest to bring the remaining unknown members of the Circle to justice.

And yet, to their shared surprise, it hadn't turned out that way. Perhaps that had something to do with the fact that Tyler had discovered a new family, of sorts – a brother he'd long given up for lost, and a niece he never knew existed. Although, as far as Mina understood it, neither of those relationships had blossomed particularly well in the intervening months. Still, whatever the reason, he'd seemed genuinely content enough with the answers he'd found, and instead of secretly investigating the Circle behind the backs of Professional Standards, as everyone had assumed he would, he'd thrown himself into the reorganisation of the Cold Case Review Unit.

Mina supposed it was possible they were all wrong, and he'd just got better at hiding things from them. But she didn't think so. For the first time in a long time – perhaps ever – the two of them had begun to share information and work properly as a team. When Diane and Suzanne Cooper had joined them, that teamwork had only grown stronger. Okay, so they all had their own responsibilities and areas of expertise, but they regularly pooled information. The department had seen better results than ever, and the top brass appeared satisfied, as far as they ever were anyway.

Of course, now she has to wonder if any of that was true.

Diane closes her eyes. 'I didn't want to say anything, but I've noticed it too. He's been different the past few weeks. Secretive. Holding things back.' She limps over to a chair and sits down, sighing lightly as she takes the weight off her bad leg. 'I tried talking to him about it but ...'

'He brushed you off.'

'I *let* him brush me off.' Diane massages her knee. 'I should have pushed him more but, well, I suppose I didn't want to upset the apple cart.' She's blaming herself. Mina supposes that was inevitable, sooner or later.

Mina's about to tell her it's not her fault but, before she can, Diane turns to Scott.

'I don't suppose he told you anything about what he was working on?'

Mina's suddenly aware that Scott has been listening, taking everything in. He crosses his arms as though holding himself together, and exhales slowly.

'I saw him earlier. We . . .' He hesitates, his eyes flicking back and forth between them. 'You're right about him being a bit distant lately. It's been the same with us. I thought he might be pushing me away, so I gave him some space but . . . I'm not sure, maybe that wasn't the right decision.'

It's such a candid exploration of their relationship that Mina almost blushes again. It's also very considered. There's no heat in Scott's words, no anger or self-justification, and his eyes are glistening with unshed tears. This is a man who wears his heart on his sleeve. How appropriate, she thinks, given that Tyler's just the opposite.

'It's not your fault either,' she tells him, and glances at Diane to make it clear who the 'either' refers to. Diane smiles and nods.

'I knew he was worried though,' Scott goes on.

'Worried?'

He thinks about this. '"Concerned" is maybe a better word?'

'What makes you say that?'

Scott thinks again before answering. 'I'm not sure, to be honest. I just got the sense he was preoccupied.' He sounds as though he's working through this for the first time even as he speaks. 'Maybe it wasn't just about the two of us.' For the first time he seems unsure of himself.

'What the hell was he up to?' Diane shouts, her voice unusually harsh. Ironically, it makes her sound more like her old self.

'You said you saw him earlier?' Mina asks Scott. 'What time was that?'

'A few hours ago. About four. We had a drink in the Fat Cat, and then he got a call and had to take off.'

Mina meets Diane's eye, and she nods. 'I'll text DI Doggett. Scott, he may want to talk to you about this.'

The door opens again and this time it is a doctor – or a surgeon, Mina supposes. He introduces himself as Mr Khan and starts talking around the houses, everything couched in medical terms that make about as much sense to Mina as an episode of *Love Island*.

'Please!' she interrupts when she feels her head spinning. Khan stops talking and she takes a deep breath. 'I'm sorry, doctor. Can you just tell us? Is he going to be all right?'

There's a pregnant pause and Mina feels her stomach dropping further and further through her body. Surely it can't keep falling forever – eventually it must hit bottom.

'It's too early to say,' Khan tells them, seriously. 'He has a number of broken bones and a punctured lung, but by far the biggest area of concern is his brain. He sustained a significant blow to the head and the swelling is considerable. We've had to induce a coma until it goes down. Only then will we know the full extent of the damage.'

'Damage?' Diane asks. 'You mean . . . brain damage?'

Mina breathes in sharply and Scott touches her arm. It's a measure of how agitated she must be that her first feeling is gratitude at his kindness, rather than discomfort at the unwelcome intimacy.

'It's too early to say,' the doctor says again, clinging to a well-honed mantra. 'But, yes, it's a possibility. Before we worry about that we need to get the swelling down or he could haemorrhage. That's our main priority. The next few hours, possibly days, are critical. I'm sorry I can't tell you more at this time.'

Diane thanks him and asks a few more questions, but Mina can't listen. She walks to the window and stares through it at whatever distant, imaginary place Diane had been studying earlier.

Tyler, what did you do?

She can't understand it. She has no idea what he could have been doing in an old, abandoned cinema. As far as she knows, it doesn't have anything to do with any of the cases they're investigating. She needs to get to the office and find out for sure. What happened in there? Did he fall? Doggett didn't seem convinced, and if she thinks about it properly, neither is she. It doesn't make sense. But that means somebody pushed him off that gantry, or at the very least there must have been a scuffle and he fell. What was he doing there? Meeting someone? But why?

The questions come thick and fast, and she can't think of a single answer before another pops into her head. She sighs heavily and rubs her hands across her face. She can't do anything to help his recovery, but maybe she can do something about what put him here.

What happened to you, Adam Tyler?

Whatever happens, Mina promises herself – promises *him* – she *will* find the answer.

5

Dark shapes rise in the garden to greet Ruth when she gets home, chief among them the small mound behind her father's old workshop. She used to put flowers there sometimes, until her father caught her. He'd left her with a gash across her eye that she'd thought might never heal, although it did, eventually. Now she only has a faint scar, just above her eyebrow.

She hurries past without really looking, as she always does. She can still feel him in the workshop, waiting for her to admit her failures. By the time she reaches the front door to the main house she already has her key in her hand, but she still manages to fumble it in the lock. She struggles for a moment or two, certain that at any moment his hand will come down on her shoulder, but then she's in and turning and slamming the door closed behind her. She forces the bolt home with a loud rattle and exhales into the darkness.

But now she can feel him behind her, and she scrambles for the light switch. The bare bulb fizzes into life on the ceiling, flickering before settling into a dull yellow glow that only adds to her anxiety.

Sleeping Dogs

The house surrounds Ruth, towering over her, dwarfing her. It feels more threatening than ever, and she can't understand why. He should be gone by now. She's done her best to be rid of him, and yet he's still there, everywhere she looks. He's there on the stairs, peering at her through the broken bannister. He's behind the dark panelled door to the front room – *his* room, as it became. He's lurking in the darkness of the old dining room and beyond the white-painted door to the cellar. She hurries past, down the corridor into the kitchen, the one room she actually uses, and only now does she feel a modicum of calm. She switches on the kettle and finds a piece of cheese in the fridge. She sits on her old stool and nibbles it while she waits for the water to boil.

She glances at the clock. Gone ten. She thought she might have heard something by now. Ruth's feet are killing her. The bus that was supposed to go from the end of Leigh Raddon's road never turned up, so she'd been forced to walk to the tram stop. Then she hadn't had enough money for the full fare, so the guard had thrown her off four stops early. She pulls off her strappy sandals and rubs her feet. She thinks back to the party and counts her blessings that she'd decided against heels. She has no doubt she would have coped even less well than the policewoman. Not that she owns any heels, of course.

After a short conflab with their hosts, the policewoman, or detective, she supposes – Mina – had rushed away from the party without so much as a goodbye. The pathologist, Leigh Raddon's wife, had followed her. And then the boyish policeman had taken off as well. No explanation given for the abrupt departures, and Ruth couldn't quite bring herself to ask.

51

The garden had erupted into a hubbub of discussion, but Ruth stood apart, as she always did, sipping at her glass of wine and wondering whether she ought not to slip away as well in the confusion. One or two of the others were beginning to drain their glasses and make noises about going.

But then Leigh Raddon shouted, 'Drink up, folks! No reason for the party to end just because one of the hosts has disappeared.' Leigh had laughed, but there was something about the set of her face that made Ruth wonder if the party wasn't already over.

Knocking back her wine, she'd felt the dress tugging at her waist, reminding her just how much bigger she was than all those other glamorous women. They were older than her as well, and it didn't seem fair that they had managed to keep themselves in shape long past when she'd been able to. She's still not quite sure how she'd got her outfit wrong, but she knew she had the moment she'd arrived, panting and no doubt red-faced from her rush. Leigh Raddon had looked her up and down in disgust, and Ruth had stood there shaking, still a little upset from the events of the day.

The dress had come from the Oxfam on City Road, and it had looked perfect on the window dummy, just the sort of thing for a summer soirée at the home of a great artist. Not one of them would guess that she cleaned toilets for a living. The whole business had seemed exciting back then, like something from a James Bond film. A new experience she could add to her list, which was, she reminded herself, how this whole business had begun.

How long ago now? It seemed like no more than a few

weeks. Ruth had just turned thirty-eight and she'd finally got her life back. She'd turned from the graveside before the first spadeful of earth hit the lid of her father's coffin and walked off into the woods. The other mourners had been shocked, but people did funny things in times of grief, didn't they? Besides, there really weren't all that many of them. There was Maureen, of course, who had come in from Macmillan Cancer Support twice a week. But Maureen wasn't the sort to judge anyone, and she hadn't known her father before the cancer got him, what he was really like.

Janice and her daughter from the Co-op had been there. They'd both loved her father but then, why wouldn't they? They'd only ever seen the charmer who wiggled his eyebrows at the ladies and winked when he went in for his baccy and stout. Yes, he could be charming enough with strangers, if he wanted to be.

Perhaps the vicar had judged her, but as she had no intention of setting foot back inside that church, she could live with that.

No, all in all there'd only been perhaps eight people who'd been there to see her shame her father's memory, and none of them would do more than idly speculate on what it might mean.

That had been ... she does a quick calculation in her head. Six months ago? More or less. Ruth had walked off through the rain, past the gates to the cemetery – *Wasn't it wonderful they'd found space for him? Not everyone made it in these days* – and on down the tram tracks towards the park. She'd stood there for almost an hour, staring out across the pond and watching the rain slant into the water, the ducks huddled closely together against the chill. She hadn't felt the water that had sluiced down her neck under the black dress she'd bought from the Sue Ryder shop the day before. She hadn't cared that her makeup had run and virtually washed itself away. She hadn't heard the school kids as they ran home through the rain, not on a conscious level anyway. She didn't feel the cold or the wet. She didn't feel much of anything.

Ruth had learned that from a young age: how to keep quiet, how to live a small life without drawing attention. How not to feel. She'd learned that lesson so well it had become second nature to her.

But now he was gone. Finally. And he couldn't hurt her anymore.

Thirty-eight. That wasn't so bad, was it? She still had plenty of time. Hopefully. She could still carve out a life for herself. At least, that's what she'd thought then.

The kettle clicks and bubbles itself back into silence.

She'd been wrong. She has to admit that now. She can't pretend to be something she isn't. The women at the party had seen right through her, and they always would.

Oh, God, what has she done?

How did it all go so terribly wrong? She'd never meant to hurt anyone. All she'd wanted was a life! Was that really so much to ask?

Somehow, she has to figure out her next steps. Can she make this right? She checks her phone. Still nothing. Maybe, if she can find a way to approach the detective – Mina.

She can still do this. She can still beat him. But she has to be strong now. Hard, like him. Like her father. And isn't that the irony.

6 months ago

I

The envelope was on his desk when he got in that morning.

Tyler had the place to himself since Mina had arranged to come in late after a dental appointment. It was a large room for just the two of them, a corner office with magnificent views across the city, and with enough space for three or four more to work comfortably.

The Cold Case Review Unit had been assigned the space by Laura Franklin, the Assistant Chief Constable who'd been brought in to 'shake things up'. That was a euphemism for the sort of ruthless performance management that fell on an institution after its previous leader was discovered to have been heavily involved in organised crime.

Franklin had certainly made her mark over the past months, hiring and firing, bringing in her own people and restructuring just about every department in South Yorkshire Police. Watchwords like *accountability* and *reputation* were now bandied around as talismans. It wasn't unusual for Franklin to 'touch base' with them when she wasn't 'reaching out'. Tyler wondered if she'd ever actually been a beat copper or whether she'd started out in business and 'executed a career path transference' or whatever it is she'd call it.

But to give Franklin her due, she did appear to be making a difference, and the higher-ups seemed happy enough with her progress. Though perhaps they were just pleased she'd managed to steer clear of too many negative headlines.

She seemed supportive of CCRU too, which had originally been conceived as little more than a PR exercise; an olive branch for the media, offered as evidence that no stone was ever left unturned in the pursuit of justice. Perhaps Franklin felt the same way, but Tyler thought it was more than that. She had instructed him to begin recruiting extra hands and had only put up minor resistance at the suggestions he'd given her. She genuinely seemed to have their team's back, to want them to succeed. He used the word *seemed* though, because you could never be a hundred per cent sure with the higher-ups. You were useful until you weren't, and then they found a way to make you go away.

This office was a good example. It was far too grand for the likes of them, and every day he expected to have it taken away again, or at least to be told they'd be sharing it. But so far, they still had this room – much of this floor, in fact – to themselves.

Still, as Tyler stood over his desk with the squatter-envelope staring up at him, he found himself glancing around at the other workstations and the water cooler, as though the person responsible for its delivery might be lurking in the corner behind the printer. It was a slim A5 white envelope with the words *FAO murder squad* written on it in what looked like blue fountain pen. The script was cursive and elegant, each of the letters precisely formed, as though the writer had taken their time and maybe had some sort of training in calligraphy. But the lettering was shaky, and there was that contradiction between the very formal 'FAO' and the misspelling of 'squad'. It spoke of someone intelligent, but perhaps with little formal education. Or maybe the writer was out of practice or elderly or suffering from some form of dementia. Or a combination of those.

Tyler picked the envelope up carefully between his fingertips and examined it closely, turning it back and forth. He lifted it into the light from the window and saw a darker shape within: a sheet of paper, perhaps folded in two but no more. Flipping it over, he saw that the flap on the back had already been unsealed. He pulled out his mobile.

'Your ears must be burning,' DI Doggett announced by way of a greeting as he answered the phone.

'What's that?'

'The Beak's been looking for you.' He meant Franklin, of course. Tyler didn't know who had started the nickname, but it had taken off quickly enough. Laura Franklin was a small, slight woman with a mighty nose, and Tyler had heard more than one commentator liken her to the secretary bird from *The Lion King*, minus the subservience, of course. Given that 'Beak' was also a nickname used for judges and headteachers, it had stuck, though Tyler personally thought it was a bit weak. Usually, nicknames were derived from personality traits, and the fact that this one seemed born mainly from appearance betrayed the complete lack of knowledge anyone had about the woman.

He ignored Doggett's comment. 'What do you know about this envelope on my desk?'

He could almost hear the other man shrug. 'What envelope?'

'White. Handwritten. Marked for the attention of the murder squad.'

'Oh, that envelope.'

Tyler picked it up and turned it over in his hand again. He had no doubt Doggett knew exactly what he was talking about.

'Arrived yesterday,' Doggett explained. 'Figured it was more within your purview.'

Purview? When Doggett started using big words, you knew you were in trouble.

'Meaning, it was an extra headache you didn't want to deal with.'

Doggett snorted something unintelligible and no doubt unflattering. 'Have you even opened it?'

Cradling the mobile under his chin, Tyler slipped his fingers under the flap of the envelope and pulled out a single sheet of lined white notepaper, folded in half. The writing on the page was the same cursive script as on the envelope, but more spidery and hesitant. In certain places the words were hard to make out.

> To whomsoever it may concern,
>   I am sorry about what hapened. It were a accident. No one was suposed to get hurt we was going to let her go. He shunt of done it. It were long time ago. No one was supost to get hurt. It was beach wh~
>   I am sorry~

The hand trailed off in a ragged line after 'beach wh' and again after the second apology. That 'wh' had to be a missing word.

'Where', maybe? Given the context of the letter, and the fact it was addressed to the Murder Team, could the writer have been about to say where they'd buried their victim? On a beach somewhere? That hardly narrowed it down.

Then, further down the page, as though added as an afterthought, but in a much firmer hand and with a black pen rather than blue:

frank weatherstone. He knows talk to frank

The letter was unsigned, but that in itself wasn't unusual. The Murder Team got anonymous tip-offs like this every now and again. They were usually short and sweet, and on the rare occasion they managed to trace the informant, it generally turned out to be somebody who'd heard someone else bragging about something down the pub. Either the whole story was a pack of lies or, occasionally, it led the team to the person they knew was guilty anyway, but without offering a shred more of the proof they needed to make an arrest. It was a complete waste of time and resources. Even so, every tip-off had to be followed up. Just not by Doggett if he could help it.

'I take it you don't know what this refers to?' Tyler asked him.

'You take it correctly. I haven't got a Scooby. Cold case though.' Doggett paused, then added, 'By my reckoning.'

'Oh, yeah?'

'Says so in the letter. "It were a long time ago."'

Tyler sighed. 'Fine. I'll look into it. But you owe me one. Any idea how it ended up on your desk?'

'No friggin' clue. Good luck. Oh, and watch out for

Franklin, reckon she had a ferret in her knickers.' And with that, Doggett ended the call.

Tyler sat down, dropped his phone on the desk and looked again at the letter. It was odd, to say the least. That floridly formal greeting, 'to *whomsoever* it may concern'. And then the next lines with their errors in grammar and spelling. A Sheffield-based speaker, judging from the transposing of the past participles *was* and *were*. Now he was looking at it more closely, Tyler could see the ink was lighter towards the end. Probably the same pen but written at a different time to the opening greeting. Perhaps the writer had started the letter and then stopped, unsure whether to go on. The substance of the letter was repetitive: two apologies, two attempts to assure them that 'no one was supposed to get hurt'. The writer was regretful, but at the same time tried to distance him or herself from the events in question: 'It were a long time ago'. Back and forth. Apologetic, guilt-ridden, denying responsibility, unsure whether to say anything at all . . . It was such a mix of style and emotion that to Tyler it had the ring of truth about it. Someone definitely knew more than they were saying. And it wasn't just gossip overheard in the pub. The writer had been involved first-hand. The two different spellings of 'supposed' were interesting too, as though perhaps he or she had once known how to spell the word but had forgotten. That spoke of age as well.

Unless it was all an elaborate joke, of course. He suspected he knew what Doggett's thoughts on the matter would be. If he'd really thought there was something worth pursuing here, he wouldn't have passed it on. But Tyler had a feeling . . .

'Ah, finally!' Franklin said from the doorway. 'I thought I was going to have to send out a search party.'

Tyler started to stand up, but Franklin waved him back into his seat. She flitted across the room, grabbing the chair from Mina's desk and rolling it into position on the other side of his own. She sat down, leaned back and crossed her arms.

Here it comes! he thought.

But in fact, she only glanced around once or twice before focusing on the letter he still held in his hands. 'New case?'

He folded it and pushed it back into the envelope. 'Anonymous note. Probably nothing in it.'

She made a low growl in the back of her throat. 'Don't waste too much time on it then.'

He inclined his head in acknowledgement. There was no point saying anything else.

'We've reached a crossroads,' she announced, unfolding her arms and crossing her uniformed right leg over the left instead. She placed her hands carefully on her knees. 'Things are finally starting to settle down after a . . . well, shall we say, a tumultuous period.'

That was one way of putting it. They'd uncovered a level of corruption within the force that still had officers looking at each other askance at every turn. It didn't help that whoever was ultimately behind the so-called Circle had yet to be uncovered. Franklin had continued to assure him that Professional Standards were still actively looking into the whole business, but he had a feeling that, as far as the higher-ups were concerned, they'd rather the whole thing quietly went away. Still, he reminded himself, that wasn't his problem anymore.

'So,' Franklin went on, 'it's time to start clawing back some good will. With that in mind, I've instructed the Press Office to reach out to the media again. We need some good news stories and I think the work you're doing here might be just the thing to strike a chord with the public. Righting past wrongs, bringing closure to families, that sort of thing.'

God, not this again! 'Ma'am, I—'

'This is happening, Tyler, so please don't waste either of our time by trying to argue with me. Jess'll be in touch to set something up, okay?'

He shrugged, which she seemed to take as good enough.

'In the meantime, how are you getting on with the recruitment drive?'

That had been one of the things that had surprised him most about Franklin's continued support of the department. Somehow – and Tyler really didn't dare ask how – she'd managed to find extra hours for him to increase their staff.

'Diane starts on Monday,' he told her.

'Well, that *is* a bit of good news. It'll be good to have her back after all this time. She was too quick to jump ship, in my opinion.' Tyler felt the urge to jump to his godmother's defence, but Franklin went on before he could speak. 'I understand though, of course. After everything she's been through, it was natural she'd want to take stock. But I'm glad she's coming back. We can't afford to waste talent like hers.' She uncrossed her legs and stood up. 'While we're on the subject,' she continued, moving to the window and looking out at the view, forcing Tyler to swivel his chair round, 'it may be that the two of you will require a period of adjustment. It won't be the same, with Diane coming back purely in a civilian capacity, and you now effectively her boss, instead of the other way around.'

'I'm sure we'll manage,' he said. He and Diane had already talked about this. It was true it might take them both a while to adjust, but they'd agreed that the benefits outweighed the potential difficulties. It would be far from the worst storm their relationship had weathered.

'I'm sure you will.' Franklin turned from the window and leant back on the glass. 'And your other civilian recruit?'

'I haven't made a decision yet.'

Franklin made the throat noise again. How she managed to convey so much with such a small sound was beyond him.

'I have to admit, she wouldn't be my first choice.'

Tyler was already aware of Franklin's thoughts on this matter but he braced himself for a repeated barrage.

'Whatever challenges Diane's return presents, you could all be knocked into a cocked hat by—'

He jumped in before she could get up a head of steam. 'You did say the choice was mine.'

Franklin paused for a moment, unused to being interrupted. 'It is,' she said eventually. 'And I'm sure you'll live and die by it. Just be careful it's the former, won't you?' She frowned suddenly. 'Where's DC Rabbani, this morning?'

'Dentist,' he said, and it suddenly sounded like such a poor excuse that for the first time he wondered if Mina had pulled a sickie. No, she wouldn't do that.

Franklin pushed herself away from the window and wandered over to Mina's desk. It was in its usual state of disarray, and Tyler felt the sudden need to justify the mess on Mina's behalf. Franklin lifted the corner of the topmost document in the in-tray and glanced underneath. She didn't appear to be looking for anything in particular. Perhaps the whole thing was just a technique designed to inspire a little wariness in him. If so, it was working.

She straightened abruptly and turned back to him. 'Results, DS Tyler. That's the key here. You – and DC Rabbani – have been performing admirably over the past few months, but I really think we have a chance to take this department to the next level. I want to hold you up as a shining example for other forces of what can be achieved if we prioritise cases that are currently unsolved. You're not going to let me down now, are you, Adam?'

'No, ma'am.' *I wouldn't dare.*

She eyed him closely for a moment or two and then nodded. 'Carry on, then,' she said, and swanned back out of the room.

Tyler let out a deep breath. Was that all Franklin had come to tell him? If so, she could easily have picked up the phone to give him the same information. So what was her real reason for coming all the way up here? She was being far too nice, and in his experience, it was when people were being nicest to you that you had to watch out for them the most.

II

It was mid-morning when Mina arrived in the office. The left side of her face was palsied from the anaesthetic, and when she spoke her speech was slurred and unintelligible. Tyler felt guilty for even considering she might have had an ulterior motive for being off. They really did need to start learning to trust each other again.

'How was it?' he asked.

'Don'g ash!' she slurred.

'Was it your uncle?'

One of Mina's numerous uncles had a dental practice just a couple of roads from where her family lived.

She shook her head. 'Par'ner,' she told him, simply. He supposed having a member of your family rummage around in your mouth and tut at your cavities might be a bit much.

He filled her in on Franklin's visit and her news concerning the media article. Mina rolled her eyes, eloquently expressing that she was as reluctant to take part in the whole business as he was.

After that he left her to her misery, and they worked in

silence for the rest of the morning. He offered to buy her lunch, but she just looked at him in that way she did when she thought he was behaving particularly foolishly. Instead, he brought her back one packet of paracetamol and one of ibuprofen, and that seemed to win her over. He wasn't a big fan of painkillers himself, and he thought perhaps she remembered that because she looked up at him with a crooked smile when he dropped them on her desk and said, 'Thanksh,' in a way that managed to convey more than just gratitude.

Despite having a number of cases he was supposed to be actively working on, there was something about the letter that drew Tyler back to it that afternoon. Maybe it was just that it was something fresh, a tangible lead that could be looked into, as opposed to the numerous dead ends his other cases presented.

He read and reread the words and tried to make sense of them. The more he thought about it, the more he became convinced there was something there. He put aside what he was working on and began to examine the letter again in earnest.

Out of the whole thing there was only one real clue that he had to work with: the name Frank Weatherstone.

It wasn't hard to find the man. Weatherstone had a record that stretched right back to the early 1970s. Assuming this was the right Frank Weatherstone, and the evidence suggested it could be, he'd had a number of arrests over the years, mostly for petty theft, but also a few for incidents that showed he was handy with his fists as well. There was a firearms offence that had led to a short custodial sentence in the early 80s; after that, he'd dropped off the radar and didn't appear to have had any further brushes with the law. Either he'd become a reformed man when he'd left prison, or he'd just got better at not getting caught. A quick DVLA check told Tyler that Weatherstone was still living in Sheffield, assuming the information was up to date – there'd been no updates for decades. He made a note of the address and sat back to examine what he'd found.

Just because Weatherstone had a record, that didn't mean it was time to start jumping to conclusions. It could just be that someone had a grudge against him and was trying to get payback, or that Weatherstone had been caught bragging about something he'd actually had nothing to do with. But even if so, there was still the fact that the letter writer had been involved in this unknown incident. It was a confession more than anything, with Weatherstone's name thrown in at the end after some considerable period of reflection, given the change in pen. To Tyler that made it far less likely that this was a prank or someone just trying to cause Weatherstone trouble. If it was, then it was a highly elaborate ruse.

He checked his watch; not quite four thirty, but he didn't want to be late. This new lead was definitely worth pursuing. But not today. He slipped the letter into his top drawer.

'I'm getting off,' he told Mina. He expected her to make something of the early finish, but she was still nursing her face and feeling sorry for herself. She simply waved him an absent goodbye over her head.

As Tyler left the building, stepping out into a late afternoon breeze, the letter tickled away at the back of his mind. He refused to let it take hold though. As he crossed the car park, he reflected that there was a time when he wouldn't have been able to do this. He would have worked long into the evening and then probably taken the whole case home with him to look over later. But those days were firmly behind him.

His life was so different now, compared to just a couple of years ago. He'd been obsessed with the death of his father, but now, while there were still questions to be answered surrounding exactly what happened all those years ago, for the first time he could remember he felt content. The man who had murdered his father was behind bars. Refusing to talk but locked up and unable to cause any more hurt to anyone.

For the first few months, Tyler had visited Mark Jackson every week. The man never refused his request, but neither did he ever answer Tyler's questions. He smiled a lot and said nothing. It had taken an intervention by Doggett to make Tyler confront what he was doing. He was losing himself again, transferring his obsession from his father's death onto his killer. Tyler had argued with Doggett for weeks, refusing to accept that the investigation into Jackson and the organised crime network he worked for was no longer his responsibility. But finally he'd recognised that if he didn't make a conscious decision to change, the whole business would be the end of him. He'd rung the prison and cancelled his next visit. He hadn't been back since.

One advantage of leaving early was the lack of traffic, and in less than fifteen minutes Tyler was pulling into an industrial estate near Meadowhall. There were a handful of restaurants and stores. He pulled into a space across from a coffee shop and got out.

Doggett was also the reason he was here now, although the DI didn't know that, of course. The talk he'd given Tyler about not getting lost in the past and seizing new opportunities when they were afforded you had been a catalyst for change in more ways than one. Tyler had first met Scott Austin when Scott had been working for the police as a Human Resources officer, but shortly after their meeting Scott had left to pursue a new career in counselling. Tyler had held onto his number though. It had been months earlier and he hadn't been sure the man would even remember him, but Doggett's words had rung in his ears, and he'd decided to take a chance. To Tyler's surprise, Scott had remembered him.

Inside the coffee shop, there was no sign of him yet. Tyler ordered a black Americano, double shot, and carried it over to a booth near the window.

Scott arrived a few minutes later, full of apologies. He hovered for a moment, as though waiting for something, then said, 'I'll just grab a drink then.'

Tyler jumped up. 'Let me get it.'

'No, really, it's fine.' Scott was smiling, but his furrowed brow suggested he was finding their exchange puzzling.

'Please,' Tyler insisted, inching his way out of the booth. 'I was the one who invited you. What would you like?'

Scott inclined his head. 'Oat latte, please. With some kind of syrup.'

'Anything in particular?'

'Whatever they've got. I don't mind. Sweet tooth,' he added by way of explanation.

Tyler went back to the counter. Not a great start. He hadn't been on a date for years, not a proper one. It was easy enough to hook up with someone these days, but he was out of practice when it came to the art of casual conversation. Of course, it wasn't just casual conversation, was it? Not really. First dates were about presenting yourself in the most flattering light, while simultaneously strip-mining your date for information. The latter, Tyler was certainly capable of, but the former was definitely not within his skill set.

He got the sense, however, that Scott could see him for who he was quite easily, even if he tried to hide it. Tyler was used to other people finding him confusing, and it was one of the things that he'd been attracted to about Scott when they'd first met. Although it had been in a professional capacity, when Scott had been assigned to make sure Tyler was coping after the death of a colleague, he'd felt that Scott understood exactly who he was, far beyond the confines of his job.

'I was glad you called,' Scott said, after they'd got the pre-liminaries out of the way. 'Although, I was a bit surprised.' He didn't say, 'after all this time,' but the words hung in the air, nevertheless.

Tyler had been surprised as well, but he managed to stop himself from saying so. He suspected it wouldn't be the best response under the circumstances. 'I'm sorry it took so long.'

Scott smiled at that. 'I did tell you not to ring until you'd sorted yourself out.'

Tyler smiled back. 'You did.'

'So, have you?'

Tyler wanted to say yes, if only because even he was savvy enough to know it was the right answer. But he had a feeling Scott would see through that as easily as everything else. Instead, he said, 'I'm sort of a work in progress.'

Scott laughed. 'Aren't we all?'

After that, the conversation began to progress a bit more smoothly. Scott told him all about his new job as a counsellor. He was studying for a qualification as well as working full time, which made Tyler wonder how they would ever find time to date considering the time constraints of his own job. But that thought made him realise something: he'd already decided he wanted to see Scott again. The conversation cycled through food and travels and favourite films – horror on Scott's part and a confession that he didn't watch much on Tyler's – until they came all the way back to when they'd met.

'I heard some of what you went through,' Scott said carefully. 'Your dad and everything. I'm sorry, that must have been hard.'

Tyler found himself clamming up again, as he always did when conversations moved perilously close to the events of that time, but he managed to nod an acknowledgement. The silence seemed to expand around them, swallowing up the good mood that had developed and sending them back to the awkward beginning.

'I'm an arse,' Scott said. 'I shouldn't have said anything. It's just, it felt like the elephant in the room.'

'It's fine,' Tyler said, looking up. 'Ancient history.' He could almost believe it too, although the look on Scott's face said he didn't.

'Still, not exactly first date material.' Scott reached across the table and took Tyler's hand. His own hands were soft and warm, his fingers long and thin. Pianist's fingers, Tyler thought, although Scott had already told him his only musical ability lay in a two-chord version of 'Scarborough Fair' he could strum on the guitar. 'Let me make it up to you. How about dinner?'

'Sure,' Tyler said, reaching for his jacket.

'Oh.' Scott grimaced. 'I meant another time. I actually have plans this evening. I thought this was just coffee.'

Tyler felt uncharacteristically foolish. 'Of course. No problem.' He wasn't sure he'd managed to keep the disappointment out of his voice.

'This weekend? On me.'

They made plans as they headed back out to their cars, and Scott left him with an awkward embrace and a chaste peck on the cheek.

As Tyler got into his car, he realised he'd been hoping the evening would play out differently. Things had seemed to be going well enough until the past had reared its ugly head again. But he forced himself to shake the doubt away: all in all, it really hadn't gone that badly. As he drove out of the car park, he was surprised to find he was smiling.

III

Staring down the barrel of an uncharacteristically free evening, Tyler's brain switched to its default setting and the letter jumped into his head all over again. He couldn't shake the feeling there was something in it he was missing. Before he'd really considered what he was doing, he found himself driving in the opposite direction to home. He was more than halfway to his destination before he realised where he was going: Frank Weatherstone's house.

He knew how to find the avenue in question, just off the Herries Road near the hospital, but he had to check his notes for the exact number. At the edge of a small council estate, it was an unusually large, detached property that stood out among the 1950s semis that surrounded it. Some kind of farmhouse, he guessed, although the accompanying farmland had long since been swallowed up by the estate. It still had a good-sized garden though, and an outhouse of some sort. He wondered again if he was wasting his time. Weatherstone could have absconded anywhere after his release from prison in the 80s and just failed to update his driver's licence. Although, the probation service would have followed that up, and Tyler had found no record of it.

The garden was a tangle of untended grass littered with piles of sand and the remains of some building equipment that didn't seem to have been used in quite some time. The house itself wasn't much better, the gutters blackened from overflowing water and the grouting between the brickwork loose and missing altogether in places. There had been some obvious attempts at repair over the years, but nothing that looked recent.

Tyler had a moment of doubt as he rang the doorbell. What was he even doing here? He had no idea what he would say. And if he said the wrong thing, he could be tipping his hand too early. If Weatherstone was guilty of a crime, he'd have time to dispose of any evidence. Being here was stupid and risky. But it was too late now – he could see a greying net curtain at the side window twitching. He smiled and raised his warrant card. There was the sound of a chain being undone, and then the door slowly swung open.

It was a woman, perhaps fifty years old, with greasy, greying blonde hair hanging down around her shoulders. She was wearing a saggy grey T-shirt, a grey woollen cardigan and grey jogging bottoms. Everything about her was grey except for the bulging black ovals under her eyes, which were red rimmed from crying. She looked at Tyler with no trace of interest or curiosity on her face. He showed her his warrant card again and announced his name and rank, but still there was nothing. He'd seen people who were high look like this, but there was no scent of weed coming from the house and her gaze didn't seem distant or untethered; she just didn't seem the least bit interested in who he was or why he was there. There was something unnerving about that.

'Can I speak to Frank Weatherstone?' he asked, and she replied with a single word.

'No.'

It didn't seem belligerent. She was stating a fact.

'But he does live here?'

The woman sighed heavily. She had rested one hand on the door jamb and he noticed that her nails were chipped, the cuticles red raw and bleeding in places. Her unkempt appearance had caused him to overestimate her age. She was in her late thirties or early forties, at most.

'Not anymore. He died.'

'Oh. I see.'

She offered no further information, so he prodded a bit further.

'And you are?'

'His daughter.'

'I'm very sorry for your loss. And your name?'

'Ruth.'

'Ruth Weatherstone?'

'That's right.'

'Can I come in, Ms Weatherstone?'

For the first time something approaching emotion flitted across the woman's face, but Tyler couldn't say exactly what it was. She seemed uncomfortable, certainly, but he had a feeling she might be like this with everyone. She certainly hadn't seemed particularly disturbed that he was a detective, and that in itself was a bit odd. She hadn't asked why he was there either.

'I was on my way out,' she told him, and he took that as a no.

He looked her up and down. She didn't look as though she was dressed to go out. Her bare feet were poking out from under her sweatpants, the toenails long and crusted with dirt.

'This won't take long.'

But she made no attempt to let him in. Instead, she continued to stand there, the blank look back on her face.

'Can I ask when your father died?'

'Two weeks ago. The funeral was today.'

He didn't think she'd said it that way to make him uncomfortable, but it had that effect. He could hardly insist on questioning her further under the circumstances.

'I'm really sorry, Ruth. I wouldn't have bothered you if I'd known.'

Nothing on her face told him whether she accepted the apology or not. He turned to leave but then had one last thought. 'I don't suppose your dad ever went to the beach, did he?'

'What?'

'The beach. You know, Skeggy, Cleethorpes. Did he have a preferred holiday destination?' Tyler was aware he must sound like a madman, but she had no greater reaction to this than she had to anything else.

'No. He didn't go anywhere.'

'Okay. Look, how about I come back at a better time? Do you have a mobile I can reach you on?'

For a moment he thought she was going to say no to that as well, and from the look of her he might even believe her. But then she began reeling off the number and he was forced to extract his notebook in double time. He read it back to her and she nodded.

'Okay, Ruth. Thanks. I'll be in touch. Once again, I really am sorry for your loss.'

As he walked away, Tyler wondered if the letter writer had known Frank was dead. It wouldn't be the first time a death had prompted a confession. Wives who had long been under the thumb of a controlling partner had been known to come forward about their spouse's activities once they were no longer a threat. Or daughters, perhaps?

Of course, it could just as easily be someone trying to pass the buck to somebody who could no longer defend themselves. If that were the case though, it begged the question why anyone would want to draw attention to something from so long ago.

He heard the door click behind him and turned to see the net curtain twitching again. He reminded himself the woman was grieving. People did funny things when they were grieving. But still, she hadn't asked him a single question about why he was there. That was extremely unusual, and he could only think of one reason. She already knew.

IV

Ruth pushed the door closed and rested her brow on it for a moment, the plastic cooling her forehead. Then she leaned over to the window and drew back the curtain an inch. He was still out there, looking back at the house. She let go of the netting and stood perfectly still. Eventually she saw the shape of him turn and walk away down the road.

She willed herself to calm down; her heart was thumping in her chest and the back of her neck felt hot and sweaty. Why had he come? What did he know? He hadn't given much away, but the whole time she'd been talking with him she'd felt as though she had the word 'guilty' stamped across her forehead. It was ironic. Wasn't it? She'd never been sure about the meaning of that word, but she thought it might apply here. She finally had her freedom and this detective turned up to take it away from her.

She checked the window again but there was no sign of him. She was being ridiculous. He wouldn't come back that quickly. Would he? No, of course not. He'd taken her number, which meant he would ring first. Didn't it?

As her heart began to settle, she started to think more clearly. He'd asked for Frank. And that meant they hadn't known he was dead. And he *was* dead. *Dead.* She had to remind herself of that. He couldn't hurt her anymore. But, no – of course he could. It couldn't be coincidence that the police turned up today, of all days. Had he left something behind that incriminated her? He certainly wouldn't have gone to any effort to protect her after his death.

Ruth shuffled cautiously into the front room. It was the room her father had lived in, and it still had his mark on it. The place stank of tobacco and the flocked wallpaper was so yellowed it was difficult to see what colour it had been in the first place. She certainly couldn't remember. And there was his chair. The sage green monstrosity he'd died in. There were stains all over it – the seat, the back, the arms – so it was difficult to say which of them, if any, were the result of the old man's life fluids seeping out of him at the end. She should have thrown it out straight away, but then she'd barely set foot in here in the past two weeks. Not since the funeral people had hauled him away. Even now the room seemed to resist her presence, as though his ghost still lingered. Perhaps it did. Maybe it was shouting at her, 'Get out, get out!', just as he always had in life. Maybe it was slapping her too, although if it was then she couldn't feel it anymore.

She sank to her knees on the gritty carpet and tears began to leak from her eyes. No! She would not cry for him. Why was she being like this? She hated him! She should be glad he was gone. She should be cleaning him out of this place and going on with her life. Finally. Finally living.

Isn't that what she'd been telling herself all these years? When he died, she'd be in charge of her own destiny. All the life she had never lived would be hers. She'd travel and meet someone wonderful. She'd get a job, a proper job that didn't just involve cleaning other people's toilets. She'd go back to school and do her A-Levels, or an access course, or whatever it was they called it. She'd go to university, and it wouldn't matter that everyone else was younger than her because the difference would be that they'd be there just to party and she'd be there to study, to be more than she'd ever dreamed she could be.

At uni she'd learn the guitar, or maybe the piano, and after uni she'd travel. She'd go to Canada and Japan and New Zealand. Canada because she'd always wanted to go across the Rockies by train; Japan so that she could see the cherry blossoms; and New Zealand because she couldn't think of anywhere further away from here.

The house creaked and shifted around her. *You're not going anywhere.* She could hear him laughing at her plans. *You think you can make it on your own? You can't even make a decent shepherd's pie. Useless bitch!* She flinched, reliving the warmth of the gravy running down her neck. One of those stains on the carpet was from that day. No way of knowing which one now. There were so many. Food for the most part, but blood too. He always made her clean it up. *Cleaning's about the only thing you're good for and you can't even do that properly.*

He'd let her get a job, eventually. But only once he was too weak to bring in any money himself. 'Cleaner,' he'd told her, relenting only after they'd had the conversation for the umpteenth time. 'Somewhere you can do by yourself, mind.

I'm not having you talking to people.' And then, just as he always did when he was worried she might be finding a way out from under him, he'd said, 'Remember, Ruth. You leave me and I'll set the rozzers on you. They'll find you even if I can't. No one's gonna want you after that. Though who'd want you anyway?'

Is that what he'd done? He'd known he was dying, after all. Could he have engineered a way to contact them in the event of his death? She wouldn't put it past him. One last attempt to control her life from beyond the grave.

You're not going anywhere.

He was right. The truth, the grubby reality of her situation, came to her as she knelt in the stench of her father's residue. She hadn't the vaguest idea how to live the life she wanted.

She wiped her face with the ripped sleeve of her baggy cardigan. The tears weren't for him. They were for *her* and the perilous situation she found herself in. He'd left her with nothing. No money, but then she'd hardly expected that. The only time she'd spent any time in this room was the day after he'd died, when she'd searched the place from top to bottom just to make sure he hadn't squirreled anything away somewhere. She didn't think he had, so she hadn't been disappointed.

But worse than that was that he hadn't left her any skills. Her schooling had been patchy at best, and he'd taken her out as soon as he could. He'd taught her no life skills and she'd had no mother to do so either. She'd never learned to drive. She couldn't even swim! The only skills she had at all she'd learned from the telly. It wasn't enough. She had no idea where to begin.

She'd only managed to organise the funeral with the help of the reverend, but she still had no idea how she was going to pay for it. She'd found no will or life assurance policy as yet; items she hadn't even considered until the reverend had asked her about them. He'd also suggested her father might have opened a funeral plan, and when she'd looked at him blankly, he'd faltered for a moment and then said he'd go ahead with the funeral anyway and they'd sort all that out later.

Without a will, she'd been told by her father's bank, she had no authority to access his accounts, but then she doubted there was anything significant in there. Still, it would have been nice even if it was just a couple of hundred, and he must have had some money somewhere because he'd gone up the betting shop often enough.

Ruth dragged herself to her feet. She was so tired. She looked around the room again one last time. She didn't have the energy for it now. She would just close the door and let it all fester for a bit longer. Maybe she'd start on the rest of the house, or maybe she'd just put the telly on.

She was shuffling back down the hallway to the kitchen when she caught a glimpse of herself in the long mirror. She looked an utter mess. What must the policeman have thought of her? She looked down at her stomach, the outline visible even under the loose cardigan. Maybe she should start by losing weight. *A healthy body, a healthy mind.* She'd heard some wellness guru saying that on *Lorraine* recently.

But something came to her now: the policeman would have seen only what he expected to see – a woman grieving the death of her father. He didn't know her past or what sort of woman she was. No one did. Unless she allowed them to. There was no need to panic. That wouldn't get her anywhere.

She felt something boil up inside her. *Useless!* But this time it was her voice she heard, not his. He was gone and this pathetic excuse for a woman was what he'd left behind. The only way she would ever truly be free of him would be if she could learn to change.

Could she though?

It had to be worth a try.

monday

1

Mina sits bolt upright in bed, gasping. Her T-shirt is sticking to her back and her hair's plastered to her forehead and neck.

The door opens and her mother leans in, a silhouette against the bright light from the hallway. 'Are you okay, Amina?'

She must have cried out. 'Yeah, sorry. I'm fine.' She puts her hand up to shade her eyes from the glare.

'You were screaming like that girl from the Essex programme!'

'Mum!'

'Okay, okay. I'm going.' Maryam begins to back out of the room but then stops and pushes her head in again. 'You need some breakfast. I'll make you something.'

Mina glances at the clock on her bedside table. 'It's only just gone four!'

'You were going back to sleep?'

She can't argue with that. 'Fine,' she says, pushing off the duvet and sitting up. 'But I'm going for a run first.'

Her mother arches an eyebrow at her.

'Thanks, Mum.'

Maryam nods and slides backwards, closing the door behind her.

Mina settles on a quick loop, down Abbeydale and back through Nether Edge. She stops outside the Picture House, its distinctive dome towering above the road, and accepts that it isn't coincidence she's come this way. *What was he doing here?* There's still a visible police presence, and she considers stopping to speak to Doggett, to see if he's found anything. She doesn't doubt he's still in there somewhere, ferreting around looking for clues. But he won't be pleased she's ignored his instructions, and it isn't as though she can help in her running gear. She jogs on.

The nightmare that woke her comes back to her in flashes. She was back at the hospital, hurrying through its endless corridors. She could hear Tyler calling out for her, but she couldn't find him, no matter how hard she looked. His cries were growing fainter and fainter as she searched down one corridor and then the next, her feet dragging through treacle. She knew she was running out of time but had no idea why.

She pushes the dream away and runs on, faster and faster. By the time she's home she's panting hard, and after a quick shower she begins to feel properly awake. Her mother is in the kitchen, cooking eggs and neglecting the fact that Mina is vegan – again.

'I'll just have some muesli.'

'Mina, you can't live on dust!' Her mother talks over her shoulder as she carries on with her cooking. 'Don't forget, your Uncle Nazir is coming this evening.'

'I'll make sure I'm on my best behaviour.'

'Amina!' her mother warns in a low voice.

'Fine. Fine. No work talk, I promise.'

Nazir had been the chief source of resistance within the family to Mina joining the force. Her mother's uncle, he was more than a little old-fashioned and there had been a lot of talk about women and their place, which had obviously only cemented her decision further. It had caused a rift in the family that hadn't so much healed as scabbed over. Now, as long as she stayed off the subject of work when he was around, they could usually get through a meal without incident. Of course, Priti, whose fashion choices were Uncle Nazir's other favourite topic of disapproval, never let an opportunity pass to remind him what Mina did for a living. For someone who got their information almost entirely from TikTok, she was remarkably up to the minute on local crime reporting.

'I'm probably going to be late tonight anyway,' Mina tells her mother now.

Before she can explain further, Maryam turns from the hob. 'Amina, would it kill you, just for once, to put this family before . . .'

Nazir wasn't the only one to disapprove of her choice of career. This particular argument already has a long history, and Mina sometimes wonders whether her mother still believes the archaic position she adopted all those years ago or is just so entrenched in it she can no longer see a way out. Normally, Mina would be up for the challenge, but today, perhaps because of Tyler, she doesn't feel like fighting.

'Where are you going?'

'To work.'

She leaves her muesli unfinished and heads back upstairs to finish getting ready, ignoring her mother's grumbling attempts to get the last word. Why does it always have to be like this? This constant war of attrition that eats away at them both. She knows – at least, she thinks she knows – that her mother's low-grade sniping comes from a place of love. Or concern, anyway. Maryam had lived in a state of almost constant fear for the first few months after Mina had joined the force. But Mina had hoped the passage of time would soften her mother's anxiety. Perhaps it never would. Perhaps that was what being a mother meant.

When she gets back downstairs, Maryam appears from the kitchen as though she's been waiting for her.

'Here,' she says, forcing a slice of toast into Mina's hands.

It's meant as a peace offering, so Mina takes it. She draws the line at saying thank you though.

'You'll get indigestion!' are her mother's final words as she leaves the house, shouted after her as Mina strides to the car.

She's in the office by five and gets to work on Tyler's desk. By a quarter to six she's been through everything she can find, which is hardly surprising given how fastidiously tidy he is. None of it, as far as she can tell, has anything to do with the Abbeydale Picture House. There's nothing in his calendar about a meeting, and the notes in his Duty Diary only refer to cases she's already aware of. She can't see how any of them link to the old cinema, but she goes over them anyway, just in case. Perhaps he'd found a lead connected to one of them, but if he had then why hadn't he mentioned it? She hasn't got access to whatever he'd looked up on their police systems, but she supposes Doggett will take care of that, as well as look at his mobile and Pocket Notebook. It all feels like a colossal waste of time. Did she really expect to find anything? If he had been there on official business, she would have known about it. And if he hadn't wanted her to know, then he wouldn't have left information about whatever 'it' was lying around at work.

Not all of their cold cases are stored on the system however, or even on computer. Far from it. Part of their remit, and the reason for their increased allocation of resources, is to correct that. But until they manage to do so, a lot of the cases they look into exist only as hard copy reports, stored in a warehouse half-way down the Parkway. She supposes it's possible Tyler pulled a file and was looking at it at home rather than in the office.

Which decides her on her second stop of the morning. But as she stands up and grabs her jacket, ACC Franklin appears in the doorway.

'Ma'am?'

'Ah, Mina. I had a feeling you might be in early.'

The Beak doesn't make a habit of visiting them at six in the morning and Mina feels an unexpected sinking in her stomach.

'Can I help you with something, ma'am?'

'I understand from DI Doggett that Tyler didn't tell you what he was working on.' As is her habit, Franklin manages to set her challenging question as a statement of fact.

It puts Mina in a difficult position, which is probably the point. 'We often work on different cases,' she offers, diplomatically.

'Hmm,' Franklin agrees, without really agreeing. 'Is there any more news on his condition?'

'When I left the hospital last night—' it was actually this morning, Mina realises '—they were saying it was a waiting game. Hopefully, in a few days the swelling will go down and then ...' The surgeon had been less forthcoming about what came after that. 'Then, I guess we'll see.'

Franklin takes this information on board without comment, as though Mina has just informed her about a suspect in one of their enquiries. She moves to the window and then turns and looks down at Tyler's screen. Mina can see it's still on, the screensaver yet to kick in, the tell-tale glow reflected on Franklin's face exposing that Mina must have been looking at it. She feels the colour beginning to rise in her cheeks.

'I need you to be focused on CCRU.'

The sudden turn in the conversation throws Mina, and she has no doubt it's intended to. 'Ma'am?'

'It might not have occurred to you, but with Tyler out of action for ... well, for the foreseeable future, I need you to step up and fill his shoes. You're a capable officer and you've been ready to take your sergeant's exam for a while now. Why haven't you?'

'I ... I just want to make sure I'm fully ready in terms of—'

Franklin interrupts her. 'Well, that aside, *you* are now in charge. You have a team who'll be reporting to you and who will need guidance.'

I'm in charge? The thought hadn't occurred to her. And if it had, she would have assumed that Diane would be the person best placed to take the reins. Either that or they'd bring someone else in. Maybe they'd asked Diane already and she'd said no.

As if reading her mind, Franklin goes on. 'Diane Jordan, and Suzanne Cooper for that matter, are both civilians now. That doesn't necessarily discount them from steering the ship, but you are the longest serving member of the team and the most au fait with the day-to-day running of the unit. I've no doubt they'll support you, as will I.' She pauses for a moment and cocks her head on one side as though confused as to the problem. 'You have my full confidence, Mina.'

'Thank you, ma'am.'

'But with that in mind, you should be aware that I do *not* want your priorities skewed by what has happened to DS Tyler.'

Ah, here it is. The sting in the tail. A silence settles in the office, with only the hum of the water cooler to break it.

'Ma'am—' Mina finally manages, but Franklin is ready for her.

'I understand it will be tempting for you to get involved in the investigation, but that will not be permitted to happen. DI Doggett is more than capable, and if I thought differently, I would have handed this whole thing over to Professional Standards.'

Something in her tone gives Mina the impression she might still do that. Could Franklin really believe Tyler was up to something dodgy?

'And I will not allow this unit to fall apart,' Franklin goes on. 'It might be weeks before we know the exact circumstances surrounding Tyler's accident and—'

'Accident?' Mina blurts. 'It didn't look like an accident. DI Doggett said—'

Franklin holds up a hand. 'I'm sure DI Doggett will keep all lines of enquiry open, but as it stands there's no evidence that anyone else was in that part of the building. It seems likely, as unfortunate as it may be, that DS Tyler simply lost his footing.

From what I understand it's a very old building in quite a state of disrepair.'

'But we can't just assume—'

'Nobody will be *assuming* anything, DC Rabbani, but *your* job is here. We've invested a lot of time and resources in this department over the past year or so and I won't let that fall apart while DS Tyler is incapacitated. *You* won't allow that to happen. Is that understood?'

Mina can feel her cheeks heating up again, though not for the same reason as before. 'Yes, ma'am. Understood.'

'Good. Well, I'll leave you to it. I'm sure you've got plenty to be getting on with.' Franklin strides back to the door and then turns. 'I think perhaps it's best if you keep me up to date with your progress. I'll set up a weekly meeting so we can examine the unit's performance. Try not to look so worried, Mina. This is a good thing.'

A good thing? Mina's face must betray her thoughts because Franklin corrects herself.

'Not regarding DS Tyler, obviously. But every cloud and all that. This is a good opportunity for you, and I've no doubt Tyler will thank you for it when he returns. Carry on.' And with that, she's gone.

Mina drops back into her chair. She'd hardly moved the whole time Franklin was in the room. *What the hell was that all about?* She'd like to think it was simply Franklin looking out for her, that they have some special relationship that warrants this close attention, that the other woman is only really worried about the running of CCRU. But Mina hasn't forgotten how ruthless Franklin had been when they'd first met, pretending to mentor Mina so she could pump her for information about Tyler. Does Franklin really expect her to sit back and not get involved with this? How far can she take what the ACC says at face value? Mina knows what Tyler would say to that.

Mina looks down at her overflowing in-tray. Maybe Franklin has a point. Tyler wouldn't thank her if she let the department fall apart on her watch. She swivels her chair to face his desk. There's one thing she knows for sure, though. If their positions were reversed and it was Mina lying in that hospital bed, Tyler wouldn't drop it, no matter what it cost him. And despite her assurances to Franklin, she has no intention of dropping it either.

She waits a few more minutes, not that she couldn't explain herself to Franklin if she was caught leaving the building again, but still . . . just to make sure. Then Mina grabs her coat and car keys, and to hell with her career.

2

It's still early when she reaches Tyler's apartment building and pulls up outside the gates. Sunlight slips between the blocks of brick buildings, but it's weak and ineffectual, and Mina shivers in the chill morning air. Summer's on its way out and this cold is the first sign of the change.

Her first obstacle is the front gate. She could ring the concierge, she supposes. She can see him sitting in his office at the foot of the first building, but she'd rather not have any record of her being here if she can avoid it. It's doubtful Franklin's going to be out here investigating but still, better to be safe than sorry. She doesn't need to puzzle over this long though, because the gates swing open to allow an office worker to drive out and she slips through before they close again. She walks slowly and purposefully past the concierge, but he doesn't even look up from his desk. Even if he had, she doubts he would have challenged her. There must be hundreds of people living in this complex, and he can't possibly know them all.

The second obstacle is entry to the building itself, but again she doesn't have to wait long before a woman leaves for work. Mina gives her a wide smile as she catches the door and strides in. She's beginning to make a habit of this, first at the hospital and now here. If Franklin does fire her she might have a promising career as a cat burglar.

The third and final obstacle is the hardest though: the door to the apartment itself. She really hasn't thought this through. If she had, she could have lifted Tyler's keys from the hospital when she was there last night. She supposes she still could, but the drive there might take half an hour or more at this time of day, and that's assuming she can just pop in, take the keys and get out again. It's unlikely she could manage that if Diane's still there. She'd have to explain what she's up to, and she's not sure how Diane would respond. Even if she were inclined to help, by the time Mina made it back here and performed her search she wouldn't make it back to the office much before lunchtime, and that's a bit of a risk if Franklin's watching her as closely as she made out.

She wonders if she could try picking the lock. She saw Tyler do it once, with a plastic credit card or reward card or something. But that had been a long time ago and the lock in question had been old and flimsy and, she suspected, a lot easier a target than the reinforced fire door of this relatively new apartment building. Plus, she has no idea how to do it.

Further along the corridor, another woman emerges from her apartment on her way to work. Mina knocks on Tyler's door as though she's just arrived and waits while the woman passes. Again, she smiles in reassurance, but this time she must not get it quite right because the woman scowls at her suspiciously.

Mina watches her push her way out of the corridor, but she doesn't glance back. Suspicious, but not suspicious enough to raise an alarm.

There's a loud graunching sound as the handle in front of her flicks downwards, and the door swings open as though by itself. Mina jumps back with a slight squeal. Jim Doggett's standing in the doorway, blinking at her with one eyebrow raised.

'You don't make much of a Jehovah's Witness,' he says.

'I was just . . .'

He steps back, holding the door open for her. 'Well, you're here now – you coming in, or what?'

Mina steps into Tyler's hallway. Doggett closes the door behind her, turns and crosses his arms.

'I thought . . .' Again, she trails off.

'You thought you'd come and have a nosey and see what Tyler was up to? Same as I did. Only, *I'm* meant to be here. Officially.'

Mina drops her eyes to the floor.

'Exactly how were you hoping to get in? You can't have expected an answer to that knock.'

Mina struggles to find an answer, so she turns the question around. 'Well, how did you get in?' she demands, looking him squarely in the eye again.

Doggett pulls a set of keys from his pocket. 'Diane gave me these.' He wiggles them in mid-air before slipping them back in his pocket.

At least that's answered one question. 'What did you find out last night?' Mina asks. It's as much an attempt to distract him as because she's desperate to know.

'Not much more than you already know,' Doggett says, and it looks as though the admission pains him.

'The car?'

'Clean.'

'What about Scott? He said Tyler got a call from someone earlier in the evening.'

Doggett nods. 'His personal mobile's missing.'

'What?'

'It wasn't on him when we found him. His work one was in the car though, so we might get something off that.'

'Well, that proves it then – someone else *must* have been there.'

'Hold your horses, Quick-Draw. It could be here. Or he could have lost it.'

'Tyler? You don't believe that.'

'It doesn't matter what I believe, it's what I can prove. Franklin still seems to think this whole thing could just be an accident.'

'Bullshit!'

'Aye. But after everything the department's been through, do you think she wants to go running to Professional Standards again? Maybe it suits her to believe it was an accident.'

Mina hadn't thought of it that way. It puts their conversation in a new light and maybe explains why Franklin doesn't want her getting involved and muddying the waters even further. Doggett doesn't work directly with Tyler, so if he does find out Tyler was up to something then it doesn't compromise them as much. It makes sense, but Mina still wants to be involved.

As though he's read her mind, Doggett says, 'Standing about

in this hallway isn't proving her wrong, so since you're here, why don't you make yourself useful? You can take the bedrooms while I finish off in there.'

It doesn't take them long to search the entire apartment. It's a relatively small place and, as Doggett surmises at one point, if Tyler is working on something secret, 'he's hardly likely to have hidden it in his underwear drawer.' Even so, what they're doing feels wrong. Mina knows she certainly wouldn't appreciate anyone rifling through her belongings if the situation was reversed, and Tyler was more private than most people. *Is!* she reminds herself. *He isn't dead yet!*

But there's nothing. No work of any description that they can find. And no phone. Doggett does find Tyler's laptop though, packed away in its case. 'I'll take it in for the "speccy-techies" to have a look at,' he tells her. Other than that, the only paperwork is an expandable concertina file that holds bank statements and personal information. Mina finds it stored neatly in a plastic box under the spare bed. Given how tidy Tyler keeps his desk at work, she probably shouldn't be surprised. All the information he ever needs is filed away in his own head.

After an hour or so she abandons her search and heads back into the kitchen-living area. She swears loudly. Doggett, on his hands and knees in the kitchen, pulls his head out from under the sink and looks at her.

'Why didn't he tell us what he was doing?' she asks. *Why didn't he tell* me *what he was doing?*

Doggett hauls himself back to his feet, wincing slightly as his knees crack. 'You have met Tyler, right?'

'I know, I know. It's just . . .' She thought they'd got past all this. For years Tyler had kept his personal obsession with his father's death from her, but after they'd arrested Jackson, it had really felt like all that was over. 'He seemed . . .'

'Different?' Doggett suggests.

'At peace,' she says, and Doggett nods.

'I have to admit, he did seem a lot more content about life recently. I figured it had something to do with him banging the counsellor fella but, whatever it was, it looked good on him.'

'So, what changed?' she asks, and Doggett gives her one of his trademark shrugs.

He wanders over to the living room windows. Tyler's is a corner apartment with a view across the same car park that Mina crossed an hour or so ago. The autumnal sun's fully up now and feels warm and comforting on her skin, through the glass at least.

'When did you notice he was acting different?' Doggett asks her.

Mina tries to think back. 'I'm not sure. He's been distant. Quiet. For a few weeks, maybe a bit longer?'

'But you definitely noticed a change?'

Mina thinks hard before she answers. She *had* noticed, but she'd been trying to ignore it, hoping he would bounce back. She'd put it down to his personal life, or maybe just the changes in the way they were working in the department – they were all still getting used to that. 'Yes,' she says finally. 'He's definitely been behaving a bit weird. 'Last week he was barely in the office. When I asked him what he was up to, he made excuses. Not even very good ones. If it were anyone else, I'd have said they were slacking but . . .'

'It wasn't anyone else,' Doggett finishes for her.

Mina shakes her head.

'And you don't think it was personal? He didn't have a row with the tight-trousered counsellor?'

'Scott said much the same as us last night, that Tyler's been distant with him lately too. They met last night for a drink, but other than that Scott hasn't seen him for a while.'

'Or so he says.'

Mina looks at him. Could Doggett really suspect Scott of being involved in this? Of course, he could: Doggett would suspect everyone, until there was evidence to the contrary. *He probably suspects me.* The thought disturbs Mina more than she would have expected.

'An old cinema would have been a bit of an odd place for a date,' she says.

Doggett taps his scuffed trainer heel on the laminate flooring, his trademark twitchiness getting the better of him. 'Hmm.' He offers no further opinion.

'So now what?' she asks.

'You find anything in the office?'

She shakes her head, wondering whether he knows she's already been in this morning or is just guessing.

'You have a department to run,' he tells her. So, he *has* spoken to Franklin.

'I can't just let this go,' she says, hearing the strain in her own voice.

'No one expects you to,' he tells her, and then adds, 'not even Franklin. But you do need to carry on as normal. Play the game, Mina. She'll turn a blind eye if you do a good enough job, but don't push your luck. In the meanwhile, I'll keep you up to date with anything I find, okay?'

'Fine,' she says.

'Talk to the others,' he adds. 'Jordan, Cooper. See if they remember anything. And I want you to jot down everything you can think of. Every conversation, every off-the-cuff remark. Anything that didn't sit right with you. Go back as far as you can but start with last week. Can you do that for me?'

'Of course.'

'Right. I'll talk to you later.'

They leave the apartment together, and Mina's pleased to see that despite their rummaging, and maybe because of Tyler's fastidiousness, they've managed to leave things pretty close to how they were when they came in.

As she arrives back at the office and gets out of the car, she experiences a sudden sensation of being watched. She glances around but can't make out anyone nearby. No doubt she's imagining it. Locking the car and heading into the building, she considers her thoughts from earlier. If Tyler had been working on something, would he really have kept all the notes in his head? It seems unlikely, even for him. But if he did have some notes somewhere, then where were they now? That they were missing, or hidden, must add credence to the theory that he didn't just fall. There was something suspicious about this, surely.

Whatever the truth is, she'll find it.

3

Ruth steps forward, ready to shout a greeting. 'Oh, hi! What a coincidence!' or something like that. But the words shrivel on her tongue and her feet attach themselves to the ground and refuse to move. She stands there, determined to press forward with her plan but totally unable to.

Mina hesitates, then turns and turns again, as though searching for someone, suddenly conscious she's being observed. Ruth slips quietly behind the wall she'd been leaning against and takes some deep breaths. Had she been seen? It would be one thing to happen across Mina accidentally but another entirely if she were to get caught stalking her.

Dipping her head back around the edge of the wall, there's no sign of her target. She really shouldn't have worried – no one notices Ruth Weatherstone unless she makes the effort to be noticed. And not always then.

She bangs her fist hard against the brickwork, the rough surface grazing the heel of her hand. Why did she freeze like that? She peels away from the building and heads towards town.

A wasted opportunity.

Maybe she shouldn't have come here, to the police station. Mina might have insisted on making things official and dragged her into a cell or something. She'd considered approaching her closer to home, but then how would she explain the fact she knew where she lived? But still, the police station. Maybe it was for the best she'd lost her nerve and Mina hadn't seen her.

Useless bitch!

No! She's better than this now. She's not a scared little girl anymore. She's a grown woman. Certainly more grown up than most of the women she's met in the past few months. They think she's one of them, these *girls* she meets at bars. To them, she's another flighty thing in heels and a sparkly frock, interested in the same things they're interested in – guys, shots, *Love Island*. They have no idea she's the cuckoo in the nest. That she constructed this life for herself barely six months ago. *Fake it till you make it!* That had been the title of the TED Talk she'd watched on the day of the funeral. She'd used it to reinvent herself.

So why hadn't it worked this time? Why can't she 'fake it' with Mina?

She crosses the tram tracks and negotiates the doorway of a McDonald's where a group of teenagers are vaping and hurling insults at each other. She's never been a teenager.

She has to find a way to talk to Mina. That other one, DS Tyler, had turned out to be nothing but a disappointment. But it would be different with Mina, wouldn't it? She'd understand. She had to. They have a connection.

Ruth wishes she could be certain of that. Maybe that's what had made her freeze. She still isn't a hundred per cent sure how to proceed, how much to say, how much of the truth to reveal.

Nearly at her bus stop now, she begins rooting through her pockets, hoping to find enough change for the fare. If not, it's going to be another long walk home.

A wasted trip, but next time she'll be more confident. She'll work out exactly what she's going to say beforehand. *Fake it till you make it.*

Mina Rabbani is going to give her what she needs.

5 months ago

I

Ruth pulled at the waistband of her dress, hitching her knickers up again. She knew she should have bought some new underwear to go with it.

Over the past few weeks she'd undergone something of a transformation. She'd managed to lose some weight, mostly through healthy eating – she'd used that unofficial Slimming World website that gave out free recipes – but she was also getting out and about a lot more. With no reason or desire to stay at home any longer, she'd taken on extra cleaning shifts, which had the not insignificant bonus of a bit more money coming in. Added to that, the reverend had helped her apply for a government grant for the funeral costs. She hadn't got it yet, but he seemed convinced it would happen, so that was one less thing to worry about. She'd still not had any luck with the bank, but even that wasn't enough to dampen her good mood. All in all, she thought she had the right to feel proud of herself, perhaps for the first time, and she'd decided she deserved a little treat.

She'd found the dress and matching clutch purse in a

charity shop just off Division Street, one of those cool places which was full of students buying flared trousers and dungarees. Everyone in there had been so chic and she'd done her best to emulate them. At first, she'd been embarrassed to be the oldest person in the place by a long chalk, but then she'd remembered the TED Talk she'd found on YouTube the day of the funeral. *Fake it till you make it!* So, she'd ignored the stares, the unspoken judgement, whether real or imagined, and by the time she left the shop she'd convinced herself she had every right to be there.

Now, standing awkwardly on the terrace at the front of the bar, she was doubting herself again. She clutched the gin and tonic in her hand and surveyed the scene before her. It was a Cuban tapas bar, and one of the high communal tables scattered across the terrace was teeming with tanned, dark-haired young men smoking roll-ups. Bar staff on their break, she assumed. She thought she recognised the young one on the end with the head of thick black curls as the guy who'd served her when she'd arrived. Her eyes met his and he winked lazily at her. Ruth swallowed and turned away.

At the next table there were two couples, one staring into each other's eyes and the other engrossed in their phones. She ruled it out.

The third table was empty, but a group of girls spilling out of the bar were starting to drift towards it. It was now or never. She launched herself forward, so she reached the table at the same time they did. Two of them shot her looks that bordered on hostile, but the third smiled. It was the sort of place where you couldn't complain about sharing a table with strangers, which is why she'd picked it. Ruth perched one buttock on a high stool at the end of the table and began to sip her drink.

They were all smoking. Everyone smoked. She'd noticed before the effortless way in which people who smoked were able to strike up conversations with each other, and had decided this was her way in. She'd practised lighting and inhaling at home, choking on the burning smoke the first couple of times, until she thought she had it down well enough not to embarrass herself.

The woman in the middle was exactly the sort of friend she had imagined having. Bright-eyed and chatty, with her hair hanging in artful waves around her shoulders in varying shades of blonde and brown. *A balayage*, Ruth thought; she'd seen it on a Holly and Phil makeover. Clearly a career woman; she was talking about some issue she had with a colleague, rolling her eyes and waving her cigarette to emphasise what a 'bell end' he was. The other two listened and inserted the occasional shake of a head or a muttered 'oh my God'.

'He sounds like a right tosser,' Ruth interjected loudly. All three women turned to look at her, and the stony silence made her worry she'd misjudged the situation. 'Sorry,' she added, waving her own cigarette dismissively, 'I didn't mean to eavesdrop. But seriously, why are we still putting up with this shit? Am I right?'

The woman in the middle held her eye for a moment, and then she smiled. 'Oh my God, I know, right? What do *you* do?'

'Advertising,' Ruth told her. What spilled out next was so elaborate and detailed that if their positions had been reversed Ruth would never have known it for the pack of lies it was. She made up stories about her work on a glamorous new campaign for L'Oréal, throwing in casual references to six-figure sums and bonuses. She invented a colleague called Gus who regularly stole her ideas and passed them off as his own. The girls on each side began to ooh and aah in appreciation, and even the one in the middle seemed impressed, although she was less vocal in her responses, maintaining her tight smile and emphasising it occasionally with a sage nod of her head. Ruth was in.

She bought a round of drinks, only slightly baulking at the price. It was an investment in her future after all. She hesitated before paying and asked the bartender to recommend a shot. When she got back to the table with a bottle of wine and four bright pink miniature glasses of something that looked like stomach medicine, the girl on the left – Amy – whooped encouragingly and Ruth found herself flushing with relief that she'd gambled well.

Laura – the girl in the middle – said, 'Oh God! Tequila Rose is soooo last summer!', but she threw back her head and downed the liquid as fast as anyone else, so perhaps she hadn't meant it as a put down, exactly. More a reminiscence.

As the evening wore on, Ruth experienced what she could only describe as an out-of-body experience. Perhaps it was the booze: she wasn't exactly used to drinking. But whatever caused it, the sensation was real enough. She could see herself sitting there on the stool, laughing and joking with these three women – Laura, Dalpreet and Amy. 'You are a darling, Ruth!' Laura told her at one point, and Ruth found herself melting under the praise. 'I couldn't bum another fag off you, could I?'

A darling! Ruth thought as she passed across her rapidly

dwindling packet. No one had ever said anything like that to her before. Was this what it was like, having friends? It had all been so much easier than she'd thought.

'More drinks!' someone shouted.

'I'll get them!' She was giddy with the newfound camaraderie.

At the bar, the dark-haired lothario was back. 'Nice dress,' he said, as he began to pour the drinks. He spoke with a laid-back drawl, in an accent she couldn't quite place.

Ruth found herself blushing. Surely he wasn't serious. But then, perhaps he was. After all, she had nothing to mark it against. She turned her head and found another man watching her. He wasn't quite as handsome as the bartender, but his slicked-back quiff had a certain elegance. He had a nice smile too; he was using it on her now.

Ruth felt wonderful. Men were noticing her. *People* were noticing her!

The bartender's smile slipped as she turned back to him. 'Those ladies,' he said, nodding his head towards the outside terrace where Laura was once again holding court. 'You know them?'

Ruth frowned. 'Actually, I just met them.'

'Ah.'

Ah? What did that mean?

'Look, love,' he said, slipping out of the indeterminable accent so completely that it took Ruth aback. 'That lot are in here pretty regularly. They have a habit of . . . well, put it this way, I've never seen *them* buy a drink. Just thought you should know. You seem like a nice girl.' The wink made another appearance.

Ruth felt her mouth begin to fall open, but no words would form. 'It . . . It's not . . .' she managed eventually.

'Look, I'm not trying to be funny, but they're taking advantage of you. I've seen 'em do it before and it just boils my piss.' The smile was gone now.

'Could you . . . ?' Cheeks burning with humiliation, she couldn't think of the right words and stuttered out a curt, 'M-mind your own business!'

It sounded ridiculously childish. The bartender raised his hands in mock surrender.

'My bad,' he said, but she saw him roll his eyes at the guy with the quiff.

The blood pumping through the back of Ruth's head and down her neck made her feel hot and dizzy. She still couldn't find any words. Nothing she'd seen on YouTube had prepared her for this. 'Wha . . . How much?' she stammered.

He rang up the total on the till and she passed him the cash. As he took it, his eyes flicked up and down her body. She saw disdain in his gaze and began to wonder if his earlier comment about the dress hadn't been flirting. He probably said that to every woman. He was probably *paid* to say that. Ruth grabbed the tray and turned away from the bar, feeling herself flush deeply. The man with the quiff caught her eye and smiled again, perhaps in sympathy, but she was too mortified to do anything other than hurry away.

Back at the table, the others let out a whoop of excitement as she put down the tray. They seemed not to notice her sudden change in demeanour as they hungrily divvied up the drinks between them. She sank back on her stool and tried, as they

chittered and giggled among themselves, to summon up whatever magic she'd employed before. To become one of them.
To fit in.

It was no use. She was acutely aware of her distance from
these women. It was in the quality of their outfits; the tightly
woven material and the shiny newness of their shoes. It
was in the thick lustre of their hair and the weight of their
jewellery. Everything about these women was so much more
substantial than Ruth. Except perhaps their waistbands.
She watched Laura's perfect fingers as she gestured her way
through another anecdote, with their multi-coloured and
immaculately manicured nails. Looking down at her own
hand, she saw the way the bright red polish she'd found in
a drawer was patchy in places, the paint bleeding into her
cuticles and failing to hide the bits of skin that she constantly chewed.

Laura and her friends emptied their glasses but made no
attempt to head to the bar. Ruth's own drink sat untouched on
the table in front of her.

She stood up slowly, feeling the tears building behind her
eyes. None of the others even registered her as she picked up her
clutch purse, for the first time noticing how dull and tarnished
the clasp was, and began to walk away.

'Ruth?' One of them – she thought it might have been
Amy – called after her, but she was already heading for the
steps leading down to the road. She heard a couple more shouts
of her name but then whoever it was gave up. She stepped out
onto the pavement, turned the corner and pressed her back up
against the stone wall as though she needed the support. Perhaps

she did. Now she was up and walking through the crisp spring evening, the drink had hit her. Tears began to roll down her face and she wiped them away savagely.

'Are you okay?'

Ruth jumped. It was the man with the quiff.

'I'm sorry,' he said, gently reaching out to touch her arm. 'I didn't mean to scare you.'

'I'm fine.' She straightened, pulling away from him, although not too sharply. 'Just needed some air.'

He smiled again. It really was a lovely smile.

'I'm Drew,' he said, and then hesitated. 'Look, I ... I just wanted to say, I heard what that guy at the bar said, and you really shouldn't listen to him. He was bang out of order.'

'No, he wasn't.' Ruth heard the crack in her own voice. 'He was right. They *were* taking advantage.'

The man – Drew – frowned. 'Well, he still shouldn't have said it. Not like that.'

'I'm such an idiot.' *Useless!* She felt the old self-pity welling up inside her. She couldn't help herself, it was all going to come pouring out in front of this stranger. 'I'm not like them. I can never be like them.' She turned away from him and felt the hot tears slide down her cheeks again.

'Why would you want to be?' he asked, and the words brought her up short.

She turned to look at him. Was he trying to take advantage of her as well?

'You're upset. I can't let you go home like this.' He nodded towards the bar opposite. 'Let's pop in there for one.'

'I don't think so.' She started to move away but he brushed

his hand against her arm again. It wasn't enough to restrain her, but she stopped anyway.

'It'll be quiet in there. You can tidy yourself up a bit while I get the drinks in. *I'm* buying,' he emphasised, the smile back again in force.

'I think I've probably had enough.'

'A soft drink then? Please?' he added.

Ruth hesitated. The humiliation was fading but she still felt silly and exposed. She wiped away the rest of her tears. She was being pathetic, allowing those idiots to get the better of her and ruin her evening. She looked again at this man with his lovely smile. Drew. He seemed genuinely concerned for her, and the bar was well-lit and looked safe enough. She nodded, slowly.

'Thatta girl!' he told her, and she let him take hold of her arm this time and escort her across the road.

The toilets were down a set of stairs that were far harder for her to negotiate than they should have been. Ruth washed her face and examined herself in the mirror. Bloody hell, she looked a mess! Her mascara had run, so she had no alternative than to scrub it off the best she could. She took some rolled-up toilet paper to her rouged cheeks as well. What a fool she'd been, playing dress-up. She looked like a clown.

After a bit of furious scrubbing, she decided it was the best she could manage. She still wasn't sure she'd take Drew up on his offer of a drink, but at least she felt a bit calmer now. She supposed she ought to at least thank him for taking the time to look out for her.

Back upstairs she found him waiting at a table near the door. He stood up as she approached and pulled her chair out for her like some sort of old-school gentleman. It seemed strange given how young he was.

They sat down, and for a moment he just stared at her. Ruth worried she hadn't done as good a job with the makeup as she'd thought, but then he said, 'Wow.'

She laughed a little, embarrassed.

'Sorry,' he said. 'It's just ... and please don't take this the wrong way. You're much prettier without that shit all over your face.'

The profanity was thrilling. Ruth pushed a stray strand of hair behind her ear and looked down at the table. 'You're taking the piss.'

'I'm really not. I meant what I said before. I don't know why you'd want to look like those ... painted idiots with their lips and faces all puffed up with chemicals. You have a natural beauty. You shouldn't hide it.'

'Oh, come off it!' She was laughing now. 'You're winding me up.'

'I'm sorry you think so.' He was laughing too, but not unkindly. 'You should have more confidence in yourself.'

She noticed he'd ignored her request for a soft drink and bought them a bottle of white wine. There was a glass already poured for her.

He explained apologetically, 'I took a chance you'd change your mind. I can still get you something soft if you'd prefer.' He started to stand up, but she waved him back down.

'It's fine. Thank you.' She took a sip. It was a very nice wine, much better than what they'd been drinking at the other place.

He told her it was a Sauvignon, from New Zealand, and she

wondered if he was showing off, trying to impress her. She sipped from her wine glass and laughed nervously as he spoke. His confidence was overwhelming. It took her a moment or two to realise he'd stopped talking and was looking at her intently.

'Listen, Ruth, I—'

'How do you know my name?'

'What?'

'I never told you.'

He looked stricken. 'I . . . I heard the woman at the bar calling after you. At least, I assumed that was you. Your name *is* Ruth?'

'Oh. Right. Yes.' She supposed that made sense.

'Okay, then. Phew!' He laughed. The confidence was back. 'So anyway, I was going to say, I'd like to get to know you better.'

'I really should be going,' Ruth said, standing up. For some reason she felt uncertain again, the panic from earlier rearing up in her once more.

He stood up with her. 'That's fine. Let me get you a cab. But please, can I at least get your number?'

Ruth felt a little flutter of something inside her but found herself saying, 'You're . . . too young.'

'I'm older than I look,' he told her, and she wondered if this was flirting.

'All right then, I'm too old.'

'I like older women,' he said, but to Ruth that made the gap seem even bigger.

'What are you? Twenty-seven? Twenty-eight?'

She saw his face fall and she knew she'd got it right. She'd always been good at guessing ages.

'It's just a number,' he said. He looked up and smiled again, shyly, and Ruth felt butterflies in her stomach.

What harm was there in a number? 'Okay,' she relented, and pulled out her mobile.

After they'd exchanged numbers, he was as good as his word and hailed her a black cab, even passing the driver a twenty to cover the fare. She attempted to argue, but not very forcefully. She'd already spent far more tonight than she'd intended. He kissed the back of her hand gently as she got in and promised to call. Again, she was struck by how gentlemanly he was.

Ruth leant back against the black plastic seat as the cab wound its way through the city streets and out onto the ring road. A lot of money, but perhaps not a waste after all. Her mobile, still clutched in her hand, vibrated and chimed, and she found herself lifting the screen to her face with a swell of hope.

> Ruth. I would like to speak to you again about your father. Would tomorrow be okay? Whatever time is most convenient for you – DS Tyler

She felt that little surge inside her tummy again, but this time it was for a very different reason.

II

Tyler checked his phone for the third time since he'd got to the office. Still no word from her. He shouldn't have been surprised but it was annoying all the same. With Diane on her day off and Mina out the whole week on some bloody nonsense training course, he had a lot to fit in today, and knowing what time Ruth Weatherstone would be available to talk to him would go a long way in helping to coordinate his agenda.

He considered ringing her but then decided against it. He should probably give her a bit more time; it had been very late when he'd sent the message. Mina would have told him off for that. Perhaps Ruth was a late riser and had yet to check her phone.

The feeling that she was hiding something had only grown in the weeks since he'd spoken to her and, given that all other leads had dried up, she might be the only chance he had of ever understanding that letter. His research into her had drawn a blank. She had no driver's licence, no criminal record, barely any presence on social media. The only thing he had discovered of any note was that she was thirty-eight years old, significantly younger than he'd assumed when she'd answered the door. Could she have written the letter? He would have guessed from the writing at someone much older, but if she was poorly educated, he supposed it wasn't impossible.

Still, kid gloves for now. He needed to keep her onside as far as he could, at least until he was sure she was involved in this somehow. Otherwise, he'd be fielding a harassment charge, and he doubted Franklin's renewed support for CCRU would protect him from that.

Instead, he refreshed his emails, hoping he'd have something from Corinne Daley-Johnson. Corinne was another Franklin addition, their own personal forensic scientist who worked out of a private lab somewhere in Leicester. Not that she only worked for them, of course, but they could call on her when needed (provided he could justify the expense). He'd sent the letter to her three weeks ago (and unless she found something conclusive, he definitely could *not* justify the expense) but so far he'd had no response. He considered chasing it up, but it was hardly urgent, and Corinne didn't respond well to people telling her how to do her job. 'Choose your battles,' Diane had whispered to him obliquely after his first entanglement with her.

Tyler sighed and pulled a copy of the anonymous letter from his drawer. Not for the first time, he wondered what it was about this whole business that kept drawing him back in. It was beyond low-priority, and it wasn't as though he didn't have a string of cases he was working on already that looked like they might have much more promising outcomes. CCRU had three arrest warrants for historical offences ready to be served, a possible lead on an unidentified body found washed out of one of the Sheaf culverts last month, and he was due in court later in the week to give testimony. If Franklin knew he was wasting his time on an anonymous letter he knew little more about now than the day it landed on his desk a month ago, she'd have plenty to say, no doubt. Thankfully, so far at least, she'd stopped short of the level of micromanagement she'd threatened. Nothing had materialised of the PR exercise either, for which he was grateful.

But there was something here ... something he was missing. It was an itch somewhere deep in his mind that he just couldn't scratch.

Tyler heard Doggett grumbling his way down the corridor long before the man himself came into view. The scruffy little DI stomped into the office, grabbed the empty chair from Mina's desk and wheeled it across to Tyler's own.

'You'll never guess what the bloody woman's gone and done now!' he announced, far louder than was wise given the office door was wide open; there was little doubt he could mean anyone other than Franklin. He dropped onto the chair with a bounce and the wheels squeaked their objection.

'I'm guessing she hasn't put you forward for a commendation.'

'The Last Laugh comedy club rang. They want you to head-line next week.' Doggett's face was deadpan. 'She's only gone and brought back that useless article, Vaughan!'

DS Vaughan had been transferred back to Doncaster a while back after spectacularly failing to win over Doggett, despite her golden girl status with Franklin.

'I thought you'd got shot of her?' Tyler was well versed in humouring this and other of Doggett's various antipathies.

'Yeah, so did I. Until bloody Max got herself up the duff. Managed to get herself diagnosed with some bloody unpronounceable condition and now it's all "bed rest" and "light duties".'

'Pre-eclampsia.'

'I don't give a stuff what she calls the baby.' But there was a glint in Doggett's eye that betrayed him. 'The point is, did Franklin really have to go and lumber me with that bloody fool again?' The wheels resumed their squeaking as he took up a rhythm with his foot on the floor. 'The girl couldn't find her arse with both hands.'

Tyler tried not to grin. 'I'm sure you'll soon knock her into shape.'

Doggett looked at him, searching his face for some sign of amusement. Instead, his eyes found the copy of the letter on the desk. He frowned as he read it upside down. Then he grabbed it and pulled it towards him.

'You're not still looking into this, are you?'

'It passes the time.'

'And have you discovered anything?'

Tyler's silence was enough to cause a grin to break out across Doggett's face. 'Well, don't let the Beak catch you wasting resources on nonsense.'

'I'm glad I've cheered you up.' Tyler tried to snatch the letter back, but Doggett jerked it out of his grasp.

'Hang on, then. Give us another look.'

Tyler tried refreshing his emails while Doggett read. After a few moments, the DI whistled and looked up.

'It's not exactly Nobel Prize-winning literature, is it?' He read from the letter, '"It was beach whuh—". I suppose some daft 'apporth might call it poetry, but I mean, who writes a murder confession but fails to mention the name of the victim?' He read on a bit. 'I take it you've looked into this bloke, Weatherstone?' he asked when he'd finished.

'He's got a short record that ends in the Eighties.' Tyler gave Doggett the potted biography he'd uncovered so far. 'The interesting thing is, he died a few weeks ago, so I wondered if that might be what prompted the letter writer. I've been trying to reach his daughter but—'

'Yeah, fascinating,' Doggett interrupted. 'Can't wait for the Netflix series.'

Tyler snatched the letter back and tucked it into his desk drawer. 'Did you come up here for anything in particular, or is this just a general wind-up visit?'

Doggett looked across at him, the grin fading from his lips. He leaned back in the chair, putting his right foot up across his left knee. He might have looked still and at peace for once, had his foot not started jiggling about in the air to some rhythm only he could hear. 'How are you?' he asked, seriously.

The question caught Tyler off guard. 'I'm fine. Why wouldn't I be?'

Doggett shrugged. 'Oh, I don't know. You haven't been back all that long, and I wondered if catching the bloke what killed your dad might have sent you west or summat.'

Tyler said nothing.

'I guess I should have known better. Nothing ruffles the Iceman, eh?'

Tyler rolled his eyes. It wasn't the first time he'd heard that epithet applied to him. 'It beats what they used to call me.'

Doggett's brow furrowed a little and he leant forward. 'And what about Jackson? All these little visits.'

'I stopped going. You were right.'

Doggett nodded. 'Well, that's the best bit of news I've had in a long time.' He dropped his right foot and swapped it for the left, which took up the same rhythm without pause. 'A little dickie bird told me you took another bit of my advice.' When Tyler frowned, he went on, 'You rang the psychiatrist.'

'Who told you th—?' But even as he said it, he realised he knew the answer. Diane. 'He's not a psychiatrist, he's a trained psychotherapist.'

'It figures you'd be dating a shrink. Come on then, give us the gruesome details. Not too gruesome, mind.'

The second date had actually been very enjoyable. The conversation had flowed much more easily than in the coffee shop, with Scott talking a lot more about his change of career. In turn, Tyler had tried to steer clear of the thorny topic of his own work, and in doing so considered that there used to be other things in his life. He'd told Scott about his university days, and his travels around the world shortly afterwards, then given him a truncated account of the series of events that had led him to change direction and brought him into the police force. He'd even talked about the incident that had led to the scar on his face. Though he'd played down the seriousness of the whole thing, just the fact that he was telling the story was a huge step forward.

All in all, the evening had been the best night out Tyler could remember having in a long time, and he hadn't even waited until he got home to text Scott and set up another date. Scott had said yes straight away.

Then had come the ill-fated trip to the cinema. It had been some ridiculous horror movie that Scott seemed to inexplicably enjoy. Tyler had found the whole thing interminable and by the time they'd come out he'd been struggling to hide his contempt. They'd planned to go for drinks afterwards, and maybe if they had they would have got past it, but then Tyler's mobile had rung. A thirty-year-old car mechanic had taken his girlfriend hostage after shooting two pedestrians outside their house and the Murder Team needed support. Scott had said he understood, but there'd been a look in his eye as they parted company that said he was having second thoughts. And the truth was, it always came down to another case, sooner or later. There would be many more broken dates. Tyler had never had a relationship last more than a few months, and if it was as much hard work as this was, and at such an early stage, that hardly boded well for the future. Did it?

Since that night, he hadn't heard anything from Scott. Tyler supposed it was probably up to him to get back in touch given that it was his fault the last date had ended early but, well, maybe it was better that it ended now before it properly began.

'I take it from your face, you've fucked it up already then?' Doggett asked. 'Maybe that's why you're looking for a new crusade.' He uncrossed his legs. 'Just a thought.' He jumped back to his feet and headed for the door without waiting for Tyler to respond. 'Right, well, some of us have got real work to be getting on with. Good luck with your cryptic crossword, Sherlock.' This last he shouted as he left the room.

Tyler found himself unusually irritated by Doggett's visit, but only because he knew the other man was right. He was wasting his time on this letter business. Still, he pulled the copy out of the drawer and read it over again. Something Doggett had said had stuck with him: *who writes a murder confession but fails to mention the name of the victim?* It was a valid point. Was that what had been bugging him? There were definitely no other names on the page, besides Frank Weatherstone's. No other capitalised words other than the beginnings of sentences. But then, Weatherstone's name wasn't capitalised either. Tyler read the letter again, looking for words that could be names. He supposed 'shunt' could be a name. Unusual though. No, it was clearly a bastardisation of 'shouldn't'. And 'supost' was 'supposed', although elsewhere the writer had spelled it 'suposed'. Did that mean something?

Beach? Was that a surname? Maybe the missing word wasn't 'where' but 'what' − *It was beach what we killed*, or something along those lines. That fitted with the Sheffield dialect displayed elsewhere.

Tyler googled the words 'Beach' and 'surname', and the first hit gave him the origin of the name: Norman ancestry, 'a name given to someone who lived near a stream, or a prominent beech tree.'

Beech.

He felt a chill across his shoulders. It couldn't be. Could it? He found himself performing another online search, this time for a full name. Alison Beech. Again, the very first result brought up the information he was looking for. It was a news report from the *Daily Mail* in the late 1990s: *Police − 'Kidnapped politician's wife feared dead'*.

He'd read the letter so many times now that the words

bounced around in his head. *No one was supposed to get hurt. We was going to let her go.*

Tyler felt a surge of satisfaction. He picked up the phone to ring Doggett. Then put it down again. He could be wrong. It might not have anything to do with her at all. And he was not about to give Doggett any more ammunition.

But that itch in his head had disappeared. The story hadn't been headline news for decades now, but for a time it was all anyone had talked about. This wasn't an anniversary year or anything that might have prompted one of the crazies to come out of the woodwork. There was a good chance that whoever had written this letter, along with Frank Weatherstone if the writer was to be believed, had kidnapped and probably killed Alison Beech, the wife of Dominic Beech, former MP and now Lord Beech.

Her body had never been found.

III

Twenty-four years ago.

The case had been big news at the time. Sheffield MP Dominic Beech had firmly hitched his wagon to Tony Blair's meteoric star and was riding high in the polls. He'd yet to achieve front bench status but it was widely agreed, by those who knew such things, that it was only a matter of time. And those commentators had been proven right; despite the tragic events of that summer, Beech had gone on to serve in three separate government departments, written an autobiography that touched on his personal tragedy without feeling too exploitative, and was currently a well-respected peer of the realm and reassuring presence on the occasional televised political commentary panel.

Tyler had still been just a kid, so he didn't remember the details first-hand. When he thought back to that time, he remembered it as an uncharacteristically blissful period of his childhood. His mother had been gone long enough that he'd almost grown used to it, and it was still a few years before his brother, Jude, would fall in with the wrong crowd and set off the chain of events that would ultimately lead to the death of their father. Tyler was doing well at school, played in the lunch-time chess club and, unlike the years that followed, enjoyed a healthy cohort of playmates. Other than a vague awareness of the fallout surrounding the death of Princess Diana, his knowledge of events taking place outside his own small bubble was fairly limited, and his biggest concerns were the upcoming move to 'big school' and attempting in vain to keep his Tamagotchi alive.

But public interest in Alison Beech's disappearance had lasted for longer than a single summer. For a few years the case had been reviewed periodically, and the local press in particular had a tendency to drag the story out on its anniversary, dusting down the details and repackaging it as a useful filler piece in case of a quiet summer. Throughout the following decade there had been a couple of books written on the subject, and a TV documentary which had tried, unsuccessfully, to reignite an active investigation into what had become of Alison. Since then, among the force at least, the case had become something of a local legend, bandied around the station as an example of a notorious vanishing, much like Lord Lucan or Shergar.

So, everyone knew *of* the case, if not its finer points. Doggett had been right, annoyingly. This *did* fall within the remit of CCRU, and it was a case Tyler himself had a familiarity with because he'd reviewed it before, if not in any great detail.

Alison had been snatched from a playground in front of her young son. A witness had seen her being bundled into the back of a white van and, despite Dominic paying the £250,000 ransom that had been demanded, she'd never been seen again.

It was widely believed that the unknown kidnappers had killed Alison and hidden her body somewhere that had yet to be discovered – an unmarked grave in the Peaks or a one-way trip out to the North Sea had been the bleak, if practical, conclusion of the TV documentary, although there was no physical evidence to support either conclusion.

As Tyler reviewed the case, he tried to keep any such suppositions at arm's length. The officer in charge of the investigation had been a DI Robert (Bob) Smith, who had retired almost ten years ago. He made a mental note to 'reach out' to him – Franklin would appreciate that one. It wasn't always easy talking to past investigators though. They were often defensive, assuming that any new information that turned up would paint them in a poor light, as not having done their jobs properly or guilty of mistakes. It didn't help that sometimes that was true, although more often than not a break in a cold case came about simply because of the passage of time – the development of new techniques in DNA extraction, or, as in this case, an anonymous tip from a pricked conscience.

However, there was nothing in the notes to imply that Smith had made any bad decisions. If anything, that in itself was a little unusual. In any investigation, there were inevitably a few inconsistencies; the odd mistake made or procedure not followed to the letter of the law. People weren't perfect and didn't do perfect jobs. But in this case Tyler couldn't see anything that warranted rechecking or following up. Perhaps DI Smith had been more perfect than most.

What there wasn't any mention of in the case notes, however, was any Frank Weatherstone. More often than not, when an anonymous tip came in it led them to a suspect that was already connected to the case, but there was nothing here about him. If the tip was real, and Tyler was becoming increasingly convinced it was, then it was seriously possible they might make some progress.

The one discordant note that did occur to him now, though it hadn't done when he'd previously reviewed the case, was that the whole thing hadn't been even bigger news, both at the time and since. Beech was, and continued to be, a highly prominent personality. In Tyler's experience, he was exactly the sort of victim who could and would cry loud and strong about any perceived lack of results from a police investigation. But he hadn't. No pressure had been applied to the Chief Constable – at least, nothing obvious. There'd been no public outcry of dissatisfaction, no attempt to galvanise support or interest in the continued investigation into his wife's disappearance. Beech had declined to take part in the TV documentary and was still notorious for being unwilling to talk about the events of the time when interviewed. Doggett's favourite watchword, 'The husband did it', sprang into Tyler's head. It wasn't exactly a smoking gun, but it was noteworthy that Beech hadn't been more vocal in his attempt to find the perpetrators of this crime. Or his wife, for that matter. On the other hand, perhaps he was just a very private person. He'd withdrawn from public life for a while after that fateful summer, and even now he wasn't one of those politicians who regularly courted the media.

Tyler sat back in his chair and considered what he had. He knew what Franklin would tell him, but it wouldn't be what he wanted to hear so he decided to leave her out of this for now. Surely an informal chat with Dominic Beech wouldn't hurt? And it was well within his purview to take another look at the case.

He made two phone calls.

The first was to Doggett to enquire after Smith.

'Old-school,' was Doggett's concise response. 'But competent,' he added, as though aware he was obliged to offer a bit more. 'Why do you ask? This isn't still to do with that bloody letter, is it?'

Tyler was ready for this. 'No, something else entirely. I'm just going over an old case and I wanted to look him up and get his opinion on something.'

Doggett grunted. 'Retired to Spain, I think. I've got a feeling he carked it though. Couple of years back.'

The second phone call, to Tyler's surprise, met with better results.

IV

The house was a modern, detached place in the leafy suburb of Fulwood. House wasn't quite the word for it, though. The place was huge, constructed of unfeasibly large panels of glass and metal that had probably been craned into place under the watchful eye of a Channel 4 design documentary team. The focal point of the impeccably landscaped approach to the building was an enormous monkey puzzle tree, which towered above a grassed mini roundabout in the centre of the driveway.

Dominic Beech opened the door himself, which threw Tyler a little. He'd half expected a liveried butler to appear, silver tray in hand and white cloth across his arm, to ask him to wait in the drawing room; the master would see him shortly.

Tyler introduced himself, presenting his warrant card, and Beech showed him into a plushly furnished living room which stretched all the way through to the back of the house. He was a distinguished-looking man, impeccably dressed in an artfully casual combo of fitted shirt and chinos. He had grey wings in his still-dark hair, but if anything they served to emphasise his youthful charms, the boyish good looks that had been his stock in trade when he had sat in Parliament. Given the man was a little over sixty, that was no mean feat. However else his wife's disappearance might have affected him, it hadn't caused him any premature aging.

'Thank you for agreeing to see me,' Tyler began.

Beech shook his head. 'Not at all, not at all. I can scarcely believe it after all this time but . . . I take it you have some news or . . . ?' He left the sentence hanging.

Tyler had decided not to mention the anonymous letter for now. It might have to come to light at some point, but until there was a good reason to believe it would lead somewhere there was no point in raising the family's hopes. 'I'm afraid not, sir. As I explained on the phone the other day, this is just a routine re-examination of the case. To see if anything could have been done differently, or if anything was overlooked.'

'Ah.' Beech nodded. 'I see.' He dropped his gaze, but Tyler couldn't decide what it meant. Was it the dying of a final spark of hope? Or just the tempering of anticipation? Even if it was the latter, that didn't mean anything. Beech had had more than two decades to come to terms with what had happened. He'd remarried ten years ago and had two more young children now. He could hardly be expected to still be grieving, at least not in the same way.

'Please, take a seat,' Beech offered, sitting down himself in a leather armchair. 'Can I get you anything?'

Tyler took the sofa opposite and waved away the offer of refreshment.

'How can I help?' Beech crossed his legs, interlocking his hands over his knees. It was a classic defensive gesture, but not unusual. When people found themselves dealing with the police, they often went straight on the defensive. It was natural, a sort of irrational sense of guilt they couldn't help displaying.

'I know it's difficult, but it would help if we could go over that day again. Everything you can remember.'

Beech snorted a small laugh. 'Difficult? I'll say it's difficult, though probably not for the reason you mean. It was a very long time ago, Detective, and to be frank with you, I long tired of fielding enquiries about this. I made a pact with myself that I would only talk about any of it when I absolutely had to.'

Tyler supposed that was reasonable, but he said nothing, waiting for Beech to intuit that this was, in fact, one of those times he absolutely had to. But the other man seemed to have plenty of experience dealing with uncomfortable silences. He smiled lightly and Tyler saw another flash of the charismatic all-rounder who had helped charm not only the Red Wall, but the Liberal and Tory voters as well.

'Okay, let me see,' Beech said eventually, leaning back and uncrossing his legs. It looked like a practised gesture, as though he might have been aware of his earlier defensive stance and was now telling the world he had nothing to hide. No doubt he would have been trained in dealing with the media and he wasn't the sort of politician who struggled with it. Tyler doubted the man ever did anything subconsciously.

'Alison took Lucas to the park that day – our son. The first I knew anything was wrong was when the police arrived at my constituency office to say he'd been found alone. That was the start of a nightmare that just seemed to run and run ...'

Tyler had watched an interview Beech had given on

Newsnight a few years ago. It was an unusually candid account from a man who famously prized his privacy, but it was clear the entire interview had been closely scripted. Beech had been there to speak in support of a new online protection bill, and his wife's kidnapping was brought up in passing to help convey his own experiences of internet trolling over the years. His telling of the story now was remarkably similar. Even that phrase, 'a nightmare that just seemed to run and run', was word for word what he had said back then.

He was a performer. The sequence of events that had unfolded all those years ago might have been a nightmare at the time, but by now it had become little more than a fairy tale, a story to dine out on occasionally. Perhaps Tyler was being unfair to the man, but he didn't think so. There was something chilling about how easily Beech talked about the fate of his wife. Something almost entertaining about the words he used to describe the police sting at the ransom drop. An operation that he certainly had not been present for, though he described it almost as though he had been. There were occasional moments when his words dried up or he choked, but even these seemed stage-managed. Tyler began to accept he was unlikely to get much of any worth from Dominic Beech. He was too schooled in the art of media politics.

As the well-rehearsed speech continued, Tyler also realised that it had been a long time since he'd dealt with a case going back this far. It was another reason Franklin would probably tell him he shouldn't be wasting time on it. The older the case, the less reliable the testimony of any remaining witnesses. It wasn't the only factor used to grade the merits of a renewed investigation, but it was a significant one. DI Smith was no longer around to answer for any mistakes he might have made; after his conversation with Doggett, Tyler had managed to confirm that he had indeed 'carked it' and had been cremated and scattered somewhere along the Costa Brava. Frank Weatherstone, if he was guilty, was also gone, unable to provide testimony, let alone be tried for any wrongdoing. The only possible reason to continue was in the hope of finding Alison's body, and without any new evidence there was only one avenue of investigation left open to him: the anonymous author of the letter. If he found the letter writer, could he find Alison?

Something Beech was saying suddenly caught Tyler's attention. 'Sorry, say that again please?'

Beech frowned as his practised monologue was cut short. 'Which bit?'

'You said, "other cases"?'

'The kidnappings,' Beech reiterated. 'Surely you've read the case file?'

Tyler was wrong-footed. There had been no mention in the file of any other kidnappings. 'I'm afraid record-keeping back then wasn't what it is today. I have very little information from the original investigation and DI Smith is no longer around to speak to.' It felt a little close to admitting fault and Tyler began to regret coming here without more of a game plan. He was rushing into things again.

Beech raised an eyebrow that could have meant anything, and as he re-crossed his legs Tyler decided the likelihood was he'd lost some credibility with the man.

'DI Smith's theory was always that the kidnappers had

actually been targeting Lucas, not Alison. When she fought them off and he got away, they took her instead, figuring she'd be worth as much to me as my son. They were right about that. I think there was a witness who came forward to corroborate this.'

'I've seen the witness statement.' Tyler had read it. A young woman named Greene had testified that she'd been out walking her dog when she saw a scuffle between a woman and two men. As statements went, though, it wasn't very detailed.

'As I understand it,' Beech went on in a lecturing tone, 'there had been a couple of other children taken from parks around that time. Smith thought the same people were responsible. That's why he encouraged me to go along with the ransom drop. In the other cases, the ransom was paid and the kidnapped child was returned. Only, this time was different.' Beech looked down at his shoes and for the first time Tyler saw genuine grief etched across his face. Perhaps he had misjudged the man.

This was all news to Tyler though, including that comment about Smith encouraging Beech to meet the ransom demand. It wasn't shocking that Smith would have left that out of his report, but why wouldn't there be mention of the other cases?

He did his best to move the conversation on. 'When the kidnappers contacted you they told you not to go to the police, but you did.'

'You're not telling me I was wrong, are you, Detective? Even then, I knew enough about personal security to realise that in these situations the victims are rarely returned unharmed. I did what I thought was best. What *was* best!' It was the first time Beech had raised his voice.

Tyler put his hand up in defence. 'I'm not suggesting you were wrong, sir. I've absolutely no doubt you did the right thing, regardless of the outcome.'

Beech seemed satisfied with this and nodded. 'Is there anything else?' he asked, simultaneously checking his watch.

'Am I keeping you from something?'

'Zoom call. But I have a few more minutes if there is something else?'

Tyler examined the man in front of him for a moment. He decided to cut to the chase. 'I get the sense you'd rather I didn't look into any of this again.'

'Your senses are remarkably acute, Detective.'

'May I ask why?'

Rather than answering, Beech placed his fingers together and rested them on his lips for a moment. Then he sprang up out of his chair. 'I'll show you why.' He crossed to a solid oak sideboard and selected a landscape photo frame from among the many that scattered its surface. He brought it across to Tyler and held it out to him.

'On your left' – Beech indicated the relevant photo with his forefinger – 'is a picture of my two girls, Zara and Catherine.' The picture showed two toddlers playing together in a sandpit on a sunny day. From the background, Tyler surmised it had been taken in the back garden of this house. The summer before, perhaps; it had been a particularly good one.

'They're very lovely,' he said, unsure if this was the correct response. He glanced across at the photo on the right. It made for a stark contrast. A teenaged boy stared sullenly at the camera. He was about fourteen or so and had jet-black hair and pale skin. He wore the classic Goth uniform of black jeans and T-shirt; the logo on the tee was a skull wearing headphones and the name of a band was emblazoned underneath. At least Tyler assumed it was a band; he'd never heard of them. It had obviously been taken in a nightclub of some sort and it was difficult to make out many of the details. 'This is your son,' he didn't quite ask.

'Lucas, yes,' Beech confirmed. 'He doesn't look like that now, of course. He put that whole rebellious phase behind him, thank God. He lives in Canada and, I'm ashamed to say, this is the most recent photo I have of him.' Beech took back the photo frame and turned it round. He stroked the glass with his thumb and examined it, lost in thought. 'He couldn't stand it. All the speculation and intrigue. Never mind the guilt he felt about what had happened. I tried my best to shield him from the worst of it but . . . well, I suppose I wasn't around enough. My bad, as the kids say these days.' Beech put the frame back on the sideboard. 'That's why I never talk about it, why I pretend none of it ever happened, why I don't want it all raked up again. Alison is gone, long gone. It was all horrible beyond words, you can't imagine. But we can't change the past, can we? All I can do is protect us from having to go through all of it again.'

By 'us', Tyler had the feeling Beech was talking about his daughters rather than his distant son.

'Unless you have some sort of new evidence . . .'

Tyler finished the sentence for him. 'You'd prefer it if I didn't go stirring things up.'

Beech inclined his head. 'I'm happy to have this conversation with your superiors if I have to.'

'That won't be necessary.'

Tyler did his best to appear as though he'd got what he wanted, apologised for causing Beech any distress, and took his leave. As the front door closed behind him, he glanced back at the great steel and glass monument that was the family residence. *Unless you have some sort of new evidence . . .* Did he? Arguably, although he knew which side Franklin would come down on if she got a phone call from Beech tearing her off a strip about her over-exuberant officer.

He turned away from the house and started down the long driveway. The first spots of a cold rain hit the top of his head.

Maybe he would even have agreed with Franklin, under normal circumstances. But unfortunately for *Lord* Beech, if he'd wanted Tyler to drop the whole business, he'd made one fatal mistake: he'd threatened him.

Now there was no chance he was going to give up. He was going to find Alison Beech, even if it killed him.

tuesday

1

Mina foregoes her normal morning run, in order to have time to visit the hospital before work. She almost wishes she hadn't when she sees Tyler. He's barely recognisable, trussed up in traction, barely an inch of him visible beneath the bandages and breathing apparatus. She feels herself on the edge of tears and has to swallow hard to fight them back as she watches him barely clinging to life. She has to be strong for Diane.

But on the bus back into town she lets them fall, doing her best to hide her face from the other passengers with her hand. By the time she gets off near the old market she's half-blinded by tears, which is maybe why she doesn't see the woman until she's almost careered straight into her.

'Oh, hello!'

Mina doesn't recognise her at first.

'Ruth,' the woman says. 'We met the other night. At Leigh Raddon's house?'

'Of course,' Mina says, smiling and wiping her eyes. 'Hi, Ruth. How are you?'

'Me?' Ruth asks, seemingly taken aback that someone would be asking that question. 'I'm . . . okay. I guess.'

There's an awkward silence. Mina expects Ruth to ask the same back, or to comment on her tears – she must look a state – but Ruth just stares at her and blinks. Her outfit's a little less coordinated than the one she had on at the barbecue: a block-print blouse and jeans, either of which on their own might look quite nice. But she's wrapped a baggy beige cardigan over the top, shapeless and shabby. Mina can't help noticing that there's a hole in the left sleeve.

Ruth is still staring at her intently. 'Have we met some-where before?' Mina asks. 'I mean, other than the barbecue, obviously.'

Ruth's cheeks colour and she stiffens slightly, as though upset.

'I'm sorry if I've forgotten, it's just, I meet a lot of people in my line of work and—'

'Can we get a coffee?' Ruth blurts out, interrupting her. She pushes a few strands of greasy hair behind her ear and now her gaze slides away, her eyes failing to make eye contact with Mina's.

'I'm on my way to work.'

'I didn't mean now.' Ruth's voice is brittle. She breathes out a little huff and seems to check herself. When she goes on, her voice is softer. 'I'm sorry. If I'm being honest with you, I don't really have many friends. I thought we got on well the other day and . . . well, when I saw you just then I thought I'd see if you'd like to have coffee sometime.'

Mina feels her own cheeks flushing now. 'Sure,' she finds herself saying. 'Why not?' But even as she says it, she finds herself worrying that this might not be such a good idea. There's something odd about the woman. On the other hand, she's not so good at making friends herself. Maybe she's being too judgy. 'Why don't you give me your number?' she goes on, pulling out her mobile. 'I can give you a call next week.'

Ruth appears to hesitate for a moment as she pulls out her own phone. 'I always forget the number. Give me yours and then I can ring you.'

Mina pushes down a little internal sigh. So much for that trick. 'Sure.' She gives Ruth her number and then watches while Ruth calls her. Mina's mobile buzzes in her hand. 'Got it,' she says, but Ruth looks on expectantly. *She's actually going to watch me put it in the address book.* Mina types the name 'Ruth' against the number and presses Save.

'So, when are you free?' Ruth asks immediately.

Mina makes a point of looking at her watch. She's had enough of this; she's beginning to think she won't be making that call after all. 'I really need to get to work. I'll text you.'

'You won't though, will you?' Ruth suddenly looks like a child on the verge of a tantrum; her cheeks are flushed and her hands are balled at her sides.

Mina glances around at the people passing by. It occurs to her for the first time that maybe the woman fancies her or something, but then she dismisses it. She really doesn't have time for this.

'Okay, look, Ruth,' she begins, determined to set the woman straight. Perhaps she should have been more forthright to begin with. She certainly has no intention of becoming friends with her now.

But once again, Ruth interrupts. 'I really need to talk to you,' she says. 'It's important. It's . . . to do with your work.'

Mina's starting to worry now, preparing herself for a very awkward confrontation on the street. Is this something to do with some old case she's worked on but can't remember the details of? She straightens her back and pushes out her chest a little – her work stance, her brother Ghulam calls it. 'Ruth, if you have a complaint or a problem, you should speak directly to the station.'

'No, no, no, you don't understand.' Ruth's beginning to sound desperate. Is she unhinged? 'I lied to you before.' She's avoiding eye contact now. 'At least, I didn't lie exactly but I didn't tell you everything . . . I'm not trying to cause any trouble, honestly. I just . . . I just need some advice about what to do. I hoped, what with you being a police officer, you could help me.'

Now that some of the fight has left Ruth, Mina relaxes a bit. 'What's this about, Ruth? Are you in trouble? If someone's threatening you or—'

'No, it isn't that exactly but . . .' She looks around. 'I don't want to talk about this in the street. If you could just meet me. Please. For coffee. That's all. Somewhere public. I'll explain everything.'

Mina hesitates, but what harm could it do? And anyway, she's intrigued now, despite herself. 'Okay. I really do need to get to work but . . .' She checks her watch. 'How about this evening? I can probably get away for five. The coffee shop on the corner there.' She points across the road. 'All right?'

Ruth nods but then frowns. 'You'll really be there?'

'I'll be there,' Mina says.

'Thank you.'

Ruth smiles properly for the first time and her face is transformed. She's genuinely worried about something. But then why all this cloak and dagger? Why didn't she just say so from the start?

'Thank you. I appreciate you taking the time. I'm sorry if I . . .' She doesn't finish the apology.

'That's okay. You'll be all right till then? You're not in any danger, are you?'

'No, no, I'll be all right.'

'Okay, I'll see you at five-ish.'

Mina hurries away but can't help glancing back. Ruth's watching her, and waves enthusiastically in her direction. The woman's clearly disturbed in some way.

What has Mina got herself into now?

2

'Right,' Danny announces as he strolls into the office, 'how can I help?'

Mina feels the blood rushing through her arms and legs. Adrenaline, she reminds herself. Because he made her jump, that's all. No other reason.

'What are you on about?'

'I'm here to help. Whatever you need. I wasn't supposed to start until next week but I cleared it with the desk sergeant.'

She frowns at him. 'We don't really have any active cases at the moment. Certainly nothing that requires a PC.' She's aware that it might sound like she's dissing him but it's too late to take it back now.

If he's offended, he shows no sign of it. 'Yeah, but . . . Tyler, right?' Now it's Danny's turn to frown. 'You must be investigating what happened to him? I figured, with DCI Jordan at the hospital and DI Cooper on leave, you might need an extra pair of hands.'

He's very well informed for someone who's only just transferred back, but then she supposes he must still have friends here. He was always one of the lads, slapping each other on the back and helping each other along when they got into trouble. Though, in fairness to him, he was never like that with her. He might have said the wrong thing now and then, but he never took the piss out of her, and he wasn't one of those who thought she shouldn't be in the job, or worse, didn't deserve to be.

'You okay, Min?' He's looking at her, concern etched on his face.

'Of course I am,' she snaps, turning her back on him and picking up some random paperwork from her desk. 'And don't call me that.'

He's quiet after that but she can still feel him there, lurking behind her. She glances over her shoulder to see that he's wandered over to the window.

'Bloody hell! That's a view!'

She sighs, drops the pages back on the desk and turns around, crossing her arms for extra defence. 'Look,' she says. 'We really don't need you at the moment. Why don't you go and find DI Doggett? He's the one investigating Tyler's attack anyway.'

Danny turns around. Silhouetted by the light of the window behind him he really does look as though he's been working out. 'It *was* an attack, then? Not just an accident?'

Mina hesitates. 'We're not sure but . . .'

He nods and crosses back over to her. 'But you think so. And so does Doggett.' He grins. 'You're not working the case though, right?'

'Right,' she tells him, failing to quite meet his eye.

The grin widens. 'Understood. Okay, I'll go see the Yorkshire Terrier and see if he can use me.'

'You're keen to get involved, aren't you?'

'What do you mean?'

'Don't get me wrong, Danny, it's good to see you, but from what I remember you weren't all that interested in CID.' *Or anything other than keeping your head down until you could draw your pension.* She doesn't say that bit out loud.

The grin returns, wider than ever. 'Maybe I saw how well you were doing, and I fancied a bit of that sweet action for myself.'

Is that supposed to be his idea of flirting? Damn Emma for trying to set them up on that ridiculous date! Now she can't stop thinking about him that way. This prize prawn who could never keep his eyes off women when they were on patrol together. She doesn't have time for this. Doggett tasked her with talking to the others and going over everything they could remember from the past few weeks. Trouble is, she's already spoken to Diane this morning and she can't get through to Suzanne, who'd mentioned something about some retreat or other when she'd gone on leave. That leaves her with her own memories, and as much as she's been over them she can't think of anything that might help. Who else is there?

She looks up to see Danny still staring at her with lazy eyes. What's he waiting for?

'Okay, I'll be off, then,' he says, still making no attempt to leave.

'I don't suppose . . .' she begins.

'Yeah?' The look of hope in his eyes is almost pitiful. He's like a puppy dog, eager to please. A suspicious part of her can't help wondering why.

'When was it you spoke to Tyler?'

'What, last? About a week ago, I guess.'

'You don't remember anything, I don't know, anything odd about him or . . .'

Danny frowns. 'I'm not sure I get what you're asking me.'

'No,' she says. 'Neither do I.'

'Talk to me, Min-a.' He adds the last letter in response to her glare.

'We don't know what he was doing there, in that place. None of us – not me, Diane or Doggett. It doesn't seem to be connected to any case he was working on and there doesn't seem to have been any reason in his private life for him to be there. As far as we know anyway.' She didn't like adding that last bit, but it didn't help Tyler if they weren't being honest with each other.

'Okay,' Danny says, his brow furrowed in a thoughtful way that makes him look like a child trying to puzzle out how to tie his shoelaces. 'So how can I help?'

'You're all right, Danny. I don't think you can. I just wondered if he said anything to you, on the off chance.'

He shakes his head slowly, clearly trying to piece together his memories of the encounter. 'Not really. We didn't talk much, to be honest. He just rang me up to say he'd squared things with the Bea—,' he corrects himself, perhaps a bit unsure of her allegiances, 'with ACC Franklin, and that I should be ready to attend the team meeting next Monday.'

'Well, lookie here!' Emma Ridgeway strolls into the office with her usual elegance, but her words irritate Mina. 'Good to see you guys getting on.'

'Don't be daft!' Mina snaps. She seems to be snapping at

everyone. 'Sorry,' she adds, but then she sees Emma and Danny exchange a look that only serves to irritate her further.

'I'll leave you to it,' Danny announces, uncharacteristically sensitive to her mood for once. Or maybe he's just fed up of being shouted at. She doesn't know this new Danny and she has to stop judging him by the old one.

Emma smiles at her, sadly. 'How is he?' she asks.

All her frustration evaporates and Mina sags into her chair. 'There's no change. I went by this morning. Diane's still with him but . . .' She doesn't know what else to say.

She'd seen the nurses' expressions as they came to check on him. She'd wondered if she was imagining it – surely nurses were trained to keep a stoic expression on their faces – but it seemed obvious that they were silently willing her to be prepared for the worst. And all the while, Tyler lay there with tubes up his nose and his limbs bound. He looked so pale; barely recognisable as the boss who constantly got under her skin. She'd thought that would be the worst of it but then she'd seen Diane's face, and somehow that brought the whole thing even closer. She was ashamed of herself, but she'd got out of there as quickly as she could.

Emma hugs her and, as much as Mina isn't the biggest fan of unsolicited tactile affection, she has to admit she needs the contact more than she'd realised. When they break apart, she can feel tears threatening to leak from the corners of her eyes. She can't afford to fall apart. She turns and pretends to shuffle the paperwork on her desk.

As always, Emma gets it and gives her the time she needs to compose herself. 'How can I help?' she asks after a few moments.

Mina speaks without turning around. 'Unless you happen to know what he was working on, I'm not sure you can.' As she says it, a different thought occurs to her, and she turns back towards Emma. 'But on another subject, that friend of yours from the barbecue – Ruth. How do you know her exactly?'

Emma's brow creases for a moment. 'Ruth?' she asks, desperately searching for a face to go with the name. 'Oh, yes. I don't, I guess. It was Leigh's party, really. She invites all kindsa folk to these things. I never know any of them. Why do you ask?'

'Can you find out how Leigh knows her?'

'Sure. What's the issue? Is she involved in this somehow?'

'What? Oh no, nothing like that.' Mina outlines the strange conversation she had with the woman earlier.

'O-kay ...' Emma says, when she's finished. 'That does sound a bit ... creepy? Well, weird, anyway. What do you think she wants? You're not going to meet her, are you?'

'Of course I am. She could be in danger or something.'

'But she said she wasn't.'

'Emma, believe it or not, people don't always tell the police the truth.'

Emma wobbles her head on her shoulders and rolls her eyes, acknowledging the sarcasm. 'Fine. I'll speak to Leigh, see what I can find out.'

'Thank you.'

'So.' Emma drops her voice to a whisper. 'You and Danny ...'

'Get out,' Mina tells her. Emma laughs, kisses her affectionately on the head and heads out of the office.

3

Mina spends the rest of the morning in the office alone, scanning hours of CCTV footage for a black (or dark blue) panel van that may (or may not) have been used in a heist on an upmarket clothes shop. It feels wrong for some reason. She's got used to having other people around. And even when it was just the two of them, and Tyler was out of the office somewhere, there was always some remnant of him left behind – a half-drunk cup of coffee, the remains of a sandwich wrapper. Now it feels as though every part of his presence has evaporated.

Added to that, she is now responsible for two other people, even if they aren't here at the moment. And by extension, responsible for all those people waiting for answers from them. The mothers with lost children, the women too scared to walk the streets, the bereaved and broken stuck in the prisons of their own imaginations. She's felt all this before, of course, but it's different now that the buck stops with her. How did Tyler cope with it?

She thinks about moving to his desk. If she's running the department now, should she establish her authority by occupying his space? It seems unnecessary though; neither Diane nor Suzanne are the sort of women who would be impressed by a ploy like that. And anyway, it doesn't feel right. *He's not dead yet!*

The email from Corinne arrives just after lunch. It's short and sweet, simply asking if Mina could ring her when she gets the chance. She ignores it for a couple of hours, never keen to talk to Corinne and happy to have the CCTV search as an excuse for procrastination, but it niggles away at the back of her mind. It's unusual, to say the least; Mina has a bit of a difficult relationship with the forensic scientist, and she usually leaves Tyler to deal with her. But that's not an option now. She also doesn't want to have to be the one to tell Corinne about Tyler. Mina sighs. She's being ridiculous. If she's going to run this department, she's going to have to find a way to work with the woman. She picks up the phone and hits the relevant speed dial.

'Corinne Daley-Johnson.'

'Corinne, it's Mina Rabbani.'

'Oh, hi, Mina, yes, sorry to bother you at this time.' She's obviously heard the news about Tyler then, which at least lets Mina off the hook in one regard.

Corinne goes on unprompted. 'I wasn't sure what to do about this, but I thought someone should know. DS Tyler requested a DNA test a few months back, on a letter and enve-lope that he'd received anonymously in the post. I carried out the relevant work and emailed him the results.' She stops then, perhaps unsure how to go on.

'That's not all?'

There's silence for a beat but eventually Corinne speaks. 'No. He rang me a few weeks ago and . . . it was a bit unorthodox.'

This is one of the things that irritates Mina about Corinne. She likes to announce things, as though she gets off on the drama of it all. 'Really?' she asks, patiently. Corinne'll get there in the end.

'He asked me not to mention it to anyone. I told him I wasn't in the habit of talking about the work we do here, not to any-body, but that wasn't what he meant. He asked me, specifically, not to mention the letter to you.'

Mina feels a cold shiver sweep through her body. 'Me? He mentioned me by name?'

Again there's a pause. 'He did, but I think he meant the rest of CCRU as well. I asked him why, and he said it was a complicated case that he didn't want to involve anyone else in at the moment. He promised he'd explain eventually, but for the time being I wasn't to bring up anything to do with it in front of you.'

Mina finds herself lost for words, and for once it isn't Corinne's fault. It briefly enters her head that the other woman might be making this up to cause trouble between them, but she discards the thought immediately. Corinne might be a pain in the arse but she's always professional.

'Obviously,' the forensic scientist goes on, 'that puts me in a somewhat difficult position. When I heard what had hap-pened, it occurred to me that the letter might be relevant, but, of course, I might also be the only person who knew about it.'

Yeah, and wouldn't you just love that! Mina thinks.

'But with Diane at the hospital and Suzanne on leave . . . I thought I'd better speak to you.'

The inference is clear: she hadn't wanted to come to Mina at all but hadn't had any other choice.

Mina pushes down her pride. 'I see,' she says, carefully. 'Corinne, could you email me the details, please?' She has a sudden worry that Corinne might think she's involved in all this somehow, but then, if she did, she wouldn't have come to Mina in the first place. Still, she adds, 'And copy in DI Doggett as well, if you could. He's the officer in charge of investigating Tyler's ... incident.' She refuses to call it an accident. That should cover her though, in case Corinne decides to speak to Franklin and make trouble for her.

'Okay, no problem.' Corinne sounds almost relieved to have the whole thing off her plate. 'Please, pass on my regards to Diane and ... well, everyone here is wishing DS Tyler a speedy recovery.' She sounds almost jolly now, a stark contrast to her previous hesitancy.

Mina ends the call and sits patiently staring at her screen for the few minutes it takes for Corinne's email to come through. When it does, all other thoughts go out of her head. So much so, she forgets all about her arranged meeting with Ruth Weatherstone.

4

Jim Doggett pushes open the door of the pub and hauls himself up the single stone step through the narrow doorway. He feels and hears his right knee click and winces, not so much at the pain as at the cliché of it all. When did he get this bloody old? The dog scuttles between his legs, causing him to stumble into the side of the bar.

'Fuck!' he announces, as he untangles the lead from his wrist and extracts himself.

'Usual, Jim?' says the woman behind the bar.

'Obliged, Chloe, love. Take one for yourself while you're at it.'

'You're a gentleman.' She moves away towards the pumps but shouts back to him, 'You can let him off if you like.'

He grunts his thanks and bends down to unclip the dog. The terrier immediately takes the opportunity to slip into the snug and out of sight. Some bugger'll no doubt end up feeding the little bastard crisps and then that'll be himself up half the night cleaning shit off the hallway carpet. The blessed thing was a martyr to its bowels.

Sleeping Dogs

When he took the animal on after its previous owner died in a house fire, he figured he wouldn't have it long before it carked it, especially since the vet guessed its age at the time as somewhere in the region of fifteen. That was a couple of years ago now, but the creature steadfastly refuses to die and costs him a fortune in special dietary supplements thanks to a dicky liver, or some such. To Doggett, that just goes to prove that no good deed goes unpunished.

Chloe delivers him a pint of Best and he settles up with her before sauntering over to a free table under the window. He sits down with a sigh and then castigates himself for it. He's always bloody sighing these days. Getting up, sitting down, taking a shit – he can't seem to move without making a bloody great song and dance about it. He stares at the foam still slowly settling at the top of the glass. Then at the empty seat next to him.

It wasn't as though they met *every* Tuesday. And maybe not so often of late, now he comes to think of it. But he can't deny it feels wrong to be here now, without him.

'This one's for you, soft lad,' he says, raising the pint to the air beside him before bringing it to his lips. By the time he lowers the glass – after another hefty sigh – a good third is empty.

He tuts at himself. What the hell is he doing? The lad isn't dead yet. But from what Diane tells him, it's still touch and go. And what if the poor sod comes out dribbling, or unable to wipe his own arse? He wouldn't wish that on his worst enemy. Well ... he could probably think of a handful of people, but no more than that.

Somewhere deep in the bowels of the pub the dog barks.

Doggett whistles and it comes bounding back to him, wagging its stubby tail.

He's well into his second pint when Rabbani turns up, looking at her phone. She's breathless, as though she's run all the way here from the station. He wouldn't be all that surprised if she had – from what Tyler's told him, running's about the only pastime the girl has outside of work. What is it with youngsters these days? It's like they don't know how to relax.

'Oh, shit!' she says.

'And a good evening to you, too.'

She looks up from the phone. 'Sorry, it's this woman that's been pestering me. I was supposed to meet her earlier and I completely forgot. I better just send her a text.'

'Let me get you a drink,' he says, and fetches her a lime and soda that doesn't exactly break the bank. He takes the opportunity to order his third pint while he's there.

Back at the table her phone's away again, and she has that hungry, eager look he's come to recognise – eyes wide, not quite grinning but close enough a gnat could starve on the difference. 'Go on, then, out with it.'

For once she doesn't waste time looking surprised or asking how he knows – perhaps she's finally getting used to it – but starts on her tale without even taking a drink. 'Anonymous letter,' she says, pulling out a piece of A4 paper folded into quarters. 'Arrived about six months back. Tyler was looking into it.'

Doggett feels his stomach clench. *Shit!* He doesn't often get things wrong but when he does, he has a habit of managing to do so spectacularly. 'That's what this is all about?'

She unfolds the letter for him, and he reads it. It's the same one. The one that landed on his desk and which he then un-ceremoniously dumped onto Tyler's.

This is your fault, you stupid old goat!

She outlines to him what the forensics people have told her about the DNA test Tyler ordered. He'd seen something in his inbox earlier from that daft looking woman with the double-barrelled name, but he'd figured it could wait until morning. Another mistake.

'And they're sure this is him?' he asks. He glances at the report. 'This Harry Foster? Who's he when he's at home, then?' He knows she'll already have looked into the man before coming to him. She's too good an officer not to have.

'Small-time crook. He was sent down a couple of times back in the early Nineties for burglary, but nothing too serious and nothing since. I've got his address if you want to head straight there.' She eyes the empty glasses on the table and adds, 'I can drive.'

'Hang on, hold your horses, sunshine. Assuming he wrote the letter – and we don't know that for sure – what's it got to do with Tyler visiting an old, abandoned cinema after hours? And, for that matter, what does the letter refer to? Let's not go off half-cocked just yet.' He looks back at the piece of paper in question and scratches at the three days' growth on his chin. 'Did he mention any of this to you?'

'No.'

'Me neither. Well, not recently. He mentioned it a few weeks after I ga— after he received it, but I assumed he'd given up on it. It's a bit thin, isn't it? Not much to go on.' He looks up at her again, anxious to see if she's noticed his slip. If he's responsible for what's happened to Tyler he'll pay the price, whatever that is, but for now he could do without her making him feel even worse than he does. But she's barely paying him any attention at all.

The dog has taken the opportunity of his distraction to jump onto the bench and curl up next to her, and she's stroking it idly, her eyes locked onto the table, her drink still untouched in front of her.

'Mina?'

She looks up but still seems a million miles away. 'He told Corinne not to mention it to me.'

'Yeah, well. You know what he's like. Plays his cards close to his chest and all that—'

'Me, specifically.' She frowns into the middle distance. 'Why would he do that? Unless he suspected me of summat or ...' She looks at him properly now. 'I've got nothing to do with any of this, you know that, don't you? I've no idea who Harry Foster is, or what this letter means or any of it! I wouldn't hurt him. Never!'

For the tiniest instant he wonders why she's protesting so vehemently. It only serves to cast doubt on her words. But he *does* know she's got nothing to do with it, not in any way she can imagine at least. That's the trouble with conspiracies, he thinks. Soon you begin to see them around every corner. But he won't doubt her, not her. Not Tyler either. They've been through enough together that they need to hold onto that much.

'Of course, you wouldn't. Mina, we'll figure it out, all right?' He reaches out and touches her arm lightly.

She nods and pushes her hair back behind her ear, shaking herself back to the present. 'So, what do we do?'

'*You* don't do anything,' he tells her.

'But you just said—'

'I said I trust you and I don't believe you had anything to do with this. But you're forgetting Franklin. She doesn't want you involved.' One word of this little development and Franklin would probably call in Professional Standards. Again. None of them needed that, least of all Tyler.

Mina picks up her drink for the first time but cradles it in her hands without taking a sip. 'I can't just sit here and do nowt,' she says, and he can't tell if she's talking to him, herself or the lime and soda.

'I'm not asking you to,' he tells her. 'Carry on with the task I've set you. Have you managed to speak to Cooper yet?'

'I've left her messages but she's at some retreat up north.'

'Talk to them all again, Mina. Diane and your forensic lass – the lot. Find out if any of them know anything more about this.'

She nods, again without looking up. 'What about Harry Foster?'

'Leave that to me.'

When she leaves, it looks as though she has the weight of the world on her shoulders, and he supposes he can't blame her for that. The sleeping dog whimpers, lost in some dream or nightmare. He reaches over and strokes its belly the way it loves so much, and gradually the twitching and moaning subsides.

Yes, best she stays out of it for now. But he's got work to do, and quickly. Because he knows one thing for sure. If Tyler was keeping this from her it was for good reason, and he doesn't doubt that reason had something to do with protecting her.

4 months ago

I

Ruth lay in bed trying not to move. She was busting for a wee, but if she got up he might not be there when she got back.

She allowed herself to turn her head a fraction, to look again at his perfect skinny body and the curve of his back as it swooped under the rucked sheet. She still couldn't believe he was there at all, but he must be because she could hear the gentle snuffling of his breath against the pillow, feel the warmth of him radiating into her. She was aware of everywhere their bodies touched: her love handle pressed against his side, her knee tucked into his thigh, her left foot draped over his, oh so casually. It was an awkward position to be laid out in, and certainly not the way they'd slept, but over the past twenty minutes she'd done her best to get as close as she could without waking him. She felt as though she was draped over him like a scarf, but still, she wanted to stay like this for hours, for days. Forever.

'Hey, you,' he whispered, and his voice rippled through her body like a caress. He lifted his head from the pillow and looked at her through half-lidded eyes from behind his fringe. She hadn't known he had a fringe until then. Who knew that all that elaborately styled hair flopped so beautifully over his face? If she had the chance, she would encourage him to wear it that way more often. He stared at her.

'What?' she asked. Was it her hair? Her breath? She was suddenly conscious that she'd pulled her knickers back on before she fell asleep but not her bra, and the angle she was lying at pushed her breasts towards him like great floppy bunny ears. They were still partially covered by the sheet but even so . . .

'You're very beautiful,' he told her.

She felt that ripple again, something that started in the back of her head and flooded its way through her body from top to toe. She dropped her eyes and felt her chin fold up on itself. *Chins*, she thought, bleakly. Then he put his hand on her face and gently lifted her head up again. He leaned in and kissed her. It was beautiful. Romantic. Not the acrobatic stuff he'd seemed so into last night, but chaste and gentle, his lips barely brushing against hers. It was the most exquisite moment of her life.

'Good morning,' he said, and took her hand, guiding it down to the hardened length between his thighs. She held him, marvelling that she was actually doing this, that he was taking pleasure in her company like this. And then his hand reached up to the back of her head and he pushed her down under the sheet.

When he was finished, she got up and ran straight to the bathroom to wash her mouth out and to finally, blissfully, empty her bladder. She was still worried he might not be there when she got back, but less so. He'd laid back down even as she jumped up out of bed, as though he fully intended to go back to sleep again. But either way she couldn't have held it any longer. The relief she felt as her furious stream hit the porcelain was actually more pleasurable than what she'd felt last night. But then, they did say it got better with time, didn't they?

He was face-down again when she got back. Still conscious of her upper nakedness, she pulled a baggy T-shirt from the drawer and slipped it over her head. He looked up at her over his shoulder through those lazy eyes and patted the bed next to him encouragingly. She wondered if it was her turn now. Would he go down on her like Michael Douglas in *Basic Instinct*? He hadn't done that last night, but she had to admit she was curious about it. But when she climbed back into bed, he merely draped an arm over her middle and snuggled into her neck.

Ruth lay awake for the next hour wondering what was next. She ought to be glad he was still here, shouldn't she? It was just that ... did he intend to sleep all day? Obviously, it was way too early to be thinking about the future, but she couldn't help herself. This wonderful man had fallen into her lap out of nowhere, had ridden to her rescue like a knight in shining armour. It was the meet-cute to end them all.

He'd rung her a few days after they'd met. She'd been beginning to worry but he immediately apologised, explained he'd been tied up with work. To make up for it, he'd take her out for a slap-up meal. It had been incredible: a French bistro on Ecclesall Road where she couldn't even pronounce the items on the menu. If she was honest, she could have done with a bigger portion, but it was certainly expensive. He'd paid for everything, including the taxi.

Then there was another meal, Greek this time, and another after that – Italian. At this rate, she thought they might work their way through the whole of Europe.

He wasn't very talkative, she'd noticed. Not about himself anyway; he asked plenty of questions about her, some of which she answered, and some she avoided. But she wanted to know everything about him as well. She didn't even know where he lived yet. Wherever it was, it would have to be better than this place. He'd been a bit vague about work as well, now she came to think of it. At the time she'd just been pleased he hadn't run a mile when she told him she cleaned pub toilets for a living. He'd barely flinched, in fact.

Finally, last night (a groundbreaking sushi bar in the city centre), he'd suggested they go back to hers. She'd almost said no. She hadn't wanted him to see her empty life, not as starkly as the house betrayed it. But if she'd said no, she might never have seen him again. She took a chance.

'Thank you for inviting me back here,' he told her now, though she hadn't, it had been his idea. 'That can't have been easy.'

She wondered what he meant. Did he know he was her first? Had she given herself away somehow? She didn't think she had. She'd watched some porn videos on the internet the other night, once she'd realised this might be on the cards. Some of it was truly disgusting and she knew she'd never do any of that, but, well, she thought she'd got the gist, at least. But what if she hadn't? There'd been a moment last night, when he was in her mouth the first time, where he'd flinched slightly and pulled away. She'd tried to apologise but he simply shushed her and turned her around. She was scared he was about to reject her but then she'd felt him, down there, pushing his way into her, and any thought of rejection was driven out of her mind by the pain. It was excruciating. So much so that she'd tried to get him to stop. But he hadn't and, eventually, the pain had subsided and she had felt some pleasure. She thought she would have preferred it the other way round though, for the first time at least. She could have stared into his eyes as he worked his way inside and kissed her. That's how she'd imagined it anyway. But her research had included other positions, so she wasn't too shocked. She gathered some men preferred it this way, and maybe it *was* better for them, how would she know?

'I'm guessing you haven't had many people back here since ... well, since your father,' he went on now.

It took her a moment to work out what he was talking about. She was relieved when she figured out what he meant.

'No, I ... well, no one. I mean, I don't really get visitors.' She shouldn't have said that. It made her sound lonely, pathetic.

'Well, I hope I get to visit,' he said, smiling roguishly. 'Often.' He wiggled his eyebrows and she laughed. Then he flipped onto his back and stretched his arms. She felt his skin pull away from hers and the places he had touched were suddenly cold. This was it, he was leaving.

But instead, he sat up. He smiled at her but this time there was a hint of sadness to it. It was even prettier than his normal smile. 'You miss him,' he said.

She'd told him about her father last night. Not all of it, of course, just that he'd died recently, and she was still learning to adjust. She hadn't wanted to say anything at all, but once she knew they were coming back here it would have been too awkward to have to explain the mess in the downstairs room. She might have been able to avoid them going in there altogether, but she decided not to take the chance. She didn't want to spoil the mood by bringing Frank's ghost into the equation at the worst possible moment.

In the end, she was glad she'd said something because he'd insisted on a tour of the whole house as soon as they got back. He'd been impressed with the size of it and wanted to see everything, not that there was much to see. She did notice a flicker of disgust on his face as he took in the stained chair and the yellowed wallpaper, but she could hardly blame him for that. The whole place disgusted her too.

'Do you want to talk about him?' he asked her now.

Did she? To her surprise, she found that she did. She wanted to tell this man everything, so that he would know every part of her and love her all the same. But she also knew it was too soon. And if he found out the truth about her past, he might reject her. Of course he would. *Useless bitch! Who'd want you?* And then she'd always wonder, was that the reason he'd never called again, or was it because she'd been rubbish in bed?

'Not right now,' she said, and heard the apology in her own voice.

He nodded his acceptance and she felt relieved that he wasn't going to push it.

'When you're ready to,' he told her. 'I want to know everything about you. Everything. If we're going to make this work there can't be any secrets between us, okay?'

Ruth's heart surged. *If we're going to make this work.* She didn't think she'd ever wanted anything more. And *he* wanted it too!

'No secrets,' she promised, and surprised herself by launching herself at him for a kiss.

He seemed equally surprised, pulling away to begin with. But then he settled into it, and she felt the hardness of him pushing its way between her thighs again. *Yes*, she thought to herself. This was it. It would be better this time, she was sure.

But then his lips parted from hers and she felt his hands grip her shoulders and twist her around. When she felt his hand on her throat she tensed, which made it hurt even more when he pushed his way into her.

It was her fault, she thought afterwards. She probably just needed to learn to relax more.

'Any chance of a bit of brekkie before I get off?'

'Oh.' She hadn't considered this. Her fridge was pretty much bare. She felt the shame ripple through her as she confessed as much.

'No worries,' he said, leaning over and scooping up his jeans from the pile of clothes on the floor. He rummaged in the pocket for his wallet. 'Here,' he said, proffering a twenty-pound note. 'Anything'll do. That shop on the corner must have bacon and eggs and stuff, eh? I can have a quick shower while you're gone.'

She knew she shouldn't take the money but . . .

It only occurred to her when she was on her way back – with a plastic bag full of breakfast ingredients, a jar of Nescafé and a pint of orange juice – that she'd just left a comparative stranger on his own in her house. She had nothing to worry about, surely, but she quickened her step, nevertheless.

As she got back she thought she saw him: a shadow hovering at the upstairs window, in what used to be the old study. But why would he be in there? Her eyes were so intent on trying to see through the grubby net curtain that she almost walked into the man waiting for her by the front door.

'Oh!'

It was the same policeman as before.

'Hello, Ruth,' he said. 'DS Tyler. Remember me?'

Of course she remembered him. He'd been texting her for weeks now and she'd been ignoring him.

They stood there staring at each other, but eventually he stepped off the path onto the uncut grass so she could shuffle past him to the door.

'Can I come in?' he asked.

'It's not really a good time,' she told him.

'It won't take long. I really do need to talk to you about your father.'

What could she say? *I don't want to talk about him. I never want to talk about him.* Wouldn't that just make him more suspicious? She needed to make it clear that whatever he thought he knew about Frank, it had nothing to do with her. She opened the door, wondering if Drew was about to appear and shame her even further. Thankfully, there was no sign of him in the hallway.

DS Tyler followed her in and pushed the door closed behind him, which made her feel trapped. She tried to calm herself down. He was a policeman, she didn't have anything to fear. But she knew that wasn't exactly true. *I'll set the rozzers on you.*

'Is there somewhere we can go that's a bit more comfortable?' he asked.

She didn't want him to see any more of the house, and she really didn't want to explain all this to Drew. Hopefully he was still in the shower, though she couldn't hear any water running. She decided to ignore the request, putting her plastic bag down on the floor as though to emphasise this would have to do.

'Okay,' he said, once it became clear she wasn't going to respond. 'Now, Ruth, your father had quite the chequered past, didn't he?'

'I don't know about that,' she said, and realised that made it sound as though she knew far more than she was saying. She needed to get better at this.

'I'm not here to try and get you into trouble but I need to find out if he was involved in something a long time ago. Twenty-four years ago, in fact, so you would only have been what, fourteen, then? Fifteen? That means you were a child, Ruth, so even if you did know something about it you don't have anything to worry about. Whatever your father may or may not have done, it wasn't your fault.'

Of course that's what he'd say, but she wasn't stupid. She'd seen enough cop shows on the telly – and heard her father tell enough stories – to know that this was how they worked, lulling you into a false sense of security and tricking you into saying more than you meant to. Best if she just kept schtum.

'Did you know a woman named Alison Beech?'

She looked up at that name, and in doing so gave herself away.

'You recognise that name, don't you, Ruth?'

'What . . . What do you want?' she managed.

'I want you to tell me the truth. There's a husband out there who wants to know what happened to his wife. A child who lost his mother. I think you might be able to help me get the answers they need. That's all.'

She refused to make eye contact with him.

He turned to go, then hesitated and turned back. 'I'm not trying to cause you any trouble, and I understand you're still grieving. But you could really help these people. You could help Alison's family. I think you want to help them, and that's why you sent me the letter.'

She frowned at him. 'What letter?'

He studied her for a moment as though looking for something. Whatever it was, he didn't find it. 'Just think about it, Ruth. You've got my number?' He pulled a business card and a pen from his jacket pocket. 'Here,' he said, scribbling on the back. 'This is my personal number too, just in case. You can ring me anytime, day or night.'

He let himself out and she pushed the door closed behind him and locked it. She had no doubt he'd be back.

She heard Drew coming down the stairs and slipped the business card into her pocket. She turned to see a look of intense concern on his face.

'What was that all about?' he asked.

She wanted to tell him. She'd already determined to tell him everything – she had to, if this was going to work between them. But it was so hard.

'Ruth,' he said, 'please. Whatever it is, let me help you. You can trust me. I hope you know that.'

She did know that. Or at least, she thought she did. She wasn't sure what it meant to really trust someone. To have a partner to share the weight of a burden, to offer advice when needed. It was so impossible to get Frank's voice out of her head.

Never trust strangers. We don't need anyone else. We're all right on our own.

No, she wanted to cry. *No, we're not all right. She* wasn't all right.

'There's something I haven't told you,' she said. 'My father . . . he was a bad man.'

After that it was hard to stop.

11

At the Monday morning meeting, Mina was in full flow. Diane and Tyler had shuffled their chairs over, and Corinne Daley-Johnson's image blinked at them all from the monitor on Mina's desk. Tyler always let Mina take the lead on these things. They'd both accepted that when it came to organisation she was far and away his superior. She enjoyed the meetings a little too much though, in his opinion. Which meant they did tend to drag on. Tyler let his mind wander.

It had been a week now since his brief chat with Ruth Weatherstone, and more than a month since his meeting with Dominic Beech. What had he actually learned from either of them? From her reaction he was fairly sure that Ruth hadn't been the one to send the letter, but he suspected she knew a lot more than she was saying. He had a sense he could reach her but there was an obvious fragility there. He didn't want to push too hard.

The same was true of Beech, though for different reasons. He'd made it clear he didn't want Tyler reopening the case; the question was why? Tyler had done a bit more digging into the family's past, and all three of the Beech children, past and present, had been sent off to private school at a pretty young age, so he wasn't sure he bought the whole concerned father act. Lucas had been shipped off barely a year after the trauma of losing his mother. It must have been unbearably hard on such a young boy. Tyler wasn't in the least surprised that, after school, he'd taken advantage of a scholarship, and moved overseas.

There was also that titbit of information from Beech about 'other kidnappings'. Tyler couldn't find any evidence of them. He'd watched the TV documentary the other night and that hadn't mentioned anything about other kidnappings either. Of course, that had been made a good decade after Alison went missing and the filmmakers hadn't worried greatly about the accuracy of the details, dramatizing the events so that the whole thing felt closer to fiction than reportage. But if he took Beech's statement as fact, why would Bob Smith not have made reference to additional kidnappings in his reports? And where were these other cases?

The whole investigation felt thin, ephemeral, as though every time he tried to grab hold of it, it slipped through his fingers. Of course, the luxury of dealing with cold cases meant there was rarely any immediate hurry. After twenty-four years Alison Beech was unlikely to be waiting for his help somewhere. She was either dead or had a new life – almost certainly, and unfortunately, the former.

So, what was it that kept tugging him back?

Mina's voice cut across Tyler's thoughts. 'Okay, well I think that's almost everything. Corinne, did you say you might have some results on Granger's DNA by next week?'

They all knew full well Corinne hadn't said any such thing. This was Mina's way of geeing her up a bit, advice she'd been given on a training course Franklin had sent her on, about dealing with agencies outside the force.

Tyler resisted the urge to undermine her by jumping in. Corinne stared out from the screen with no particular expression on her face. She was far too clever to fall for this blatant attempt to trap her into a commitment. 'I think I already mentioned the current backlog,' she said, calmly. 'If you want to prioritise the sample though, I can upgrade your request to urgent? I'll just need an email from you, DS Tyler, confirming the additional expense.'

Mina managed a half-successful attempt not to roll her eyes. 'Just get to it when you can.'

The scientist nodded her satisfaction, bid them farewell and ended the video call.

'Subtle, Mina,' Tyler chastised.

'It doesn't hurt to keep the pressure on,' she told him, unapologetically. 'They might be under-resourced, but so are we. I don't want her prioritising more active cases and forgetting all about us just because we deal with historic stuff.'

She drew the meeting to a close and Tyler and Diane went back to their own desks.

As he sat down, a box popped up in the corner of his screen and he was surprised to see it was an email from Corinne. His first thought was that this was going to be a complaint about Mina, but he discounted that even before he opened the message. It wasn't in Corinne's nature.

DS Tyler,

    I wasn't sure if you wanted me to mention this in front
of the team – you implied a certain level of discretion
was advisable – but we've had a hit on the sample from
the anonymous letter.

    Details attached.

    Regards,

    Corinne

Finally! He clicked on the attachment and examined the contents of the document. The results regarding fingerprints were inconclusive: too many people had handled the thing before it reached Tyler and there were only partial, smudged prints. But the envelope had come through for them. It used to amaze Tyler how few people considered that when they licked the sticky strip on the back of an envelope, they were essentially depositing their DNA all over it. In more recent years, self-sealing envelopes had largely put paid to that, and though touch DNA could still sometimes be recovered from any folds in the paper, it was much less reliable. Thankfully, as in this case, some people still used old-school lickable envelopes.

The result matched a record in the database, with a 'Strong Possibility' that the sample belonged to one Harry Foster. That was the highest level of probability, and Tyler glanced through the table of statistics to find that the chances of anyone other than Harry Foster having licked the envelope were millions to one. That would do well enough for him, even if the defence might try to sow doubt.

Foster was on file because he'd done a stretch for burglary

back in the early 90s. There was a Sheffield address on his parole file and a quick DVLA check confirmed it was the same they had for him as well. It was a long shot. Would the man really still be there? Then again, Frank Weatherstone had been. It was worth a try.

III

As he drove up City Road later that afternoon, Tyler again wondered why he was keeping this whole business from the others. Neither Diane nor Mina had any control over how he spent his time, nor what cases he deemed best to look into. But the whole point of their Monday meetings was to go over their priorities and he couldn't justify why he thought this case deserved attention over the hundreds of others they had on file. He'd told Diane he was leaving the office early to get ready for a date. Her eyes had lit up at the information, and the barrage of questions he'd then had to endure had left him regretting the ruse, even if it was, at least, factually accurate. He did indeed have a date.

Scott's call had come out of the blue. It had been a few weeks since the disastrous cinema trip, during which time they'd exchanged a dozen or so texts, skirting around the issue of another date without really committing to anything.

'I got that job,' he'd announced by way of a greeting.

'Oh, wow! Really? That's brilliant.' Tyler had worried that maybe his response was too much. Did it sound like he was

189

surprised Scott had got the job? 'Really great,' he'd tried to clarify, only making it worse, followed by, 'We should celebrate,' more to cover his embarrassment than anything else.

'Yeah,' Scott said. 'That's why I rang. This is my first proper job for, well, quite a while. I'd like to take you out, properly. My treat.'

It had occurred to Tyler after the call that maybe the reason Scott hadn't been keener to solidify another date was because he was short of money. If that was true, then what was his own excuse? He'd heard the excitement in Scott's voice though, and it was nice to think that Tyler was the person he wanted to share that with. Navigating the late-afternoon traffic, Tyler was surprised to find that he was excited as well. Whatever this fool's errand he was on led to, he knew one thing for sure – he wasn't going to let it make him late.

The Foster residence, if that was what this still was, was a terraced house on an estate just past the City Road Cemetery. It wasn't the most well-to-do area of Sheffield and the house itself looked as though it hadn't had any care and attention for a good many years, the pebbledashed walls starting to moult in places. Tyler knocked on the door.

The man who answered was clearly not Harry Foster. A son, perhaps? Or a grandson even. He was a few years younger than Tyler, in his late twenties, and dressed casually but smartly in jeans and a navy soldier shirt. Tyler introduced himself and showed his warrant card.

'Oh,' the younger man said, but failed to add anything further.

'Can I come in?'

The man hesitated. 'Harry ... Well, can I ask what this is about?'

'I'd like to ask Mr Foster a few questions.'

'About?'

Tyler regarded his interrogator for a moment. He could just be an overprotective relative, but somehow he didn't quite fit that role. If anything, he seemed curious more than anything else.

'That's between me and Mr Foster,' he said, following it up with, 'Who are you, exactly?' It was blunt, but he had the feeling he needed to be.

'Oh,' the man said again. 'I'm Zac. Harry's carer.' He held out his hand and Tyler shook it. 'You do know Harry has dementia?'

He didn't. That was going to make things a lot more difficult.

Zac finally opened the door and allowed Tyler to step into the hallway. The place smelled of damp and tobacco. Tyler thought about the anonymous letter and a few things fell into place. If Harry *had* written the note, it might explain why it seemed so conflicted, even between sentences. He imagined an older man suffering from dementia probably had good days and bad. But which days were the ones when he felt the need to unburden himself, and which was he having today?

He followed Zac into the front room where Harry was sitting, nodding in an old, faded armchair. Tyler glanced around the room, which looked like a time capsule from the 1970s. It certainly hadn't seen a lick of paint since then. One wall was dominated by an enormous trophy cabinet, the glass thick with dust; another by a brown tiled fireplace that was old enough to be retro now, but hideous enough that any new owner would rip it out in a heartbeat. On the mantelpiece above were an array of packets and plastic bottles of medication.

Zac must have seen him looking. 'He's just had his pills,' he said in a whisper. 'He might be a bit out of it.'

Tyler looked at the carer, who was standing awkwardly near the door, as though he didn't want to come all the way into the room but still wanted to know what was going on.

'How bad is it?' Tyler asked him.

'The dementia? Some days are better than others,' he said, echoing Tyler's thoughts. 'Look, I'm really not sure you're going to get much out of him—'

But his words were cut off as Foster twitched and opened his eyes. He stared ahead of him without moving, but Tyler was right in his eyeline. He didn't really want to have this conversation with Zac in the room, but he also didn't know how long he would have before the man closed his eyes again.

'Mr Foster?' he asked, squatting on his haunches next to the chair. 'Harry? My name is Detective Sergeant Tyler. I'm with South Yorkshire CID. I wanted to ask you a few questions about a letter you sent us.'

Did the man's eyes flicker for a moment? Maybe. Or maybe Tyler was just seeing what he wanted to see. He pulled the copy of the letter from his inside jacket pocket and presented it to Harry.

'You did send this, didn't you, Harry? Do you remember?'

Tyler was aware of Zac shuffling closer. He was either concerned for his charge or a nosy bastard, Tyler couldn't decide which. Either way, he couldn't read the contents from where he was.

Harry's eyes seemed to focus on the letter for a moment. His head moved away from the back of the armchair, but barely. He lifted a wizened hand and touched the paper lightly. His lips parted and Tyler leaned in close, trying to hear if the old man was trying to speak.

'Weatherstone,' Tyler whispered. 'Frank Weatherstone?'

The hand started to shake, and Tyler felt a momentary pang of doubt. This man was plainly very ill, and he didn't want to add to his troubles. But this was the last lead he had.

'What happened to Alison, Harry? Do you know? Alison Beech? Do you remember her?'

Harry's head shook, but it wasn't clear if he was answering or if it was a symptom of his illness. His hand dropped into his lap, his head sagged back against the chair, and his eyes closed.

Tyler leant back on his heels and pushed his way to standing. He stepped towards Zac, carefully sliding the letter back into his pocket.

'He's really not good today,' Zac said, redundantly. He seemed a bit shaken by the scene, but he got over it quickly enough. 'Tell you what,' he said, 'if you want to leave me with a list of questions or something, I could ask him later? He does have his good moments.'

Tyler looked at the man. 'I'll tell *you* what, why don't you call me the next time Harry's having a good day and I'll pop back?'

Zac nodded. 'Sure. If you like.'

Tyler took another glance around the room. One thing did

stand out to him; there were no photographs. 'Does Harry have any family?'

Zac shook his head. 'No. No one that I know of. It's a real shame. But I guess that's why I'm here,' he said brightly.

A thought occurred to Tyler. 'Is he housebound?'

Zac's brow furrowed. 'Sorry?'

'Supposing he wanted to post a letter. Could he manage it without help?'

The furrowed brow creased even further. 'Well, he's not completely infirm. I mean, on good days we can still get to the park and back, and he's been known to pop up the local shops now and again for his tobacco, but not so much recently. There's a post box at the end of the road though, so it's possible.'

Tyler nodded. 'And you've not posted anything for him recently?'

The carer shook his head. 'No. Never.'

'How often are you here?'

'Me? Three, four times a week. It depends. There's a team of us, actually: it's not just me. Do you want me to ask the others? I can pass your details on as well, if you like? That way, if he's having a good day, whoever he's with can call you.'

Tyler began to think he'd misjudged the man. Perhaps he really did just want to be helpful. 'I'd be grateful.'

Zac opened his mouth and then hesitated. Finally, he asked the question that must have been burning away in the back of his mind the whole time. 'Do you mind me asking what this is all about?'

Tyler smiled, bleakly. 'I don't mind, no.' Then he turned to look back at Harry one last time.

Maybe this whole thing was a waste of time – he could hear Mina's tut from here. Presumably Harry had heard about Frank Weatherstone's death somehow and then his old . . . what? Friend? Colleague? Boss? Whatever he was to Harry, he was dead, and that knowledge had freed Harry enough to take action. He'd written what he'd probably meant as a letter of confession, perhaps trying to unburden himself before the inevitable end, but in his confused state he'd barely got half the information across. Whatever had happened to Alison Beech was lost in this man's broken memory or Frank Weatherstone's grave. Who else could possibly know what had happened all those years ago?

'Terry!' Harry shouted, causing both Tyler and Zac to jump. He was sitting upright now, wide awake, his eyes bright and shining fiercely. 'Where's Terry?' he asked. He seemed confused.

Zac glanced at Tyler as though asking permission to step forward. Tyler nodded. Zac seemed reluctant to cross the room, but he did, slowly.

'It's all right, Harry. Nothing to worry about, eh?'

'Where's Terry?' the old man asked again, and this time his voice was strained and anguished, like a child who's lost a favourite toy.

'He's not here, Harry.' Zac turned and shrugged, as if to say he had no idea who Terry was.

'Who are you? I want Terry.'

'It's me, Harry.'

'No, *I'm* Harry.'

Zac looked up at Tyler again, grimacing with embarrassment. 'I'm Zac, Harry, you remember.'

'Zac? You're not Zac. Zac's the poofter!'

Zac flinched a little at that, but his voice stayed calm. 'That's me. How about a cuppa? There's a policeman here to talk to you.'

'Copper? I don't talk to coppers!'

'Cuppa. Nice cup of tea. I'll put the kettle on.'

Harry snorted something, and Tyler stepped aside so Zac could pass him on his way out of the room. 'Go easy.' He said it almost as a question and tapped Tyler gently on the arm in a manner that pleaded caution.

Tyler stepped forward again and reintroduced himself.

'I don't talk to coppers,' Harry repeated.

'But you sent me this letter, Harry.' He pulled the copy back out. 'And before you deny it, it's covered in your DNA. What do you know about Alison Beech?'

'Who?' This time Tyler was sure the question had nothing to do with dementia.

'Alison Beech. She went missing twenty-four years ago, and here—' he pointed at the relevant part of the letter '—you blame it on Frank Weatherstone.'

Harry shook his head. 'Never 'eard of 'im.'

'He's dead, Harry. Do you remember that? Frank's dead.'

For a brief moment he thought he might have got through to the man. Harry's eyes flicked to the doorway and then back to Tyler.

'Whatever it is you want to tell me, he can't hurt you now.' But as soon as Tyler spoke, he knew he'd made a mistake.

Harry's face creased into a sneer. 'I'm not afraid of the likes of him.'

196

'So you did know him?'

The sneer deepened briefly, but then Harry frowned as though remembering something. 'She weren't supposed to get hurt.' He stared at Tyler, as though asking for forgiveness. 'It was ... She shouldn't have given her ... Terry said—'

'Here we are then!' Zac pushed his way back into the room with his shoulder, carrying a tea tray.

Tyler jumped to his feet. 'Wait outside!' he shouted. The carer looked taken aback but slid the tray onto an occasional table littered with newspapers and hustled back out of the room.

When Tyler turned back, he knew instantly that whatever Harry had been about to say was gone. The vacant look was back. Whatever it was he was seeing now, it wasn't Tyler. 'Terry?' he managed once more, and then closed his eyes again.

Tyler hung on for a few minutes, but he was confident Harry wasn't faking it. The gentle sound of his breathing grew heavier, and it became clear he was firmly asleep. Tyler stepped back into the hallway where the irritating carer stood sanitizing his hands.

'I'm sorry, I didn't mean to ...' Zac trailed off.

Tyler looked the man up and down. He couldn't blame him, he supposed, though he sorely wanted to.

'This Terry he kept mentioning. Any idea of his surname?'

Zac shook his head. 'An old mate, I guess. He mentions him every now and again, but whoever he was, I don't think he's still around.' Zac smiled sadly. 'I'm not sure he has anyone. Except us, I guess.'

Tyler thought back to the abusive name Harry had used and found himself feeling sorry for Zac. 'It must be hard,' he said.

'Putting up with that shit.'

Zac frowned for a moment as though unsure what he meant, but then he seemed to get it and nodded. 'He's not always that bad. And he doesn't mean anything by it. Just a different generation, i'n't it?'

Zac let Tyler out with another promise to ring if it looked as though Harry was having a better day and Tyler strolled back down the road to his car.

What had the old bugger been about to reveal? Was it even worth coming back? Or would he get more of the same? He wasn't just relying on Harry being more lucid; when he was fully compos mentis he'd clammed up tight. What he needed was for him to be coherent enough to tell him about the past but lost enough that he forgot he was talking to the police. Tyler wondered for a moment whether Zac had been right: maybe the carer would stand a better chance of getting the truth from Harry. But he wasn't a trained interrogator, and anything he did find out would be inadmissible in court anyway. 'Terry said what?' he wondered out loud, and a young woman with a pushchair shot him a cautious look as she passed.

Whatever it was, it implied that Terry had been there as well, unless that was just part of the dementia? Maybe it was something. But even if it was, it wasn't very much.

IV

Tyler's date was at an upmarket Italian place in the city centre. He was the first to arrive again, and the maître d' showed him to the table reserved under Scott's name. Perhaps he was finally getting the hang of this dating lark. He ordered a pint of ale, and the sommelier tried his best to stifle his disgust.

Scott arrived full of apologies, though he wasn't all that late. He was wearing an immaculately fitted white shirt that flattered his toned muscles. Glancing once, with a slight smile, at Tyler's half-finished pint, he ordered a large glass of Sauvignon.

'Make it a bottle,' Tyler told the sommelier, largely to impress Scott, although it was the sommelier who positively beamed with pleasure.

They ordered their starters and snacked on bread and olives while they waited.

'So,' Scott said, immediately jumping to the heart of the issue. 'Any chance you're going to get called away to a scene of bloodshed and mayhem tonight?' His smile went a long way towards taking the sting out of his words.

'There's always that chance,' Tyler replied seriously.

'I really didn't mind, you know. Last time. It wasn't an issue.'

Tyler was about to say, *It will be one day*, but stopped himself. Instead, he said, 'I should have rearranged something sooner. I'm sorry.'

Scott grimaced. 'It wasn't all down to you. I wasn't sure after last time whether you wanted ... Well. I blame my choice of film.'

'It wasn't really my thing.'

'Yeah, I figured that when you got your mobile out to check for messages. Twice.'

Tyler glanced down at his phone on the table and nodded. He picked it up and slipped it into his pocket. 'Old habits,' he said.

Scott grinned. 'Slasher flicks are a bit of a guilty pleasure of mine.'

Tyler smiled back. 'Maybe I can learn to ... appreciate them.'

After that, things seemed to get back on track. Scott spoke lovingly of his expansive family. His parents were still alive and happily married, and they and his siblings got together regularly for big gatherings at their childhood home in Nottinghamshire.

'Three older brothers,' Tyler said. 'That must have been a challenge.'

Scott laughed. 'You have no idea. But Sarah, my younger sister, and I ... we learned to hold our own soon enough.'

He outlined his relationship with each of them: the oldest and youngest brothers were married, with families of their own, whereas the middle brother was something of the black sheep of the family, although even here there was a fondness to his words. The youngest, his sister, was still at uni. Tyler tried to take in the details, but he was soon lost in a sea of names and anecdotes about the various scrapes they'd all got into when they were growing up. He wondered what that must have been like, but it was so very far removed from his own childhood that he struggled to picture it. Despite that, he found himself enjoying the conversation.

'What about you?' Scott asked, as they tucked into their mains. 'You have a brother, don't you?'

When they'd first met, Tyler had asked Scott for his professional opinion about how best to help his brother. Scott had given him the telephone number of a colleague who might be able to help with Jude's PTSD, but Tyler had never got around to using it.

'Yes,' Tyler said. 'He's in prison.'

There was a pregnant pause, amplified by the sound of Scott's knife and fork clinking against his plate.

'Oh. Right. I'm sorry, I didn't realise.'

'No reason you should.'

This is what happens, Tyler thought. He could feel the situation slipping away from him again. There was just no good way to explain it all. So maybe he shouldn't. 'It's a long story,' he said, smiling to try to mitigate the damage. Scott had that familiar look on his face, as though he was trying to analyse him in some way.

Tyler went on. 'I will tell you though. One day.'

Scott put down his fork and leaned back for a moment. 'I'd like that. When you're ready.' He changed the subject. 'So, any other family?'

'I have a niece.' But that, of course, was part of the same story. He had to make an effort at something though. 'Edith.

She's almost seventeen. We only found out about each other recently and . . . well, then I arrested her dad.'

He'd wanted to do more for her, and for her mother, but Janice wouldn't allow it. She'd agreed to the DNA test, but only, he suspected, because Edith had begged her. After that, she'd made it very clear to him that he should stay away. He supposed that was fair enough given the circumstances. 'I try and keep an eye out for her.'

Scott seemed to understand that he shouldn't ask any more questions. 'I'm sure she'll appreciate that,' he said. 'One day.'

Tyler cast around for something to say to bring the conversation back on course. *Is this the problem?* he wondered. He had so little going on, other than work, that there was nothing to talk about. It was easy enough if you just hooked up with someone at a bar or a club, but dating was hard! *How do people do this?*

'My father died when I was a teenager,' he found himself saying. 'But I guess you already know about that.'

Scott nodded. 'What about your mum? I don't know anything about her.'

Tyler had a sudden image of her from the last time he'd seen her. She was wearing a paisley-patterned summer dress and her auburn hair cascaded down her shoulders in thick waves. She was screaming at his father, accusing him of some treachery – infidelity was her favourite topic, though there'd been others.

'She left us when I was a kid,' he said, aware that once again there was no good way to tell this story. 'She suffered with mental health problems that went undiagnosed for a long time, and she walked out on the family when I was still young. After that it was always just me, my dad and Jude.'

'Have you ever tried to find out what happened to her?'

'I suppose I—' Tyler stopped abruptly.

Was that it? Was that the reason he was becoming so obsessed with Alison Beech's fate? Because her case reminded him of his mother? She hadn't been kidnapped, but the parallels were there. A young boy whose mother leaves one day and never comes back, with no goodbye, no explanation. There he was, patting himself on the back for giving up his obsession with finding his father's killers, and all he'd done was swap one crusade for another.

'I'm so sorry,' Scott said. 'This is none of my business.'

'No, no, it's all right. Really. I just thought of something, that's all. To answer your question: yes, I have thought about it but, well, it was her choice to leave. It never felt right to go chasing after her.' He'd tried asking Diane about his mother on a couple of occasions, but nothing had ever come of it. Now he thought about it, Diane had always seemed as reluctant to talk about his mother as he was. But that was a can of worms for another time. 'Maybe I should,' he added.

Scott nodded, but there was a look of concern on his face that hadn't been there earlier.

'Anyway,' Tyler pressed on. 'You got room for dessert?'

They shared a tiramisu – one plate, two forks – and Scott joked that they must look like a proper cliché. 'If you even mention *Lady and the Tramp*, I'll deck you,' he said. Tyler laughed, though he had no idea what the reference meant.

At the end of the meal he offered to pay, but Scott was adamant that he pick up the tab. 'I said it was my treat.'

'At least let me buy you a drink to say thank you then.'

The grin slid back onto Scott's face. 'Fine by me,' he said.

The bar they picked was one of those Spanish places that had salsa lessons going on inside. They sat at a communal table outside on the terrace and switched to shorts – a dark rum and coke for Tyler, and a vodka, lime and soda for Scott.

It happened almost by accident. Tyler noticed a woman eyeing up the stool next to them and leaned across to retrieve his jacket so she could sit down. Scott misinterpreted the manoeuvre and leaned in for a kiss. It was awkward and un-expected and they both laughed. But it was electric as well. Their eyes locked, and Tyler forgot all about the jacket and the woman left standing.

A few minutes later the drinks were abandoned, and Scott hailed a black cab and gave the driver an address in Crookes. It was a modern apartment complex on the edge of the Bole Hills. Tyler knew the area well from his childhood. His father, Richard, used to bring them up here to watch the fireworks on Bonfire Nights.

They were barely through the front door before they began tearing at each other's clothes. The first time was frenzied and desperate, and they finished together in a heap of tangled limbs, half on the bed and half off. The whole thing had lasted no more than a few minutes and there was an air of embarrass-ment as they each gathered enough clothing to look vaguely respectable, before returning to their metaphoric corners and commencing round two.

They joked self-deprecatingly about their own staying power, or lack thereof, while at the same time reassuring each other that it was their innate desirability that had forced things to such a quick conclusion. Scott made them gin and tonics and they sat together in bed, sipping and talking, at first anyway, until the fizz of the tonic water and the clinking of ice became the only accompaniment to the sound of their kissing.

The second time started much more slowly and built. They took turns, as equals, and Tyler had never experienced anything like that before. Always, in his experience, partners either demanded everything of you, or gave all they had. This felt different. It felt shared.

The third time waited until morning. Tyler was late to work.

wednesday

1

What would Tyler do?

Mina's sure about one thing, he wouldn't be sitting around the office shuffling paperwork for Franklin. If she didn't know better, she'd almost think Doggett was trying to keep her out of this for some reason. She shakes her head. First Tyler, then Franklin, and now Doggett? This place is enough to make you paranoid.

But paranoia or not, Tyler has definitely been keeping her at arm's length. For weeks now. She'd put it down to him reverting back to his old ways, getting secretive and not sharing information with her, but now that she's had a chance to think back, he wasn't like that with the others. Just a few days before his so-called accident she'd seen him laughing and joking with Cooper as though they were old friends. That in itself should have been enough to make her see he was behaving oddly, but it was the way he'd shut down when she walked in that had disturbed her. For a moment it was as though she was back in the playground with the girls all clamming up the minute she arrived. Except of course Cooper hadn't. She'd been perfectly pleasant and personable. It had been Tyler who'd avoided her eye and then, maybe ten minutes or so after she'd come into the room, made a flimsy excuse about checking some evidence at the lock-up and disappeared for the rest of the day.

Now she realises: that was the last time she saw him. She really needs to talk to Cooper, but she's not due back until Monday. She'd said she was going on some wellness retreat in Northumbria and Mina's already left two messages for her. Cooper can be touchy about stuff like that. Since coming back, she's been very vocal about leaving on time and switching off outside of work. After all she's been through, Mina can't blame her for being a bit quick to start talking about the union whenever she feels she's being put upon. But still, this is a bit different, surely?

It occurs to her suddenly that maybe Cooper doesn't even know what's happened to Tyler. Has anyone else rung her? Should she have done it? She picks up her mobile and tries Cooper's number, but once again it goes straight to voicemail. She leaves another message. 'Hi, Suzanne, it's Mina. Sorry to bother you on your holiday and all that but ... something's happened. Something pretty serious. Can you call me please? As soon as you get this. Sorry.'

She drops her phone on the desk and sighs. Well, that was pathetic. And now Cooper will probably think she's in trouble about something. She'll turn up at the office tomorrow morning with the union rep right behind her.

Her phone immediately lights up with an incoming call and Mina grabs it. It's not Cooper though.

'Diane?' she answers, hoping to convey every question she wants to ask with a single word.

'Hi, Mina. No change, I'm afraid.' Diane's voice is as controlled and measured as always, and not for the first time Mina's grateful for the other woman's incredible ability to remain professional in even the most trying circumstances. 'I just wanted to make sure everything's okay there at the office?'

Mina freezes. Has Franklin not told Diane that she put Mina in charge? She definitely isn't the sort of person to consider bruised egos when making appointments. 'Erm ... yes. Everything's fine here.'

There's a lengthy pause and then Diane asks, 'What's going on? Mina, is something wrong?'

'No! No, nothing like that. It's just ... well ...' She comes right out and says it. 'Franklin asked me to look after the unit until ... well, for the time being.' *Look after.* That sounds better than 'run', she thinks.

There's the briefest of pauses and then Diane says, 'Mina, of course she has.'

She can hear the smile in Diane's voice.

'I thought maybe ...'

'You thought my nose might be put out of joint taking orders from someone who used to be a subordinate. Mina, I went through all this with Adam when I first came back. I'm not that sort of person and, frankly, the fact that either of you thinks I am makes me a little sad. We're colleagues now, and, I hope, friends. And I'm old enough and ugly enough to accept I'm not the one calling the shots anymore, okay?'

Despite the words, Mina can feel the warmth of the speech. 'Thank you,' she says.

'That said, if you think that means I won't be making my opinions heard, you can think again.'

Mina smiles. 'I wouldn't have it any other way. Boss.'

'I was just ringing to see if you needed me to come in or . . . well, it's just that I haven't had a lot of sleep and—'

This she can do. 'Don't you dare!' Mina tells Diane. 'Your priority is Tyler . . . Adam.' She still finds it weird that Diane calls him that – she's the only one who does. 'Stay there, or go home and sleep, but you are not to come to the office. Is that understood?'

'Yes. *Boss.*'

This time the pause is less charged. But when Diane goes on, her tone has changed. 'Is there any more information about what happened?'

Mina hesitates. She doesn't want to add to Diane's worries – she has enough to cope with – but . . . 'You said back in the hospital that you thought he'd been different the past few weeks. More secretive, I think you said.'

'Yes. I thought, just as you did, that he might have been getting hung up on the past again. Looking into Jackson and the Circle and everything.' As Diane mentions this her voice drops a little. They're all a bit skittish when it comes to talking about what isn't supposed to be spoken of.

'You said you'd tried to talk to him about it.'

'That's right. He came over for dinner a couple of weeks ago and I asked him outright – why he was pulling away again, shutting people out. He denied it all, of course, and changed the subject. But I'll be honest, Mina, whatever it was he was going through, I genuinely don't think it had anything to do with that. If I had to put money on it, I would have said it was something more ... personal. More current. I figured it had something to do with Scott.'

Something to do with Scott, not something to do with her.

'Did he ...' Mina doesn't know how to word this. 'Did he mention me at all? Like, whether it had something to do with me?' She trails off, and Diane fills the silence.

'No, he didn't mention you. Mina, what's going on?'

She's already said too much. Diane has enough on her plate. 'Don't worry about it. Ignore me, I'm just being daft.'

'Mina ...' Diane stops for a moment. 'It's perfectly natural if you're feeling overwhelmed. This is a big step up for you, but I've absolutely no doubt you can do this. Yes, you've got some big shoes to fill, and the circumstances aren't exactly ideal, but you've got this. And Suzanne and I will help you any way we can. You'll have our full support.'

It takes Mina a moment before she fully understands what Diane's talking about. She thinks this is about Mina taking over the department. The kindness of this woman! Her godson is in hospital at death's door and she's taking time to reassure Mina about her job. But at least it gives her an out.

'You're right,' she says. 'I'm really sorry, I shouldn't be bothering you with all this.'

'Now you are being daft,' Diane tells her. 'You can come to me any time. I'm sure Suzanne will tell you the same. And, if you ever get truly stuck, just think to yourself, what would Adam Tyler do?'

She means that last as a joke, Mina thinks, after the call has ended. But the words reverberate in her head long after she's put down the phone.

What would Tyler do?

She knows full well what Tyler would do. He'd go and see Harry Foster and find out what this letter is all about. Of course, that's exactly what Doggett told her not to do. But Tyler would ignore him. That's what Tyler would do.

She thinks about it for a good half an hour as she sits in front of her screen and fails to read the case notes she should be working on. Then she picks up her car keys and heads out of the office.

2

Harry Foster's house is a run-down terraced property close to the cemetery.

She rings the bell and waits, but after a few minutes there's no sign of any response. She tries again, but still nothing.

'Help you with something?' A voice reaches her, not from the house she's stood outside, but from somewhere off to her left.

The neighbour's house is in better repair than Harry's and has obviously had some money spent on it at some point because it now has a cupboard-sized porch extension. Which means its front door directly faces Harry's. The woman addressing her is standing in the open doorway and looking straight at Mina. She's in her mid-to-late fifties and wearing a dressing gown that at some point might have been pink. It's only loosely fastened, but fortunately she's wearing jogging bottoms and a T-shirt underneath.

'I'm looking for Harry Foster.'

The woman nods, as though about to impart some obscure piece of arcane human knowledge. 'That's the right one. I ain't seen him though. Not for a few days now.' She clears a thick wad of catarrh from her throat that would have announced her as a smoker even if Mina couldn't smell the stale scent of tobacco wafting from the doorway. 'Can I help you with something?'

'No,' Mina says, 'not really.'

The woman grunts a noise that's clearly designed to show how affronted she is.

Not a great start, Mina. Pissing off the neighbours. She should probably set some limits to this whole 'What would Tyler do?' business. She pulls out her warrant card and shows it to the woman, introducing herself properly.

'Oh,' the woman says, her mouth turned down almost into a pout. 'Thought you was selling summat. *The Watchtower.*' She looks Mina up and down. 'Or whatever your version is.'

Mina forces herself to smile. 'So, is that unusual, Mrs ...?'

'Craig,' the woman says, clearly still unsure whether she should continue with her defensive position or thaw a little in the chance of obtaining some juicy gossip.

'Mrs Craig. Is it unusual not to see Mr Foster for that long?'

'You usually see him of a morning. Goes for his baccy at the corner shop. 'Course, he's going barmy so he misses some days.'

Barmy? Mina thinks. She doesn't ask but Craig tells her anyway.

'You know, up here.' She taps her temple with her forefinger. 'Demented or whatever they call it now. Me grandad went doolally, but that's just what happens when you get old.'

Mina swallows hard, the smile on her face beginning to hurt. She forces herself to unclench her teeth. Perhaps this was one of those times when maybe it wouldn't hurt to be a little bit more like Tyler after all. He would have put the old bigot in her place by now.

Which gives her an idea.

'You haven't seen this man here, have you?' She flicks through the photos on her phone until she finds one of Tyler. She has to go back quite a way, but eventually she finds one from the day they did the interview with the paper. He'd looked so uncomfortable standing by his desk with the photographer trying to get him to relax that she hadn't been able to resist. She shows it to Craig.

Another grunt which, this time, may or may not mean yes. Luckily, she follows it up with, 'Might have seen him. It would have been a while ago now though.'

'How long, do you think?'

'Mmm. Few months. Can't be sure it were him though.'

Mina would bet that it was. She doubts much gets past Mrs Craig. She definitely recognises Tyler's face, but seems to like being unhelpful as a matter of principle.

'So, when was the last time you saw Mr Foster? Can you remember? Exactly.' She says the last word with a sharper inflection and Mrs Craig jumps a little. When she speaks, she's a bit more defensive.

'Well, I don't know exactly. I mean, I definitely saw him Sunday because our Karen was round and – no, wait, that would've been *last* Sunday.' She smiles for the first time, and it goes a long way towards softening her face. 'The days run into one, don't they?' She thinks a bit more. 'Not sure. Maybe a week. Maybe more.'

Mina thanks her for her help and turns away, hoping that

it's enough of a signal to send the woman packing. Mrs Craig lingers for a moment but eventually, reluctantly, shuts her door. Mina has no doubt her eye is still pressed to the spyhole.

A week, maybe more. A man with dementia. Is it grounds enough to break in? He can't be all that bad if he's looking after himself and living alone, but a week's still a fair amount of time, assuming Mrs Craig's testimony is reliable. Added to that, he could be a material witness in an attack on a police officer.

Of course, if she's wrong about this, Franklin will suspend her. Mina stares at the PVC door. She's not sure she could break in if she tried, so instead, she crouches down and pushes open the letter box.

The smell hits her with force and she knows instantly what it is. Her head recoils of its own volition but she forces herself to look back. He's lying on his back at the foot of the stairs, a few feet from the door. Her eyes focus on his hand first – aged, fingers twisted into a claw-like position. Even if she could reach in and feel for a pulse, she doesn't need to.

Mina slowly lets go of the letter box, stands and looks again at the neighbour's front door. At least Mrs Craig's in for a memorable afternoon. So is Mina, but she doubts it'll be as enjoyable. She unclips her radio and makes a call that might be the last of her career.

3

Doggett watches from a safe distance as ACC Franklin rants at Mina. He'll do his best to rescue her in a minute but it's important Franklin gets some of it out of her system first. Sometimes that's all they needed, the bigwigs – a chance to vent.

The poor girl looks like she's shifting between crestfallen in one moment, and liable to blow in the next. *Hold your tongue,* he wills her. Some battles are worth fighting, some worth rolling over for. His ex-girlfriend, the poet, would probably call that a mixed metaphor, but mixed or not, it was the stark-bollocking truth.

He wonders what she's doing here, the Beak. An old fella with dementia falling down the stairs is hardly the stuff of Assistant Chief Constable concerns. What *is* her interest in Mina? Did Tyler know anything about it? Bloody hell, the lad couldn't have picked a worse time to go flying off a gantry.

Dr Ridgeway emerges from the house, snapping off her polypropylene gloves and hooking a finger behind her ear to liberate her mask strap.

'And?' he asks, before she can reach him.

'Y'all wanna know if he was pushed or if he fell.'

'No,' he tells her, without any real heat in his voice. 'I wanna know who he had in the 4.15 at Kempton Park.'

She flips her eyebrow up at him but doesn't bite. 'No signs of struggle or defensive injuries. It looks consistent with a fall down the stairs. He's been dead a week, max. Can't say for sure, but if someone helped him on his way there's no obvious sign of it. PM could show somethin' else . . .' She spreads her hands.

'Yeah, yeah, yeah. "Don't quote me on that", you'll need to wait till you get him on the slab, other fizzy drinks brands are available.'

She shoots him a wry smile. 'You got it, Detective.'

In truth, what he likes about Ridgeway is the fact that she's willing to give him even this much, where most aren't. Maybe it's an American thing, but she's a lot less highly strung than her predecessor and, from Doggett's point of view at least, that's a bloody big bonus.

'If he *was* pushed,' she goes on, 'there may be some faint signs of bruising on the flesh, but it's unlikely. I reckon your best bet will be the CSI guys.'

'Okay, doc. Thanks for coming out.'

'I was kinda surprised to get the call. Is there a reason you think Mr Foster didn't just fall?'

Other than the fact he was a material witness in a case Tyler was investigating before he, too, had an unexplained fall from a great height?

'Just being thorough, doc. Just being thorough. Excuse me.' Mina's getting braver and starting to answer back; it's definitely time to intervene.

' . . . just saying that if he was working on a cold case when he was attacked then surely it makes sense for us to investigate.' Mina's face is growing redder by the second. 'Ma'am,' she adds, just a fraction too late.

'Chip off the old block this one, eh?' he interrupts. Both of them turn and glare at him, but he's well used to fielding hostile looks from women. He does what he always does and ignores them. 'Seems he fell,' he says. Best to get the pair of them back on track as soon as possible. 'If there was foul play involved, it isn't obvious yet.'

'There must be,' Mina snaps.

He widens his eyes, knowing full well that his bushy eyebrows will be climbing his forehead. He has his own range of looks and this is his patented 'shut-the-fuck-up' face. If Mina notices, she makes no show of it.

'I mean, it can't be a coincidence, surely?' she goes on.

Franklin's bird-like mouth twitches. 'Detective Constable Rabbani, I still haven't heard a reasonable explanation as to why you are here.'

Mina opens her mouth to snap back, but for once she seems to falter over the best course of action.

Doggett jumps in again before things can get any worse. 'My fault, ma'am. Apologies. Mina came to me with some information last night concerning an anonymous note her department received a few months ago. We think it might have been what DS Tyler was looking into when he was attacked.'

Franklin rolls her eyes and huffs. 'We still don't know for sure DS Tyler—'

But he's been waiting for this. 'Actually, ma'am, I've just come from speaking with the surgeon who stitched up our lad's scalp. He's of the opinion that Tyler couldn't have come by the injury solely as a result of the fall. It was more consistent with a violent blow to the head.' He waits for this to settle before delivering his own killer blow. 'It was definitely an attack, ma'am.'

Franklin's face betrays nothing of what she's thinking, but she's not stupid. He doubts she's missed the fact that, by his own account, that means he asked Mina to come here *before* they had this new information.

'He's sure of this?' she asks, but she doesn't wait for his nod before she goes on. 'That changes things then.' He has to give the Beak her due: as unyielding as she can be when she's set on a course of action, once she has new information she pivots without batting an eyelid.

'Yes, ma'am. I thought perhaps the best route forward would be for DC Rabbani and her team to remain focused on the letter DC Tyler was investigating, while I pursue any leads pertaining to the attack on Tyler himself.' *Pertaining.* He's particularly proud of that one. 'Where things overlap' – he raises his hand to the victim's house, now crawling with techs – 'we can join forces and work together. I suggest we touch base with each other on a daily basis going forward.'

Touch base. Going forward. He wants to vomit but it sounds like the sort of office-speak bollocks she revels in.

Franklin nods slowly, though there's a curve to her lip that says he might just have overplayed his hand.

'What about the tech side of things?' she asks.

'I'm still waiting on the phone people. The team are going over his laptop right now, but they're snowed under, apparently.'

She takes the hint. 'I'll see what I can do to expedite matters.'

'I'd appreciate that, ma'am.'

He doesn't mention to her that Tyler had wiped his browser history recently, which he feels pleased about when she launches into her next topic.

'I must say I'm less than thrilled that one of my officers was working on something that neither I, nor any of his other colleagues, knew anything about.'

'No, ma'am.' There's not much he can add that isn't going to fan the flames higher.

'I really don't want to have to involve Professional Standards in this, but if you don't find anything soon . . .' She leaves the threat hanging.

'Yes, ma'am.' All this yes-ma'am-no-ma'am-ing is giving his spleen the earache but it seems to do the trick.

'All right, Jim. You've obviously got things under control. But I'll expect regular updates. An attack on one of us is an attack on us all. Understood?'

'Yes, ma'am.' His jaw is aching from the smile. *Where does she get this crap from?*

She turns to Mina. 'DC Rabbani. I shall be watching. Closely.'

Mina opens her mouth and Doggett clears his throat ostentatiously. *Just let her have the last word!*

'Yes . . . ma'am,' she says, and it's all Doggett can do not to let out a sigh of relief.

They watch Franklin walk away and, once he's sure she's out of earshot, he rounds on Mina. 'What the flamin' hell did you think you were doing?'

She opens her mouth to defend herself, but he goes on before she can speak.

'I specifically told you to leave this to me and you blunder in here and fuck it all up! I'm not finished,' he says, forcing her to close her mouth once again. 'I know what you thought: *Oh, poor me, I'm being left out again.* Boo-hoo. So sad. Poor old Mina always gets the short straw. Did it occur to you I might have a valid reason for not letting Foster know we were looking into him?' He waits just long enough for her to decide that isn't rhetorical before he pushes on. 'Did it occur to you that he might be the one who tried to murder your friend and colleague? And that by coming here you might put into jeopardy any chance we have of convicting him?'

She's going bright red and he feels her pain, but she's had this coming for a while now. She needs to learn, and just because he saved her from Franklin's wrath doesn't mean she's safe from his. He lets her stew on his words a moment before he goes on.

'I wanted to look into Foster myself before I decided what the best course of action was. Did *that* not occur to you? Well, did it?'

By the end he's virtually shouting, and he sees Dr Ridgeway looking across at them with concern. Mina's close to the doctor, which should only serve to add to her discomfort. All to the good as far as he's concerned.

When she finally finds her voice, it's cracked and faint. 'I just thought . . . I mean, I tried to think what he would do.'

He's about to ask who, and then he gets it. Tyler. He has to admit, it is the sort of bullshit move he'd expect of the lad. He finds his anger waning, but he stokes it back up.

'You're not Tyler. And if you were, you wouldn't have the glittering career ahead of you that I know you have. You wouldn't have the Beak twitching around at crime scenes, checking up on you. For Christ's sake, Mina, you're a detective now, you need to start engaging your brain now and again!'

She looks up at that, confusion writ large across her face.

'You think she turns up for every junior officer who fucks up and disobeys orders?' He's been thinking about it and after this latest run-in with the Beak he's pretty sure he's got it right. 'She's grooming you for something.'

'What?'

'It's the only explanation, as far as I can see. I don't know what she's got in mind, but I've seen it happen in the past. Trust me, you're on the fast track, and if you play the game, you'll be light years ahead of Tyler and me both. But you do have to play the game. There's a reason Tyler won't ever be Assistant Chief Constable. You don't have to follow in his footsteps.'

He doesn't enjoy talking about the lad like this given his current situation, but she has to understand where to draw the line. She has to learn the lesson he never did.

'You have to be better than the rest of us,' he tells her.

She doesn't say anything, but he can see he's given her food for thought. Good enough, if it stops her running headlong into trouble every chance she gets. If it stops her ending up in a hospital bed with her skull caved in.

'He was dead anyway,' she tells him with trademark belligerence. 'Foster, I mean.'

'Lucky for you. But less lucky for Mr Foster.' He keeps the

smile off his face but chucks her on the chin, enjoying her scowl. 'Come on, the photographer's been through. Let's get suited up and see what the boys and girls in white coats have got for us.'

4

While Mina's suiting up she manages to get her trembling under control. Emma's supervising the loading of the body into the back of the van and keeps trying to catch her eye, but Mina's mortified enough at her public flogging without fielding sympathy from a friend into the bargain. She can still feel the heat radiating from her cheeks.

The worst part is, Doggett's right. She knows he is. She should never have come here after he specifically told her not to. What had she been thinking? Was it really just that she was trying to be like Tyler? She has the utmost respect for Tyler, but Doggett was right about that, too – she doesn't intend for her own career path to match his. Why on earth was she trying to out-macho him? It was the sort of stupid crap she might have expected from Danny back in the day. But even Danny's moved on since then. Everyone else is moving forward in their development and she's regressing. She owes Tyler more than that. She has to do better.

She bends over and pulls the sterile boots on over her shoes, sighing as she straightens up. There's no point dwelling on it.

Doggett's said his piece and he'll leave things at that. He isn't one to hold a grudge or to retread old ground. She has to do her best to just put the whole thing behind her and, since Harry Foster had already been dead a good several days before she got here, at least she hasn't jeopardised the case or caused any longstanding harm. In fact, without her early intervention they wouldn't even know he was dead yet. Her thoughtless action might turn out to have a silver lining after all.

As she pulls on the polypropylene gloves and tucks her hair under the hood she chews over Doggett's other bombshell. What had he meant she was on the fast track to something? Was that really what he thought? Franklin had her earmarked for . . . what, exactly? She'd wanted to ask him more about what he thought, but even she has enough sense to know when it's best to shut up and retreat. Sometimes.

Her mobile vibrates and Mina tuts. Doggett raises an eyebrow at her. She can't just ignore it though – it could be important. She snaps off the gloves again and extracts her phone from under the suit. She glances at the incoming call information on the screen – Ruth Weatherstone. Damn! She'd forgotten about the woman again.

'Take your time, by all means,' Doggett tells her. He turns his back and walks away.

She doesn't have time for this. She hits the call cancel button and slips the phone back in her pocket. Glancing across at Emma, she wonders if she's yet had a chance to ask Leigh how she knows Ruth. But Doggett's already disappearing into the house, so she follows him in.

Even through the mask, her nostrils are once again assaulted by the scent of death. It's muted though, and edged with industrial plastic. Doggett steps across the patch of bodily fluids staining the carpet at the bottom of the stairs and disappears into a room. Above them the SOCOs are largely crowded around the compact landing area, dusting the walls and bannisters for fingerprints.

Mina follows Doggett into the front room. It's pretty standard for the home of an elderly man living alone. There's a cream-coloured armchair that once had a pale pink and blue swirled pattern, now mostly faded, and an elaborate hem with gold thread that has frayed and come loose in places. The chair still shows the print of the man who used to sit in it, with its bowl-shaped dent in the cushion and hair-lacquer-stained backrest. The mantelpiece is heaving with bottles of medication and packets of pills. She recognises many of them from the pharmacy: statins and some heart-related medications from the look of it, as well as all the usual digestive regulators. 'Stoppers and Starters', her dad likes to call them.

'We'll need to talk to his GP, I suppose,' Doggett tells her, following her gaze. 'And any care providers he's had in.' He lets out a low snort. ''Course, that'll be a bloody ball-ache. Like prising a pint out of a Yorkshireman.'

There's very little in the way of decoration or ornamentation in the room, other than a barometer on the wall and a rusted horseshoe nailed to the fireplace. Two items do stand out though. Above the mantelpiece there's a Jack Vettriano print of a man and a woman in black, dancing. The woman's knees are bent and she's staring up at the man, her hands clutching his waist while his are arched behind him in an exaggerated dance pose full of bravado. She thinks it's probably an Argentine tango. Her *Strictly*-obsessed mum would know. She wonders if Harry Foster had a romantic streak. Or did he just think of himself as a Jack-the-lad?

The second object that catches her attention is a trophy cabinet against the back wall. It's plain enough in and of itself, possibly handmade since the wood doesn't seem to have been varnished properly. The glass is dusty and thickened with decades of grime, so if it was handmade, it was fashioned a long time ago. Inside, there are a number of statuettes and ornate lumps of silver and gold, sculpted into columns and spheres. For a moment she's reminded of Leigh Raddon's garden, but these are on a very different scale and probably worth a great deal less, in monetary terms, at least; they obviously meant a lot to Harry. Moving closer, Mina can see that many of them are labelled with his name and have dates and titles under them. *Young Featherweight Champion, Heeley, 1965. Junior Boxing, 2nd Place Runner Up.* All variations on a theme, the latest date she can find inscribed on any of these treasures is 1968. Harry was in his seventies, so he can't have been much more than eighteen back then. Whatever glorious fighting career he had must have ended while he was still in his prime. Mina has a moment of sadness for this man she's never met, holding onto a past he couldn't get back to.

'I think we can rule out a burglary gone wrong,' Doggett says, and for a moment she thinks he's talking about the trophies. But when she turns to him, he waves a wad of cash at her. 'Top drawer. Must be a few grand in twenties in here. Some old lags just can't break old habits.'

As she turns back to the cabinet something catches her eye on the floor at the back of the armchair. She bends down and sees what looks like a corner of paper sticking out from under the frayed hem of the chair cover. Sliding it out carefully, she turns it over. It's an envelope – empty, but with a scrawl of handwriting on the front. It says *To Police* and nothing else.

'Looks like he was definitely our letter writer,' she tells Doggett.

She lifts the flap of the hem and tips the back of the chair a little so she can see underneath, but there's nothing else of interest. As she moves round to the front she notices the thin edge of another object wedged down the side of the cushion.

Doggett joins her and she holds the envelope out to him. He takes it in a gloved hand and turns it over. Mina bends over and extracts another crumpled envelope from the side of the chair, this one sealed. There's a name on the front – Mr Beech – and an incomplete Sheffield address.

'Hang on,' Doggett tells her, tapping her wrist with the tips of his gloved fingers. He bends over this time and raises the sagging seat cushion. Underneath there's a mass of half-written scraps of paper and scrunched-up envelopes.

'Looks like he wrote to a lot of people, not just us.'

Doggett lets the cushion drop again without disturbing the rest of the letters. 'Let's let the white-coats do their work before we do anything else.' Mina nods. She's done with blundering in and causing trouble.

Her mobile rings again and she swears. Doggett glances at her with raised eyebrows.

'It's this bloody woman,' she tells him. 'Won't leave me alone.'

'I have the exact same problem,' Doggett says.

Mina snaps off a glove and pulls out her phone. She supposes she's being unfair. After all, she did stand Ruth up. But then she glances at the display and sees the incoming call isn't from her at all.

'It's Cooper.'

Doggett grunts. 'At last.' He wanders off into another room. She answers the phone. 'Suzy?'

'Mina. Sorry, I've only just got your message. It's the retreat, they don't let us have our phones during the day, and anyway there's not much signal up here.'

Mina hadn't asked too many questions about the nature of this retreat. She knows Cooper's had issues with alcohol in the past, and she suspects this 'wellness' week has something to do with that, but she hadn't wanted to pry.

'What's up?' Cooper asks.

Mina tells her everything she knows, from Tyler's injuries to the anonymous letter which is now their only tangible lead. It takes a depressingly short amount of time. Cooper listens without passing comment. She's always professional, maybe too much so – none of them really feel like they know her that well yet.

When she's finished, Cooper asks, 'What can I do to help?'

'I'm not sure. Do you know anything about this letter? What he was working on?'

Cooper doesn't answer straight away, which gives Mina pause for thought and, perhaps for the first time in days, a glimmer of hope.

'Alison Beech,' she says eventually.

Mina's heart leaps in her chest. Finally, they have a name. 'Go on.'

More silence, but finally Cooper speaks. 'I don't know much, to be honest. But I know this is all about kidnappings. He came to see me a few months ago, before I joined you guys.'

'Suzy, please. We need to know what you know.'

'Of course. But honestly, it really isn't much.'

'That's fine. Just tell me whatever you can.'

It would be more than they had now.

3 months ago

I

Suzanne Cooper lived in a run-down block of flats on the Arbourthorne Estate, not all that far from Harry Foster's place. The whole area had become synonymous with crime in Sheffield over the past few decades. Ironically, or perhaps thankfully for those who lived there, it also had some of the best views over the city on offer: originally, it had been where all the posh nobs lived, breathing in fresh air and looking down on the working classes trapped in the industrial smog below. How times had changed.

When Cooper let him in, Tyler saw boxes piled up around the place.

'Moving day's Friday,' she said, by way of explanation.

'Going far?' he asked.

'Not as far as I'd hoped.' She smiled to take the self-pity out of her words. 'I guess the Caribbean will have to wait a bit longer.' She offered him a drink and he settled for a black coffee.

When he'd first met Cooper, she'd been a DI working on Missing Persons' cases, but not long after that she'd made some bad decisions and found herself suspended on disciplinary charges. It hadn't all been her fault and, luckily for her, after Franklin came in and shook up the department, she'd been allowed to resign quietly with her pension intact.

He hadn't had much to do with her since, although he knew Mina had stayed in touch. Cooper had spent a good few months wallowing in self-pity and self-recrimination after she'd been forced to resign, but lately, according to Mina at least, she'd managed to turn things around for herself. When Mina had last visited, she'd described Cooper's place as being littered with empty bottles and used ashtrays. Now it was clean and tidy, apart from the packing. Perhaps she really had turned her life around.

'How are things on the work front?' he asked, while she fiddled with a coffee pod machine. She obviously wasn't short of money at least.

She must have read his thoughts because she grinned. 'It's been tough,' she said. 'But I've been getting by with some consultancy work. I could definitely do with something more permanent, but for now it pays the bills. It's the only reason I've been able to afford this new place. God, I can't wait to get out of here.' There was the *thump, thump, thump* of footsteps overhead and she raised her hands as if to say, *See what I mean?*

She served up his coffee and invited him to sit at the breakfast bar that separated the kitchen from the living area, moving a box of crockery over to the couch so they had some space.

'Right,' she said, as she sat down and took a sip from her own mug. 'How can I help?'

'I'm not sure if you can,' he admitted. 'It's a bit before your time, but I'm hoping you may have looked into the case or at least that you're aware of it.'

Tyler outlined to her what he knew about the disappearance of Alison Beech. While he talked, she nodded, giving the impression she was at least partly familiar with the details.

When he'd finished she didn't say anything straight away, but stared into the middle distance and sipped at her coffee.

'You're right,' she said, finally. 'That's way before my time. But I do remember the case, obviously. Not in enough detail to tell you anything you don't already know though. Who was in charge of the original investigation?'

'Bob Smith.'

'Ah,' she said. 'Now I see why you came to me.'

'I'm sorry?'

She frowned at him. 'He came up the ranks with Superintendent Stevens. I'm assuming that's why you're here?'

Stevens. Was that name ever going to go away? He was the man responsible for most of the problems Franklin had been sent in to fix, including the death of Tyler's father and, of course, Cooper's disgrace.

'I'm never going to be forgiven for the past, am I?' She put down her mug. 'If you're wondering if I ever had anything to do with Smith, I didn't. I never even met him. He retired long before I joined the force.'

'Okay.'

'Okay?'

'If you say you don't know anything, I believe you.'

Her eyes bored into him, perhaps trying to figure out his angle.

'I didn't say I didn't know *anything*. I said I never met him. Heard plenty about him though. Word was he was bent as. Only reason he retired was because he knew they were coming for him. I'm guessing that's why he went overseas. No doubt Stevens helped ease him out of the situation before the shit hit the fan.'

'That's interesting, but it's not the reason I came to see you.'

She tilted her head, giving him permission to go on.

'According to Beech, Smith thought Alison's abduction was a mistake. A woman at the scene gave evidence she'd seen the kidnappers grab the son first and Alison got in their way. It was only after the boy got free that they bundled her into the van.'

Assuming he could trust Beech, and assuming he could trust the unnamed eyewitness. And assuming, after what Cooper had just told him, that he could even trust Bob Smith. The man might have been on the take, but was he on the take in this case? Even bent coppers did a good job some of the time. Stopped clocks were right twice a day.

'I don't remember that,' she said, frowning.

'It doesn't appear to have been common knowledge. If it's true, and I only have Beech's word for it at the moment, they kept it away from the media.'

Cooper picked up her mug again but didn't drink from it, instead just turning it around and around in her hands as she thought. 'When was this?' she asked. 'The exact date.'

He told her and she thought about it some more. Tyler liked that about her. She thought about things before she gave an opinion. Perhaps that was something else she'd learned the hard way.

'There *was* another kidnapping,' she said, eventually. 'It

would have been around that time, I think. Maybe a bit before. I remember reviewing the file a few years ago. A young kid was taken from a park ... the daughter of a local businessman and his wife. They paid the ransom that was requested. Fifty thousand, I think, from memory. Left the money in a litter bin in a park and the kid was dropped off a few hours later, unharmed.'

Tyler's ears pricked up. The details sounded remarkably familiar.

'What was the outcome?' he asked.

'The perpetrators were never found. I seem to remember the kid was having nightmares and the parents decided to leave well enough alone. They refused to let her be interviewed so we couldn't get a description of the attackers. After that they stopped co-operating. The mother, fearful of what the kidnappers might do, hadn't wanted to involve the police in the first place, but the father convinced her. He had some crazy notion he could offset the ransom money as a tax expense or something. I don't know if he succeeded.'

'Why haven't I heard about this?' Tyler asked. If it was an unsolved case, he should have come across it by now.

Cooper looked at him sharply, as though checking whether he intended the question as a rebuke. 'Like I said, the parents stopped co-operating and eventually I think they withdrew their initial complaint.'

'So how did you come across it? You said yourself you weren't around back then.'

She was still staring at him intently, as though trying to gauge if he was friend or foe. Perhaps he wasn't that sure of the answer himself.

'It came up on MisPers. The initial police report had been copied across but not the declassification, so I ended up looking into it quite deeply before I clocked it was a closed file.'

'Did you ever re-interview the victim or her family?' That, too, sounded like a rebuke, but he couldn't help it. There was nothing on file, but that didn't mean Cooper hadn't spoken to them off the record.

'Kidnappings didn't really fall within my remit,' she told him without emotion. 'And given that the child had been returned unharmed, and there were no further abductions, I didn't deem it a priority.' She was speaking more carefully now.

He nodded. That was fair. 'What if there *were* more?' he asked.

'Look, there was no evidence—'

He cuts off her defensive response with a wave of his hand. 'I just mean, let's assume Alison's kidnapping was actually a bungled attempt to take her son. If they'd succeeded, hypothetically, the picture would look a bit different. Two well-to-do families with kidnapped kids. Both taken from parks. Maybe they weren't the only ones who paid up and got their kids back. Maybe there were others, but they didn't report it.'

She thought about that for a moment. 'It's possible. There's one other thing I do remember.'

He met her gaze. 'Go on.'

'Bob Smith was the original investigator on that case too.'

'That is interesting.' Could Smith have been involved in some way? 'Do you remember the name of the victim?'

Cooper stared at the ceiling for a moment. The noise upstairs continued intermittently. 'Williams,' she said finally, looking back at him. There was no hint of doubt in her voice. 'Derrick

Williams. That was the name of the businessman. The girl's name was . . . Abigail. Yes, Abby.'

'Thank you.' He should be able to find the relevant info from that. Though how he'd find any other victims, assuming there were any to find, was another matter.

She showed him to the door, and he thanked her again, for her time and for the coffee.

'You've got a good memory,' he said.

She laughed a little, but it was a self-deprecating sound. 'I remember all of them,' she said. 'But mainly the ones who didn't make it.' The smile died.

She'd turned a blind eye when Stevens had pressured her. She'd chosen the easier path and that meant there were victims out there who would never receive justice. At least, that's how Cooper saw it, according to Mina. It seemed that for all her efforts to move forward, there was a part of her still stuck in the past.

'Do you ever think about coming back?' he asked. It sounded like a whim, but it wasn't. He'd wanted to see what she was like first, with his own eyes, and what he saw now impressed him. She clearly still had issues, but she was dealing with them. More importantly, she'd been good at her job.

'To the force?' Cooper laughed, loudly. 'I think that ship has long sailed.'

'Not necessarily,' Tyler told her. 'They're not about to let you be an officer again, but what if I had a position coming up? Civilian. Would you be interested?'

She gawped at him. 'Are you serious?'

'Missing persons are still cold cases. Someone with your

speciality – and memory,' he added with a grin, 'could be of great use to us.'

She shook her head, but it didn't seem like a hard no.

'Look, think about it,' he told her. 'I'll give you a ring in a couple of weeks and we'll talk some more. Good luck with the move.'

He left her standing on her doorstep with her mouth open.

II

The playground wasn't dissimilar to any other across the city. Tyler wandered around comparing the geography as it was now with the scene of crime photos from twenty-four years ago. The first thing he noticed was that there weren't all that many pictures, at least not in comparison with the number of photos that were taken these days. It would have been the pre-digital age then, of course.

But holding up the few images he had, he could see a number of striking changes. The park had been re-landscaped in the intervening years, perhaps more than once, and it looked very different now. For example, visible in the background of several of the photographs was a large ramshackle shed that had sold teas and coffees and snacks. It had long since been demolished, and park visitors now had to make do with the expensive chain coffee shop up on the main road. Conversely, the playground equipment was in far better condition, an elaborate wooden wigwam that housed a tall double slide replacing the worn-down roundabout that used to be there. There was also a separate, fenced-off area for people who wanted to exercise their dogs, and what had once been an unkempt field for impromptu ballgames was now kept trimmed and neat, with white lines marked out for rugby and football.

Tyler wandered up and down the grass verges, fielding suspicious glances from wary parents who were supervising their kids with a vigilance that was no doubt a lot more honed than it had been two and a half decades ago.

He thought he'd located the spot where the actual snatch had taken place, although it was difficult to be a hundred per cent sure. Some of the houses in the pictures were no longer there and a new block of apartments stood in their place, so there was a certain amount of guesswork involved.

According to the interviewed witness, Ms Greene, two men had leapt from the bushes and snatched Lucas Beech from the swings before Alison ran forward to tackle them. In the ensuing struggle the boy had got free, and Alison had called out to him to run. She had then been bundled into the back of a van waiting a few metres beyond the bushes on the cul-de-sac that led to the main road.

It was odd though. Tyler couldn't work out why the kidnappers would choose this particular point from which to launch their attack. The bushes were long gone, perhaps removed because of what had happened, but from what he could make out they'd been nowhere near the children's play equipment of the time. If they'd been lying in wait there, the kidnappers would have had to sprint across several metres of open ground to reach the swings, giving Alison plenty of time to react.

Moreover, yes, the bushes would have provided cover, but it was a public park, and a fairly empty one at the time. Unless the kidnappers were particularly distinctive in some way, which he supposed was a possibility, they wouldn't have stood out any more than any other walkers in the place. Was there something about them that would have occasioned comment from potential witnesses? If there was, Greene hadn't mentioned it. In fact, now he came to think of it, wasn't hiding in some scrubby bushes even more suspicious than merely walking through the park in plain sight? It sounded like a cartoon ambush.

The more Tyler puzzled over the landscape, the more Greene's story didn't add up. If Lucas had been on the swings, then why hadn't Alison been with him? She might have wandered over to sit on a bench, but they were only a few feet away. And the van. It must have been a good twenty or thirty metres from the swings. Did they really drag her all that way? And if so, why didn't Greene get a better look at them?

There were a number of possibilities. It could just be that the woman had got things wrong. Witnesses were notoriously vague when it came to important details, and memory, even short term, could be extremely unreliable. Or he could be misinterpreting the layout of the pictures. But he didn't think it was that. The only other alternative he could think of was that the woman had lied. But why? Unless she was involved somehow.

More importantly, why hadn't Smith picked up on any of this? He was either incompetent or he could have been in on it too. The statement Greene made had backed up his purported theory of a child-kidnapping gang, and yet he hadn't made reference to any other kidnappings in his report. It wasn't unheard of, especially at that time, for an investigating officer to disregard evidence, but usually when that happened it was because they had a particular suspect in mind and some small part of said evidence didn't match their theory. In those days, the police had not been obliged to turn over evidence that contradicted their sequence of events to the defence. But in this case, there hadn't been any suspects. At least, none that Smith had included in his reports.

'Are you DS Tyler?' The woman who spoke blinked at him myopically through a pair of thick lenses. She held a short lead with a Chihuahua on the end whose eyes bulged even further than its owner's.

'Abby?' Tyler asked.

The woman nodded and shuffled nervously on the grass bank while the dog took the opportunity to sniff at Tyler's shoes.

'Stop that, Hercules!' She jerked on the lead, which was attached to a harness that lifted the dog clean into the air. It scrabbled for a moment before resuming its snuffling. 'Sorry,' she went on, 'he's a bugger with new people.'

Abby Williams was so exactly not what Tyler had pictured that he was momentarily thrown. Of course, he'd only seen pictures of her as a five-year-old girl, so it shouldn't have been all that shocking that she'd changed over the years. But still, there was very little to connect that chubby, cheeky-faced five-year-old with the scrawny, slightly crumpled-looking woman standing in front of him. For one thing, Abby Williams would be twenty-nine now, but this woman looked closer to forty-five, and her face was so completely obscured by the oversized glasses that it was almost impossible to see her features.

'Thanks for agreeing to meet me,' Tyler said, and only then considered that she might have had issues with the choice of meeting place. It wasn't the same playground she'd been kid-napped from, but he supposed it could be considered triggering for her. When he'd discovered she lived just down the road from here it had only occurred to him to kill two birds with one stone. Now he watched as she glanced around nervously at the treeline.

'I hope this isn't bringing back too many unpleasant mem-ories for you,' he said.

Abby turned back to him and squinted through her lenses. 'Oh, no! It's not that.' She grinned a little. 'It's my sight. Wide-open spaces make me a bit nervous. There's nothing to focus on. You're lucky I picked you out, actually.'

'I was wondering how you managed that.'

'You're the only one here without a dog,' she said, wiggling a pair of thick, unsculpted eyebrows, as though implying Tyler wasn't the only one who could deduce stuff.

They walked back to the path and Tyler had to help her negotiate the steep bank leading up to the pavement. He felt guilty about forcing her onto the grass in the first place. He'd lost track of the time while he was examining the park and hadn't realised their meeting was so close.

They sat down on a bench not far from the kids' playground and Abby lifted the Chihuahua up onto her lap and wrapped it inside her jacket. 'Shoot!' she said to him.

Tyler considered where to start and decided on another apol-ogy. 'I really am sorry. It never occurred to me this might not be the best place for our chat.'

She waved away his concern, but he noticed her hand was shaking a little. 'Really, I don't have very many memories of the whole thing. In fact, I'm not sure how much use I'm going to be to you. Maybe being here will jog something though.' Her jollity was endearing, but he suspected it was a little forced.

'Just tell me what you can remember.'

Abby thought for a moment, her face screwing up with the effort. 'Thing is,' she said, 'I'm not really sure what I remember and what my parents told me afterwards. That's the thing with childhood memories, isn't it?' She scratched the top of the dog's head and it shivered with pleasure. 'I suppose I could start with the story my mum told me before she died. Up until that point, I didn't remember anything really.

'I think she felt guilty. Maybe Dad did too, in his own way. She was the one that was with me though, so I suppose that made a difference. She was talking with some friends and the next thing she knew I was gone. I can't imagine how that must have felt for her, but I could hear some of it in her voice when she told me what happened. I'm guessing the fear never really goes away after something like that. It would explain why she was always so bloody possessive.' She laughed. 'Anyway, she rang my dad and they searched the whole park for me, and that's when the woman approached them.'

'Woman?'

'Yeah. One of the kidnappers, I guess. She just thrust a note at them and said, "This is for you!", or something like that. By the time they figured out what was happening she was gone. The note told them what to do. Fifty grand, in a bag, to be left by the litter bin at the edge of the park at midnight on such-and-such a date.'

'And they followed the instructions?'

'To the letter. Lol.'

'They didn't call the police?'

'Not until after. The note told them not to or I'd be—' She made a cutting motion across the dog's throat and clicked her tongue. 'They paid up. Dad was a hedge fund manager and pretty well-off, so I suppose in the grand scheme of things it wasn't a lot compared with the life of his daughter.' She chuckled. 'I doubt he still thinks I was worth it.'

Tyler glanced at her and she interpreted his unspoken question.

'We haven't really talked since Mum died. No biggie. Just one of those things. He doesn't exactly approve of what he calls my *life choices*, and frankly, I don't approve of his.' Her laugh was light-hearted despite her words, and Tyler began to warm to this cheerful, pragmatic woman. 'I once joked with Mum that it must have been why he refused to support me at uni: he'd already spent so much on my childhood that he felt *I* owed *him*. Thing is, fifty grand doesn't seem that much, really, does it? For a wealthy banker.'

Tyler agreed, it didn't. But on the other hand, maybe it was clever. Ask for two hundred grand or a million, and suddenly the family had a problem, one that might cause them to start thinking about picking up the phone and calling for help. But make it affordable and straightforward to rustle up without provoking attention, then throw in the threat of violence, and you made it easy for them to do exactly what you wanted. Especially if you acted quickly, while they were still reeling from shock, which, by the sounds of it, was exactly what they'd done.

'There was another note,' Abby went on, 'sellotaped to me

251

or something when they found me. It basically told them not to go to the police or they'd come back and finish the job. It was Dad's idea to ignore it and go to the cops anyway. Mum apparently begged him not to, but in the end he needed the police report for insurance purposes.' She laughed again, but this time there was no doubt it was forced. 'Thing is, the insurance never paid out. Probably another reason he hates me.'

'And what about you?' Tyler asked. 'What do you remember?'

'Like I said, not very much. I think I can remember being in the back of a van, you know, bouncing around and banging myself on things. Mum said I was pretty bruised when they got me back so that might have been why . . .' She trailed off.

'Do you know where you were held? Or for how long?'

She shook her head. 'I know it was a house. They kept me in a bedroom. Other than that, I don't remember.'

Tyler hesitated. 'I'm sorry to have to ask you this but, do you remember . . . if they did anything to you?'

She smiled, but it was a pained expression. 'Truthfully? I don't know. I think that's the hardest thing, really. Not knowing, I mean. I was only gone a few hours and . . . you'd remember something like that. Wouldn't you?'

He didn't answer. Memory loss in children who'd been through trauma was a common defence mechanism, but what was the point in giving her more to worry about? The whole business clearly still affected her, even after all these years.

'I sometimes think I can remember their faces,' Abby added. 'A woman . . . a skinny South Asian guy maybe? But I don't think I'd be able to pick them out of a line-up or anything.'

She stroked the dog with trembling fingers, and Tyler

wondered again how much of the laughter and bluster was an act.

'And there was the dog, of course.'

'Dog?' Tyler looked at her in surprise. There'd been no mention of a dog at the scene of the kidnapping.

'Bloody great big thing. German Shepherd, I think, or at least that's how I remember it. I love Alsatians, don't you? I can't have one in the flat though. I'm not sure if it was one of them or if I've made that up since, but the dog itself was definitely real. They kept me in a room with it. I remember being really scared at first, but then it came over and put its head on my lap and I stroked it.

'I think that's probably where my love for animals comes from. It's why I went into animal rescue instead of banking like Dad wanted. Mind you, he probably wouldn't have minded if I'd been a vet. It's how much money you earn that matters to him.' She laughed again. 'I suppose you could say that what happened to me set the entire course of my life. Maybe I should thank those kidnappers. Dad would love that!'

Tyler thanked Abby and gave her his card, asking her to ring him if she thought of anything else over the next few days. He watched her shuffle away with the tiny little dog still tucked up inside her jacket.

A dog. That would certainly help as cover if you were hanging around a park looking for potential victims, negating the necessity of hiding in the bushes. Not that these victims were randomly selected. The kidnappers must have known Derrick Williams had the ability to pay the ransom, and possibly that he would be inclined to pay as well. That would all have taken a lot of planning. He wondered how many other times the gang had employed this technique and got away with it: how many other children had been taken, and where were they now? If the victims didn't go to the police afterwards the kidnappers could have been at this for years before they got unlucky.

They'd got unlucky with Derrick Williams. He had gone to the police. He'd spoken to Bob Smith and then, just a couple of months later, Bob Smith had been involved with another kidnapping attempt. Was it the same gang? Was Smith's involvement a coincidence?

Tyler's thoughts were interrupted by his mobile vibrating.

'Where are you?' Mina asked when he picked up.

'Hello to you too.'

'Don't give me that crap – Franklin's after your blood! You're meant to be at this press thing.'

'Shit!' He'd forgotten the photoshoot that was supposed to be happening.

'Don't worry, I covered for you. Said you had to interview that witness about the soft play robbery, so if she asks, could you maybe stick to that story?'

'Sure. Thanks. So how was it?'

'Oh no, you're not getting out of it that easily. The report-er's here now. I told her you were on your way. Please tell me you're in the city.'

Tyler found himself smiling. 'I'm ten minutes away. Fifteen, tops. Do your best to stall.'

'Fine,' she said, and hung up. It didn't sound like she was fine though.

III

Fourteen minutes and thirty seconds later Tyler was pulling up at the office. He could have done without this, but Franklin wouldn't let it go. She was determined to make CCRU a good news story and after all the extra resources she was throwing their way this wasn't a hill he wanted to die on.

In their top-floor office Diane was chatting casually with a wispy-bearded millennial holding a camera, while Mina was talking to a much older woman Tyler recognised as Jessica Gaskill from the local paper. It looked very much as though Mina was being as co-operative as a cat in a sack, and he might have pitied the journalist had he not known her well enough to be confident she could more than handle herself.

'Ah, here he is,' Mina said, somehow managing to position herself behind Tyler even as she introduced him.

'Long time, Tyler,' Gaskill said, shaking his hand.

'Not long enough,' he told her, and she barked out a laugh.

He'd only half been joking. Gaskill had tried to interview him about the Stevens business a while back, and had hounded him regularly for a good few weeks before she'd got bored.

Then she'd written the piece anyway. To be fair to her though, it hadn't been a complete hatchet job, and she'd done him the courtesy of leaving the rest of his family out of it.

'I wanted to thank you for taking the time to speak with us. I know you must be super busy.'

Tyler wondered if that was a dig, but she sounded genuine enough. He apologised for keeping her waiting and she introduced him to the cameraman, whose unlikely name was Leonardo. The lad rolled his eyes as she spoke, and Tyler noted the smirk on Gaskill's face. This was obviously a regular wind-up.

'Mum was a bit of a film buff,' the cameraman rushed to explain. 'Leo's fine.'

They settled down into what in the end was a very affable couple of hours. Gaskill took turns interviewing each of them, starting with Tyler. Her questions weren't exactly probing, and it was a refreshing change from the encounters he was used to when it came to the press. Normally, journalists shouted at them at crime scenes, rushing to hold them to account for some failing. Gaskill was fair and seemed interested in their work, asking relevant questions when she needed to clarify something, and without it sounding like she was looking for an angle. He began to think that perhaps Franklin had known what she was talking about when she'd arranged this puff piece. That said, there was a world-weary professionalism to Gaskill that kept him on guard. He wondered what she had been offered in exchange for all this.

'What makes you select a case for re-examination?' she asked, at one point.

'It might sound cut-throat,' he told her, choosing his words carefully, 'but everything is rated and given a score. There are various factors, but largely it comes down to whether it's in the public interest, combined with how likely we are to get a result. For example, new forensic techniques might shed light on a murder where a sample found on the victim was never tested because we didn't have the technology for it at the time. That case might score highly. On the other hand, a rape committed in the 1960s might score lower because the chances of the perpetrator still being a risk to the public is pretty small.'

'That's interesting,' Gaskill told him. 'So, you don't prioritise rape cases?'

Tyler studied the woman, trying again to work out her angle.

'That's not what I said, and it's also far from the truth. In fact, former DCI Jordan's main priority is the examination of outstanding sexual assaults.'

That launched a further flurry of questions. It really was shocking just how many sexual assaults were outstanding on their system, but he didn't try to sugarcoat the statistics. Maybe this article would prompt someone to come forward with information about a crime. If he could prick someone's conscience, he was more than willing to suffer a little criticism surrounding the numbers. Besides, he knew that comparatively their solved crime rates were good.

Leo photographed each of the three of them in turn and then, at the end of the interview, they all lined up behind Tyler's desk with the expansive view across Sheffield beyond them. 'Yeah,' Leo said, as he flicked through his digital work to check he had something suitable. 'That's sick! We've definitely got something for the centre page.'

Diane laughed. 'I never thought I'd be a centrefold at my age. Just make sure you put those staples in the right places.'

Gaskill came over to thank Tyler while Leo was packing up his equipment.

'Don't worry,' she said. 'It'll be a good piece. I think it's important, the work you're doing here. My sister was raped back in the Nineties, when she was at uni. It wasn't here, she was at Leicester, but the point is she's never really got over it. I was already a junior reporter back then and I was sure I could fix everything for her. I spent years looking into it, and other cases, trying to work out who did it.'

She sighed in a manner that conveyed the outcome of that particular crusade.

'It's easy to get obsessed with these things,' he told her. 'That's why we have to try to be dispassionate in our decision-making.'

She eyed him closely.

'It's not always easy though,' he added, and she accepted that with a lopsided nod.

'I wonder sometimes, if they found the person responsible, whether that would make a difference to her.'

'In my experience it does,' he told her. 'Somewhat.'

She held out her hand. 'Sorry I gave you a bit of a hard time, and don't worry, I won't stitch you up.'

Something occurred to him as he shook her hand. 'Were you reporting in this area in the Nineties?' he asked.

'I was, actually. I went down south at the turn of the

millennium and came back a few years ago when I split from the bastard ex.'

'Do you remember the Alison Beech case?'

'Dom Beech's wife? I remember it well. It was my first front page byline.' She paused, a hunger coming into her eyes. 'Don't tell me you've found her?'

'Nothing like that,' he said, holding up a hand to fend off any further enquiries. 'And before you start, I can't talk specifically about any active cases.'

'Uh-huh, so what do you want to know?'

Tyler hesitated. Gaskill was a clever woman and there was no way of asking this without giving away to her at least some of what he shouldn't be telling.

'There's a rumour that the prevailing theory at the time centred on an organised kidnapping gang; that they were after Alison's son and she got in the way.'

'A rumour? Meaning, you don't have any record on file?'

'It's . . . complicated.'

Gaskill thought for a moment. 'I seem to remember something mentioned, but I don't think anything came of it.'

Tyler pressed on. 'There was a woman, a witness at the scene who reportedly gave an account that the kidnappers went for the kid first, but that Alison fought them off. I'm trying to trace her.'

Gaskill put down her bag and leant back against his desk. 'I want an exclusive,' she said. 'Total access to your investigation.'

'Hang on, there *is* no investigation at the moment. It's way too early to be reporting anything.'

'Fine,' she said, narrowing her eyes. 'I don't mind keeping

quiet for now, but I want exclusivity when you're ready to tell the story.'

'It might be months. It might be never.'

'I'll take that chance.'

'Fine. I'll call you as soon as I have something. Promise. Can you find me the witness's name? All I've got is a surname. Greene.'

'Find it?' Gaskill told him. 'I remember it.'

He frowned. 'Really?'

'I'm hardly likely to forget. She said it was her mum's idea of a joke. Much like our poor Leo over there.' She grinned. 'It was Theresa. Theresa Greene.'

'You're kidding.'

'Straight up. I remember wondering if she had a brother called Soylent.'

'So, you interviewed her?'

'Well, sort of. I tracked her down and she seemed pretty eager, especially when I mentioned there might be money in it for her. But in the end she never turned up for the interview. I figured she got cold feet. It happens. I tried getting hold of her, but she never returned my calls after that.'

'Wait, Theresa? Did she go by anything else?'

'Eh? Yeah, she hated the name. Used to call herself Teri. With an I.'

Teri. Not Terry. Harry Foster had been calling for Teri. That couldn't be a coincidence.

'Can you dig out any information you have on her?'

'I'll do my best, but I don't know if I've kept anything. What's this all about?'

'Seriously, Jess. I can't, not right now. But I promise, as soon as there's anything concrete, you'll be the first person I call.'

She hesitated, but finally nodded and picked up her bag. 'I'll email you whatever I find. But you owe me big time for this!'

'I'm good for it,' he told her, grinning.

IV

Ruth was on her way home from work when she saw his picture on the front cover of the local paper.

It wasn't the main article – that was something about the council giving the go-ahead for a new cinema complex which didn't really interest her. She couldn't remember the last film she'd been to see, although she could remember Frank reluctantly taking her to watch *Home Alone* when she was a kid. She'd been scared by the burglars trying to break into the house, and Frank had laughed at her and ruffled her hair. It seemed incredible now that she had such a bright, happy memory among all the bad. She certainly couldn't remember him doing anything like that ever again. Later that night she'd had a nightmare and woken him up. He'd told her if she didn't shut up and go back to bed, he'd take his belt to her. She'd lain awake most of the rest of the night, too frightened to sleep. Not because of the nightmare itself, but in case she cried out and woke him. She knew from experience he'd go through with his threat, and he never stopped until he'd drawn blood.

Still, she remembered him laughing at her in the cinema.

And ruffling her hair. She supposed that just went to show that no one was completely evil.

So no, the cinema didn't interest her at all. But the banner at the top of the page did. It had a picture of two women and a man posing for the camera in an office. And positioned alongside it the headline: DIGGING AT THE PAST — THE COLD CASE SPECIALISTS BRINGING CLOSURE TO VICTIMS OF SERIOUS CRIME *(p54)*.

She felt her entire stomach flip over and the blood rush to her face. She found herself looking around as if someone there in the shop might recognise her and point her out. *Her! She's the one! Guilty!* That made no sense, of course, but it was all she could do to force herself to pick up a copy of the newspaper and flick through to the relevant page. Her hands were shaking so much it took her several attempts to separate the last two sheets of paper.

By the time she'd opened it to the double-page spread in question she knew she wasn't going to be able to read it there in the shop: the words were dancing in front of her eyes and the paper was shaking so violently in her hands that any onlooker would think she had a condition. She folded it closed and hurried to the self-service machine to pay for it as quickly as possible, leaving the basket of shopping she'd come in for on the floor.

By the time she got home she'd calmed down a bit. It wasn't as though the article would say anything about her, was it? The man on the cover, DS Tyler, wouldn't go talking to journalists about active cases. Of course not. There'd be rules about that sort of thing.

Still, she read the article through twice while she still had her coat on, examining it line by line for anything that might, however obliquely, give her a clue as to what he knew. There was nothing though. At least, nothing obvious. He made reference to a couple of specific cases but, reading between the lines, these seemed to be things they'd put to bed.

She was still in a bit of a state when Drew arrived and let himself in. He found her with the newspaper open in front of her on the kitchen table, still wearing her outdoor coat. He frowned at her, but she didn't think he'd picked up on her disquiet. He was more interested in why she'd bought the paper in the first place.

'I thought we'd talked about unnecessary expenses,' he said, flipping it closed and examining the price. 'One pound twenty's a bit extravagant for stuff we can easily read on the internet for free.'

She nodded. He was right. They'd only had this talk last night, and here she was breaking her commitment already. That didn't bode well for their future, did it? Despite everything she'd told him, about her father, about the past, he'd still offered to move in and help with her financial problems, and here she was adding to them.

'I'm sorry,' she said, 'but look!' She pointed to the banner on the cover. He looked puzzled at first, so she clarified for him. 'That's him! That's the policeman who came to talk to me.'

Drew picked up the paper and turned to the relevant page. He read the first couple of paragraphs, but his brow was still furrowed.

'I know I shouldn't have bought it,' she rushed to add, 'but I couldn't read it there in the shop, I just couldn't. And I needed to know if he'd said anything.'

Drew nodded absently, still intent on the article, so Ruth got up and went to switch the kettle on. He liked a brew as soon as he got through the door; she should have thought of that sooner.

'I just thought it makes sense,' he'd said a couple of weeks ago, when he'd first brought up the idea of moving in. 'I'm virtually living here anyway.'

Except, he hadn't been 'virtually living' there. He hadn't been there much at all. She worried she wasn't offering him something that he wanted and assumed it was sex, or a certain kind of sex. She'd done some research online and, although many of the practices she encountered seemed a bit bizarre to her, she'd dropped a casual suggestion into conversation one day.

'Feet?' he'd said, looking at her as though she'd grown a second head. 'Why the hell would I want to touch those trotters?' He'd laughed to show he meant it as a joke, and she hadn't mentioned it again. It had been much the same with anything else she'd come up with, though there were a few things she'd yet to raise as options and wasn't sure she ever would.

She'd given in, of course, letting him have Frank's old key. She wondered why she felt so reluctant for him to have it. It was, as he pointed out, the next logical step. But since he'd got it, he no longer bothered to knock or ring or tell her he was coming. He turned up when it suited him, let himself in and then left again. Sometimes he stayed the night, but not always, using the excuse of an early start for work the next day. When he did stay they rarely made love anymore, and when they did, it never got any more complicated or sensual than that first time.

His job was another bone of contention for Ruth. He was vague about it, meeting any enquiries on her part with a line about how boring it was. Logistics, he said, although what that meant she had no idea. All she knew was that he worked in an office but didn't have to wear suits, and that he often had to work late. And sometimes go in very early.

By the time she'd made the tea, he'd finished reading.

'I don't see how any of this helps us,' he said. 'There's no mention of your dad or . . . that woman's case.'

'No,' she agreed. He'd taken her place at the table with the paper laid out in front of him, so, after she'd delivered his tea, she pulled out another chair and sat down next to him. 'I'm sorry.'

When she looked up, his lips were tightly closed and there was no sign of whether he accepted her apology or not. Then he sighed and the tight lips turned inward to form a dimpled smile.

'You must have had quite a shock,' he said, patting her thigh with his hand, his touch rippling through her with such heat she almost pulled away. He left his palm resting on her leg, and its sticky warmth sent her heart racing all over again.

'I thought . . . I don't know what I thought.' She looked back down at the page.

'This doesn't change anything,' he told her. 'Why don't we go over it all again? Tonight. Everything you remember.'

'Oh, I don't know, Drew . . . I'm tired of thinking about it.'

Contrary to what she'd most feared, when she'd told Drew

about her past, he hadn't run a mile. Quite the opposite, in fact. He'd insisted she go through it with him, examining every detail she could remember. He told her that was the way to deal with trauma. To re-examine it, catalogue it, until it became just a series of facts rather than an emotionally charged story you told yourself. It seemed quite close to a mindfulness thing she'd seen on YouTube once, so she thought it sounded right enough. He asked her questions to try and jog her memory, and refused to believe her when she said she couldn't remember a particular detail or sequence of events. Not that he thought she was lying, she knew that, but he was convinced it was all locked away in her head somewhere, the truth of what had happened back then. If she would only let herself live in the moment, he told her, it would come back to her eventually. Sometimes it almost seemed as though he was getting off on watching her relive it all, but she always shook the thought away.

It wasn't as though she was lying to him, not really. Maybe she'd played down her involvement a bit, but surely she could be forgiven that? She understood his theory about unburdening herself but, at the end of the day, was it fair to involve him, or anyone else, in her shame, her problem? She supposed it was like having an affair and then confessing just to assuage your own guilt.

She still wondered if the best thing to do would be to ring the number on the card the detective had given her and tell *him* the truth. But when she'd hinted this to Drew his temper had flared up and she'd really thought he was going to hit something. She mustn't do that, he told her, under any circumstances. Whatever the policeman said, she could still get in a lot of trouble for the part she'd played in things. Especially for having kept quiet about it all this time. He made her promise never to do anything so stupid, and after she'd hurried to agree, he'd grabbed her fiercely and wrapped his arms around her so tightly she could barely breathe.

After that she'd not mentioned it again, though she still thought it might be for the best. She was sick of all the lies and trying to keep things straight. But if she did go to the police, Drew might find out what she'd kept from him. Sometimes, she thought that maybe he already knew, and that's why he kept digging. Why he got angry with her. But she just couldn't bring herself to tell him everything. She knew she'd lose him forever.

She tried to change the subject. 'I was just wondering, were you in the attic yesterday?'

'What?'

She felt his hand tighten on her thigh.

'It's not a problem, I want you to feel at home. It's just that I noticed the light on and—'

'Ruth, why don't you let me worry about the electric bill, eh?'

'Oh, it isn't that, it's just . . . well, I wondered why you'd go up there.'

She looked up again from the paper to see him studying her. Just for a moment his expression had seemed almost disgusted, but then his eyes softened and his beautiful smile came back.

'I was seeing how much space there was. For when I move my stuff in properly.'

She supposed that made sense. Relief washed through her in a wave.

'I'm so sorry,' he said. 'I've been pushing too hard on this, haven't I?' The pressure on her leg eased. 'It's just, I want you to be happy, Ruthy.' It was the pet name he had for her. She'd never had a pet name before, unless you counted the disparaging names her father used.

He turned to face her, took her hands in his. 'Look, if you want, we can never mention it ever again, okay? But I really don't think that is what you want, is it? You want to know the truth about what happened back then. This has become a part of you, and I don't think you'll ever be whole without dealing with it. And if you're not whole in yourself . . . well, I don't see how you can be there for anyone else.' He let go of her hands abruptly and pulled back. 'Ultimately, it's your decision.' He stood up. 'I think maybe I'll sleep at my place tonight, give you some space.'

As he gathered his things, her eyes fell back on the newspaper and she focused on the picture. For the first time she read the caption beneath it: *DS Adam Tyler (centre) and the CCRU team, Diane Jordan (left), DC Amina Rabbani (right).*

Her breath caught in her chest. 'I know her!' she rasped.

Drew, who was already opening the kitchen door, turned back.

'I mean . . . I know that name.'

Drew stared at her and quietly re-closed the door.

thursday

1

'Penny for 'em.'

Mina shakes her head and turns to see Danny staring down at her, a mug in each hand and the usual inane grin stretching across his face.

'What?' she asks.

'You were miles away. Anywhere nice?'

Mina looks at her watch. It's gone eleven. Where did the morning go?

Danny slides the steaming Yorkshire tea onto her desk. 'Thought you might need a pick-me-up.'

She smiles and thanks him, but then catches herself. 'Are you supposed to be here?'

He holds up his hands in mock surrender. 'Hey! I'm legit this time. DI Doggett cleared it with the Beak. I'm here to give you a hand with whatever you need. Legwork, paperwork. Chief cook and bottle-washer, that's me. Or I can just be on tea duty if you like.'

She can't help smiling again, much as she might prefer it if she could take him down a peg or two like she used to do in the old days.

He grabs a chair and pulls it over next to hers. 'What are we up to then?'

She briefly considers that he's being a bit chummy for her liking, but lets it go. She fills him in on what they know so far about the Alison Beech disappearance. He listens intently – another first. In the past when she tried to explain anything to him, he'd simply stare into space and give off the air of someone listening to a song repeating in his own head.

'You think that's what Tyler was working on then?' he asks when she finishes. 'This missing persons case?'

'Suzanne thought he'd linked it to some other cases involving the kidnapping of kids around the same time, but there aren't any notes on his desk or computer, and nothing on Holmes. I can't even find the original anonymous letter. Luckily, Corinne scanned it, so we at least know what it said.'

She pulls up the file and lets him read it for himself.

When he finishes, he nods as though absorbing the information he's just been given and filing it away somewhere. 'Bloody hell,' he says. 'Lord Beech, eh? That's gonna be an interesting one.'

'Too interesting for the likes of us,' Mina tells him. 'The Beak doesn't want us anywhere near him for now.'

'So all we've got's this Foster bloke. You reckon he wrote the letter?'

'Looks that way, and others besides.'

'What do you reckon? Some kind of paedo ring?'

'God, I hope not! There's no evidence of it at the moment. Doggett's looking into the other letters though, and I'm supposed to be running a background check on Foster. Old associates, etc. There's a lot to get through and no bloody Uniform to help, as usual.'

'Okay,' Danny says, grinning. 'You've twisted my arm. Divide and conquer?'

She nods, and the two of them get to work. It's dull, tedious stuff, and before long Mina finds her mind wandering yet again. More disturbingly though, her eyes wander too. She finds herself drawn back to Danny. The muscles under his tight shirt ripple as he moves the mouse. He senses her watching and looks up, smiling.

Mina turns back to her screen and a name jumps out at her. Odd but familiar. Where has she heard that name recently? She switches windows to look at the letter from Corinne, and there it is again: *Frank weatherstone. He knows talk to frank.*

But there's something else – something about the name she hadn't noticed before.

'Shit!' She isn't aware she's spoken aloud until Danny turns.

'What?'

'Weatherstone,' she says. 'Frank Weatherstone. He was Foster's cellmate back in the early Nineties.'

'O-kay,' he says hesitantly. 'Well, that's good, right? He's the one mentioned in the letter.'

'Yes, but I met this woman at the weekend. She was called Weatherstone an' all.' That can't be a coincidence, can it?

If he thinks she's making something out of nothing, Danny doesn't say so. 'I guess it's a little unusual,' he says, allowing her room to entertain the notion this could be something significant.

She tells him about her encounter with Ruth at the barbecue and, though she half expects him to – wants him to – he doesn't tell her she's clutching at straws.

'I don't remember her,' he says. 'What are you saying? You think it wasn't a coincidence, her being there?'

'She's been mithering me for days now about meeting her. Kept saying it were important. But with everything going on I brushed her off.'

Danny puts his hand on her arm and Mina becomes very aware of the heat of his hand.

'Don't be hard on yourself, Min, eh? You couldn't know it were connected. We still don't.'

'It was odd though.'

'What sort of odd?'

She glances down at his hand on her arm and, registering her gaze, he pulls away.

'Intense. I bumped into her in the street and she wouldn't let me go till we'd swapped numbers.'

'Ring her,' he says. 'Go on. Arrange to meet.'

Mina nods, pulling out her mobile and finding the contact details. While it's ringing, Danny says, 'Don't let her know you're onto her though.'

Mina tuts. 'All right, I'm not an idiot!'

He grins at her.

But the phone rings on and on, and eventually goes to voice-mail. 'Hi, Ruth?' Mina says, cursing the hesitancy in her voice. Then again, that could probably be explained by her feeling guilty for not calling sooner. 'I just wanted to say sorry for missing our meet-up, the other day.' She almost said 'date', but that didn't feel right. Or maybe that *was* what had disturbed her about the other woman – was it a romantic thing after all? 'I got snowed under with work so, well, again, sorry.' This is useless. 'Look, can you give me a call back? Maybe we could arrange summat else. I'm free tonight,' she adds, and then, in case that sounds too desperate, 'or whenever. Okay. Thanks. Bye.'

'Smooth,' Danny says as she ends the call.

'Oh, fuck off!'

'What next?'

Mina thinks for a moment. 'Research.'

There's not very much out there on Ruth Weatherstone but it takes them most of the afternoon to figure that out. No driver's licence, no criminal record, no Facebook page, no internet presence at all as far as they can tell. They find a couple of other Ruth Weatherstones, but the closest geographically is a woman living in Whitley Bay just outside Newcastle, and a glance at a photo online tells them it isn't her.

'Who the hell is this woman?' Danny asks, as he gets back to the office with a couple of sandwiches and bags of crisps from the deli over the road. 'I mean, who doesn't have at least some online presence these days?'

'It's certainly noteworthy,' she tells him, 'but it's hardly indicative of a crime.'

Danny snorts, choking on his can of Fanta. 'Sorry, but you know who you just sounded like?'

'Who?'

'Indicative?'

'Oh, shut up!' she tells him, but his joke makes her think about Tyler again and the mood in the room grows darker as they go back to their separate research.

She's tried calling Ruth another three times, all told, by the time they give up on finding anything. Mina's long past caring how it might look, to have ignored her this long and then barraged her with a succession of calls. The last message she leaves is curt, almost rude; a demand that Ruth call her as soon as possible.

'Yeah, even I wouldn't ring back after that,' Danny tells her.

And that's what helps her reach a decision. It's time to go on the offensive.

Danny insists on going with her. 'If you find this woman, you'll need someone with you. She could be unstable for all you know. She could be the one that knocked Tyler on the head.'

She wants to argue that it's a ridiculous idea, but she has to admit that Ruth could have done it. It would have been tight for her to make it to the barbecue afterwards, but not impossible. And she *had* looked a bit red in the face. Had she arrived just before Mina, still flushed from rushing?

Her first instinct is to tell Danny she can look after herself, but then Doggett's words ring in her ears, and she has to admit he's right. Ruth didn't look particularly dangerous, but since when could you tell from looking at someone? She could have mental health issues they know nothing about; medical records aren't something they have easy access to. She makes her decision.

'I'll even drive if you want,' Danny suggests.

'No, you bloody won't!' Mina grabs the keys off the desk. She remembers his driving all too well.

2

With Mina driving, that leaves Danny to make the call to Emma. He chats to her on the phone like she's an old friend and Mina pushes down a little wave of jealousy. She's not sure she likes these two palling up with each other. She doesn't make friends easily and would prefer to keep the ones she's got apart from each other. Why? In case they compare notes on her? She chides herself for being ridiculous.

'She didn't get a chance to ask,' Danny says after he rings off with a chirpy 'cheerio'. 'Em said Leigh should be at home. If there's no answer we're to just go straight round the back, she'll be in the shed.' *Em!*

Sure enough, when they arrive at the Ridgeway-Raddon residence there's no answer to their polite ringing of the bell on the front door, so Mina retraces her steps from Sunday night, Danny close behind her, through the gate at the side of the house, along the path of stepping stones, and into the garden of delights. It looks almost more impressive now that there are no other people around. As they step between the imposing monoliths, Mina realises she's not looking forward to another encounter with her friend's artist wife. What is it about Leigh that reminds her so much of the worst girls she was at school with? It isn't that she has anything in common with them; she highly doubts Leigh Raddon went to a comprehensive school. But there's something about her that makes Mina think of a school bully. Maybe that isn't fair. Maybe she's just suspicious of any woman who's that confident. But then Emma's also confident, and she never feels that way about her.

Mina pushes her thoughts away. She's here for professional reasons, nothing more.

The 'shed' is in fact a large brick-built structure tucked behind the patio, and is big enough to house at least two cars comfortably. It was originally a garage, Mina remembers Emma telling her, before they moved in and converted it into a comfortable studio for Leigh to work and teach in. Mina hadn't had a chance to see it properly the other night but it's much as she might have expected. Grandiose in design but with a practicality that's also obvious – the bi-fold doors concertina all the way along the front of the structure, allowing Leigh to spill her giant work out into the garden. Mina doesn't remember them being open on Sunday; maybe she's a bit particular about who she allows inside.

Leigh answers the door with a vacant expression that morphs into a frown when she recognises Mina. 'Oh,' she says, glancing once at Danny and dismissing him just as quickly. 'Ridge isn't here at the moment.'

'Actually, we're here to see you, Leigh.' Mina speaks with quiet authority. 'We have a few questions for you.' She berates herself. It's a cheap shot. There were two ways to interview people as far as she saw it: you could either put them at their ease or come in guns blazing in the hope you might throw them off. She doesn't need to treat Leigh as a hostile witness, but she admits there's a little part of her that wants to throw the woman off balance. The fact that Danny's in uniform probably helps as well.

'Me? I don't know what I could . . .'

Mina just blinks at her until the woman relents.

'All right. I suppose you'd better come in, then.'

The inside of the studio is as impressive as the outside. There are a number of half-finished sculptures scattered around, or at least Mina assumes they're half-finished; for all she knows, that's how they're supposed to look. A great many tools line the walls – hammers, chisels, pincers, pliers. If the sculpting doesn't work out for her, Leigh Raddon has everything she needs to start a decent career as a serial killer. At the back of the room there's a potter's wheel sitting alongside a small kiln oven with an improvised chimney jutting out through a homemade hole in the wall, as well as a large barrel in one corner topped with glass-blowing equipment. Every other conceivable surface is littered with pieces of material – stone, clay, glass, metal, much of it abandoned in clamp or vice, waiting for its creator to pick it up again and shape it into something beautiful.

Though there are a number of folding chairs stacked against the right-hand wall of the room, Leigh makes no effort to offer them one. There's nowhere else to sit but a small three-legged stool positioned in front of the potter's wheel, so the three of them stand in an awkward triangle in the middle of the room. It occurs to Mina that it would have been much more convenient for all of them if they'd spoken outside, but Raddon – it seems easier to think of her that way now – obviously decided she needed the advantage of home territory, a theory confirmed by the way she now folds her arms in front of her and waits for battle to commence.

Mina supposes she only has herself to blame for the hostile atmosphere, and decides to proffer an olive branch. 'Sorry to barge in like this without warning,' she begins. 'We're following up a lead regarding a case we're working on, and we thought you might have some information that could help us.'

Raddon's arms relax a little, but she still looks confused and a little blindsided.

'It's related to DS Tyler's accident,' Mina goes on, assuming Emma would have filled her wife in on the situation as far as she's allowed.

'Oh, yes, I was sorry to hear about that. How's he holding up?'
How's he holding up?

'Still in a coma,' Mina says, deadpan. What is it about this woman that puts her back up so much? She wants to like her but . . .

Danny shifts his weight to his other foot and repositions his hands behind him. Somehow the movement takes some of the tension out of the room.

'Actually, this is about a woman that I met here on Sunday. Ruth Weatherstone.'

This time Raddon's – *Leigh's* – frown is more puzzled than aggressive. 'Ruth? What's she got to do with anything?'

'That's what we're trying to find out. Obviously I can't go into any details, but we have reason to believe she might be able

to help us with our enquiries.' *That's it, Mina, keep it professional.*
'Perhaps you could tell us a bit about how you know her.'

Leigh's eyebrows rise and she spreads her hands in a gesture
of innocence. 'I don't, really.'

'I understood from Emma that you were the one who invited
her to the barbecue?'

'That's right, along with my other students.'

'Students?'

Leigh sighs a little, as though what she's saying is obvious;
as though, if she had a modicum of sense, Mina would be able
to keep up. She gestures at the folded chairs at the side of the
room. 'I teach a small pottery class once a week on a Wednesday
evening. Ruth's one of my students. She hasn't been coming very
long and, to be honest, she isn't very good at it. Hardly a natural.
In fact, I'm not sure she has much interest in art at all, but that's
not all that unusual. The bored housewife is very much my audi-
ence these days.' Even when she's trying to be self-deprecating
she manages to sound superior. 'But I always invite all my students to my little dos. I wouldn't dream of playing favourites.'

Mina suddenly has an image of the barbecue of a few nights
ago. She had assumed all the women there, the majority of them
of a certain age and demographic, had been invited because they
were friends and contemporaries of Leigh's. But now she re-
evaluates the scene. They were students; it seems obvious now.
The way they'd huddled together, almost physically giving the
cold shoulder to anyone else. The way they'd sycophantically
hung on Leigh's every word. And Leigh herself, holding court
so proudly, displaying her latest pieces. No wonder Mina had
felt so out of it.

And now the room around them also transforms in Mina's head, with its half-finished projects of varying form. Why is Leigh Raddon, once the doyenne of Radio 4 and *Newsnight* specials with Mary Beard, teaching evening classes to middle-aged beginners? This intimidating woman is no longer riding high on a wave of adulation but struggling to find her way in an arts scene that no longer finds her relevant. For the first time Mina sees behind the curtain and catches a glimpse of her vulnerability.

'When did you first meet Ruth?'

Leigh thinks for a moment. 'A few weeks ago, I think. As far as I remember, she came to three sessions. She should have been here last night, but she was a no show.'

Danny and Mina exchange a look. After pretty much haranguing Mina for most of the past week, Ruth now appears to have disappeared. Is she in trouble of some sort? Or is she the one causing trouble?

'How did you meet Ruth?'

'She rang up to enquire about the evening class, I explained how it worked and she came along the following Wednesday.'

'Leigh, can I ask you to think back on any conversations you had with her? Was there anything at all that struck you as unusual?'

'Yes.' Leigh answers straight away without having to even think about it. 'Yes, there was, actually. She said she knew you.'

Mina feels the blood drain from her neck, and a cold shiver rattles along her spine. 'Me?'

Leigh nods. 'When we first met, she told me we had a mutual acquaintance, at least, through Emma. You.'

'She said she knew me?'

Leigh rolls her eyes at the repetition but then frowns. 'Yes, although, now I come to think of it, she didn't say how. To be honest, I didn't know you then, so I didn't pay a great deal of attention. Sheffield's a small world, isn't it? Everyone's only a degree or two of separation from everyone else. But I remember that when I mentioned the barbecue, the first thing Ruth asked was whether you'd be there. I didn't know at that point, but I said I'd be sure you got an invite.'

That stings a little. So, the only reason Mina got an invite at all was because Ruth requested it. She needs to put her bruised ego aside for a moment though; there are bigger considerations here.

'Inviting me to the barbecue was Ruth's idea?'

Leigh has the good grace to look a bit sheepish at that. 'I mean, Emma and I had talked about having you over for months now, so when she mentioned it, I thought it was a good idea. It wasn't as though I needed persuading or anything.'

'But the initial impulse came from her. This is important.'

Leigh nods. 'Yes. And, now I think of it, she also asked me not to mention her name to you.'

'She did?'

'She said it would be a good surprise, catching up with you. I honestly didn't think anything of it.'

'Risky strategy,' Danny offers, quietly. 'She couldn't know for sure Ms Raddon wouldn't say anything to you, or mention it on the night.'

Mina thinks back to her interaction with Ruth that evening. Had Ruth been about to tell her something when Emma and Danny had interrupted them? Did it have something to do with Tyler? Had she been there to confess?

It's past time she spoke with Ruth Weatherstone properly, and this time, it'll be Ruth who'll be at the disadvantage.

'Leigh, I'd like you to do something for us.'

3

Ruth hasn't been out for two days now. Stupid really. She's running out of food. Yesterday she had a Cup a Soup and two stale Bourbon biscuits that she'd found tucked right round in the corner cupboard. This morning she's had nothing but endless cups of tea, and her stomach is rumbling and growling like it's possessed.

Useless bitch.

The voice is back. Why is she like this? After all her hard work, to end up back where she started, a virtual shut-in. It's humiliating. And she really only has herself to blame.

It isn't as though she's scared of him. Not really. But she has to admit, she'd rather he didn't come back. There was no reason he would now, would he? No, she'd dealt with him firmly on Sunday. She's quite proud of herself. She won't even need to change the locks, which is useful since she can't afford to. All she'd done was flick the bolt across so he couldn't use the key, then told him through the door in no uncertain terms that she didn't want him back there. And he'd gone. She's seen nothing of him since. Hopefully all that's behind her. Hopefully.

But he still has a key. Which means she's only really safe as long as she stays in.

If only Mina had listened to her the other day, met with her. Ruth had waited in that café for over an hour nursing a glass of water. They'd thrown her out in the end. More humiliation. She couldn't believe the girl had stood her up like that! Even so, she'd given her the benefit of the doubt. Mina was a busy policewoman: maybe something very important had come up and she hadn't had access to a phone. Ruth had imagined any number of increasingly outlandish scenarios, in which Mina had been held hostage for the best part of the day, or something to that effect. So she'd made the effort to ring her, and she hadn't answered once. Worse than that – Ruth wasn't stupid – when she'd called twice in a row, in case Mina had got to her phone too late, sometimes it had gone straight to answerphone, as though Mina had refused the call deliberately.

And now, out of the blue, she wanted to talk. Well, fuck her! There, she'd thought it. Fuck Mina Rabbani. She didn't deserve to hear what Ruth had to tell her.

Her mobile rings again, making her jump.

Ruth looks down at the screen, but this time it isn't Mina's but Leigh Raddon's name that lights up the screen. She feels her heart skip a little. *The* Leigh Raddon, calling her. She can't imagine what it's about, unless ... Of course, she should have been at class last night. She answers the call with a shaking hand and butterflies in her stomach.

'Ruth? Darling! We missed you yesterday.'

She'd completely forgotten, what with her worries about leaving the house, but then, in truth, she hadn't had any interest in pottery to begin with. She hadn't given the class any thought but, if she had, she doubted she would have gone anyway.

'Yes, I'm sorry. I ... I had ... I had an appointment that I couldn't get out of. I'm sorry I didn't ring—'

'Oh, don't worry about that. The thing is your, er, ashtray, is it? I've fired it and I was wondering if you could drop by and collect it this afternoon.'

Ashtray? 'You mean the bowl?' she asks. 'Oh, erm ... that is ... Well, I've got quite a lot to—'

'I wouldn't normally insist, but I need the space, you see. I'm afraid I don't have room in the studio for my students to leave their work hanging around the place.'

'You can throw it away if you like,' Ruth tells her.

There's silence on the line for a moment or two before Leigh Raddon goes on. 'You can't possibly! After all the work you've put in. It shows ... such promise!'

'It does?'

'Ruth, my darling, you're a natural. I'd keep it myself, of course, but I just don't have the space.'

'Well, I suppose ...'

'Why don't you just pop over now? I won't keep you.'

Ruth doesn't answer.

'Or later, then, if you're super busy? I can be here all day. Just give me a rough idea of a time.'

Ruth supposes it isn't as though she really has anything else to do, and she can't stay in forever. She's going to have to go out for food at some point.

'I guess I could be there in about half an hour?'

Leigh reassures her how delighted she is and says she'll be

ready for her. 'Just come straight round the back,' she says. 'I'll be in the studio.' Then she rings off.

Maybe Ruth really does have a talent for this sort of thing. After all, it isn't as though she paid very much attention to Leigh's instructions during the class, so she must be a natural if Leigh thinks she's made something halfway decent.

It's close to forty-five minutes by the time Ruth steps off the bus and walks up the long driveway to Leigh Raddon's home. It's still impressive, even on her fifth visit. She imagines for a moment a future in which she becomes Leigh Raddon's protégé. Perhaps moves in with her and studies under her. Becomes as celebrated as Barbara Hepworth or ... well, that's actually the only sculptor she can think of, but she'll do.

She opens the back gate and finds herself straightening her back as she steps through the sculpture-dotted garden, following the irregularly paved pathway to the studio door. She knocks twice, quite firmly she thinks, and hears Leigh's loud voice call, 'Enter!'

The first thing Ruth sees when she opens the door is Mina Rabbani standing right in front of her. She lets go of the door handle and takes an unconscious step backwards. Only then does she become aware of the uniformed officer stepping around the side of the studio to cut off her escape. Not that she would consider running; she'd hardly be able to outdistance Mina, who is much younger and fitter than her.

'Hello, Ruth,' Mina says, quietly. 'I think we need to talk, don't you?'

4

Leigh gives them the use of the kitchen and withdraws to somewhere deeper in the house. Mina has to give her credit: she doesn't seem even slightly embarrassed about the ruse she used to get Ruth here.

Ruth sits at one end of the huge oak dining table and Mina pulls up a chair next to her. Danny remains standing, taking up a position slightly behind Ruth but in eye contact with Mina. She wonders if it's a deliberate move, designed to throw Ruth off balance but also conveniently positioned in the direction she would run in, if she tried to abscond. It's what she would do, but the old Danny wouldn't have thought of it. He really has changed, and she begins to see what Tyler must have seen when he talked to him about joining the unit.

Not that either of them have any right to stop Ruth if she does decide to leave. She's not under arrest. Her body language says something different though. She's hunched over on herself, staring at her hands on the table. She starts to pick at the skin around her fingernails. She has the look of a suspect who knows she's in trouble, but isn't quite sure how much.

'I don't think you've been completely honest with me, Ruth,' Mina starts.

She gives the woman room to speak, but Ruth doesn't look up or register she's being spoken to in any way.

'Okay, let's start with the easy stuff.' Mina opens her notebook. 'Your name is Ruth Weatherstone. What's your date of birth?'

Ruth begins to answer, in a small, hesitant voice. Mina jots down a few particulars – her address, her job, where she works.

'And what relationship do you have with Frank Weatherstone?'

Now Ruth falls silent.

Mina tries again, flicking back through her notes for the relevant details. 'Frank Weatherstone – part-time labourer and full-time villain. Convicted of burglary and aggravated assault, grievous bodily harm. Served two terms—'

'Yes,' Ruth snaps. She looks up and makes eye contact with Mina for the first time. 'Yes, all right. Frank is – *was* – my father.'

Mina's head is full of questions, but now it comes to it she can't decide the best way to approach this. They need to know Ruth's connection with Harry Foster, and with Alison Becch, assuming she has one. But more than that, they – *Mina* – needs to know why Ruth sought her out, and what she knows about Tyler.

'Why did you tell Leigh Raddon we were old friends?'

'Because . . .' Ruth glances around the room as though she's only realising now that she's sitting in Leigh Raddon's kitchen, her home. She shakes her head, in resignation, perhaps, before she goes back to her nails, worrying at a piece of skin on her left thumb. The area is red and swollen. 'Because I wanted to meet you,' she says.

Mina opens her mouth to speak but Danny catches her eye. He barely moves, just the slightest twitch of his head, but she gets it. He's telling her to stay silent. She knows it's the right course of action. It's what Tyler would do. But it irritates her that he saw it before she did. She's too close to this, too wrapped up in Tyler's attack. Maybe Franklin was right to warn her off.

'I followed you home from work a couple of times,' Ruth admits without any further prompting. 'I knew you were friends with Dr Ridgeway, but I couldn't see any easy way to approach her without her being suspicious. But her wife's number is freely available online, because of her pottery class. So, I joined up in the hope of finding a way to meet you.'

There's something chilling about Ruth's tone; it's as though the words are being spoken by an automaton.

'Why?' Mina can't keep the bite from her voice, and again Danny twitches slightly in her eyeline. She tries to temper her tone. 'Why, Ruth? Why did you want to meet me so badly? And why not just contact me directly?'

'I . . . I didn't want you to hate me.' Ruth's voice cracks with a first audible hint of emotion.

'Why would I hate you?'

'Because of what I've done.'

Again, Mina opens her mouth to speak but then stops, this time of her own volition rather than following any prompting by Danny. Ruth has torn the piece of skin from her thumb, which is now bleeding. She sucks it clean and then presses her other thumb over the wound to help it clot. It's a practised motion. She barely reacts. She's done this a million times.

'I should have told you the truth from the start. I wanted to. I just wasn't sure how you'd react and . . . I didn't want to get into trouble.'

'Why would you be in trouble, Ruth?'

The woman looks up at Mina. There's a smear of blood on her bottom lip, transferred from her thumb when she sucked it.

'I didn't lie to Leigh Raddon,' she says, abruptly more sure of herself. 'I never told her we were friends. I said I knew you. And I do.'

'How do you know me?'

'Because we've met before.'

Mina glances at Danny, who makes a little twirling motion with his hand by his head. It's something the old Danny would have done and somehow the gesture calms her. Some things change but some things stay the same. She's glad he isn't a completely new man.

'When was this?' she asks.

'A long time ago. You were just a kid, so I'm not surprised you don't remember.' There's something about the way she says it that makes Mina think she means the opposite. As though she does expect Mina to remember.

'How did we meet?'

'My father kidnapped you.'

Mina shudders, a bolt of electricity running down the back of her neck and raising the hair on her arms. The words hang in the room between them.

'No, Ruth,' she says. 'He didn't.'

'He did. You were only three or four. He took you from your back yard while you were out playing and brought you back to ours. Then he drugged you and kept you in a locked room. He'd done it before, with other children. It was my job to look after you, or at least, it would have been if you'd been there very long. As it was, you were only with us for a few hours.'

She's very convincing, but then fantasists always are, aren't they? Danny's trying to catch Mina's eye again but this time she refuses to look at him. He'll only suggest they end this. That they take Ruth back to the station and interview her properly. Or better yet, get Doggett to do it. He'd be right. It would be the correct procedure. But she doesn't want to hear it.

'I'm not surprised you don't remember me,' Ruth says. 'But I bet you remember Heathcliff.'

'Who?'

'Our dog. He was a German Shepherd. He's buried in my back garden now. Frank wouldn't pay for the vet when he got sick so he . . .' She trails off.

'Ruth, you need to . . .' Mina stops. An image flies into her head: lying in a bed that's too big for her. There's a large dog at her side and she's stroking it and wondering where her mummy is. There's someone watching from the doorway . . .

'You *do* remember!' Ruth says.

'No, I . . .'

'I think maybe we should stop for a moment,' Danny suggests.

Mina stands up. Her head spins and she feels as though she's going to be sick. Her arms are shaking, her whole body. This can't be real. It's the power of suggestion or something. She tries to keep hold of herself, make her voice firm. 'I think I'd know if I'd been kidnapped as a child.'

At some point Danny must have stepped forward because he's suddenly right next to her with a gentle, restraining hand on her arm. She pulls away from him sharply. What does he think she's going to do? Nevertheless, she takes a couple of steps back and turns away.

'I didn't mean to upset you,' Ruth says. 'You see? This is why I thought it'd be better if we could get to know each other first. Imagine what you would've thought if I'd just walked up to you in the street and told you this.'

She would have thought Ruth was mad, and she's not sure she doesn't now. And yet ... Mina can feel the dog's warm chest under her hand, rising and falling. She can smell the damp fur round his chin and the meat on his breath. She *is* going to be sick. It's a recurring dream she used to have when she was younger, and which she'd long forgotten about. She used to wake in a sweat, screaming for her mother, positive that her whole family had left her. That she was alone in the dark, with only the smell and the sound of the dog for company. And then Maryam would be there, the hallway light spilling in behind her, soothing her with a hand on her back, shushing her, calming her down. Sometimes she'd be allowed to climb into bed with her parents and fall asleep next to them, though when she'd wake up the next day she'd always be back in her own bed, as though nothing had happened. But the nightmare had been real. If she let herself, she could still feel the terror that it had brought with it. That awful feeling that her family was gone forever and would never come back.

Ruth couldn't know any of this. Mina had never told anyone. How could she have, when she hadn't thought about it herself in years?

'I have to go,' she says, stepping unsteadily out of the back door and into the sculpture garden.

Danny comes after her. 'Wait!' Again, he grabs her arm, but this time she doesn't pull away, just turns and stares at him. He lets go as though dropping something hot.

She sees the look of concern on his face, and whatever professional part of her still exists kicks into gear. 'I'm all right. I just need a moment to think.' She tries to smile at him, but the grin feels awkward and false, as though the skin on her cheeks is too tight. 'I'll meet you back at the office.'

'What about her?' he asks, and he's like the old Danny again, out of his depth.

'Let her go,' she tells him. 'We know where to find her and I don't think she's exactly a flight risk.'

'Mina,' he says, more sure of himself now. 'We need to talk about this. Is what she said true?'

'I don't know,' she admits. Then she turns and walks away.

She doesn't know, but she intends to find out.

5

Afterwards, Mina will realise it wasn't the best place to have this confrontation, but in the moment the thought doesn't occur to her. She pushes open the door to the pharmacy and hears the familiar chime of the doorbell announcing her.

Maryam's so used to the sound that she doesn't look up from the customer she's serving. It hasn't occurred to Mina until now that her mother might not be alone, and all at once her plan falters. What little plan she has.

She has to know the truth. But even as she thinks it, she can feel that she already knows. Somewhere, deep down. It isn't a bad dream; it isn't the power of suggestion coming from a mentally unstable stranger. It's a memory. The room, the dog, the shadowy figure in the doorway. The more she accepts the possibility, the more real the image becomes. Even when she tries not to think about it, feelings and sensations tickle across the back of her mind like feathery ghosts: the taste of strawberry jam . . . a gritty residue between her teeth . . . the scent of wet dog . . .

Mina slips down one of the aisles in the shop, pretending to examine the shelves – the blister packs of tablets, the bottles of medicine, the haircare products. This place had always seemed so magical to her when she was a child, with its rows upon rows of packets and potions, like something from Harry Potter. She'd thought her parents were wizards and, as she'd grown older, she'd decided they were, in a sense. They cured the sick, helped people when they were at their lowest. She'd looked up to them both, admired them for their dedication and hard work, even though it had meant she hadn't seen them quite as often as she might have liked.

It wasn't as though she'd been neglected as a child, far from it. She'd had any number of uncles and aunties to dote on her, and she'd always been the favourite among all of her many cousins. Or at least, she'd always felt she was. But she supposes, if she's honest, she's always felt a bit ... untethered. Over the years, she's put that down to the fact that her childhood was largely spent being passed from one relative to another for babysitting duties, some not even blood relatives, although they were all still Auntie and Uncle, of course.

But was it more than that? Was there a reason she felt a little adrift – like her connection to the people closest to her was more tenuous than it should be? Was it because once, when she was three or four years old, she *had* lost her family, for however short a time? She had lost everything. Maybe she had never really found her way back.

'Amina?' Her mother's voice is high, almost shrill, in her surprise at this unprecedented daytime visit to her place of work.

'Where's Abbu?' Mina asks without preamble.

'What's wrong? You look ... Amina?'

'Where's Dad?' she says again, almost shouting, but not quite. Even now she's not sure what it would take for her to shout at her mother.

'He's at the cash-and-carry.' Maryam holds the back of her hand out to Mina's forehead, feeling for her temperature. 'You're scaring me, Beti.'

'Who took me?' Mina asks.

'Amina? I don't understand. What's gotten into you?'

'When I was kidnapped!' This time it's much closer to a shout. Maryam's earlier customer looks up from a display she's examining and then quickly looks away again.

As soon as she looks at her mother's face Mina knows it's all true. Something snaps inside Maryam, Mina sees it – a severing of whatever string has been holding in this great burden all these years. And yet, still she tries to prevaricate.

'I don't know—'

'Please, Ammi, don't! No more lies.'

'I ...' Maryam looks around the store, searching for a way out, for answers, for a distraction, for divine intervention – Mina isn't sure. 'Where are you getting this nonsense?' she asks finally, finding resolve in a lifetime of deceit.

Mina shakes her head. 'You're going to deny it, aren't you?'

'Amina Rabbani!' It is Maryam's hard voice, reserved for when her daughter has done or said something particularly unforgivable.

For once it doesn't work. 'Why would you keep this from me? It doesn't make any sense. Who took me? Why?'

Maryam shakes her own head now, trying to set the denial in place even though she must know the genie's out of the bottle.

300

'I won't have this nonsense,' she says, finally. 'Go on, be gone from here. I have work to do.'

She's really going to deny everything! Mina has never seen her mother like this before. If she didn't know better, she'd say she was scared.

'Mum, I . . .'

'Amina, please! If ever you were going to listen to me, for Peace, let it be now!'

'Mum, I'm not going to just—'

'Beti. Please.' Maryam's voice is strained near to breaking. 'Do not speak of this again. Promise me!'

Now it's Mina's turn to feel scared. She allows Maryam to push her out onto the pavement, and watches as her mother turns the Open/Closed sign around on the window and heads straight back to her customer.

Mina slaps the glass with the flat of her palm. Maryam jumps but doesn't turn around. The customer stares at Mina with horror.

With perfect timing her mobile rings, and Mina pulls it out with a curse. It's Diane, and even as she answers, a premonition runs through her. Somehow, she knows this is going to be bad.

'Diane?'

'Mina. Oh, God, I'm sorry. He's bleeding. On the brain. They've rushed him back into theatre.'

'I'm on my way,' Mina tells her. And then, because she senses one of them needs to say it, she adds, 'He's strong, Diane. He's a fighter. He'll be okay.'

In truth, she's never felt so unsure of anything in her life.

2 months ago

I

Theresa Greene was, in fact, her real name, although she generally went by Teri, and who could blame her? Teri with an I. Not Terry with a Y.

Tyler had traced her to a high school in Doncaster where she was still known as Ms Greene. She'd never married as far as he could see. He'd decided on a surprise visit, and timed it so that school was just finishing when he arrived. He supposed he could have visited her at home, but he wanted her off balance: the threat of any sordid past coming out while she was in the classroom might be just what he needed.

On the other hand, he couldn't be a hundred per cent sure he had the right woman. There were a surprising number of Theresa Greenes on the internet, and that was assuming that the supposed witness from Alison's kidnapping hadn't used a false name. He was also relying on the supposition that the witness was in on it – Harry Foster's ex-girlfriend, perhaps – and that the name connection wasn't just a coincidence. That was either an awful lot of assumptions or an awful lot of coincidences. He didn't like either.

But the general details seemed to fit. This woman was in her late fifties, and although that put her a good two decades younger than Harry, it wouldn't be the first time a younger woman had fallen under the spell of a charismatic bad boy. It also meant that she would have been in her mid-twenties when the crime took place. A DVLA check indicated she'd been living in Sheffield at the time, and a licence change a couple of years later placed her somewhere down on the south coast. He supposed if she had been involved in the kidnapping of a politician's wife she might well have moved as far away as the land allowed. She'd moved back to Rotherham six years ago or thereabouts, as far as he could tell from his search.

However, she hadn't been in trouble with the police before, or at least nothing serious enough to be on file, and though not outstanding in any way, her teaching career spanned a good twenty years by this point and was solid enough not to raise any red flags.

Her social media accounts were few and far between, and rarely updated. But that was hardly a smoking gun. She was a teacher after all, and Tyler knew many used pseudonyms online so their students couldn't find them.

Could a woman whose past had involved kidnapping and association with a criminal gang really have reinvented herself as a prim and proper high school teacher? He knew that anything was possible, but without concrete proof it was a stretch that a jury might struggle to make.

Still, Tyler had a feeling in his gut that he was on the right track. And he had one ace card to play.

He enquired at the main office first and, once he'd shown his credentials, was escorted by a reluctant secretary through the school hallways. There were a few kids still knocking about, as well as a number of teachers looking shell-shocked and despondent after their long day at the coal face, but no one paid him any attention. He supposed visitors weren't uncommon.

Greene's classroom overlooked the school fields and Tyler could see a rugby match taking place outside. It was a good job she taught English and not PE or he might have been in for a long wait.

It was her reaction when the secretary introduced him that told him he'd hit pay dirt. It was almost as though someone had punched her in the gut. He saw her flinch, her whole body turning in on itself at the sudden pain in her centre. She managed to thank the secretary and dismissed her, turning her back on Tyler for a moment as she finished tacking something to the wall, no doubt in an attempt to compose herself.

'One second,' she told him, but he could hear the telltale catch in her voice. How long had she been waiting for this day? Unfortunately, whatever she knew was a lot more than he did, and he only had that one ace to confront her with. One was rarely enough. He was playing with a very weak hand here; he would need to be careful.

She turned around, a bit more composed but still shaky. 'Yes, officer, what can I do for you?'

'It's Detective, actually.' He needed her as off balance as possible.

'Yes, sorry. Detective.' She made no offer of a seat, but that suited him fine since he had the height advantage. She pulled down the sleeves of her lemon-coloured cardigan and crossed her arms, the little plastic tub of pins still clutched tightly in one hand. He searched her face, trying to see the woman she used to be. Harry Foster's Teri. Was it her?

'Are you acquainted with a man named Harry Foster?' It was a risk phrasing it as a question. He could have told her she was and made it harder for her to deny, but if he could catch her in a lie she might just give him the angle he needed.

She was too clever for that though. She made an effort to look as though she was searching her memory, her gaze drifting up to the ceiling as though the answers lay there. 'I'm not sure,' she said. 'I can't picture him, but it sounds like a very common name.'

'You may have to think back,' he told her, trying his best not to let any frustration enter his voice. 'It might have been quite a while ago.' He left a short pause. 'Say, twenty-four years ago.'

He saw her swallow and she coughed away some phlegm or bile before she spoke. 'That is a long time.'

'I understand you were living in Sheffield then?'

Her eyes scanned the room, searching for answers anywhere that meant she didn't have to look directly at him. He made sure he stayed focused on her. On the odd occasion her gaze did slip back to him he wanted to be staring directly into her face.

'Yes.' She left it at that.

'Perhaps this will jog your memory.' He pulled out his mobile and found the photograph he'd downloaded earlier.

It had been a stroke of luck, but sooner or later every investigation had one. He'd been going through Harry Foster's record again, checking known associates, trying to firm up the links between him and his old mate Frank Weatherstone. After getting out of prison Harry had gone back to his old stomping ground of Attercliffe, and had been cited in a number of minor offences centred in and around a sex club called Honkers. The place had been something of a ground zero for criminal activity at the time, and everyone seemed to have been aware of it. When he'd asked Doggett, the DI had smiled dreamily, and said, 'Ah, yes, those were the days,' in a manner that implied his association with the club may have gone further than the professional.

Honkers had closed down in the early 2000s, but after a number of enquiries at Companies House, Tyler had found a list of employees who had worked there over the years. Teri's had been the name that had virtually leapt off the page at him. After that he'd spent a number of quiet evenings ignoring Scott's puerile television consumption and trawling the internet for pictures of the club. They were surprisingly numerous despite the fact the premises had a strict policy against them, evidenced by more than one image of an enormous plastic sign that took up almost an entire wall and informed 'guests' that photography was 'strictly forbidden'. He even found a fan site dedicated to the place, where nostalgic gentlemen of a certain age could peruse the vestiges of their youth to their hearts' content – or that of other bodily parts, he imagined.

The pictures were pretty grainy, taken at the cusp of the digital age and before camera phones were readily available. In most cases, the photographers had simply taken a photo of their original print and uploaded it, and their skills varied from adequate to awful. Eventually he'd stumbled across the photo he was holding out to Greene. A padded booth, like something from a 1920s speakeasy, and four faces smiling for the camera. Well, three; Frank Weatherstone's expression was stony. But the unknown girl draped across his knee was beaming at the camera, as was a wide-eyed, much younger and much more handsome Harry Foster. And the woman on *his* lap, or draped around his shoulders at least, was Teri Greene. Both women were topless.

So, luck, yes, but luck born of a fair amount of painstaking commitment and bloody-mindedness.

'This is you,' Tyler said, and this time he didn't phrase it as a question. He wasn't sure he could prove it, but he'd seen her profile picture on the school website and been pretty sure he was right. It had been a gamble, on a single ace. But now he'd seen her in person he was more certain than ever. He'd won against worse odds in the past.

Greene's entire demeanour altered, and he knew he had her. She sagged, almost collapsing against the table behind her, the plastic tub of pins dropping from her hand and sending its contents cascading across the classroom floor. She put her face in her hands and let out a cry that he thought might bring someone running from outside the classroom. Thankfully, it didn't.

She wasn't actually in tears, but her face was screwed up in such anguish that she might just as well have been. She tried to grab the phone from his hand, but when that didn't work she pushed it away from her.

'Please,' she begged, 'just put it away. Please!'

He slipped the phone back into his pocket and she folded her arms again, pulling the lemon cardy tightly around her waist as though trying to cover the nakedness she'd seen in

310

the picture. Tyler felt a stab of guilt. Teri Greene had no doubt been exploited in the past, and here he was, using some seedy internet snapshot to exploit her all over again. But then he remembered why he was there. Alison Beech. He was confident Teri knew something about what had happened to her, and if she didn't? Well, he would live with the guilt if he had to.

Still, maybe it was time to offer her a way out. Not that it would stay open to her if she truly was guilty. 'I'm not here to cause trouble for you,' he said carefully, not wanting to promise too much. 'No one at the school knows why I wanted to talk to you, and I'm sure you can think of a legitimate reason that won't cause you any problems. I can also let you know where I found that picture and give you advice on how you might get it taken down.' He wished her luck with that – it would be nigh-on impossible and she might be better off pretending it didn't exist, though he would help her if he could. 'But I need you to tell me everything you can about your relationship with Harry Foster and Frank Weatherstone.'

He stopped talking to allow her time to think, but she just shook her head, still in denial about her position. Which made him think she was probably more involved than he'd suspected. That was a problem. If she was guilty of kidnapping, or murder, then the threat of exposing her Page Three past wasn't going to go very far. Before he could say anything else though, she began to speak.

'I knew Harry. We ... Well, I suppose you could say we were an item for a while.' She continued to avoid Tyler's gaze, looking down at the floor. She seemed to notice the spray of multi-coloured drawing pins carpeting the area around her feet and crouched down to pick them up. He bent down to help.

'He was a lot older than me but – God, this sounds sordid! – he had money, or at least, a lot more than I had. That club,' she said, pausing for a moment in her pin collecting so she could look at Tyler directly for the first time. 'It wasn't as bad as it looks, okay? Just a bit of dancing and, occasionally, some stripping . . .' She glanced at the classroom door. 'We weren't sleeping with them or anything.'

A redness crept into her cheeks, and he wasn't sure he totally believed her, but then he wasn't here to judge. She went back to the pins.

'Harry was sweet. And handsome. And he looked after me.' Teri picked up the plastic pot, which now had a cracked lid, and poured the pins from her hand back into it. She offered it to Tyler, and he brushed the last of the pins from his own palm. They both straightened up.

'I didn't know Frank, not closely, only as Harry's mate. I didn't know what they got up to, not in detail anyway, but I began to figure out it wasn't above board. That's why I got out in the end. I moved away. So, I guess if I'm guilty of anything it's not reporting them to the police but, like I say, I didn't really know what they were doing.'

Tyler didn't believe her. It was too easy for her to distance herself from what had gone before, and it wasn't the way an innocent person would behave. She hadn't asked what this was all about, for a start. He was more convinced than ever that she'd been part of it in some way: maybe only a small part, maybe a coerced part, but she still knew more than she was saying. She was Bob Smith's ephemeral witness who'd claimed that Lucas Beech had been the target of the snatch that had ultimately resulted in his mother Alison's disappearance. Maybe she was also the woman who'd approached Abby Williams' parents in the park with the ransom demand. How many other kidnappings had she been part of? She was guilty, he was sure of that now, but pushing her on it would only make her clam up, or start calling for lawyers to be present, and if that happened he had nothing. Nothing but a handwritten note from a dementia patient, a well-connected husband who didn't want his wife's disappearance raked up again and an unco-operative schoolteacher who he'd coerced into talking to him with a dodgy photo from her seedy past. The minute Franklin got wind of this, the whole thing would be over.

But at the moment, Teri Greene *was* talking. Trying to distance herself from events, but talking nevertheless. If he gave her enough rope, would she hang herself?

'I understand,' he said. 'Can you remember anyone else who used to hang around with them at the time?'

She began to shake her head again, more confident now that she might still be able to wriggle clear of this.

'Think hard,' he told her. 'Anyone at all who might be able to shed more light on events from back then. A friend? Someone else that used to drink with them in the club?'

She was thinking, but what was she thinking about? Was she considering whether to offer someone up to him? That's what he hoped. He'd given her a way out precisely for that reason. But, of course, if whoever she referred him to revealed too much about her own involvement she'd be right back in the frame. Abby Williams had given him one other small piece of the puzzle. He decided to throw the dice one last time.

'A South Asian man, perhaps?'

It was an odd thing to ask, but the 90s had been a very different time. He doubted Harry Foster and Frank Weatherstone would have had a great many South Asian friends.

Teri glanced at him, hesitating, perhaps trying to guess how much he already knew. 'There was one guy. Harry's accountant, I think. They didn't drink together though.'

'Do you happen to remember his name?'

She hesitated a fraction too long, weighing up just how much this man might know that could implicate her, and setting it against the thought that if she gave Tyler something, he'd leave her alone long enough for her to come up with a plan. In that moment he lost any qualms he'd had about manipulating her. She might have cleaned up her act, but if he found out she was involved in the kidnapping of Alison Beech, or anyone else for that matter, he would throw the book at her.

'His name was Kamal,' she told him. 'Kamal Rabbani.'

II

Kamal Rabbani.

The name burned away at him over the next few days and Tyler found it difficult to concentrate on anything else. At first, he couldn't be sure it had anything to do with Mina. He knew she had an Uncle Kamal, but not much more than that. She'd only mentioned him once. They'd been discussing Tyler's own newfound role as uncle and she'd been trying to make him feel better about how inadequate he thought he was, hoping that tales of the uncle who had once dandled her on his knee and tickled her cheeks with his whiskers, but who she no longer saw, would offset the fact that Tyler hadn't even known he had a niece until she was a teenager. It had been a misguided attempt, and she'd shut up pretty quickly once she'd figured that out. Tyler hadn't been actively listening anyway, but he did remember that she hadn't said whether the man was her paternal or maternal uncle – he might not even be a Rabbani.

He could run a systems check on the man, obviously. But as soon as he did that there'd be a record of it. What if Mina knew about her uncle's involvement in crime? Had she declared it when she'd joined the force? If she had, that would be between her and Professional Standards, so he'd have no way of knowing. And if she hadn't, well, as long as she didn't know about it, it shouldn't do her any harm. He knew a DCI in London whose brother was high up in organised crime; it didn't always count against you. But questions would be asked. Hard questions that she might or might not be able to answer. Questions that could tear her family apart.

There'd been no Kamal at Mina's brother's wedding. Tyler had been something of a guest of honour at the occasion, which had made Mina remark on the double standard – her parents had never wanted her to join the police, yet they were happy enough to show him off to the extended family as the famous detective. Maryam had made sure to introduce him to everyone, and he was confident he didn't remember anybody named Kamal.

And none of this meant it was the same Kamal Rabbani; it wasn't a particularly unusual name. Tyler had googled it – on his own laptop, just to be safe – and found scores of them on Instagram, Twitter and Facebook, along with scores more using the alternative spelling 'Kemal'. Some were even accountants, although none were based in Sheffield. The man who Teri Greene remembered could have been any of them. But as much as Tyler tried to come up with alternative possibilities, he kept coming back to the one he didn't like.

He tried finding some information on social media. Mina wasn't particularly active on Facebook, but he found a link to her cousin Priti's account. Priti fancied herself something of an influencer, and that led him to other family members and other social networking sites. But hours of scrolling through unboxing videos on TikTok revealed nothing more than that he was even more out of touch with the younger generation than he'd thought.

He opened one of those trace your ancestry accounts under a fake name and started looking into Mina's family tree, confirming only that Mina's father, Hakeem, did indeed have a younger brother named Kamal. It was progress of a sort, but he almost wished he hadn't found it.

He'd been careful not to do any of this at the office, of course. In fact, he'd packed up every scrap of info he had on the Alison Beech kidnapping and carted it all home with him. Not that 'all' constituted a great deal more than a slim folder that included the letter from Harry Foster and the original case report by Bob Smith, but it was still totally against procedure. He'd also copied the few notes he'd made on the work computer to his laptop and deleted every trace of them, then rung Corinne Daley-Johnson and had an excruciating conversation in which he'd tried to secure her silence about the letter. She hadn't liked it, but she'd agreed not to mention anything in front of Mina for now. It was massive overkill on his part, and the digital scrub wouldn't hold up to a forensic search anyway, but that wasn't his worry. He didn't want Mina stumbling across any of it while she was looking for something else. He'd have to tell her at some point, obviously, but there was no point in worrying her unnecessarily. He still had no idea how involved Kamal had been.

He also had no idea how long he could keep all this from the rest of the team. He was aware his behaviour had changed enough for the others to notice it. Diane had asked him on more than one occasion if he was okay, and he'd even caught Cooper, only a few days in the office now, looking at him askance from across the room, wondering perhaps why he was even quieter than usual. Mina was the only one who hadn't seemed to have picked up on anything, but believing that would be to grossly underestimate her. She knew something was up. She was merely biding her time before she ambushed him about it.

After a few days he found he had another problem – Scott. Their relationship had been progressing slowly, but Scott had a way of reading Tyler that was unlike anyone he'd ever met before. He'd spent a lifetime disguising his emotional responses to the world around him and he knew he was good at it, but Scott had a way of seeing through all of that and intuiting exactly what he was thinking. He rarely challenged Tyler directly, but he let it be known he understood. A gentle tap on the arm, a small smile or an arched eyebrow. It was enough. Tyler read it as a simple way of saying, *I get it.* Maybe it was a trick – perhaps all it really meant was, *I understand something's wrong but not exactly what,* but Tyler didn't think so. *I get it. I get you!*

They'd started staying over at each other's places once or twice a week, and on these occasions, at least, Tyler tried his best to focus on Scott and whatever it was that was growing between them. He couldn't help himself though, and at some point in the evening, usually when they were ensconced in front of some TV drama that Tyler had little interest in, he'd slip out his laptop and begin more research into the Beech case.

Scott didn't complain, he only looked amused. But he noticed. And he knew that something was preying on Tyler's mind.

One evening he'd even gone as far as to ask, 'Who is it you're so worried about?'

Tyler had been thinking about Mina again, and somehow Scott had got to the heart of things just by watching him. He'd let Tyler brush off his concern and deny everything, but he knew something was up. So, Tyler did what he always did. He shut down. He moved all his notes and his laptop into his car, and he began to avoid working on the case when they were together. Then, inevitably, and because he couldn't leave it alone, he began thinking up reasons to avoid spending time with Scott altogether.

The truth was he knew what he had to do. He just didn't like it.

III

The text came through as he pulled up outside their house.

Now where are you??!!!

Mina had a way with exclamation marks that he found ... endearing. At times.

He looked up at the house and had an uncharacteristic moment of doubt. If they told her he'd been here, he wasn't sure their already fractured working relationship would survive. Or, worse than that, what if she came home right in the middle of their conversation?

Tyler sat back in the driver's seat and let out a deep breath. That wasn't going to happen. He'd worked with Mina for years now, and he'd never known her to pop home in the middle of the day. For anything. That was the whole reason he'd chosen this time in the first place, and from what he knew of the Rabbanis' working practices, there was a good chance at least one of them would be here. It wasn't guaranteed, but he could see Maryam's car on the drive.

He forced himself to get out of the car, glancing around the neighbourhood like some kind of cat burglar – too many people round here knew who he was – and walking up the steep brick-laid drive to the front door. He pressed the doorbell and waited.

Maryam Rabbani answered the door with a frown that instantly turned into a beaming smile as soon as she recognised him.

'Adam!' she cried, and threw her arms around him as though he was some long-lost son returned to the roost. 'Come in, come in!' She virtually pulled him through the doorway and stepped out onto the front step to look down the driveway. 'Where is Amina?'

'It's just me, Maryam.'

She glanced back at him and the smile dissipated, replaced by a furrowed brow. She stepped back into the house and closed the door behind her. 'Come,' she said, unable or unwilling to ask why he was there on his own at this strange hour. She wouldn't even look at him now.

She encouraged him into the guest living room at the front of the house that he knew was reserved for important visitors, or those to be impressed. He'd been to the Rabbani family home a number of times – always with Mina – and the only time he'd even been permitted to glance in here had been on the day of Mina's brother Ghulam's wedding. Close family were always received in the large kitchen-dining area at the back of the house where people came and went pretty much as they wanted. When he'd first met Mina, the Rabbanis had lived in a terraced house not far from the Bait-ul-Mukarram Jamia Mosque in Sharrow. But after Ghulam had got married, they'd upped sticks and moved to the opposite side of Abbeydale Road, into the leafier suburb of Nether Edge. Mina's parents – and Mina herself – lived in this semi-detached Victorian town-house, while Ghulam, his wife and young sons lived in the house next door. Mina had been horrified with the plan, but Ghulam's young bride, Aamira, seemed to be fine with it.

There was never a lack of people hanging around the two houses, and the extended family of aunts and uncles and cous-ins made full use of the larger grounds to park their cars, play cricket in the garden and 'eat them out of house and home' as Mina often described it. However, there was an unusual silence hanging over the place today, as though it or the larger family had somehow anticipated his coming and given him the space he needed.

Tyler tried to reassure Maryam with a smile, but she didn't react; she just stood in the centre of the room with her hands clasped neatly in front of her. She was still wearing her white pharmacist's coat.

'Is Hakeem . . . ?'

'At the shop,' Maryam said. They always called it 'the shop', when actually it was a very successful pharmacy. In point of fact, they now had three branches across the city, although 'the shop' always referred to the original, just down the hill on Abbeydale Road.

'It is always good to see you, Adam, of course, but . . . well, you've never paid us a visit without Amina before. So, I can't help wondering . . .'

'It's . . . a little delicate,' he said. 'Do you think Hakeem could join us? It's important.'

'Please, you're scaring me now. Has this something to do with our daughter? Just tell me, please!'

Tyler had really hoped to have this conversation with both of them, but he decided not to leave her hanging. She looked terrified. 'It's about Kamal,' he said, and as soon as he spoke the man's name, Maryam's demeanour changed.

She didn't fall apart exactly, but it looked as though something had broken inside her. She staggered backwards, collapsing into an armchair, her eyes dropping to the floor. Tyler unconsciously took a step forward to catch her, but it was as unnecessary as it would have been unwelcome. She raised a hand to ward him off and then took three deep breaths, in and out. Then she looked up at him.

'I see,' she said. 'Please wait, I will call Hakeem.' She got up again, no sign now of the anguish that had caused her to sit down in the first place, and disappeared into the hall.

Tyler moved to the doorway and listened to her speaking on the phone in the kitchen. He hated listening in, but he couldn't afford to treat this any differently to a normal case. Maryam spoke in Urdu though, so there was no way he would have been able to understand what she was saying even if he could hear her properly.

He retreated back into the room, and she joined him a few seconds later.

'He is coming,' she said. 'Can I get you something to drink while you wait?'

It was an indication of how much he'd unsettled her that she hadn't asked before now.

'Perhaps a pot of tea?' he asked, and she smiled as warmly as she had when he'd arrived. He didn't drink tea, but she needed something to focus on and it gave her a chance to get away from him for the few minutes it would take Hakeem to drive from the shop. He owed her that much.

Less than three minutes had gone by when he heard Hakeem's Mercedes pull into the drive, the sun glinting off its bonnet and sweeping over Tyler as though it was picking him out as an interloper, a cockroach exposed on the kitchen floor when the light comes on. Hakeem got out and rushed to the front door.

Maryam moved to meet him, and he heard them talking quietly in the hall before they came into the room to join him. *Getting their stories straight*, a treacherous little voice told him, and he hated himself for thinking it. His loyalty was to Alison Beech though, he reminded himself. *She* was his main priority. Then Mina, and only when he was assured of her safety would he do his best to protect her parents too, if he could.

Hakeem's face when he walked in was far less welcoming than Maryam's had been, but still he stepped forward with his hand outstretched.

'Salam alaikum.'

'Walaikum assalam,' Tyler replied, shaking his hand.

'Good to see you, Detective, despite the circumstances.' Hakeem spoke with a Leeds accent. He'd lived in Sheffield for more than thirty years now, but the patterns of speech learned in his childhood were still evident.

'It's good to see you too, Mr Rabbani. I also wish the circumstances were better.'

Hakeem gestured for him to sit down, and Tyler chose the

chair that Maryam had collapsed in earlier. Hakeem sat opposite, but Maryam remained standing, close to her husband.

They glanced at each other and something unspoken passed between them before Hakeem turned back to Tyler.

'Aye well, you better ask your questions then. How can we help?'

'Tell me about Kamal.'

'What do you want to know?'

'He's your brother.'

'My youngest. There's five of us, all told.'

'But he wasn't at Ghulam's wedding, was he? Or did I just miss meeting him?'

Again, Hakeem exchanged a look with his wife before answering. 'He wasn't. We don't have owt to do with him anymore.'

'Why is that?' Tyler asked, once it became clear the story wasn't going to be offered up.

Hakeem sighed, perhaps resigning himself to the truth. Whether or not that was the case, when he spoke next it was to volunteer a little more information.

'Kamal was the baby. He's only two years younger than me but it always felt like a lot more. He's also the reason we left Leeds.'

Maryam shifted a little, and Hakeem glanced at her before going on.

'He was always in trouble at school, always hanging out in the wrong places and with the wrong people. He ended up getting in with a bad crowd, you know? It's not a new story. My brothers and me tried to sort him out, keep him on the straight and narrow and all that, for Dad's sake as much as anything. But he just didn't seem to know how to stay out of trouble.

'So, we brought him here. Tried to keep him tied to the faith, keep him involved in the community as much as possible. Trouble was, he's too bloody clever by half. He might not have paid much attention at school, but he didn't need to. Numbers always came naturally to him. We got him a job with an accountants up the road. Friend of the family. Till they figured out he was a bit too good with numbers, if you know what I mean?'

'Was he arrested?' If there was a criminal record, Tyler had yet to find it.

'No. No one round here wants the police involved if they can help it. No offence.'

'None taken.'

'We handled it ourselves. Paid the firm back so he owed us, not them. Then put him to work on the family books, keeping him on a short leash, obviously. Marrying Maryam helped.' He looked up at his wife fondly. 'She's always been good with numbers herself, so she kept an eye on him for us.

'But eventually he went back to his old ways. And ... well, maybe we took our eye off the ball, thought he'd really turned over a new leaf. We were wrong.'

'What was he involved in?'

'That I can't tell you. It were rumours mostly. Theft, bad company. Once we figured out he'd gone back to his old ways, we kicked him out. You get a second chance in this family, but you don't get a third. Maybe that sounds harsh to you, but that's the way we are.'

Did it seem harsh? To be kicked out on the basis of rumours. Tyler wasn't able to judge, but from what he knew of Hakeem Rabbani it certainly seemed out of character. Still, he didn't want to accuse the man of lying. Not yet.

'That's one more chance than some would have given him,' he said. 'How did you know he was up to something illegal then, if you don't know exactly what it was?'

'After he'd made a success of the family books he decided to go independent, strike out as self-employed. Problem was, most in the community wouldn't have anything to do with him after what had happened before. Memories last a good while round here. But one or two took pity on him at our request.

'It wasn't enough to explain the cash he suddenly started throwing around though. Naeem noticed first. He'd started getting generous with stuff – presents, food and that. Then he got a new car out of nowhere. I think we all knew by that point, but we still didn't do owt about it until . . . Well, he started to get jittery. We cornered him one day, the four of us and a couple of cousins, and demanded he told us what was going on. He refused to explain himself and that's when we made the decision. We told him to leave. A cousin in Pakistan said they'd take him in if he wanted. We gave him the option and he took it.'

'He didn't have any alternative,' Maryam said. Tyler imagined not all of her discomfort was to do with the shame Kamal had brought down on them; some of it was guilt too, that they hadn't done more to help him.

'So, he's in Pakistan now?'

Hakeem opened his mouth to speak but Maryam shifted again and lightly touched his arm.

'No,' he said. 'He lasted a couple of years there but eventually he came back. The last I heard he was living over in Leeds.'

Tyler wondered if Hakeem had been about to lie to him before Maryam's intervention. Had he lied about anything else? If so, why?

'Do you know anyone he was involved with here in Sheffield? A name, anyone you can remember Kamal mentioning?'

'No,' Hakeem said. 'We don't know anything about that, we never did, and we don't want to, neither.'

It wasn't that Tyler thought he was lying as such. In fact, there was something about how quickly the heartfelt statement had been made that told Tyler it had been used before. Perhaps it was one of those family stories the Rabbanis told each other on a semi-regular basis, although he suspected it was more likely Kamal's name was never mentioned.

But there was something in the way Maryam was avoiding his gaze now that said there was more to this. Why were they so reluctant to talk to him? They hadn't even asked him why he was interested in Kamal. Perhaps that was understand-able if they wanted nothing more to do with him, but there was something else going on here and he couldn't put his finger on it.

'Exactly how long ago did all of this take place?' he asked.

Hakeem made a show of trying to remember. 'It was . . . I dunno. Twenty, twenty-five years ago?'

Tyler was certain Hakeem actually knew to the day, and he'd bet any amount of money that it was twenty-*four* years ago. 'What aren't you telling me?' he asked them outright. Sometimes it was better not to mess around and, in truth, he respected these people too much to play games with them, regardless of their intentions with him.

Hakeem opened his mouth to speak, but again Maryam touched his arm.

'You have to understand, Adam,' she said. 'We never told Amina about any of this. She remembers her uncle only as a happy man who used to play with her sometimes when she was little. As far as she knows, he moved to Pakistan and that was that. When she decided to join the police, we ... well, we didn't support her. I know this caused a great rift between us, but the truth was we weren't just worried for her safety. We worried that if any of this came out it could damage her in some way, harm her career. Or worse.'

'It would only affect her career if Kamal had been involved in something and she knew and failed to disclose it.'

'I see. Then perhaps we were wrong to hide this shame so well, but we only wanted what was best for her. For the whole family.'

'Do you know where I can find Kamal?'

Hakeem hesitated before speaking. 'You haven't told us why you're looking for him.'

'No.'

Hakeem nodded, perhaps realising he wasn't going to get any more out of Tyler and resigning himself to it. 'I know he were in Leeds somewhere, about five year' ago. But I can find out for you. Put the feelers out.'

'Hakeem, I wouldn't want him to know I was coming. This is important, and if you or any of your family hampered my investigation by warning Kamal to disappear, for instance, well, that *could* harm your daughter's career. It would also break her heart.'

Hakeem straightened his back. Tyler realised he'd offended the man in his own home, and he wondered if that meant he'd used up the last of his credit with Mina's family. If so, he'd miss coming here for lunches and family gatherings. But his job was to find Alison Beech.

'No one will warn him,' Maryam said, and Hakeem nodded. 'You have our word.'

'Good enough,' Tyler told them.

'I'll be in touch,' Hakeem told him as he showed Tyler to the door.

As Tyler turned to leave though, Hakeem grabbed his shoulder and spun him back around. Behind him, Maryam was hovering nervously.

'Promise me, Tyler, whatever happens with Kamal, whatever new shame he brings down on us, promise me you won't let it hurt her.'

He wanted to. He wanted to promise that more than anything. Instead, all he could say was, 'I'll do my best.'

Then he turned and walked away.

IV

'Well?' he asked her.

They were sitting together on the new sofa, Ruth picking at a piece of hard skin that had formed in the nailbed of her little finger, and Drew next to her, a cup of tea cradled in his hands. He hadn't asked her if she wanted one. She didn't, but he hadn't asked.

'Well, what?'

Drew flinched as though she'd lashed out at him. 'I don't know why you have to take this out on me.' He turned to look out of the window.

It wasn't a very comfortable sofa, Ruth thought. All lumpy, and nearly as badly stained as the 'hideous monstrosity' that had been there before – his words, not hers. But she supposed she should be grateful. It *had* been a lovely thought, and it must have cost him a fair bit even if it was second-hand. Also, as he'd pointed out, there was no point holding on to the past. Frank's chair had only been a constant reminder of what she'd been through. Still, she wished he'd checked with her before he'd got rid of it.

Ruth glanced across and saw him reflected in the window. The disappointment on his face, beneath that elaborate quiff he loved so much. It was physically painful to her. 'I'm sorry,' she said. She reached out and put a hand on his leg, stroked it gently through the thick denim of his jeans.

'Do you even know what you're apologising for?'

She hesitated, not wanting to get it wrong. 'I'm snappy today. It's just the stress of the situation. I shouldn't have taken it out on you.'

He continued to stare into the distance like a hurt little boy, so she apologised again, and eventually he forgave her with a heavy, put-upon sigh.

'So. How are you getting on?' he asked, going back to his favourite subject. 'Have you made any progress?'

'I don't know, Drew. I'm beginning to think this isn't such a good idea.'

He sighed again, louder this time, and began to pull away.

'No,' she said, grabbing his arm. 'I mean, I've got an idea but ... I'm just not sure it's going to work.'

'Tell me,' he commanded.

She told him what she'd managed to work out so far about Mina Rabbani's movements. As she spoke, she realised she was trying to put a good spin on things but, in truth, she was genuinely proud of what she'd achieved. She'd found out Mina's address by following her home. She'd watched her house on a number of occasions now, working out her running routine. She couldn't follow her then, obviously – there was no way Ruth would have been able to keep up – but she'd worked out the route through trial and error, lying in wait each day in a different spot. It had taken quite a few attempts, but slowly she'd pieced it together. She'd followed Mina to a coffee shop after work one evening, taking up a position at a table directly behind her and her friend. In doing so, she'd established that the friend was married to the famous artist, Leigh Raddon. Of course, all of this she made sound much harder to Drew than it actually had been.

Even so, he didn't seem impressed. 'Why haven't you spoken to her yet? You said yourself it was our best chance of finding her uncle. If we could track him down, maybe he could give us . . . give *you* the answers you're looking for.'

She hadn't told him she'd already remembered the uncle's name. She wasn't really sure why she was keeping it from him.

'I . . . I don't know what to say to her.'

Again, he pulled away, and she hurried to tell him the rest.

'I thought . . . if I could get closer to her, via the friend, she might be more inclined to speak to me.'

'And do you know her friend?'

'Well, no, not yet, but that's the clever bit.'

She started to fill him in on her plan – the pottery class she'd found listed online – but Drew suddenly stood up.

'I need to be getting off,' he said.

'What? But you've only just arrived.'

He hadn't been here much over the past couple of weeks. She could feel him slipping away. Sometimes she wondered if that was even a bad thing. It occurred to her that she could end it. She could. She'd thought about it several times. Well, once. When he'd shouted at her for something she didn't even know she'd done and stormed out of the house. But then, after a day or two, or three, alone with nothing but the loud tick of the grandmother clock on the wall and Frank's voice in her head, she'd found herself relenting. Whatever she had with him was better than that, surely.

'Ruthy, you're supposed to be finding out about Rabbani. Where he is, how much he knows about what happened back then. Not making new friends and starting up with new hobbies. I mean, how much is this all going to cost?'

'No, it's not much and—'

'I just don't think you're taking it seriously enough.'

'I am!'

'We talked about this. We need to know how much trouble you might be in, and piecing together what happened back then is the only way to work that out. Do you want to be arrested?'

'What? No, but . . . I was only fourteen.'

'That's old enough to take responsibility for your actions. You have to accept you were at least partially responsible for what happened back then. You knew what they were doing, didn't you?'

You leave me and I'll set the rozzers on you. They'll find you even if I can't. No one's gonna want you after that.

'Yes,' she said. 'Of course.' She knew he was right. All he was doing was echoing the same thoughts she'd had day after day for more than twenty years. But then why, when he said it, did it not sound right? She wanted to argue with him. She *had* only been a child, her every move controlled by her father. It wasn't as though she'd had any choice. At least, that was the way it had felt at the time. Surely, a court of law would understand that?

He rapped her on the head with his knuckles, bringing her sharply back to the present. 'You do *want* to remember what happened, don't you?'

She nodded.

'Unless you've already remembered something that you haven't told me?'

Ruth shook her head, not trusting herself to speak.

'Ruthy, you are telling me everything, aren't you? I can't help you if you're not being entirely honest.'

'I am being honest, Drew. I was a kid, it was a long time ago.'

'You have to keep on trying. You never know when some-thing else might come back to you. And you have to tell me when it does, so I can help you process it.'

Ruth nodded again, but her head was suddenly full of images she didn't want there. A keyring with a picture on it of a boy wearing Mickey Mouse ears. An upturned plate with its spilled sandwich scattered across the floor. The smell of days-old urine and faeces. She pushed it all away.

But she was certain now that she had to keep feeding pieces of her past to this man, to keep his attention. She tried to work out exactly when this had become about *them*, rather than just her. She wasn't sure why she was lying to him. She told herself she was being ridiculous. He wasn't with her just because of this. Why would he be? And yet . . . he seemed so interested in her past, and it was when she told him she couldn't remember any more that he started drifting away from her. She couldn't lose him.

'I wanted to make us something nice tonight,' she told him, changing the subject and completely ignoring the fact he'd just told her he was leaving.

'I can't stay tonight.'

'But I thought . . .'

'Ruth.' He took hold of her hands. 'I can't stay with you every night. I have my own life to live as well.'

'Of course,' she said. She didn't ask what that other life entailed. Perhaps everyone had one. Perhaps she was supposed to have one, as well. In truth, she wanted them to share a life together. Or she thought she did. She knew it was pathetic but, as much as she'd craved her independence, it was so much easier with someone to tell you what to do.

Useless bitch! You think you can make it on your own?

He kissed her gently on the cheek, pulling away when she tried to angle her head to meet his lips.

'I'll give you a ring tomorrow,' he told her, getting up and making for the door. 'See how you're getting on.'

'What if he comes back?' she asked, desperate for something, anything to keep him there.

'Who?'

'The policeman! He rang me again last week. And the week before that.'

'Oh.' He screwed his face up in disinterest. 'I dunno. Just refuse to speak to him. He can't make you tell him anything.'

'Should I mention . . . Rabbani?' She'd almost said 'Kamal'. It was getting increasingly difficult to remember what she'd told him and what she hadn't.

'No, of course not!' He was already turning away from her again.

'What about Alison?' she blurted, realising her mistake even as she made it.

He stopped with his hand reaching for the living room door handle and turned very slowly on the spot. 'You didn't tell me you knew her name.'

'What?'

'You said you didn't have anything to do with her.'

'I didn't. But . . . I heard them say her name a couple of times. Is it important?'

His mouth falls open with incredulity. 'Is it important? Of course, it's *fucking* important!'

He reached her in moments, grabbing hold of her wrists and pulling them up and towards him.

'I'm sorry,' she said, trying to pull away. 'Drew, please! You're hurting me.'

He was staring at her, but it was almost as though he was looking through her rather than at her. His lips twisted, and his grip on her wrists tightened until she could feel the throb of her blood against his fingers.

'Drew?' she whimpered.

He started, looking down at his hands as though they didn't belong to him. Finally, he let go.

'Alison,' he said, the word sounding uncertain in his mouth.

'Yes. Her name was Alison.'

'Why didn't you tell me this before?'

'I don't know. I . . . I thought I did or . . . I'm not sure when I remembered it.'

'Do you know what happened to her? Is that something else you've forgotten to tell me?' He spoke slowly and calmly, but somehow still seemed angry.

'No. No, of course I don't know.'

He examined her now with a cool gaze that scared her more than when he'd turned on her a minute before.

'If you don't start making a bit more of an effort, I'm really not sure what's left for us.'

He was giving her one last chance, she thought. If she got this wrong, she'd never see him again.

'It's difficult,' she said. 'Sometimes . . . sometimes it's like I can almost remember.'

He stepped forward and she thought he was going to grab her again, or worse. But then he was wrapping his arms around her and patting the back of her head with his hand. 'Shuuuush,' he soothed her. 'I know this is difficult for you, but you've done really well. Now. You must try to remember the rest. It's important. For your own sake.'

She rested her head on his chest, and for a moment she thought this might become something else. Like it did in the TV shows. He would hold her head in both his hands, look down at her with love clearly visible in his eyes, and kiss her passionately. Then he would lift her up and carry her to the bedroom.

But they hadn't done anything in the bedroom for weeks now.

Instead, he kissed the top of her head fondly, like she used to do with the dog. Then he turned and walked out of the room.

She heard the door slam a few moments later.

friday morning

1

'Bloody hell,' Doggett says when he sees her. 'You look like you lost a grand and found a fiver. Covered in shit.'

'Yeah,' Mina says. 'That about sums it up.' Her face is pale, and she has thick bags under her eyes as though she hasn't slept.

He takes a wild stab in the dark. 'You've been up at the hospital?'

She nods.

'You can't help him sitting up there worrying, you know.'

'I can be there for Diane!' she snaps.

He supposes she has a point. He'd wondered if he should go up himself but he's not what most people would consider a shoulder to cry on. Too bony for one thing. And he really hates hospitals.

'He'll be all right, you know? Diane said they thought he came through the op well enough.'

'They don't know. They're just guessing. He still hasn't woken up.'

'Yeah, but he could, though. He could wake up at any moment and start barking orders at you.' He doesn't mention that Diane had said they were worried about how much brain damage Tyler might have suffered; he has no doubt Mina knows already.

'Yeah, 'course.' Her voice is drained of hope.

Doggett looks up at the dilapidated cinema and wonders again why the lad would have come here on his own so late in the evening. As always, he can only think of two explanations: Tyler was looking for something – something urgent that couldn't wait until morning. Or he was meeting someone. Someone he trusted not to bang him on the head and throw him off a gantry.

Which is why Doggett's arranged to meet the manager here. If this place has any connection to Alison Beech's kidnapping, he wants to know about it.

He glances back at Mina, who's staring into space. *She's going to be less than useless*, he realises. *Where the bloody hell is Vaughan?*

'Come on,' he tells her. 'Out with it.'

She looks at him and lets out a long slow breath. 'I think Tyler was investigating me,' she says. 'Or my family.'

'Uh-huh,' he says, carefully.

She isn't stupid though, and she immediately fixes him with one of her challenging frowns. 'You knew.'

'I knew he was keeping things from you, and not in the usual way. He asked the forensics lass not to tell you what he was looking into, and he hid his tracks. No notes, no official paper trail. Whatever he was up to, I guessed it might have something to do with you. And the only reason he could have for hiding everything so well is that he thought what he'd found was something that could hurt you.'

'You think he was protecting me?'

'I know he was.'

'But ... why? From what?'

'Or who? You tell me.'

He can see her weighing up how much to tell him. She knows something, he'd put money on that. But she still doesn't know how hard whatever this is could impact her, or her family, perhaps. She's wondering how far she can trust him with the truth. He isn't hurt by that. It's sensible. But still, he hopes she knows he'd cut off his right hand before he'd do anything to hurt her. So would Tyler.

'I was kidnapped,' she says. 'As a child.'

Doggett says nothing, but his mind is suddenly racing, filling in gaps. He slots this knowledge in, tries it for size, turns it round and tries again. How is this connected to what Cooper told them? To Alison Beech and the kidnapping of the short-sighted lass from the dog's home? He'd been up there yesterday morning and spoken to Abby Williams, confirming that Tyler had interviewed her a few months ago, but it hadn't sounded like the kid had been able to provide much additional information.

'My family won't talk to me about it,' Mina goes on. 'But I'm fairly certain it's true. Ruth Weatherstone told me.'

She correctly interprets his frown and tells him all about the woman she'd met at Emma Ridgeway's barbecue on Sunday. It can't be a coincidence.

'So,' he says, as she finishes explaining all about her confrontation with Ruth yesterday, 'Tyler gets an anonymous letter half-confessing to the kidnap of Alison Beech.' Doggett conveniently leaves out the fact that he was responsible for that bit. Why hadn't he remembered? He should have seen how obsessive the lad had been about it. He'd found him poring over it a good few weeks after he'd passed it on. And then shortly after that, Tyler had rung him to ask about Bob Smith. He'd denied it had anything to do with the letter, but Doggett should have made the connection.

There's no point dwelling, what's done is done.

'The letter implicates Frank Weatherstone,' he goes on, organising his thoughts. 'But Tyler can't interview the man because he's died a couple of weeks earlier. Which is the reason Foster wrote the letter in the first place, we're guessing. He's trying to get everything off his chest before he pops his own clogs, and with his old mate Frank no longer around, he can do so.'

'Tyler would have spoken to Ruth though,' Mina says. 'He had Weatherstone's address.'

Doggett nods. 'We'll need to speak to her again, obviously.' He doesn't tell her off for letting the woman go in the first place, but she looks sheepish enough that he knows she hears the unspoken criticism anyway. 'The DNA on the envelope leads him to Foster, but whether or not he got anything out of the man, we don't know. Given he was suffering dementia, the old fella might have told him everything or nothing, but we know Tyler would've tried, at least. Frank Weatherstone and Harry Foster were cellmates and old pals. I don't think it's a stretch to assume that Tyler figured they were in on this kidnapping business together.'

'And then, through Suzanne, he made the connection to a number of other kidnappings that happened at the time.'

'Including yours.'

Mina closes her eyes, as though she's trying to will the information away. 'But how? My parents clearly never reported it or there'd be a record somewhere. There isn't, I checked.'

'He must have spoken to them,' Doggett tells her.

She absorbs this information slowly, seemingly unwilling to consider he might have gone behind her back at first, but eventually coming to the same conclusion. She nods. She should have got there sooner. She's not thinking straight.

'We'll have to speak to them, too.'

'*I'll* speak to them,' she tells him, and he decides not to argue.

'Whatever they told him brought him here. That's the piece we're missing.'

'We're still missing lots of pieces,' she tells him. 'My family aren't responsible for this.' She sounds as though she's trying to convince herself more than him.

They fall quiet for a moment, each lost in their own thoughts.

He wonders if that comment about missing pieces was meant as a rebuke. The information he'd requested about Tyler's police systems searches had finally come through that morning, but long after it was of any use. All it did was confirm that Tyler had been looking into Frank Weatherstone, Harry Foster and the Beech case; info they already had from elsewhere. He was still waiting on his request to the phone company and the forensic reports on the scene here at the cinema. And no amount of pressure seemed to be helping with that. The techies were being less than useless, as usual. He'd rung them again this morning, tried to reiterate how important it was they got access to Tyler's deleted search history. 'Yeah,' the cocky little bastard on the

345

other end of the phone had told him, 'they all say that.' He'd
politely reminded the little shit that this was one of their fucking own but had still only succeeded in extracting a promise
that they'd 'do their best'.

'I remember it,' Mina says, quietly. 'Like a vivid dream. I was
held in a bedroom somewhere. There was a dog with me, asleep
in the bed. I think they gave me something to make me sleepy.'

Abby Williams had mentioned a dog.

'That's all I can remember. I can't remember being taken or
returned. I don't know if they ... if they did anything. All I
can remember is the bloody dog.'

It isn't often that Doggett has to think about what to say. He
tends to blurt out whatever comes to him, whenever it comes
to him, and to hell with whether it upsets anyone. There's only
ever the thought that's in his head at that moment, and he voices
it, no matter the consequences. But now, he hesitates.

'You'll drive yourself mad trying to second guess,' he says,
eventually. 'Imagination is far crueller than truth, in my experience.' He reaches out to pat Mina on the back but stops, his
hand a few inches from her jacket. 'Speak to them. I'll come
with you if you want.'

'I'll be okay.'

A mobile phone trills, interrupting the silence, and Mina
pulls it out and checks the display. Doggett doesn't need to see
it to know who it is; it's written all over her face.

She presses answer, and Doggett can hear the woman on the
other end as clearly as if she were standing with them.

'Amina? Amina, is that you?'

'Yes, Ammi.'

'Can you come home, please?'

'Are you going to talk to me this time?'

Doggett thinks he hears her mother sigh, although it could be the line.

'Yes,' she says. 'It's time. You might hate me afterwards, but you need to know now. This has gone too far.'

'Finally, something we can agree on.'

'Just come home. Please.'

'Fine,' Mina says, and she ends the call without saying good-bye. She hesitates, not wanting to ask.

'Go home,' he tells her. 'Now.'

'But you need me here.'

'I can manage,' he tells her, then gestures to the car park where Vaughan is finally pulling up. 'And I've got Speedy Gonzales over there to fuck things up for me, I don't need you as well.'

She smiles at him, but it's weak and evaporates quickly as she turns to walk away.

2

She rings the doorbell.

It feels weird, but not as weird as letting herself in after everything that's happened. Why does she feel like a stranger in her own house? Last night she stayed at the hospital, as much because she didn't want to go home as through concern for Tyler.

When Maryam opens the door, she looks tired. Mina has a sudden image of her mother as an old woman. Is this that moment? she wonders. When the roles reverse and you become the adult, and your parent the child? Maryam isn't all that old, not yet out of her fifties; her mother and her mother's mother are still going strong back in Pakistan. But the future is there, lurking in her features. Has Mina caused this? With her threats and temper? No. She hardens herself to the image of her mother as victim. She's here to learn the truth, and she has to accept that there will be a cost to that truth. For her, or her family, or possibly for both.

'In here,' Maryam says, as she closes the front door behind them and ushers Mina into the front room reserved for big family meetings and important guests. Her father's waiting, standing next to the faux fireplace like some upper-class lord of the manor, the effect only slightly spoiled by the fact he's still wearing his dispensary overalls. Mina tries to remember the last time she saw him wearing anything else.

'Come 'ere,' he says, with his thick Loiner accent, and beckons her forward.

She lets him hug her, but without making any attempt to return the sentiment. When he lets go, his smile falters.

'Eh, Mina, don't be like that. Your mam and I only ever wanted what were best for you.'

'By keeping the truth from me?'

'You were only a child at the time,' her mother says. 'And later . . . you never asked about it. We hoped you'd forgotten.'

'I used to have nightmares,' Mina says, failing to keep the accusation from her voice. 'You let me sleep in your bed.'

Her mother looks down at the floor and her father takes up the explanation. 'We just thought the whole thing was better left.'

'We?' Mina asks. Her mother's always been one for a quiet life, for ignoring what doesn't fit her cosy narrative and pretending it doesn't exist.

'Hey!' her father says, in his stern tone. 'That's enough. This were a joint decision between the pair of us. Don't go blaming your mother for everything.'

Mina takes in a deep breath, then lets it out. She sits down in one of the leather armchairs and tries to keep her cool. She can't stop herself crossing her legs, but she stops her arms before they meet and forces her hands down into her lap.

'Just tell me,' she says. 'Please. Tell me the truth about what happened.'

Hakeem and Maryam exchange a look and, surprisingly, it's her father who nods slightly, giving her mother permission to speak. Mina would have expected it to be the other way around.

Maryam sits down on the edge of the opposite sofa and Hakeem joins her, taking up a position by her side, his hand gently resting on her shoulder.

'It was a weekday afternoon,' her mother begins. 'A Thursday, I think. We were both at the shop, so we only heard about what happened after. You were at the old house with your cousins and Auntie Zoya. You kids were all outside in the yard, playing cricket most likely. You were always playing cricket.'

Her father massages her mother's shoulder, squeezing it gently. For the first time Mina realises all of this isn't just about her. She sees the pain in her mother's eyes as she recounts the story, reliving the worst moment of her life – her child, taken.

'Auntie Zoya didn't see what happened, but a couple of the older children said it was quick as a flash. One moment you were there, the next gone. They saw a white van driving away. They didn't even know you were in it at first. It was only later, when Zoya called for you, that she began to put things together. By then, of course, we'd already had the call.'

Her mother looks up at her father, willing him to go on in her place.

Her father clears his throat before he speaks. 'You remember your Uncle Kamal?'

The sudden change in direction confuses Mina. She remembers Kamal, vaguely. A kind man who used to play with them in the yard, teaching them how to play cricket. But before she can ask any questions, her father goes on.

'He came to the shop and told us what happened. Some men he was involved with had taken you as leverage, to make sure he did something. He never told us what that was and there weren't really time to argue. He told us to go home and wait, and above all, we shouldn't call the police.'

'What . . . ? Why . . . ?' Mina can't make sense of any of this, can't think which question to ask first.

'Hold on, love,' her father says, raising a hand to forestall her questions. 'There's a bit more and then we'll get to it.'

'You have to understand,' her mother goes on. 'We didn't know what was going to happen to you. It was only a few hours, but you cannot imagine what went through our heads.'

'Your mother wanted to ring the cops anyway, but me and the lads convinced her to wait a while.' By 'lads' her father means his brothers.

Then it's her mother's turn to go on the defensive. 'They went looking for you, your uncles. The whole community.'

Did everyone know what had happened except her? How had she not heard about this? She'd thought she was part of the community, but suddenly she's not so sure.

'Kamal just kept telling us to trust him,' Maryam goes on. 'That he would fix everything. And he did.' It's almost a question at the end, her mother turning once again to her father.

He picks up the story. 'Kamal came back with you a few hours later. He was all banged up, cuts and bruises all over his face, but you were okay. A bit sleepy but otherwise you seemed unharmed.'

'You kept asking about a dog – could you keep him.' Her mother's voice catches in her throat. 'I think they must have drugged you with something. But we got you checked over. There was . . . there was no real harm.'

Mina knows what her mother is telling her, and relief floods through her. She hadn't realised how much this had been worrying her until now. She's seen the worst things that can happen to children when they're taken. She's sat with victims while they've been examined, seen the misplaced shame in their eyes, the horror their parents try so hard to hide.

This whole situation still feels surreal though. How could it have happened? Why doesn't she remember it properly? Was that an effect of whatever they'd given her? If so, what other damage did it cause?

She mentally shakes herself. What use is thinking like this? She has to remember there's a bigger picture here.

'Tyler came to see you, didn't he?'

Her mother and father exchange another look and come to another unspoken agreement.

'He came to ask us about Kamal,' her father says. 'We didn't know where he was then but I . . . I put the feelers out for him, and it paid off. Tyler went to see him.'

'What did he say?'

Instead of answering, her father gets up. He moves to the hallway and shouts in Urdu. Mina's a bit rusty but she thinks it's, 'Bring him in.'

Until now, Mina had assumed they had the house to themselves, which was a stupid assumption to make in this family. Now they file into the room: her uncles, although two are not strictly speaking her uncles at all, but her father's cousins. Still, they're all 'the lads'.

Uncle Nazir is with them as well. Her mother's uncle. He's the last to enter, pushing a suited younger man in front of him. The younger man's glasses are cracked, and he has a large bruise forming on his right cheek.

'What's going on?' Mina demands, leaping out of her seat and defaulting to police mode rather than the deferential dutiful-niece persona she usually deploys with these men when she sees them.

But rather than lecture her on respecting her elders, they all, to a man, look ashamed of themselves. Even Uncle Nazir, who under normal circumstances never fails to make it clear to her that he doesn't find her life choices respectable. Even he has his head bowed.

Only the bespectacled, suited man looks at her. He has a half smile, or possibly a grimace, on his face. It seems familiar.

'Uncle Kamal?'

'Been a long time, Mina. You grew up well.'

Mina looks from one man to the next, searching their faces for explanations. 'You brought him here?' She means the accusation that comes through in her tone. 'Let go of him!'

Nazir lets go but steps back, very obviously blocking the doorway. 'He needed a bit of persuading,' he tells her. 'But he understands now he must tell you the truth.'

'I don't believe this. You kidnapped him?' Mina's voice comes out screechy and unrecognisable. 'For the love of—' She bites off the blasphemy. 'What were you thinking?'

'Tell her!' her father says, and his voice is as hard as she's ever heard it.

Kamal actually flinches.

'Tell her what you told us!'

Her uncle raises his hands in supplication. 'Okay, okay. Peace!'

She knows she should take control of the situation, but part of her needs to hear what's coming. If she can use her father's anger to get to the truth – God help her! – she will. She's pretty sure Tyler would approve.

'Well?' she asks.

'Your friend,' Kamal says. 'The copper.'

'DS Tyler,' she tells him. 'He has a name.'

Nazir steps forward again and Kamal jumps. He nods, hurriedly.

'DS Tyler,' he says. 'Yes.' He looks her squarely in the eye and she doesn't see anything but truth there.

'I think I know who might have attacked him,' he says.

1 month ago

I

The receptionist who showed Tyler to the waiting room was tall and skinny with bright red hair. He couldn't have been much over twenty and still had acne staining his cheeks and neck, with one particularly sore-looking eruption at his hairline that was inflamed and weeping. There was a faint pink bloodstain on the collar of his shirt. He looked as though he wouldn't last five minutes in a confrontation, whether with a pissed-off client or an overly demanding solicitor.

'If ... er ... If you could wait here, I'll go and tell Mr Rabbani you're here?' he said, or possibly asked.

'I'd appreciate that.'

The spotty youth sidled out of the room, glancing back through the glass panel in the door as though unsure whether he should be leaving Tyler unattended on the premises. Maybe he shouldn't. In Tyler's experience, solicitors were sticklers for rules and regulations as much as anyone else involved in the legal profession, at least until they decided to break them.

The room was standard waiting room fare, with magnolia-painted walls lined with cheap plastic seats. Four glass-topped coffee tables were scattered with recent magazines, mostly upmarket ones like *Country Life* and *Vogue* – there was little room for a *My Weekly* in here. One wall had been left unplastered, the bare brick itself a feature designed to emulate the latest hipster-chic coffee shops and complemented by the industrial air vents dangling on metal wires from the ceiling.

Tyler wandered around the room idly while he waited, his hands clasped behind his back. He wondered what Kamal Rabbani LLB (Hons) would be thinking right now as the young receptionist informed his mentor that a police detective was here, and consequently how long he would have to wait. There was a small chance Rabbani might be hightailing it down the back staircase while Tyler was standing here twiddling his thumbs, but he thought it was a *small* chance.

It was the letters after Rabbani's name that had decided him on a course of action. When Hakeem had got in touch to tell Tyler the family network had tracked down his prodigal brother, he hadn't been overly surprised. What had been more notable was how long the process had taken, since he was fairly certain Hakeem had known exactly where his brother was all along. Cutting a brother off was one thing; not keeping track of him, for a man like Hakeem anyway, would be unconscionable. But perhaps conscience had been the problem: Hakeem had been forced to weigh up his loyalty to a disappointing brother and to his detective daughter.

The biggest surprise, however, had been Kamal's change in status. In the twenty-plus years that he'd been gone, he'd seemingly turned his life around as effectively as Teri Greene, completing a law degree and qualifying as a solicitor, before joining this prestigious law firm in Leeds. It was a remarkable feat, if Hakeem's version of the man was to be believed. Twenty-four years was a long time, but these kinds of Damascene conversions usually came about only after a significant stretch inside, or at least a close brush with one. And as far as Tyler could establish, Kamal had never served any time. Had Alison Beech been his reformative moment? A near miss that had scared him straight?

Regardless, Kamal seemed to be a changed man, at least on the surface. He had a good career and plenty to lose, which made him less of a flight risk. Tyler eyed the fire escape, just visible through the waiting room window. Of course, that depended on just how deeply Kamal had been involved in Alison Beech's disappearance. He'd already taken one risk by going to Hakeem and Maryam instead of finding the man on his own. But without the resources of the department and on his own time it would have been a Herculean task. Not to mention that it would have raised questions he didn't want to answer just yet.

And Tyler had been wrong before. After his meeting with the Rabbanis, he'd tried to reach Teri Greene again, only to find that she'd resigned from her job unexpectedly. The head-teacher he'd spoken to had been more than happy to vent his displeasure at teachers who took off without warning midway through term. He'd tried visiting her at home as well, but he'd got no answer. There'd been no car outside. She could have just been out; she could have decided on a sudden career change, or that she needed a holiday. But Tyler figured she was in the wind. He'd obviously unsettled her much more than he'd thought. Either that, or she too was more culpable in Alison's disappearance than he'd suspected.

The door opened behind him, and he turned to see Kamal Rabbani walking into the room with the spotty receptionist hovering behind him.

'Thanks, Sam. I can manage from here.'

Sam stared blankly for a moment before retreating down the corridor as Kamal closed the door.

'Detective Tyler?'

Tyler nodded and stepped forward to accept Kamal's handshake.

'I apologise for the delay. Please.' Kamal held out his palm towards one of the seats and pulled another around so that they faced each other. 'I'm sorry to have to see you in here, but my office is currently unavailable.'

Unavailable, or he didn't want his colleagues to know about this visit. Tyler imagined that, later, Sam would be getting an incentive of some sort to keep his mouth shut about today's visitor.

Kamal was an imposing figure, in height at least. He was taller than Tyler, who rarely felt dwarfed by anyone, and must have been well over six feet. But he was slight of build and didn't look as though he spent much time down the gym. Tyler couldn't see this man handling himself particularly well in any physical confrontation; in fact, height aside, it was easy to see how Kamal might be considered the runt of the litter – the other Rabbani brothers were all on the stocky side. But Tyler could see the strong family resemblance.

He introduced himself formally, and Kamal nodded and

smiled. He seemed calm, but then he'd had ample time to compose himself. He had to be worried about why Tyler was here, and yet you'd be hard pressed to guess it from his demeanour. That said, he was unable to completely hide the curiosity in his eyes.

'So, what can I do for you, Detective?' He spoke softly, projecting a peculiar sense of serenity as he crossed his right leg over his left knee and interlaced his long fingers around his kneecap. If it was an act, it was a good one. Whether this newfound sense of inner peace extended to a fit of conscience Tyler was yet to discover, but if it had, then maybe he would actually get some answers.

'Kidnappings,' Tyler said, simply, and left it at that.

If Kamal's equilibrium was ruffled, he didn't show it. '*Kidnappings*, plural?' he asked. 'I'm not sure I follow.'

'For the most part, I'm interested in what you might know about the kidnapping of Alison Beech.'

This time the smile on Kamal's face did falter slightly. His right index finger twitched, and Tyler knew in that moment that Mina's uncle was involved. He'd hoped he was wrong, and now he knew he wasn't. He pushed down the wave of regret and sadness that surged within him.

'I'm afraid I've never heard of her,' Kamal said.

'Really, Mr Rabbani? A well-educated man like you? I would have thought solicitors needed to be well up on their political history. You've never heard of Dominic Beech? Lord Beech.'

Kamal inclined his head as though acknowledging the point. 'Ah, yes. The name didn't ring a bell at first. She was his wife?

The woman who went missing? But that must have been … what? Twenty-something years ago?'

'Twenty-four years ago, shortly before you left Sheffield.'

Kamal remained calm. 'I assume you have something more that connects me to this woman besides the fact I left town at about the same time? Because speaking purely in terms of the law – and that is, let's be honest, what counts here – that's a very flimsy case you've just outlined. If you were prosecuting my client, I would urge you to come up with something a bit more solid before you took any of it to the CPS.'

'You're right, Mr Rabbani, I don't have any evidence that would convict you in a court of law, but I do have an interesting theory that I hoped I might put to you. Perhaps you could use your expertise to tell me where I might be right and where I'm barking up the wrong tree.'

Kamal flexed his hands in an inviting gesture. 'Go ahead. I like a good story.'

'I think that twenty-four years ago you were … acquainted, shall we say, with two men named Harry Foster and Frank Weatherstone. They were career criminals and I'm not sure as yet how you came into contact with them, though if I had to guess it would probably be through Harry, as he seems to have been the more sociable of the two. They heard about your financial prowess and came to you with a significant amount of money they were trying to clean, namely the proceeds of a number of kidnappings they'd committed. Now, I don't think you personally had much to do with the kidnappings them-selves, you just dealt with the money side of things afterwards. How am I doing so far?'

'It's very entertaining,' Kamal said. 'I'll give you that.'

'Then, this enterprising pair upped the ante and decided to turn their sights to a prominent local politician and his wife, the aforementioned Mr and Mrs Beech. They attempted to abduct the couple's young son, but Mrs Beech put up more of a fight than expected and they ended up with her instead. They decided to go ahead with their plan anyway and demanded a ransom. It was paid. And then ...'

'And then?'

'Well, that's as far as my story goes,' Tyler admitted. 'So far, at least.'

'It's not much of a story then.'

'I was hoping you might provide the ending.'

Kamal shook his head. 'I'd love to help you, but I've never been all that keen on fantasy.'

'What happened, Kamal? Did she fight back? Was she harder to handle than a five-year-old? Maybe Weatherstone lost his temper with her.'

'I really don't understand why you're here.'

Tyler was brought up short. In truth, he didn't understand that either. Had he really expected Kamal to just roll over and tell him what he wanted to know?

'I could bring you in,' he said.

Kamal remained calm. 'Are you arresting me, Detective? Because if so, I'd recommend you have some solid evidence to produce, or my partners here are going to go to town on you and your fascinating little story. Do you have a single witness to any of this?'

This wasn't going to work – Kamal wasn't going to be

intimidated as easily as Teri Greene. Tyler suspected that even if he had some leverage over him, the man still might not crumble. But the truth was, he didn't.

'Like I said,' Tyler told him, 'it's just a story. But I want you to know that I'm not going to stop digging. A woman is missing, and I intend to find her. If you know something about that, it's in your interest to tell me now before I find out about it some other way.'

Kamal tapped his thumbs together. 'I have a niece who works for your lot,' he said.

'Yes,' Tyler told him. 'I know her.'

Kamal didn't seem surprised at this, and Tyler would have bet he'd already known.

'Family is important, wouldn't you agree?'

'If you think I won't take action against you out of some misguided loyalty to her, you should know that I arrested my own brother not all that long ago.'

Kamal waved away his words.

'As I understand these things, cases like this, they must be a nightmare for you, yes? Little in the way of evidence, witnesses dead or untraceable. Even if you manage to get them to court, and that's assuming you get your superiors on board, someone like me comes along and blows them out of the water, eh? I don't know, maybe I muddy the waters by pointing out that the original investigator messed up in some way. Perhaps the man had some financial difficulty that mysteriously went away shortly after your victim's disappearance. I might suggest that this man was in on the crime all along, and facilitated the ransom drop in such a way as to ensure the perpetrators got away. Of course, no doubt that fellow's long dead by now, so there'd be no way of proving that either. Still, it might be enough to derail your case.'

Tyler's ears pricked up. Was Kamal trying to imply that Smith had been in on it? His words seemed a little too close to Tyler's own suspicions to be coincidental. He got the feeling Kamal was trying to tell him something, if only to get Tyler off his back. He made his decision.

'What if I told you I'm not interested in pursuing anything in court? That all I want is to find Alison Beech and lay her to rest.'

Kamal nodded and stood up. 'As I said before,' he said, reaching for Tyler's hand, '*family* is everything.' He held Tyler's gaze for a moment. 'I wish I could help you further, Detective, but I really can't.'

Kamal showed Tyler out himself, escorting him to the elevator in the corridor. The solicitor remained cool and collected, a thin smile on his face, until the doors closed. Even if he had some evidence that implicated the man, Tyler thought as the lift descended, he'd be a tough nut to crack. And without it, as Doggett might tell him, he was pissing in the wind.

II

The second Mrs Dominic Beech was not at all what Tyler had been expecting. She was a large woman – not fat, but statuesque – with dark, luxurious hair piled around her face in well-coiffured waves. She wore a moss-green V-neck peasant dress that accentuated her curves in a manner that brought to mind certain Greek goddesses; her sleeves were pulled up to her elbows and there were smudges of what he could only assume was flour on her face and hands. It wasn't the only detail which made him think of a particular celebrity TV cook – when she spoke, her deep, plummy accent fitted the glamorous image perfectly. In looks at least, she couldn't have been further removed from her petite, blonde predecessor.

'Excuse my appearance, Detective,' she told him after he'd identified himself, her voice betraying no hint of concern. 'You're here for Dom, I take it? He's in the garden with the girls. Won't you come in?'

He stepped past her into the hallway he'd stood in once before, but this time, rather than escort him into the living room, she led him down a short corridor and into a small study on the other side of the house. After he declined her offer of refreshments, she encouraged him to make himself comfortable. 'I'll fetch Dom now,' she said, but failed to make any move to go. 'I assume this is about Alison?'

Tyler smiled in a manner he hoped was noncommittal.

'Awful business,' she said, shaking her head. 'I mean, you hear about things like this all the time, but you just don't expect it in Sheffield, do you? Manchester, maybe. London, certainly. But not here.' She continued shaking her head, seemingly lost in thought.

Something occurred to Tyler. 'Did you know Alison?' he asked her.

'What? Oh, no. No, no, I didn't meet Dominic until years later. It was ... oh, twelve years ago now. We've been married ten. I remember the whole business though.' She brushed some of the flour from her fingers. 'When I met Dom, I worried it might get between us, you know? My friends all warned me, "Christ, Monica, don't get involved! You can't compete with a ghost."' She chuckled. 'But the truth is, Dom's always been brilliant about it.' She paused after that and stared at the wall. 'Perhaps a bit too brilliant.'

'How so?'

She snapped out of her reverie. 'Oh, no, I just mean, I worry he's keeping it all bottled up so it won't affect me. And the girls. He's just so ... so stoic, sometimes. I wish he'd just let it all out.' She laughed again, but this time it sounded forced.

'It must be terribly hard for him,' Tyler told her. 'In my experience losing someone is hard enough, but never knowing what happened to them ...' He left the thought hanging.

She nodded. 'Yes, yes, that's it exactly. I used to think that perhaps it helped him, the fact that they weren't all that close towards the end. But now I'm not so sure. Somehow, I wonder if that makes it worse.'

This was news to Tyler, but he kept his face straight. 'You think perhaps they would have patched things up, given the chance?'

'Oh no, I don't think so. From what Dom's told me, it was pretty much over between them by that point. Though of course it would have been nice if they'd had the chance to at least end things civilly. You know, apologise for all the things said, all the hurt, then move on, become friends maybe. My ex and I managed it and I think it's awfully cathartic, that sense of closure. But instead, she went and got herself kidnapped.'

She suddenly seemed to register what she'd said and for the first time Tyler saw her lose her composure. She wrung her hands, distress clearly visible in her eyes. 'I'm so sorry. That must have sounded very callous.'

Tyler assured her he took no offence, but after that she couldn't get away from him quickly enough. She slipped out of the room, leaving the door propped open, and hurried off into the house. He turned away and began studying the framed pictures on the walls as he waited for her husband to appear.

So, Dominic and Alison had been having marital problems. That put an interesting spin on things. Especially since it had never been reported anywhere else, to his knowledge. It wasn't surprising that Dominic might have wanted to keep it from the press, and the police, but it was interesting nonetheless.

Most of the pictures in the study were of Monica and the

girls, alongside other friends and family, but there were plenty of Dominic too: smiling widely for the camera with a young Tony Blair; perched inelegantly on the arm of a red sofa while fending off advances from the Spice Girls; chatting animatedly with a panel of guests on *Question Time*. There were quite a few certificates of achievement too – Dominic's degrees, accolades from charities and councils, as well as, somewhat incongruously, a number of swimming certificates. It seemed as though Beech had framed every accolade he'd ever had.

There was one certificate that wasn't Dominic's though. A school prize for reading with the name 'Lucas A. Beech' picked out in an ornate font in the centre of the page. Above it there was a picture of Lucas, perhaps only eight or nine, holding up the same certificate and doing his best to smile. He didn't look anywhere near as withdrawn and damaged as the teenage Goth Dominic had shown Tyler on his last visit, but his eyes were wide and watery, the half smile painfully sad. Perhaps at that age Lucas had still hoped to see his mother again someday.

What was most curious to Tyler, however, was the lack of any pictures of Alison herself. He went back over the wall but, try as he might, he couldn't find a single one. Perhaps that wasn't so surprising given what he'd just learned about their relationship. Might they have patched things up if they'd been given the chance? How did it feel to live with that thought for all those years?

'I thought I made myself clear the last time we spoke, Detective Sergeant Tyler.' Dominic Beech marched into the room as though ready for combat.

Tyler held up his hands in surrender. 'You did, sir, and I'm really not here to cause you any further pain or trouble.' The words stuck in his throat a little, but he could do this. For Mina. If Beech made a complaint about him, everything would come out into the open, and he couldn't let that happen. 'But you'll appreciate that your family wasn't the only one affected by events back then.'

Beech's eyes narrowed and Tyler put him out of his misery.

'You told me yourself that DI Smith's theory involved a kidnapping gang. It seems there might have been something in that, and I'm sure you wouldn't want to deny any other victims their own chance at justice.'

From somewhere deeper in the house came the sound of children squealing. Beech glanced over his shoulder and then back at Tyler. 'Just ask what you need to ask,' he said. And then, as though he couldn't help but assert his own authority, he added, 'But make it quick.'

Tyler nodded and decided to get right to it. 'How well did you know DI Smith?'

Again, Beech frowned. 'What the hell does that mean?' His voice was raised and he glanced over his shoulder once more as sounds of family life echoed through his home. When he went on, he'd tempered his tone. 'He was the man *your* people put in charge of my wife's kidnapping.'

'But you knew him before that, didn't you?'

'I was acquainted with him. As I was – and still am – acquainted with a number of your colleagues.' The implied warning was stark, and again Tyler held up his hands in an attempt to placate the man.

'I just wondered if you noticed any change in him, while he was in charge of your case?'

'Change? What sort of change?'

Tyler tried again, aware that he was dancing on the head of a pin. 'Did he ever give you any reason to think he wasn't doing his job to the best of his ability?'

'Are you implying DI Smith was incompetent in some way? That he messed up?'

'He was in charge of the botched ransom drop. The perpetrators got away with the money.'

Beech seemed to consider this. 'Smith was the one who counselled against paying the ransom. He only agreed to it because I was adamant that we do everything in our power to ensure a favourable outcome.'

A favourable outcome. Even now the man couldn't stop talking like a politician.

'But it was Smith who told you about the other kidnapping cases? And the previous ransoms that had led to favourable outcomes.'

The politician levelled a hard gaze at him, but Tyler kept his face straight.

'Yes,' Beech said. 'But hang on . . . you're not implying Smith was involved in some way, are you?'

Tyler tried his best to backpedal. 'We always have to consider the possibility that the original investigation wasn't handled as well as it should have been. Normally I'd be directing my questions to the investigating officer in question, but in this case DI Smith is no longer around. I just wondered if he might have said something to you, or done something, that you remember thinking was strange. Or wrong in some way. Anything at all, no matter how insignificant it might seem now.'

Beech did at least think about it, but after a couple of seconds he shook his head. 'It was a long time ago. I'm sorry.'

'If you think of anything ...'

The other man nodded. 'Fine. Is there anything else?'

Tyler hesitated. He wanted to ask Beech about his relationship with his missing wife, but he knew the moment he mentioned it the interview would be over. Was it worth it? What new information would he gain?

The decision was taken out of his hands by the appearance at the door of a young girl, perhaps six or seven, wearing dungarees covered in grass stains.

Tyler raised his hand. 'Hi there.'

Beech spun on his heel. 'Zara! I told you to stay in the kitchen. Off with you.' He bustled her out into the corridor and sent her running with a gentle tap to her bottom that made her squeal with laughter.

'If there's nothing else, Detective? I don't get a great deal of uninterrupted time with my family and I like to make the most of it.'

Tyler hesitated, still unsure how far to push it. Before he could decide, Beech went on.

'I saw your ACC Franklin at a civic do the other week. I'd hate to bother her again so soon. Especially on a Sunday.'

Tyler heard the threat loud and clear. He nodded. 'I've taken up enough of your time. Thank you for all your help.' He followed Beech up the corridor back to the front door.

Beech opened the door for him, and as Tyler turned on the

doorstep to say goodbye, he saw Zara watching from the other end of the hallway.

'Who is he, Daddy?' she announced without any sense of impropriety.

Beech looked Tyler directly in the eye. 'No one, darling,' he said. 'We won't be seeing him again.' Then he closed the door.

It was as Tyler was driving home that he saw the sign for the storage place. He hadn't been there for a while. He glanced in the rearview mirror at the box on the back seat that was the sum total of his investigation so far and laughed. He just couldn't break old habits, could he? The business with the Circle and Stevens had made him beyond paranoid. So much so that he now minimised any electronic trail almost by default, regularly erasing search histories and rejecting digital storage in favour of paper. He found himself flicking the indicator and following the sign to the uStore facility.

He was used to making hard decisions, whatever the cost. But this felt different. Was there really any decision to make? He had five suspects who he thought had likely been involved in Alison Beech's disappearance: Frank Weatherstone and Bob Smith were dead, Harry Foster was barely alive, Teri Greene was in the wind and Kamal Rabbani knew the law well enough to know that it was in his best interests to keep quiet.

He should let the whole thing go. Nobody wanted him to look into this any deeper – not Franklin, not Dominic Beech, not the Rabbanis. Despite his words, he doubted Beech would go to Franklin just yet, but another visit might well convince him. Tyler had zero evidence, only theories, and exposing what he knew ran the risk of derailing Mina's career, or at the very least stalling it considerably. Especially if her parents knew more than they were saying, and he had the nagging sense that they might.

But at the end of it all, Alison Beech was still out there somewhere. Didn't he have a responsibility to find her? If he could?

He pulled into the car park, grabbed the box from the back seat and let himself in via the rear entrance. His unit was on the third floor, five-by-five-feet with a combination padlock on the door. He spun the wheels – 4942, Jackson's prison number – and laughed at himself again. He switched on the light inside and found everything exactly as he'd left it, months ago now. He'd been true to his word to Doggett, he really had given up his crusade. But he couldn't get rid of his research. The best he could manage was to put it away. Out of sight, out of mind.

He looked down at the box in his hands. Perhaps it was time to do the same with this. For now.

He slid the box inside the unit, switched off the light and closed the door.

friday afternoon

1

The first thing Mina does is clear the room. She throws them all out, everyone except Kamal, and, to her surprise, they agree to go. She'd expected some small resistance from her mother at least. But in fact, only Nazir makes any sort of protest and, again to Mina's surprise, it's her mother who backs her up and orders her uncle out of the room. Mina hears him protesting all the way down the hallway, but Maryam's having none of it.

Mina turns to find that Kamal has taken the opportunity of the respite to sit down on the settee and take off his glasses. He's examining the crack with his finger and thumb, assessing the damage. He sighs a little, puts them back on and looks up at her.

'I'm sorry they did that,' she says.

He shakes it off. 'I'm rather used to it,' he says, the implications of which Mina tries not to think about.

He looks up at her. 'You really do look quite different, Mina. I'm not sure what I was expecting but ... well, this wasn't it.'

Mina has no idea where to begin, but she's not about to start reminiscing about old times. 'DS Tyler came to see you to ask about the kidnappings.'

'Straight down to business, eh? Fair enough.'

'Don't stall! Just tell me! This is important.'

Kamal hesitates. 'I don't know if you know this, Mina, but I'm a solicitor now. If I tell you anything, as a police officer you're duty-bound to report it. It's as good as a confession.'

'Why are you here then?'

'I wasn't given a lot of choice.'

Mina looks at his swollen lip, puffed up and bisected by a thin red cut. The blood has had time to clot, but the wound still looks shiny and new. Does she know her family at all? For years they've kept this huge secret from her, and now she discovers this ... this propensity for violence. Her own father had been part of whatever they'd done to Kamal or, at best, had *allowed* it to take place. This is for her benefit, she reminds herself, but has to swallow down a wave of revulsion.

'They won't hurt you again. I won't let that happen. But give me one good reason why I shouldn't arrest you right now.'

'You don't have any evidence.'

'I thought you were a solicitor. I don't need evidence, just "reasonable grounds to suspect an offence has taken place", and "reasonable suspicion" that you're guilty of it. I might not be able to make anything stick, but I doubt twenty-four hours in a cell will do a lot for your reputation.'

He dips his head at that, acknowledging the point. 'You're as hard as your mother, I see. She never did like me.'

'Seems like she might have had good reason. What did you and Tyler talk about?'

'He told me a story. I listened. He had most of it right, but he didn't get all the way to the end.'

Sleeping Dogs

'And you know the end?'

Kamal looks back at the door, maybe assessing his chances of escape. Then he seems to resign himself to his fate.

'He was looking into the disappearance of Alison Beech twenty-four years ago,' he tells her. 'He'd uncovered a kidnapping operation, led by an ex-con named Frank Weatherstone and his partner in crime, Harry Foster. This group were involved in a series of child abductions. There were a couple of other members – a young woman, Harry's girlfriend at the time, who helped look after the children. And a naïve young accountant, the money man, who was willing to turn a blind eye for the sake of a quick buck. We'll leave them name-less for now.

'The gang were clever. They only targeted people who had money, and they never asked for more than these families could afford to lose. They made it clear to them that if they went to the police their little darlings wouldn't survive. The families always paid, and afterwards, they rarely reported the kidnappings. If they did, Frank had a friend on the force who could muddy the waters for them and stall the investigations. The cases were never linked.'

Bob Smith. Doggett and Cooper had filled her in on his chequered past, but hearing he was definitely involved in the kidnapping of children turns Mina's stomach again. She'd never met the man, but he'd been a police officer. First Stevens, now Smith. How many others were out there right now, taking advantage of their positions to commit heinous crimes? *We're supposed to be better than this.*

'Okay,' her uncle goes on. 'Speaking purely hypothetically now, let's say the last kidnapping went a bit differently. Frank and Harry ended up grabbing the mother instead of the son. The rest of the gang thought it was a mistake, but actually it had been Frank's plan all along. He'd cooked up the whole thing with his police officer friend and the woman's husband. Five hundred grand was a lot cheaper than the divorce he was about to have to pay out for. All they had to do was make sure she never came home. Frank's friend was in charge of the investigation and organised the ransom drop so they'd get away with the money. It worked like clockwork, just like always, except this time the woman had seen their faces. Frank had made sure of that. The others were horrified when he wanted to dispose of her, especially the young accountant. He decided it was time to get out. But he wasn't going empty-handed. He took the ransom money with him.'

Kamal falls silent. Mina can't believe what she's hearing. Did her family know about all of this? How could they have kept quiet all these years?

'Anyway, he got clean away, our hero. Made it all the way to Leeds before he got the message. Frank had taken something of his – something valuable. Some*one* valuable. The only member of his family he'd ever really given a toss about. His favourite niece. He was given a choice. Come back with the money . . . or they'd kill her.'

Mina's ears are ringing, threatening to drown out his words.

'The accountant had seen first-hand just what Frank was capable of, so he did the right thing. He took the money back and rescued the little princess.'

The use of that pet name triggers a vivid memory of him, smiling and gurning at her, pulling funny faces to make her laugh. She feels a sudden rush of affection for this man she used to know, but she pushes it away.

'Am I supposed to be grateful?' she asks.

'No,' he says, his shoulders slumping as he drops the hypotheticals. 'You don't owe me anything. But if you could see your way clear to not arresting me, I'd certainly appreciate it.'

'How do you know all that stuff?' Mina asks him. 'About Frank and Beech being in on it together?'

'I overheard Frank talking to the detective, Smith. I was always listening at doors back then. It's no picnic growing up with four older brothers and I'd got used to keeping an eye, and an ear, open for trouble.'

Mina sits down, hard, opposite her uncle.

'I could point out what I mentioned to your colleague, that there's no evidence I was involved in any of this. The only witnesses are long dead, and you'll never get a conviction in court.'

He's probably right, but the insufferable righteousness of the man makes her want to arrest him anyway, to cause him some difficulty at the very least.

'What happened to Alison Beech?'

'I honestly don't know. After I got you out, I never went back.'

'Why should I believe you?'

'I don't know that either.'

'And DS Tyler?'

'He was fine when I last saw him, which was in my office back in Leeds.'

She doesn't want to believe him, but she thinks she probably does. 'You said you knew who attacked him.'

He touches a finger to his swollen cheek and winces. 'More an educated guess. I tried to help Tyler as much as I could – please believe me, Mina.'

'But you didn't tell him everything.'

He opens his mouth as though he's about to object, but evidently thinks better of it. 'I told him that all this was about family. It was the only way I could think of to point him in the direction of Beech without overtly admitting to being involved.'

Mina draws in a sharp breath. 'So, you think Beech attacked him?'

Kamal snorted. 'I doubt that very much. He's never been a hands-on kind of guy, which is no doubt why he hired Frank in the first place.'

'Who then?' She can feel her temper rising, and maybe he picks up on this because he nods as if to acknowledge her impatience.

'There was someone else there when this all went down.' He pauses, looking her square in the eyes. 'Frank's daughter.'

'Ruth?'

Again, he nods. 'She kept a low profile mostly – had to, with a father like Frank. I felt sorry for her but . . . there was always something off about her as well. For all that he led a dog's life, she was quick enough to defend him. She watched everything, and she was much cleverer than she let on. If anyone knows the full story of what happened back then, it's her, and if Tyler went to see her . . . Well, let's just say I don't think the apple fell far from the tree with that one.'

Mina shakes her head, trying to fit this new information

together with what she already knows. Her mind reels. It doesn't seem possible. Could Ruth really be capable of attacking Tyler? Physically, she has to admit that it wouldn't be beyond her. She doesn't really know the woman at all, and what she's seen doesn't conflict with Kamal's assessment of her 'being a bit off'. But then why would she seek Mina out? She'd genuinely seemed to want Mina to know about the kidnapping. Was that all just to throw her off somehow?

Mina stands up again, frustrated. There's nothing to support that what Kamal says about Tyler's attack is true. He's only guessing, and guesswork will get her nowhere.

'Can I ask you something?' her uncle asks abruptly.

'You just did.'

He smiles at this, as though it's a great joke rather than a childish attempt at a comeback, but when he speaks his voice is reflective.

'Was it hard for you, growing up in this family?'

'What's that supposed to mean?'

He probes the cut on his lip with his fingertip. 'No one else ever seemed to have a problem but, I don't know, I just never seemed to fit in. Looking at you now, I know you might not like to hear it, but I think maybe you take after me in that regard.'

'I'm nothing like you.' She's turning away before she's even finished the sentence.

Out in the kitchen they're all gathered around the table, eating, her mother fulfilling her duty as the consummate host. They fall quiet as she enters the room and look up at her almost as one, waiting for her to speak. When had she suddenly taken charge of this family?

'Let him go,' she says. 'And no one touches him again, am I clear?'

There's some grumbling from one or two of them, but the rest go back to their food as though the whole thing's over and done with.

Her mother follows her out into the back garden, where a couple of her cousins' kids are crawling all over the slide and climbing frame. They wave when they see her, and she raises a hand in greeting back. She isn't the favourite auntie, not by a long stretch; she thinks maybe she has a certain level of cool in their eyes because of her job, but she doesn't cook for them or bring them treats and toys.

The sun is setting over the trees and dark clouds are rolling in from the west. 'Manchester's weather', Ghulam used to joke with her when they were playing in the yard, just like the kids are now.

'I'm sorry, Amina. We should have told you a long time ago, but we were trying to protect you. I hope you can come to accept that one day.'

'Was that the reason you didn't want me to join the police?'

'Eh?'

'I was thinking back to when I applied. You were so against it. I never thought for a moment you'd be thrilled, but I didn't expect you to try quite so hard to talk me out of it.'

'We were worried,' her mother admits. 'There were all those checks you had to do. We hadn't heard from Kamal for many years, but we knew he was back in England. If he was involved in something bad it could come up and cause trouble for you.'

'For me? Or for the rest of the family?'

'Ah, Amina! This is not fair!'

Isn't it? she wonders.

They stand in silence and watch the children playing for a minute or two. Eventually her mother speaks. 'What will you do now?'

'Am I going to arrest him, you mean?'

'This won't be good for your career, huh?'

'Please don't pretend that's what you care about when you're really only bothered how this affects our standing in the community.'

'When did you become so hard? Is it so wrong for me to wonder how this will affect us? Your father? All our lives.'

Mina sighs. 'No, it's not wrong. And to answer your earlier question, no, it probably won't be good for my career. But covering up for him's not likely to be either.'

'I'm not asking you to do the wrong thing. I know you're better than that.'

The words eerily echo Doggett's from the other day. *You have to be better than the rest of us.* Better than the likes of Stevens and Bob Smith.

'Ultimately, it's not going to be my call to make, but that's not what matters right now.'

Her mother nods. 'Adam. How is he?'

Mina has to admit she doesn't know. She assumes either Diane or Doggett would have called her if there'd been any change and squashes down the guilt that she hasn't even thought about checking in since this morning.

'I have to go,' she says, glancing towards the garden gate that will take her back to her car without having to negotiate the rest of the family again.

'Amina.' Her mother grabs her hand, pulling her back. She wraps her arms around Mina. 'You will do the right thing. I believe in you. I love you, and I'm proud of you.'

Mina feels tears beginning to prick the corners of her eyes. She pulls away and makes for the gate, trying not to run as the first few spots of rain begin to fall.

2

Ruth trudges home through the rain without bothering with her umbrella. She doubts it will be any good in this wind, anyway. It's not a particularly heavy downpour and after the state of the urinals she's just had to contend with, it feels refreshing, almost cleansing.

She's not far from home when it occurs to her that she still hasn't bought any food, so she peels off at the top of the road to see what she can afford from Aldi. She comes away with a giant packet of pasta and the smallest jar of pesto she's ever seen. It should do her for a few days if she's careful.

She should have told Mina everything, she knows that. She'd meant to. That had been the whole point of this, surely? Drew was right. She'll never truly be free of the past until she unburdens herself of the things she's done. But it had been so hard, and Mina had been so cross, and had she really expected anything different? It isn't every day a complete stranger tells you they kidnapped you as a child. She's asking Mina for something she can probably never give. Forgiveness.

Ruth knows she doesn't deserve to be forgiven. Maybe that

was why she hadn't told Mina everything; not because she hadn't had a chance to, but because she knows, deep down, that Mina will punish her for her sins and she's still scared.

Useless bitch!

'No!' she tells the voice. 'Leave me alone!' She doesn't realise she's spoken aloud until she sees one of the neighbours glancing at her suspiciously as she walks by. Ruth shoots her an embarrassed smile and hurries on towards the house.

She notices something's wrong as she gets there. The door to the old outhouse, Frank's workshop, is ajar. She's sure it wasn't like that this morning, although, now she thinks about it, had she even looked this way when she'd left the house? She hasn't set foot in there for the longest time. That had been his domain, and she'd never gone in there while he was alive; she certainly has no desire to now that he's dead.

She forces herself to investigate, stepping across the yard and negotiating the assorted crap Frank has left behind. She wraps the handle of the plastic bag around her wrist, bringing the glass pesto jar closer to her fist as a makeshift weapon.

As she pushes the outhouse door, it grinds open with a familiar scrape. The noise awakens a realisation; Frank had stopped using the workshop long before he died, but she's heard the sound much more recently than that. Hearing it again now, recognising it for what it is, she knows what it means: someone must have been in and out of here a number of times over the past few days.

Inside, the old workshop is dark but someone has cleared an area and placed some mats and old rugs down on the floor. There's a bowl next to them, with the last dregs of some milk and a spoon. It's from the kitchen – her kitchen.

Drew's been living here, maybe ever since she threw him out. But why?

She turns, intent on getting inside the house now. But he has a key, she remembers. He can get in any time he wants. He must have already been in. She's just considering how she'll go about changing the locks when she sees it. There's mud everywhere. She hadn't noticed properly on the way in, but the more she looks, the more she sees. Dirt and earth, scattered across the grass and pathway, footprints of it leading to and from . . .

The old mound is gone. In its place, there's an irregular hole dug into the ground, bordered by more piles of displaced soil. She finds herself drawn closer. She doesn't want to look, but she can't help herself. Heart pounding, she peers down into the shallow grave and sees them. The remains, a heap of yellowed and soil-encrusted bones now, but enough to tell the shape they once held.

Ruth lets go of the bag in her hand. It unravels from her wrist, falling with a dull thump onto the grass. She feels the fear she's been running from all her life spreading over her like a cold wave. But then, it had never really left.

2 weeks ago

I

'Hello, er . . .'

'Zac,' prompted the young man who'd answered the door.

'Zac,' Tyler agreed.

They stood there for a moment on the doorstep, Tyler refusing to ask the obvious.

'He's not great today,' Zac explained.

'I won't stay long.'

The young carer hesitated, then nodded and opened the door wider for Tyler to come in.

Harry Foster sat in the same place as before, hunched over in the armchair that was much too big for his wasted frame. He was staring at a football match on the television, but if he was taking in any of the action it wasn't obvious from his glazed expression.

'Hello, Harry. It's DS Tyler. You remember me?'

Harry failed to respond, or even to acknowledge Tyler's presence. Zac wasn't wrong about it being a bad day, the man might as well not be in the room at all. How the hell was Tyler going to get the truth from him when he slipped so easily in and out of each moment in time? Tyler glanced across the room at the trophy cabinet full of boxing memorabilia and wished he could search the place properly. It would be highly unethical, and anything he found would be entirely inadmissible in court, but they were way past that now. Then again, with the ever-present carer hovering in the background, even a cursory search wasn't about to happen.

Again, he wondered why he was bothering. Why couldn't he just leave this alone? For Mina's sake if nothing else. Let this old bastard go to the grave with whatever secrets he had and allow the survivors some sort of peace. Wasn't that pretty much what he'd decided when he'd shut away the evidence in his storage unit?

But Alison Beech wouldn't let him rest. If she couldn't, why the hell should he? He'd tried his best to shut out the lingering questions, to rekindle his relationship with Scott, to focus on the cases that he had a chance of solving, but Alison's face returned again and again to haunt him. A young mother whose life had been cruelly cut short; somewhere another bereft son, looking for answers where none could be found.

So here he was again, back with the man who'd started all this.

'Has he said anything?' Tyler asked Zac. If the annoying sod was going to hang around, he could at least be useful.

'No, not really.'

The rapid response irritated Tyler. 'What, nothing at all? Since I was last here?'

'Well, I mean ... nothing about any letters or anything ...'

So much for helping out and keeping him informed. Tyler took a deep breath. It wasn't Zac's fault. What was it about this guy that riled him so much?

Glancing down, his eye was caught by a mark on Foster's wrist. He cautiously lifted the man's shirt cuff with a finger, but Foster didn't make any move to stop him. Tyler could see there were faint bruises on the man's papery skin. He looked up and noticed some bruising around his right eye as well.

'A fall,' Zac explained. 'He's getting worse. I think they'll have to find him accommodation soon.'

Tyler ignored him. These didn't look like the sort of marks you'd get from a fall. They looked like pressure marks, from fingers. He met the young carer's eyes. 'How long have you been caring for Mr Foster?' he asked.

'Just a few months,' Zac said. He seemed nervous. Was he responsible for Harry's injuries? Or was he covering for one of the others?

'It must be difficult, your job.' Tyler tried to tread carefully. He wasn't about to accuse the man directly. He had no proof.

Zac smiled tightly. 'It has its ups and downs.'

The smile, though, never really touched his eyes. He was saying all the right things, but it was as if he didn't really mean them. Tyler supposed that wasn't unusual for someone in Zac's position. Nurses and carers had to go along with you, listen to all your stories and nonsense and pretend they were interested. The best ones could fake it well, but Zac clearly wasn't one of the best ones.

Again, it seemed too incredible to Tyler that Harry hadn't said something since his last visit. He was reliving the past. He'd written that letter, full of apology and remorse. This must be a subject that had been weighing on his mind, and as such it seemed unlikely he hadn't let something slip to Zac. Maybe the carer was being professional and protecting his privacy, though that hadn't seemed to bother him last time.

'How often are you here?' Tyler asked.

'Three or four times a week. Like I said, there's a team of us. I only really do mealtimes.'

Tyler looked at his watch ostentatiously. 'You're a bit early for dinner, aren't you?'

'Oh. Yes. I . . . had some spare time so I came in early to see if I could help with anything. If nothing else it's company for them, you know?'

Tyler nodded, but he was increasingly sure the man was hiding something. 'You mentioned the rest of the team before. Did you get a chance to speak to any of them?'

'Yes. Yes, I did. But no one knew anything.'

It didn't add up. Harry Foster would have said something to someone, even if they hadn't known what it meant.

'I might need to talk to them myself. Do you have a number for your home office?'

'You're him, aren't you?' Harry spoke suddenly and loudly.

'Mr Foster? Harry. I'm DS Tyler.'

'The lad,' Harry went on, and Tyler crouched down so he was at eye level with him. Harry's eyes were still unfocused. Wherever he was and whoever he was speaking to seemed to be far away from the room they were in. 'No one was supposed to get hurt . . . I didn't know, you see? None of us did. Except him.'

'Who, Harry? Who are you talking about?'

Harry frowned and looked back at the TV. 'Not a bad little game, is it?' Suddenly he was back in the room, but was he coherent enough to focus on the topic at hand?

'Do you remember, Harry? Do you remember what happened to Alison Beech?'

Silence. Harry stared at the television screen with a beatific smile on his face. Outside, Tyler was dimly aware of a car pulling up and the engine being switched off. Some small part of him wasn't sure he had the right to upend this man's last days. Wherever he was now, he seemed happy. But if he was responsible, even partly, for Alison's disappearance, then did he really deserve happiness?

He tried one last time. 'Harry!' he said, gently shaking the man's shoulders to get his attention. 'Alison Beech. What happened?'

Harry's eyes settled on Tyler's for the first time. 'He was never gonna let her go,' he croaked. 'He done a deal. With that copper.'

'Who?' Tyler tried to piece it together. 'You mean Frank? Frank had done a deal. With Smith?'

Tyler couldn't be sure, but he thought he saw Harry's eyes widen a little at that.

Just then the front door closed, and a woman's voice called out: 'Only me, Harry!'

Tyler stood up as a petite woman in a blue uniform walked into the room.

'Oh!' she said, as she took him in. 'I'm Jordie.' She didn't ask outright, but the implied question was there. He introduced himself, showing her his warrant card.

There was relief on her face when she discovered he was police.

'Sorry,' she said, 'but we tend to get a bit protective, don't we, Harry?' This last was directed to the chair.

The change that came over Harry was enormous. The grin on his face widened into something genuine and slightly mischievous.

'Gorgeous girl!' he said. 'Gorgeous Jordie!'

'That's me!' Jordie said, immediately setting to work tidying the room around him, collecting used glasses and tissues in a whirlwind of professional activity. 'Goodness me, you've got yourself in a right old mess today, haven't you?'

Something was niggling at Tyler. 'You work with Zac, I take it?'

'Zac?' she said. 'Yeah, I think we have a Zac.'

'Queer fella!' Harry announced.

Jordie frowned. 'No, Harry, that's not nice. We don't say that.'

He grunted something that might have been acquiescence.

'He's here now,' Tyler said.

'Who, Zac? No, he only does Thursdays, I think.' She continued about her business as she spoke. 'Unless he's covering for someone, but he can't be, can he? 'Cos I'm here, isn't that right, Harry?'

'My angel!'

Tyler stepped out into the hallway and poked his head into the small kitchen at the back of the house. Then he checked upstairs, though by this point he was fairly certain he wouldn't find Zac, who must have slipped out as Jordie arrived. What was he up to, if he wasn't supposed to be here? Abusing Harry in some way? Stealing from him?

Back downstairs, Jordie couldn't remember Zac's surname, if she'd ever known it – it was clear they weren't close.

Tyler pointed out the marks on Harry's wrist and she seemed horrified.

'I can't imagine . . .' She trailed off.

'I'll need to speak to your head office,' he told her, and she gladly gave him the details.

Before he left, he made one last attempt to ask if Harry had ever mentioned anything about a woman called Alison Beech or a man named Frank Weatherstone.

Jordie frowned at him. 'If he had, that would be privileged information, wouldn't it?'

'I wasn't aware carers had a code of conduct regarding these things.'

Perhaps that had been the wrong thing to say, because after that he couldn't get a word out of her other than a repeated line about speaking to 'the office'. He assured her he would and let himself out.

II

Tyler ended the call and sat back in his chair with an impatient sigh. He was in a coffee shop on Ecclesall Road, trying to convince himself he had a legitimate reason for being here that had nothing to do with avoiding Mina. He'd had dinner with Diane last night and the whole evening had been awkward silences and shrugged one-word answers on his part. She'd finally come right out and asked him what was going on, accusing him of emotionally shutting down on them again. He'd brushed her off, but she wasn't stupid. And neither was Mina. He couldn't avoid her forever.

The manager of the care company had been a little more helpful than Jordie had during the previous day's visit, especially once Tyler had started making noises about the possibility that one of his staff might be abusing clients. Even so, he wouldn't furnish him with Zac's number over the phone, instead agreeing only to pass on Tyler's own contact details to Zac.

Given the sharp exit the lad had made, he wasn't really expecting Zac to call, and was only finishing his coffee while he decided on his next course of action – a visit to the office to follow up on the suspected abuse was an annoying prospect but seemed inevitable now. The problem was, it would make things just that little bit more official. He'd almost certainly have to explain his interest in Harry Foster, and it was unlikely that news of his visit wouldn't get back to Franklin somehow. But it looked as though Foster might be being abused in his own home; Tyler couldn't ignore what he'd seen. While he sat there ruminating, his mobile buzzed with an unknown number.

'DS Tyler.'

'Oh, yes. Hi. This is Zac Davies. I was told you wanted to speak to me?'

Tyler tried to hide his surprise. 'Yes, Zac. Thank you for calling me. I needed to ask you a few more questions regarding Harry Foster but you left very quickly yesterday.'

After a pause, Zac answered with a question of his own. 'Yesterday?'

'At Mr Foster's home. You left when your colleague arrived. Jordie, is it?'

There was another pause, longer this time, and Tyler was just on the verge of checking whether the man was still there when he finally spoke.

'Sorry, DS Tyler. I think you must be confusing me with someone else.'

This time it was Tyler's turn to go quiet. Had he somehow got the wrong man? The voice on the other end of the line did seem a little different.

'You weren't there yesterday?'

'I haven't been to Harry Foster's home for months. I asked them to transfer me. There were some issues with Mr

Foster's . . . er . . . worldview, and well, to be honest, I couldn't put up with his shit any longer.'

Tyler thought fast. 'This might sound a bit odd, but could you do me a favour, Zac? Do you think you could text me a recent photo of yourself? For identification purposes.'

'Of me? What, like a selfie?'

'If you've got something.'

'Er, yeah, sure. No problem.'

Tyler waited while Zac did as instructed, and after half a minute or so his mobile chimed with a new message. There were two subjects in the picture, but one was a young woman. As Tyler examined the features of the man in the photo, Zac's tinny voice came over the speaker with a nervous giggle. 'I'm the one on the left.'

The man in the picture was clearly not the man he'd spoken to yesterday, or on his previous visit.

'Zac, are you still there?'

'Yes, I'm here.'

'I'm sorry for the mix-up, but you might still be able to help me identify the person I spoke to. Perhaps he's a colleague of yours? He's about six foot two. Rake thin. Quiff hairstyle.'

Zac must have been thinking about the description because he went quiet again for a bit. When he spoke, it was a little hesitantly. 'Erm, I went on a date with a guy like that a few months ago. We met on a dating app. He wasn't really my type, but he seemed keen to meet and . . . well, it's sometimes hard to meet anyone who isn't looking for only one thing so I thought, why not? Only, all he wanted to do was talk about work. He was a bit dull, really.'

'And he fits the description?'

'Yeah, especially the quiff. Bit old-fashioned.' There was a beat and then Zac went on, 'Hang on a sec, I'll see if I can find his pic on the app.'

This time the pause lasted a lot longer, but eventually Tyler's phone beeped again, and this time the photo that appeared was very familiar.

'Yes,' Tyler said. 'That's him. I'll need to interview you properly about this, but for now, do you remember the guy's name?'

'Yeah, I've still got the message history. The name on his profile says Drew. Only . . .'

'Go on.'

'Well, when we met in person he introduced himself as Luke. I mean . . . it's not unusual for people to use nicknames on these things but I remember thinking it was a bit weird.'

Luke. Short for Lucas? Like Lucas Beech.

'Thank you, Zac. I'll be in touch.' Tyler was about to hang up when the other man spoke again.

'Erm . . . am I in trouble or anything? My manager says I need to come into the office straight away and . . .'

'No, you've been really helpful, Zac. I'll ring your manager back now and straighten out the confusion.'

Tyler ended the call and sat back again. *Family is everything.* That's what Kamal Rabbani had said. Tyler had assumed he was talking about Mina, but what about Alison's family? Lucas Beech had only been four years old when his mother went missing though, so he couldn't possibly have been involved in her disappearance.

Of course, that didn't mean he wasn't involved now.

friday evening

1

Mina waits impatiently on the doorstep. It hadn't occurred to her to ring ahead – she'd been fairly certain she'd find Ruth at home. It had felt inevitable, as did the sense that Ruth would tell her the whole truth this time. But it's late, the house is dark and it's possible she's in bed already. Mina feels the burden of politeness telling her to go away and come back in the morning.

No, she thinks, *to hell with that*. She's done being polite. At the very least, Tyler would have been to see Ruth, and there was a distinct possibility she'd been involved in what had happened to him. She presses the doorbell again and again, pulsing it with her finger. Still nothing.

Except ... was she imagining it, or was that the muffled sound of movement from somewhere inside?

Mina bangs her fist on the door. 'Ruth, can you open the door please? I know you're in there, I can hear you.'

There it is again, a faint whisper of noise.

'Ruth, if you want me to, I can get on the radio and call for backup, but if I do that we're gonna be banging your door down and I don't think you want the neighbours hearing all that fuss, do you?'

It's a complete bluff but it does the trick. A light switches on somewhere in the house, and she can hear Ruth shuffling towards the front door and fumbling with the latch.

As the door inches open, Mina sees the defeat in Ruth's eyes. This is a woman who's ready to talk, the pressure of whatever secrets she's been holding on to these past twenty years weighing down on her so heavily that Mina can see it in her hunched shoulders, her bent back. And yet, she only opens the door a crack and peers out.

'Ruth, can I come in?'

'It's late.'

'I realise that, but this is important. You can't keep running.'

Ruth hesitates, then seems to come to a decision. She nods and unhitches the chain.

'You'd better come in then.'

Mina steps into the hallway. The house is much larger than it seems from the outside. It's an ex-council property, and in an advanced state of disrepair, but it has high ceilings and big rooms. The residence of some bigwig politician or industrialist of the Victorian era. Done up and put on the market, it could fetch a tidy sum, even in this not entirely desirable area.

Ruth sees Mina looking around. 'Frank bought it off the council in the Eighties,' she explains.

Mina follows her into a front room that, other than its much larger dimensions, is similar in design to Harry Foster's place. Given that Foster's letter was what had originally tipped them off as to Weatherstone's involvement, she supposes that, in later life, they hadn't remained friends. Even so, their endings had mirrored each other.

Ruth doesn't offer Mina a seat or take one for herself. They simply stand in the middle of the room, facing each other. Only now does Mina notice the state Ruth is in. Her clothes are dishevelled and filthy, her cardigan torn at the sleeve. Her face and hands are smudged with dirt and her eyes are red and raw from crying.

'Ruth, what happened to you?'

She shakes her head, her voice trembling. 'It doesn't matter. He's not here, I checked.'

'Who?'

Ruth ignores her. 'You know the truth now, don't you?'

Mina's thrown, unsure where to start. 'I know your father kidnapped me when I was a child. And I know why.'

Ruth slowly nods her head. 'I looked after you a little bit,' she says.

Suddenly Mina's very aware of the fact that she's likely been in this house before. She doesn't know if she was ever in this actual room, but it's still a disconcerting feeling. 'I suppose I should thank you for that, then. Was it . . . was it here?' she asks, a chill running up her arms and down her back.

'I'm sorry,' Ruth says. 'I wanted to tell you that. It's all I ever wanted from you. To tell you how sorry I am that . . . that I didn't do more.'

Her hair is tangled and there's something stuck in her fringe. It looks like a piece of moss. Whatever anger Mina's stored up over the past few days evaporates in the face of this broken woman. She can't find it in herself to hate Ruth. She doesn't particularly like her; in fact, Ruth disturbs her on some visceral level Mina can't pinpoint. But she doesn't hate her.

'It wasn't your fault. You were just a child.' She knows the words are true, but she's not sure she sounds convincing enough to give Ruth what she needs. Regardless, Ruth nods in mute thanks. Mina continues, 'But I still need to know what happened to DS Tyler. And Alison Beech. I think you know the answers to both of those questions, don't you, Ruth?'

Ruth doesn't answer her directly, but she doesn't deny it either. 'I thought things would be different once he was gone,' she says, staring around at the nicotine-stained walls of the room. 'But he's still here.'

It takes Mina a moment to work out who she means. 'Your father?'

'I thought you'd find out. When Detective Tyler came to the door, I thought that was why. And it wouldn't have mattered. I was always going to tell the truth if anyone asked. It's just . . . they didn't.' She falls silent again.

Mina can hear a clock ticking somewhere. 'Ruth?'

Ruth jumps, pulled out of her reverie. 'I . . . I'll tell you everything I know,' she says. 'But not here. I don't want to be here anymore.'

Mina nods. 'Okay, we can head back to the office. I'll take your statement.'

In the dim light Ruth takes a step closer to her, her expression unreadable. 'There's something I need to show you first. It won't take long, I promise.'

Mina's not at all sure she likes the sound of that, and

something on her face must give her away because Ruth hurries to qualify, 'It isn't far, really. And I'll tell you most of it on the way. I promise.'

last week

I

Ruth knew something was wrong as soon as he came clattering through the back door. That in itself was a sign. She'd never seen him come in that way before. He looked ... she supposed dishevelled was probably the word. The ever-present quiff had flopped over his face, but whereas before she'd found it sexy, now he just looked as though he'd been dragged through a hedge backwards. She hadn't seen him for weeks, and though at first she'd tortured herself with anguished thoughts of what she'd done wrong, now she was surprised at how little she felt. He'd left it too long, perhaps, and she'd got used to being without him. She'd finally begun to wonder if she wasn't better off. Even if she was alone, at least she was free to do as she pleased.

'What's wrong?' she asked, priding herself on the fact that she hadn't leapt up from the table where she was sitting to rush forward and help. It had been her instinctive reaction, but she'd resisted it.

'Nothing.' He seemed distracted. Was he shaking?

His skin was pale and sweaty, and she could make out two dark, wet semi-circles under the arms of his shirt. There was a dark red patch on his left cheek as well. Had someone hit him? He was breathing heavily, as though he'd just run all the way from his place. Maybe he had.

She still didn't know where he lived. 'Over Parsons Cross way,' was the only information he'd ever volunteered. He had housemates, he told her, which was why he couldn't take her there. Only, once, he'd said Gleadless. She hadn't had the guts to ask him about it, so instead she'd followed him one time. She was getting quite good at the whole spycraft business, and the thought that he was inadvertently responsible for that added to the thrill. Luckily he didn't drive, and she'd managed to tail him all the way to some huge place in Fulwood, in a quiet neighbourhood swathed in greenery. She hadn't been able to believe he was living there; it certainly didn't seem the sort of place you'd live with housemates. As she'd waited outside for him, she'd wondered if he was having an affair, and later, she wondered if she cared. In the end though, he'd only been in there for a few minutes, ten at the most. And when he had come out, it had been a man who'd accompanied him, not a woman. A much older man, smartly dressed, and who seemed vaguely familiar, though it had been hard to see him from her hidden position in the bushes further down the driveway. They'd been arguing about something but she hadn't been able to hear the details. Before long, Drew had stormed off and she'd had to duck down so he didn't see her. She heard the older man's parting words though. 'Lucas,' he'd shouted. 'Just stop this!' She'd been so shocked she'd forgotten to follow him until it was too late, so she never did find out where he actually lived.

'Drew, you look terrible!' she said now, aware that, even a

few weeks ago, she wouldn't have dared say anything like that for risk of upsetting him. 'What's happened?'

His lip curled with a snarl, his face screwed into something she could only describe as anguish, but the expression was gone as soon as it appeared. She got up and let him drop into the kitchen chair she'd been sitting in. She touched his forehead to see if he had a temperature, and he didn't even pull away from her like he usually did when she initiated contact now. She couldn't tell if he was sick or just upset, and as she put her hand on his leg, she surreptitiously wiped his own sweat onto the leg of his jeans. There was a dark stain just above his knee. His hands were shaking.

'It w-was . . . It was an accident,' he stuttered.

'What was?' She turned away from him to fill the kettle. She wasn't sure she really wanted to know, and if she looked away from him maybe he'd have a chance to compose himself. He could get his story straight.

'S-some . . . Somebody died.'

She turned to face him again. 'That's terrible! I'm so sorry. What happened?' Inside she was screaming, *Don't tell me! Don't tell me who you are, Lucas. I don't want to know.*

He screwed his face up again, gazing down into his lap. When he straightened, he seemed more like his old self. 'Look, can we just not talk about it, all right?' His voice was hard.

Again, she fought her own instincts, to run across and put her hand on his shoulder. To beg forgiveness for upsetting him. She needed to stay calm. She took a deep breath.

'Okay,' she told him. 'You just tell me when you're ready.'

He rolled his eyes, but she thought maybe that was something to do with shock. Then he exclaimed suddenly, banging his palm down on the tabletop and making her jump. 'Shit!'

She stared at him and he met her gaze, eyes blazing.

'I need you to do something for me,' he said, looking at her from behind that lank fringe of hair. He really was quite an ugly man, and it wasn't just his looks. The kettle clicked off behind her and the boiling water slowly calmed.

'What?'

'I need a place to stay.'

'But you—'

Again, the palm came down on the table. 'Just—' he shouted, but stopped himself, going on in a more reasonable tone. 'Please, this is important. I wouldn't ask if it wasn't.'

She turned around and began pouring hot water into a mug, only vaguely aware there was no teabag in it. 'I don't think so,' she said, without turning back, trying to keep her voice level. She wasn't sure if she could get this out while facing him. 'I don't think that would be a good idea.'

She was ready for him to argue, though it wouldn't matter. She'd made her decision, and she wouldn't go back on it. But he didn't argue.

'Where is she?' he said, his voice full of anguish. 'Just tell me!'

A cold chill ran down Ruth's back. The silence that followed seemed to stretch out forever.

'If I tell you . . .' she whispered, 'will you go?'

Her voice was so faint she wasn't sure he'd heard her, but then the chair scraped as he stood up and she felt him closing in on her, imagined him grabbing her by the throat, choking the life out of her.

He didn't do any of those things. He only said, 'Yes.' So she spoke the words she'd been keeping from him and prayed it would be enough.

After she'd finished he didn't answer. But after a few moments she heard the back door open and close again, and the relief was so palpable her whole body sagged against the counter. She turned and rushed to the back door to lock it. She didn't have a choice now. She'd go to the barbecue at Leigh Raddon's place just as she'd planned, and meet Mina properly. The girl deserved to hear the truth. They all did, of course, but Mina was the only one she knew. She'd make things right, as best she could anyway, and then when Drew, or Lucas, or whatever he was called, sent them, they could lock her up and throw away the key. Before any of that though, she had one last call to make.

II

'Hi,' Scott said, offering the kind of chaste peck on the cheek that indicated even to Tyler that he was in the doghouse.

We need to talk, the text had said.

It made Tyler sad that it had come to this. He didn't blame Scott. He'd been incredibly patient, more so than any other partner Tyler had ever had. Even now, he didn't think Scott would have forced the issue were it not for the fact they hadn't seen each other for almost a month. They'd arranged to meet at the Fat Cat, which was pretty quiet at this time of the day and not too far from where Scott worked. Tyler owed him that much at least. 'Can I get you a drink?' he asked now.

'G&T. Thanks.'

Tyler ordered while Scott took off his coat and got settled. He glanced over at one point and saw Scott watching him. As always though, Tyler couldn't decipher the expression on his face.

When he got back to their table, he decided to take the initiative. 'I'm sorry.'

Scott nodded, that inscrutable half smile hovering about his lips. 'Do you know what you're apologising for?'

420

'I . . .' Tyler hesitated. He didn't want to get this wrong. Was there a chance he could still rescue the situation? 'There's something,' he said. 'I can't go into details but it's important. Really important. And I'm trying to figure out what to do about it.'

Still nothing from Scott. There was simply no way to tell if he was going to accept what Tyler had to say or get up and walk away. Either way, Tyler supposed he didn't have a choice. He'd started now.

'I let this thing get in the way of us though.'

'I think, the question is, did a part of you want it to?'

They were treading dangerously close to psychoanalysis, something Scott had promised he would never do. Not overtly, at least, or unless Tyler asked him to.

'I don't know,' Tyler said.

Scott let out a deep breath. 'One thing no one can ever accuse you of being is dishonest.'

He's not sure how to respond to that.

'Look,' Scott went on, 'I'm not going to offer you ultimatums and I'm not going to pressure you into something you don't want.' He sighed a little. 'I'm breaking my own rules just forcing matters this much but, well, I suppose I don't want to wait around forever.' As soon as he said it, he backtracked. 'Oh God, that's already an ultimatum, isn't it? This is so much easier when it's other people.'

'I don't expect you to wait.'

Scott's voice grew louder. 'No, you expect me to walk away. Like everyone else has. But do you *want* me to? That's all I need to know.'

'No,' Tyler said, without the slightest hesitation. 'No. I don't want that.'

There was a moment of silence, and then Scott smiled. 'Okay, then. That's something.'

'Is it enough?'

Scott's head wobbled. 'I guess we'll find out.'

Tyler's phone vibrated in his pocket. He rolled his eyes, but at least Scott was still smiling. He cocked his head a little, which Tyler took as permission to answer, though he then worried it might have been meant as more of a test. If so then there was no hope for them, because Tyler could more easily have cut off his right arm than leave the phone unanswered.

'DS Tyler.'

'It's Ruth,' the voice on the other end of the line said. 'Ruth Weatherstone.'

Tyler stood up and Scott waved him away. He *was* giving permission, if it was needed. He wasn't upset.

'One moment,' Tyler said. The line was faint, and he was struggling to hear over the clamour in the pub. He pushed through the back door and into the yard, where a couple of drinkers were enjoying the late summer's evening. 'Yes, Ruth. What is it?'

'You ... You wanted to know about my father. And that woman. Alison.'

Her words pushed on something deep in Tyler's stomach. This was it. He'd pretty much given up on hearing from Ruth, sure she wouldn't answer any more questions unless he had something concrete to leverage when questioning her.

'Yes,' he said, carefully. 'I still do.'

'I ... I'm ready to tell you what I know.'

He checked his watch. The rush hour traffic would slow him down. 'I can be at yours in about half an hour.'

'Do you think ...?' She trailed off. 'Could it wait until tomorrow? It's late and ... I just don't feel up to this right now.' Her voice was trembling.

'Of course. Ruth, are you okay? Are you in some sort of danger? I can help if you are.'

'No, it's not ... I don't think so. I don't think he'll come back.'

'Who?' Tyler was suddenly sure he knew the answer. 'Who, Ruth? Who might come back?'

The line was quiet, and he wondered if she'd rung off, but then, her voice small and weak, she said, 'Lucas. I don't know his surname. But he calls himself Drew.'

'Ruth, listen to me. He isn't there now, is he?'

'I think he's done something. Something bad. He seemed really upset and there was blood on his clothes.'

'Where is he, Ruth?'

'I told him what he wanted to know. I mean, I'm not completely sure but ... I think it's where she is. Where he put her.'

Tyler was desperate to ask more but he held his tongue, scared she'd clam up again.

'That old cinema,' she said at last. 'On Abbeydale Road. The one with the big dome.'

'The Picture House?'

'I think that's where he took her after ...'

'Okay, Ruth. I want you to make sure all the doors are locked and then sit tight. If you think you're in any danger at all, you ring 999. Immediately. Do you understand?'

'Yes.'

'Okay, I'll be in touch.'

Only as he hung up did he think about Scott. But by the time he got back to the table, Scott was already draining his glass and slipping on his jacket.

'Don't!' he said, as Tyler began to apologise. 'Really, it's fine. The job isn't the problem. I know it's always going to be like this. But that's the point, it's *always* going to be like this. So, when you're with me, I need you to be *with* me.'

Tyler opened his mouth to speak but had no idea what he wanted to say. Instead, he just nodded. There was hope, at least. And that was all he could ask for.

'Take your time,' Scott told him. 'Do what you have to do, and call me when you're really ready.' This time the kiss was on the lips.

Tyler hung back for a minute or so, allowing Scott time for a proper exit. He wondered if it would be the last time he'd see him. He really didn't want it to be.

Perhaps that was the answer Scott had been looking for.

III

He shouldn't have gone back there. Lucas knew that now.

He'd panicked after the business with Harry Foster and acted without thinking. All he'd wanted was to shower and change and scrape the blood from his clothes, and he'd gone to the first place he'd thought of, and the nearest.

But she'd just sat there, looking at him as if he was some kind of stranger. God, he hated her. It was all he could do to keep his hands from wrapping around her neck and squeezing the truth out of her. The thought of what he'd done to get close to her made him feel physically sick. And then she'd told him what he'd waited so long to hear, and he almost had been sick.

The door at the back of the cinema had been locked but it hadn't been hard to jimmy it open with a discarded metal bar he'd found by the fence. He still held the bar in his hand as he searched. And searching was now the problem. The place was huge, much bigger than he'd realised from outside. He should have made her tell him more before he'd left. He should have made her tell him exactly where that monster had buried his mother.

As he searched on, room after room, many of them without lighting, many more full of junk, he thought about her, sifting through the few memories he had. As though, if he could just summon up a clear enough image, it would lead him to her. He'd tried to find pictures when he'd gone home the other week but there hadn't been a single one anywhere in the house.

Home. Did he even really think of that place as home anymore? It might have been the place where he'd grown up, but it had also been the place where he'd spent the worst years of his life. Why had he ever gone back in the first place? He should have known the reception he'd get.

Nine months ago, more or less. That's how long it had taken for his life to fall apart. People had babies in that time, he supposed, so why shouldn't a life end just as quickly?

He'd just lost yet another job, broken up with yet another clingy girlfriend, and more or less decided on a whim he was done with Canada. He hadn't expected to be welcomed with open arms exactly, but he couldn't have known just how bad it would be. He'd been there less than three months when he'd overheard their conversation.

'He's my son!' His father, pleading his case to his sparkly new wife. 'I can't just throw him out.'

'He's weird, Dom,' she'd told him. 'I don't want him near the girls.'

He didn't really blame his father. Dominic had tried to love him, in his own way. But Lucas thought he must have been a constant reminder of her, of all that Dominic had lost. Never mind the fact that her disappearance had been Lucas's fault. It was him they'd been after. His mother had fought back to protect him. If she hadn't have done that, everything would have been different. His whole life. Their whole lives. He couldn't hate his father for hating him.

Since that overheard conversation, he'd known his card was marked. That's what had sent him rifling through his father's office looking for cash that day. But what he'd found was the letter. *I know who killed her,* it said, and a lot of other crazy nonsense besides, but it was signed plainly enough. *Harry Foster.*

He'd nearly thrown up all over his father's desk. Before he'd even thought about the ramifications, he'd gone to Dominic to ask about it.

'It's just another crank, Lucas,' his father had told him. 'Do you know how many of these I've had over the years?' No amount of cajoling had made him take the letter more seriously. In the end, after a week of being harangued, Dominic had put his foot down. 'I think you need to start looking for your own place,' he'd said.

Finding out where Harry Foster lived hadn't been hard. It was useful sometimes, having a father whose name you could drop when you needed something, especially if you could also throw cash at anyone who was being particularly unco-operative.

But getting in had been harder. Foster never answered the door, and the nosy neighbour had been there too often to attempt a break-in. He'd watched the place for a bit and discovered the carers who came in once or twice a week, though he'd never once managed to get a good look at the combination of the key safe on the wall. That had taken real ingenuity.

He'd clocked the male carer as a mincer the minute he'd seen him. And that was the thing about the gays, wasn't it? They were all on one or other of those hook-up apps. He'd only had to follow the bloke for a few hundred metres before his name and face popped up. After that, it had taken two drinks, a carefully steered conversation and a bit of sleight of hand to access the guy's phone and find the code among his work messages. It had all been surprisingly easy. He wondered if he would have slept with Zac if he'd had to. Probably. It couldn't have been any worse than what he'd had to do with Ruth.

Harry had been a tough nut to crack, but he'd got there eventually. And that was what had led him to Ruth, who, in her own way, had turned out to be even tougher than Harry. By then his father had run out of patience and he was being given his marching orders, but she'd been more than happy to take him in. All it had cost him was a roll in the sack now and again. Only it hadn't taken him long to figure out that he couldn't stay in that house. The same place his mother's killer had been living a few weeks before. He couldn't bear it, any more than he could bear Ruth's hands on him before long. He'd booked into a hostel, using up the last of the guilt-money his father had given him.

His mother had brought him here once, he suddenly remembered, as he turned a corner and found himself in the cinema's vestibule. They'd shared popcorn in the plush seats of the darkened screen. He pictured her beaming smile full of bright white teeth, her long golden hair cascading around her shoulders. She was there somewhere, waiting for him, calling him.

Lucas knew she'd forgive him for the things he'd done. For Harry Foster. Why had the stupid old goat followed him upstairs? In an instant, everything had changed. He'd spent months gaining Foster's trust, gently prodding his memory. It had been hard work, learning the real carers' routines and slotting his own visits into the days in between. But he'd been making real progress, and the man had seemed to be remembering more and more with each passing day. It would surely only have been a matter of time before Lucas could have pieced together the whole thing, and in the meantime he'd searched the place for the answers he was looking for.

Why had Harry chosen that moment to recover his senses well enough to tackle him head on? The man had been unfeasibly strong, and quiet too. Lucas hadn't heard him coming up from behind until the very last moment, far too late to stop Harry's right hook from connecting. Who would have known the old codger had so much strength left in him? It had been shock more than anger that had made him lash out, pushing Harry away and towards the stairs. Although, if he thought about it, there had been a moment when he could have reached out and saved the old man. But he hadn't. He'd watched Harry fall backwards, the look of horror on his face proving he understood what was finally waiting for him at the bottom of those stairs. Judgement for his crimes.

He had watched Harry bounce down the stairs, imagining his brittle bones snapping with every thud. He'd smelled the warm, coppery tang of Harry's blood flooding out of his head even as he carefully stepped over the body on his way out. He'd made no attempt to call for help, to aid him in any way. Did that make him a murderer? Perhaps. But still, he knew she'd forgive him.

Lucas was moving through the main auditorium for the

second time when he heard the noise coming from the bar by the main entrance. He stopped mid-stride and listened carefully. It was definitely footsteps. Backtracking quickly, he jumped up the short staircase to the stage, only realising at that point that he'd cut himself off from the exit. His hand tightened on the metal bar. It was an offcut from an old fence post, he guessed; something left behind by whichever set of builders had last worked on the place. It was the kind of thing that would be easily forgotten, he thought. Left to lie for decades; discarded, useless, just existing with no awareness that it had a future purpose waiting for it. He knew how that felt. Well, now he had a purpose. He was going to find her.

He could feel himself on the edge of panic as he heard the metal door at the back of the auditorium begin to grind open. Before he'd even thought about what he was doing, he'd grabbed the metallic rungs of a ladder and was hauling himself up into the gantry running above the stage.

He willed his feet not to make any sound, though the rungs creaked and groaned as he moved. *Calm down*, he urged himself. It was unlikely that whoever it was would be able to hear him over the noise they were making themselves. Just as he reached the top, a torch beam sliced out across the room. He shrank back into the corner, tucked behind one of the flats.

'Hello?' Tyler's voice echoed through the darkness. 'I'm Detective Sergeant Adam Tyler of South Yorkshire Police. If there's someone else here, you need to make yourself known. You're not in any trouble.'

Of course it was him. There was a certain inevitability to it. But how the hell had he found him here? Did the police know about Foster already? There wasn't usually a carer in on a Sunday; he should have been safe for a few more days yet.

You're going to have to sort out your own mess this time, Lucas. That's what his father had told him just a few hours ago. He'd gone there before heading to Ruth's, to throw himself on Dominic's mercy, begging him for help. Surely, with his father's clout – his money, his connections, his lawyers – they could find a way to beat this. Lucas hadn't meant to kill Foster. He had grounds for diminished responsibility, surely?

His father hadn't thought so. He'd been strangely calm about the whole thing, though his voice had been icy as he'd spoken. 'You think you didn't leave some kind of DNA evidence on Foster, or in his house? Let me tell you, son, you did. But that's okay, you don't have a criminal record, so they won't connect you. At least, not yet. This Tyler fellow's seen you there twice, so it's only a matter of time before he works it out. The fact you were there at all, that makes it premeditated. You'll definitely do time for this.'

He'd panicked, grabbing Dominic by his shirt collar, begging his father to help him. He couldn't go to prison. What could he do?

Dominic had shaken him off. 'Do what you want,' he'd said. 'But leave me out of it. For once in your life, be a man.' Then he'd thrown him out of the house.

Now Lucas hefted the metal bar in his hands, feeling its weight. *For once in your life, be a man.* Could he do it? Could he murder someone in cold blood? How did that make him any different to Frank Weatherstone and Harry Foster? If he let himself think about the mechanics of it, the fact that he would have to bring the heavy bar down on the head of an innocent man, to end one life so that he could get away with having ended another ... The metal post trembled in his hands. He tightened his grip.

But he had to do it. Dominic wasn't going to help him. He was on his own. Maybe his father would even be proud of him after this.

Again, the fence post trembled. He could sense, more than see, Tyler moving in the darkness below.

What an idiot he'd been! Getting himself into this position. He was a sitting duck up here, and if he tried to climb down now Tyler would hear him coming a mile off.

He heard the rungs of the ladder creak in the darkness. Tyler was on his way up. Lucas couldn't believe it. He'd had the upper hand and now he was just sitting there, waiting to be discovered. The bar was still in his hands, but it wasn't trembling anymore.

He could see Tyler now, an indistinct shape in the gloom as he hauled himself up onto the gantry. If the policeman looked this way, would he see him? With that torch in his hand, probably. All Lucas could do was keep still.

Then something on the far side of the stage caught Tyler's attention and he turned the other way. 'Police!' he shouted, the noise echoing around the rafters and sending a chill down Lucas's spine. 'Come out!'

It all happened very quickly. As Tyler inched his way across the precarious gantry, a pigeon came flapping out of the darkness on the other side. He fell backwards, his torch spinning away and smashing on the stage below. For a moment, Lucas thought his job had been done for him. But no, the detective had managed to cling on to the gantry railing and was climbing back to his feet. What choice was there? Tyler would have to come back this way, and there was zero chance he wouldn't see Lucas crouching there in the shadows. It was now or never.

In the end, it was surprisingly easy. The gantry shook under the weight of the two of them, but there was no longer any time for thought. He moved fast, decisively, the bar coming up and over his head before he brought it down hard on the back of Tyler's skull, the reverberation thrumming up the length of his arm. And then he pushed.

Tyler tumbled away from him, the rail giving way beneath his weight. The gantry swung wildly, and it was all Lucas could do to hold on and not follow the policeman to his death.

He heard Tyler hit the floor, and then a further crash as the rotten boards of the stage collapsed with the force of the impact.

Lucas hung on, the gantry swinging slowly to a halt. The silence settled around him. He could feel his heart beating so hard in his chest that it felt like it would burst right out, and his hands shook as he crept back towards the ladder and down to where Tyler had landed.

Edging towards the hole, he could just about make out the policeman's body in the darkness below. He wasn't moving. Lucas knew he should go and check if the man was dead, but he couldn't bring himself to do it, even if he'd had any idea how to get down to where Tyler lay. Fear seized him. He had to get out of there. He picked up Tyler's fallen mobile more from instinct than anything else, fumbling the metal bar still clutched in his hands. He'd throw them both in the river – with any luck, no one would find the body for a while yet.

He hurried back to the door and out into the night. Despite everything, he felt a fleeting pride that he had the forethought and nerve to check for cameras before crossing the car park. His heart was still racing as he slipped away down the road, keeping his head down, just in case.

Now what? He couldn't go to his father, and he'd no more money for a room anywhere. Also, if Tyler had found him here, maybe that meant the police knew more about him than he'd thought and were out looking for him. He should probably head straight back to Canada, but his passport was still at home. It might take time to convince Dominic to help him with that. There was only one option left. He had to go back to Ruth's.

His stomach clenched as he thought about being in that house again, but then a thought came to him. Her old man's workshop out in the yard. It would be warm enough at this time of the year, and dry. And he still had a key, so he could slip into the house when she was at work and get food, maybe even take a nap. He doubted she'd notice. She wasn't all that observant. He steeled himself. It would be difficult staying there again, in that place where his mother's killer had lived. But he'd done it before, and he could do it now.

Then, once he'd had a chance to get himself together and he was sure the police weren't looking for him, he'd confront her. This time he'd make her tell him everything she knew. After all, he'd killed before. Twice, now. And, if he had to, he'd do it again.

Sleeping Dogs

This time, there'd be no more secrets, no more lies. Ruth would tell him where his mother really was, and the full story of what had happened to her twenty-four years ago.

24 years ago

I

The girl is asleep in the dark with only the dog for company.

Ruth holds the bedroom door ajar and watches her through the crack. The light from the hallway doesn't quite reach the bed, but she can see the outline of the girl's body. Beyond that, a blanket of brown fur betrays its owner and tells Ruth her guess was right.

'Heathcliff,' she calls in a whisper.

She isn't supposed to come in here. Only Teri is, when she takes the girl food with the crushed-up tablets mixed in to keep her sleepy. The penalty for breaking this rule could be harsh, but the dog needs his dinner. She suppresses a wave of shame; her motives aren't quite as pure as all that. If she's honest with herself, she's jealous that they've let the girl have the dog. It's her dog! Her bedroom as well, though she's used to that sacrifice. Whenever her father has these 'guests' to stay she's relegated to the zed-bed in the pantry off the kitchen. It's cold and cramped but, unless it's mid-winter, that isn't what bothers her. It's the thought that someone else is in her room. She knows she shouldn't blame the kids. It's not their fault, after all, but still, she can't help the irrational fear that one of these days he might decide to keep one of them and then she might be confined to the pantry forever. Or worse, discarded altogether.

She hates the way Frank makes the whole gang live with them when they have a job on. She knows when they're up to something; when they're committing some awful crime somewhere, innocent people getting hurt because of it. Shame ripples through her again, as she remembers their other 'guest's' situation.

Mind, the others do bring life to the house when they stay. Teri with her feminine clothes strewn around the front room, drying on the radiators. Harry pulling funny faces in his daft attempts at making her smile. He's been doing that for years and hasn't figured out she's way too old for it now. The urgent sounds of their lovemaking in the early hours of the morning.

And Kamal. He's a bit more sober than the others; literally, since he doesn't drink anywhere near as much, but in his nature as well. He always has a smile and a kind word for her, especially when she brings him his tea while he's working in the study, his sleeping bag rucked up under the radiator.

Most importantly, they all distract Frank from taking everything out on her. He very rarely hits her when the others are here.

'Where the *fuck* is he?' Her father's voice reaches her all the way from downstairs in the kitchen. Heathcliff raises his head and growls, his ears twitching in response to his master's rage. Ruth acts without thinking, slipping into the bedroom and closing the door behind her.

Something crashes across the room downstairs. She thinks

it's probably a mug or a plate; it shatters, but with a much deeper sound than glass would make. At least that means the windows are still intact. The last time he smashed a window he made her tape it up with brown paper and they'd had to go through the winter with it like that before he'd finally got round to fixing it.

Ruth presses her ear against the door in order to hear better, aware that if he hears her moving about up here, she'll be the one who cops it. She can hear Harry trying to calm him down, talking in that gentle, reasonable way he has. Harry's the only one who can talk her father down from one of these episodes. She's tried copying him, when it's just her and Frank, and Frank gets upset about something, but she never seems to get it right. Instead, she's learned to keep out of the way when he gets like this. As far as that's possible in this house.

She glances at Heathcliff, his ears still twitching as he sits on the bed, body relaxed, but ready to launch himself up if necessary. The girl – Mina – sleeps on next to him, undisturbed.

She's grateful for Heathcliff. They've only had him a few months – a gift from Harry, who'd won him as part of a bet. Frank had accepted the gift with his usual grace and gratitude, that is to say, none. But since then, he's come around to the idea. And best of all, since the dog arrived she's noticed her father has become far less likely to give her a clip round the ear, or worse. *Thank you, Harry.*

Heathcliff – despite his fearsome German Shepherd pedigree – had turned out to be a big softie for the most part. Unless he was protecting Ruth. The first time her father had hit her after they'd got him, Heathcliff had launched himself at Frank, Ruth watching in amazement from where she'd lain on the floor, her hand pressed to her face. Since then, she's kept him as close as possible, and Frank's taken to ignoring her more than ever.

It had been her idea to name him Heathcliff, after a character in one of her precious library books, but Frank had knocked that idea on the head pretty sharpish. 'I'm not shouting that down the park,' he'd snapped at her, as though he'd ever be the one taking the dog for walks. 'We'll call him Vince, and that's the end of it.' And he does.

Something else crashes downstairs, and her muscles tense, readying her body for flight. But this time, she recognises the duller, deeper thud – a chair going over maybe, or the Argos catalogue being swept off the table. Whatever it is, it's a sign he's de-escalating; the worst of this particular incident is over. Harry's still talking to him, his voice soft and soothing. Ruth moves across to the bed and looks down at the girl. She pats Heathcliff's thick fur. 'There, there,' she says, calming the beast, just as Harry is doing below. She wonders if her words are really meant for the dog.

'*Ruth!*' Frank's summons echoes up the stairwell, and Ruth jumps and runs to the door, Heathcliff leaping off the bed after her.

She pulls it open no more than a foot and glances out. He's standing at the bottom of the stairs with his back to them, still talking to Harry.

'I'll kill the slimy little fucker, you see if I don't.' The 'slimy little fucker' is Kamal. She's heard her father call him worse, and others too, but he's the only one not currently in the house. He's the reason the girl's here too. Mina. She's his niece.

442

'Frank,' Harry's saying. 'I know he's a twat and all, but are you sure this is a good idea? I mean, what if the family—'

'Ruth!' her father shouts again, turning and catching sight of her.

'What?' She doesn't mean to sound cheeky, and she knows it's a mistake as soon as the word's out of her mouth. But for some reason she can't help it. There's a rebellious streak opened up in her lately.

She really shouldn't poke the bear.

'Get down here. Now!' he shouts, and her courage flees.

She edges reluctantly through the door and Heathcliff takes the opportunity to bound down the stairs ahead of her. Ruth thinks she sees her father flinch slightly, and she finds the strength to straighten her back.

'All right, lad,' he tells the dog. 'I wondered where you'd got to. You looking after our guest, eh?' It's a stark contrast to the way he talks to her, and she finds her resolve stiffening as she steps out onto the landing, pulling the door closed behind her. Frank looks up at her as she hovers at the top of the stairs, his hand brushing the thick, long fur of Heathcliff's coat. 'Come down here,' he tells her, sternly, but not too sternly. In fact, he seems strangely calm given his behaviour a few moments ago. That raises the hair on her neck. It's worse when he's calm. He likes to make sure she doesn't see it coming.

She inches her way down the stairs, trying not to take too long but reluctant to get any closer. He wouldn't hit her with Harry and the dog right there, would he?

'All right,' he says, as though they're coming to some

compromise. 'We won't be gone long. Teri'll keep an eye on them, just do as she tells you.'

Them. It's the first time he's openly acknowledged their other guest. The woman in the cellar. Ruth doesn't want to be alone in the house with both of them, and she worries Teri won't stick around long if Harry's not there. But she nods her agreement.

He tickles Heathcliff behind the ears. 'You be good for your Auntie Teri, all right?' He must be talking to the dog. He never talks to her like that.

Behind Frank, Harry's nodding at her gently, an encouraging smile on his face. *Just do as he says. Keep him sweet.* That's always Harry's attitude.

'Should I give her some food or—?'

Frank tenses. He doesn't like questions, and normally she'd avoid them. But sometimes it's better to risk asking, rather than get it wrong. The dog begins to growl, a low, deep rumble. Frank lets go of his collar and straightens up.

'You stay out of there, you hear me? The cellar *and* the bedroom. Just do what Teri tells you.' Then he turns and heads out the door without looking back.

Harry ruffles her hair and gives her a peck on the top of her head. 'You'll be all right, sweetheart. We won't be long.' Then he, too, is gone. Ruth feels the tension ebb out of her shoulders.

Heathcliff takes the opportunity to head into the kitchen to see if there's anything on offer, leaving Ruth standing alone in the hallway. She can hear the TV on in the front room, Teri watching her soaps. *Home and Away* and *Neighbours*. She glances at the door leading down to the cellar. The key is in the lock. That's unusual. He tends to take it with him when he goes out.

She walks slowly towards the door and presses her ear against the wood. She listens for a couple of minutes, but she can't hear anything. Her hand reaches for the key but stops, hovering a few millimetres from the metal. She pulls back.

She heads into the front room and, sure enough, Teri's lying on the sofa in nothing but a frilly pair of panties and an old check shirt of Harry's that's buttoned so low that one breast is poking out. She's painfully thin, and she has that glassy-eyed look that says she's taken something.

Ruth doesn't dislike Teri. In fact, sometimes the woman's really friendly to her. Ruth's got to know her quite well over the past couple of years, and it was Teri she'd gone to when she'd discovered the first spots of blood in her knickers. Teri had bought a box of tampons for her and told her what to do. She'd even given Ruth some advice for the stomach cramps and once, when Ruth had got drunk on Frank's whisky while the men were out, she'd got her to bed and covered for her when he'd noticed it was missing, owning up to drinking the remnants of the bottle herself. Now she thinks of it, Ruth supposes Teri's the closest thing to a mother she's ever known. Even if she's barely ten years older and has a tendency to be semi-naked and off her head a lot of the time.

'Hi,' Ruth says now.

Teri grunts something that might be a reply and waves her delicate hand in the air without taking her eyes off the telly. On the screen, two beautifully tanned young people are having an argument on a beach.

'Do you know where they've gone?' Ruth asks, moving around the sofa into Teri's eyeline.

The young woman peers at Ruth through half-closed lids and seems to notice her properly for the first time. 'You all right, hon? Here.' She hauls her skinny legs off the sofa and pats the cushion next to her in a manner that's almost conspiratorial. 'Why don't you come and watch this with me, eh?'

Ruth's unexpectedly touched. Teri knows Frank doesn't like her watching TV; doesn't like her leaving her room – or the kitchen – unless it's on an errand of some kind. She circum-navigates the glass-topped coffee table to reach the other side of the sofa. The surface is littered with half-empty beer cans and overloaded ashtrays, the latter mostly stolen from the local pub. Around these are scattered the remnants of Rizla papers, discarded roaches and tobacco strands, a glass of water, its rim smeared with lipstick, and an empty packet of Durex. There's even one of those green bar towels with the Tetley logo on them. It's mostly used for mopping up beer spillages, although Ruth did once find it wedged down the side of the sofa, and when she pulled it out it was all crusty and hard. She'd changed her mind and left it where it was. Thankfully, Frank rarely makes her clean in here.

She sits down and tries to focus on the telly. Teri does her best to explain the storyline, but she doesn't sound as though she properly understands it herself. In any case, all Ruth can think about is the woman in the cellar.

She's been there for four days now, longer than any of their other 'guests', and as far as Ruth knows she hasn't been allowed out once, not even to use the toilet. Ruth isn't supposed to know about her – isn't supposed to know about any of what they get up to – but they don't make any real effort to keep things from her. She's invisible to them much of the time, and what she does see, she's expected to ignore. She sees – and hears – a lot more than any of them realise, though. They still think of her as a child, but she's older now. Old enough to know. She's seen Teri take down food once or twice and come back out with a bucket. She's heard the woman crying out hysterically, begging to be let go. She's felt the reverberation of the cellar door slamming when Frank goes down to 'shut her the fuck up!' She knows the woman is called Alison Beech, and she knows what Alison Beech looks like because she's seen her picture on the cover of the national newspapers at the local shop when she goes round for extra toilet paper and the like. She knows the police are looking for her everywhere across the city. And finally, she knows that none of the gang know what to do with her.

What she doesn't know is whether the woman's all right. She'd tried to sneak down yesterday, and when Frank had caught her he'd nearly taken her head off with the smack he'd given her. He'd shaken her, hard, taking full advantage of the fact the dog was in the garden. He'd screamed at her to mind her own bloody business and, if she couldn't, she wasn't too old yet that she couldn't get a good hiding. She'd thought that hiding was imminent, until Harry had intervened.

Despite Frank's reaction to her attempt at rebellion, Ruth had lain awake last night and thought about the woman – Alison – in the cellar. The temperature had dropped, and it wasn't as though the place was heated. She'd considered trying again, sneaking down in the dead of night with a blanket, but had seen no way she could do it without Frank finding out. He had an instinct for these things, and she'd no doubt she'd get caught. But that defiant part of her just won't shut up.

'Do you think we should give her some food?' Ruth asks, quietly.

'Hm?' Teri's gaze stays fixed, if not on the telly itself, then somewhere in its general direction.

'Has . . . Has she had anything to eat today?' She only narrowly avoids using the woman's name. She has to remember what she isn't supposed to know. 'I could fix her a sandwich or . . . ?'

Teri's head turns, and she frowns through whatever drug-induced haze her brain is fogged with. She looks at her watch and the frown deepens, before she glances at the soap opera on the telly, as though weighing up how urgent the request is against her need to stay rooted where she is.

Ruth attempts to solve the dilemma for her. 'I don't mind taking it down.'

'I don't think . . .'

'Really, it's no problem. Dad said I was to do what you said.'

'Did he?'

'I thought maybe just a glass of water. And a sandwich.' Ruth risks one extra gambit. 'I could empty the bucket for you as well.' She's seen the way Teri's mouth twists into a grimace when she's forced to carry the thing up to the bathroom.

'Well, I suppose it couldn't hurt . . .'

'Okay, great.' Ruth jumps up and makes for the door.

'Hang on,' Teri says, half raising an arm.

Ruth stops in the doorway, her heart thudding in her chest.

'There's a sandwich in the fridge already made. On a plate, on the top shelf. Don't give her anything else, yeah?'

Ruth agrees and hurries out before Teri can change her mind, but she's confused. Why is there a sandwich already made? Teri's never struck her as anywhere near that well organised.

In the kitchen, Heathcliff looks up at her and whines. He's sitting next to the back door with his big, pink tongue flopping out between his teeth. She empties some chunks of Pedigree Chum into a metal bowl for him – the last of it, since Frank's told her he's only to have the cheap stuff from now on.

'Good boy,' she tells him, stroking his fur as he wolfs it down. 'Make the most of it.'

When he's finished, she lets him out the back door and he races off to chase a squirrel down the bottom of the garden. She supposes she should probably get out there later and clear up some of his mess. If she leaves it too long, Frank will start threatening to get rid of him.

The sandwich is exactly where Teri said it was: on the top shelf, with a small square of clingfilm clamping it to the plate. She takes it out, and then, as an afterthought, grabs a Capri-Sun as well.

It's as she's closing the fridge door that she sees the handbag on the worktop next to the microwave. She's seen it before and wondered about it, but she's never had the guts to look inside. She's pretty certain it's not one of Teri's. Besides, it hasn't moved for days. If it was Teri's, it would flutter around the house just like the rest of her belongings. There's something about it that looks both dangerous and inviting. Ruth couldn't stop herself from looking now even if she wanted to. She puts down the plate and the glass.

Inside there's a small pack of Kleenex and a brush – a thick-handled, wiry-bristled thing with blonde hair caked around it. She pulls a strand loose and lets it drop to the kitchen floor. Then there's a plastic tube of some sort. It takes Ruth a moment to work out what it is. It's for holding an emergency tampon. This unexpected connection to the woman makes her hands tremble. There's a purse inside as well, but when she opens it, she doesn't find any cash. She supposes Frank will have already taken that for himself. But there are three credit cards – a Visa card, a Mastercard and a Diners Club – each with her name picked out in embossed lettering. MRS A. BEECH. Nestled beside the purse are a set of keys, with a small plastic picture frame attached. The picture is of the woman, her husband – Ruth recognises him from the newspaper reports – and a young boy, standing in front of an enormous fairy-tale castle. On the reverse, the same boy is hugging an oversized Winnie-the-Pooh. The only other thing in the bag is another plastic tube of some kind. It looks more pharmaceutical though, and is covered in tiny text that lays out some kind of operating instructions. It says 'EPIPEN' on the side in large letters. As she examines it, Teri's words come back to her. *Don't give her anything else.* That must be why the sandwich is already made. Alison must be allergic to something. Ruth looks down at the Capri-Sun in her hand and the extensive list of artificial ingredients. She couldn't be allergic to any of those, could she? She decides not to take the chance and leaves the drink on the side. Instead, she grabs a pint glass from the sink, rinses it thoroughly and fills it with water, letting the tap run for a bit first so that it's nice and cold.

Back at the cellar door, she has to hold the glass in her left hand with the plate balanced precariously on her wrist while she turns the key with her right. Even then, it's stiff, and she has to push her weight against the door to get it to open. As she eases herself carefully down the steps, she's pleased to see the lights are on. At least Alison hasn't been in the dark all this time. Teri's work, no doubt.

It's a big cellar, stretching away under the entire house, with separate divided spaces formed by the structural walls. Ruth hasn't been down here for a while, but she used to come down all the time. She'd played down here when she was little, and she knows the layout well. She'd never been a skittish child and, anyway, the risk of spiders and rats had always been preferable to the risk that Frank might decide to lash out.

She finds Alison sitting on a kitchen chair near the old coal chute. She looks wary at first, as well she should if she's had a taste of Frank's hospitality – a black eye and a cut on her forehead tells Ruth she has. When Ruth gets closer and Alison can properly make her out, the light of hope enters her eyes.

'Please!' she says, her terror and urgency burning through in that one word. 'You have to let me go. Please.'

Ruth can't say anything. She holds out the plate and glass as though they explain everything. Perhaps they do, because the light in Alison's eyes dies again. Her lips are cracked and split in places, and her hair, long and blonde as in the newspaper picture, is now a tangle of dull straw. If she didn't know who she was, Ruth would have difficulty identifying her as the same woman she's seen smiling in a glossy colour photograph on the front cover of *The Daily Star*.

'What is it?' Alison asks, defeat settling around her and weighing down her shoulders.

It's then that Ruth sees the bicycle chain wrapped tightly around one of her legs and padlocked to a bolt on the wall. It must stop Alison from moving more than a few inches in any direction. Just far enough to reach the bucket. She does at least have a couple of old blankets to lie on, but Ruth can't imagine it would be easy to sleep with her leg trussed up like that. Her clothes are a mess, and she has on a cardigan that Ruth recognises as one of Teri's. It's too small for her and is filthy with dust and dirt from the brick floor.

'Corned beef and pickle, I think.' Ruth walks forward, crouching to avoid the low beam, and puts the plate and glass down on the floor. She inches them both closer, ready to run if the woman makes a grab for her. Even if Alison were capable of it though, the fight has long gone out of her.

'It's all right,' Alison says, her tone resigned. 'I won't hurt you.'

'He'll . . . He'll let you go soon.' Ruth wants to say more, but in truth she's not even sure of this much.

Alison laughs, but there's no humour in the sound. 'I've seen his face,' she says. 'I've seen your face.'

Ruth takes a step back, suddenly aware that Alison is right. She should have thought of that: Harry and Teri always wear balaclavas when they come down here. Just by being in the cellar she might have endangered this woman's life.

Alison shuffles down off the chair and reaches for the sandwich. She lifts the topmost layer of bread and examines the contents for a moment, then lets it drop again. Picking up the glass, she downs the contents in one before putting it back on the ground.

'Please,' she says. 'Can I have another?'

Ruth looks at her watch. Frank had said they wouldn't be gone long.

'Please!' Alison begs.

Ruth nods. She picks up the glass and turns to leave, glancing at the bucket with its dark contents blessedly unidentifiable in the dim light. She decides to leave it until she comes back. She hurries back up the stairs without turning around.

When she goes back into the kitchen to refill the glass, she sees the handbag again and stops for a moment, Teri's words playing in her head. *Don't give her anything else.* But she'd meant food, surely? Nothing else could hurt. She reopens the bag and at first thinks she'll take the keys with the photograph attached. Surely Alison would appreciate seeing her family again. But then she wonders if there's a chance, however small, that one of the keys on the ring might fit the bike lock. It's probably impossible. But what else might Alison use the metal for? Could she scrape away at the mortar around the bolt on the wall? Ruth shakes her head. It's too risky. Her father would kill her. She could take the keyring off, but the ring itself is still metal. Alison might be able to refashion it into some kind of lock-picking device. Ruth wants to take something back with her though. Something small as a gesture of defiance against her father, and which might make Alison feel better. Her eyes fall on the hairbrush. Maybe Alison wouldn't appreciate it but ... where was the harm?

Ruth refills the pint glass at the tap, picks up the brush

and retraces her steps back to the cellar door. She pauses for a moment. There's still no sound coming from the front room other than the telly, and no sign of her father or Harry. She pulls open the door and begins her descent.

She hears Alison before she sees her: a strangled, gurgling sound like the noise Harry makes sometimes when he's pulling a funny face. At first she thinks it *is* Harry, and she looks behind her, expecting to see both him and Frank standing at the top of the steps, looking down and catching her in the act. But that doesn't make any sense. If she'd been caught, the first she'd know of it wouldn't be one of Harry's comic turns. And the sound is much more sinister than that. It raises her hackles. A small part of her knows what she'll see even before she's reached the bottom of the steps and turned the corner.

It's a scene from a nightmare. Alison is on the floor, writhing, and the sound is definitely coming from her. Her legs are bucking and flailing. One of them connects with the bucket and sends it careening against the cellar wall, where it hits with a hollow slosh and upends, spilling urine and faeces out across the ground. Alison's hands are clawing at her throat, and to Ruth it looks as though she's trying to strangle herself. Opening her hands, she dashes across the cellar, barely registering as the glass shatters at her feet and water splashes up her legs. Her instinct is to stop Alison, to pull her hands away and end this futile attempt at self-harm. But now she's closer she sees the truth. Alison's throat has swollen to twice its normal size. Her whole face is bloated and red, the skin mottled with a terrible rash. She isn't trying to strangle herself; she's desperately struggling to breathe.

Next to her lies the overturned plate, and around it the

remnants of the half-eaten sandwich. As soon as Ruth sees it, she understands. The EpiPen. She turns and runs, shouting, 'Hang on!' behind her, as though that will make the slightest bit of difference. She races up the stone steps and crashes through the doorway back into the hall. 'Teri!' she screams. And again, 'Teri!' But she doesn't wait for a response. She runs on, into the kitchen and towards the handbag by the microwave. She rummages through it but can't find what she's looking for; her hands feel non-responsive, swollen and useless like Alison's neck. She picks up the bag and upends it, scattering the contents across the worktop.

There! She grabs the pen and turns and runs. All her actions feel too slow. Like she has to think about everything before it happens. Raise left foot, move it forward, put it down. Raise right foot ...

Teri is in the doorway to the front room, still red-eyed and scratching her head as though she's some cartoon caricature of confusion. Ruth doesn't stop to explain, but Teri must see the pen in her hand because suddenly her eyes widen and clear.

'No!' she says, but Ruth's already turning towards the cellar door.

Down the steps she hurtles, still feeling as though she's moving in slow motion, her whole body crashing against the brick wall at the bottom. Her socks soak up the spilled water and a shard of glass pierces the sole of her foot, but Ruth doesn't stop. She races to Alison's side.

Alison's movements are sluggish now, her legs no longer flailing, her hands still at her throat but no longer clawing.

'No! No, please!' Ruth begs. She raises the pen but she has

no idea how to use it. She tries to focus on the writing on the side, but in the dim light and through her unshed tears she can't read anything.

Suddenly, Teri is there. Teri, who, before she met Harry and Frank and took up a life of crime, was training to be a nurse. *Thank God!*

Teri stops for a millisecond, staring down at Alison's pitiful face. 'Shit!' she says. 'Give it to me!'

She grabs the pen from Ruth's hand and pulls at something, maybe a tab on the cap – it's hard for Ruth to see.

'What the fuck—' Teri fiddles with the pen in her hand. 'Come on, come on!' She bends over, puts the tip to Alison's swollen neck. 'Why isn't it . . . ?' All at once, she stops. 'It's empty. Oh Christ, it's empty! Why would she—?'

'What?'

'It's fucking *empty!*' Teri screams it, frustration cracking her voice. She bends over again and lifts Alison's wrist, feeling for her pulse. 'Shit!' she says again. She lets the hand drop, and there's a finality to the movement that sends a chill rippling up Ruth's spine.

'Shit, shit, shit!' Teri shouts. There's a moment of absolute silence, and then she stands up and walks away, leaving Ruth still hunched over Alison's lifeless form.

'You can't stop!' Ruth tells her, but Teri's standing with her back to them, staring at the cellar wall.

'She's gone, hon,' she says, her voice shaking. Then she swears again, a long, anguished scream. 'Shiiiiiit!!'

'We need to call someone. Call an ambulance!' Ruth can't believe she hadn't considered this before.

'No!' Teri shouts, turning back to her. She looks down at the sodden floor, where a slice of corned beef is soaking up a puddle of urine. 'What did you give her?' she demands, and now she's grabbing Ruth by the shoulders, pulling her to her feet, shaking her. 'She was allergic to shellfish! She told us! What did you give her?'

'Nothing! Just the sandwich. And a glass of water.' Ruth's cheeks burn as she remembers the hairbrush she'd intended to bring Alison. But that couldn't have had anything to do with this, and she'd never got the chance to give it to her.

Teri suddenly lets go, and her hands fly to her mouth. 'Oh my God! He did it.' She seems to be speaking to the room at large rather than Ruth in particular.

'Who?' Ruth asks, but even as she says it, she knows the answer.

'That bastard! He's insane. I thought it was weird when he offered to make it earlier but ... Oh, Jesus! Oh, Christ! I ... I need to get out of here.'

Teri lets go of Ruth and runs up the cellar steps. Ruth follows, but stops at the bottom and looks back at Alison's crumpled body, still chained to the wall. It was the sandwich, it had to be. No one died from drinking a glass of water. Either way, whatever it had been, it had been Ruth who had given it to her. *She* had killed Alison. She had wanted to help her, and instead she had killed her.

On her way up the steps, she becomes aware of the pain in her foot, and when she gets to the top she sits down on the topmost step to take a look. She pulls off her sock and digs out a shard of glass: a stinging sensation shoots up her leg, breaking through the numbness, and she almost revels in it. The blood is thick and dark red, spilling out over her fingers. She uses the soaking wet sock to wipe it away, concentrating hard on the task at hand. In this moment, nothing else feels real.

Teri reappears from the front room, stuffing her clothes into a shoulder bag. She stops when she sees Ruth, but then she seems to gather her resolve and goes for the front door.

'Please!' Ruth begs her. 'What should I do?'

Teri stops, her hand on the Yale catch, the door still closed. 'I'm sorry,' she whispers, without looking back. Then she pulls open the door and is gone.

II

Ruth isn't sure how long she sits there, poking at the wound in her foot. It might be only seconds or minutes; it might be hours. However long it is, she comes to herself only when she hears the van pull up in the driveway. Then she moves without thinking.

She pulls the sock back over her foot, wincing at the stinging cut, then jumps up and slams the cellar door, turning the key in the lock. She hobbles into the kitchen and lets the dog in, only now becoming aware that he's been whining to come in for a while. If she has to face Frank, she wants Heathcliff next to her.

The front door crashes open and it's Kamal she sees first, his face a mass of bruises and cuts. He falls through the doorway and onto his knees. Frank appears behind him, snarling, 'Get in there!' He grabs Kamal by the shoulders of his shirt and pulls him up, pushing him into the front room and slamming the door.

Frank turns to find Ruth watching from the kitchen doorway, and she knows he knows before he even says anything.

'What happened?' he asks, his voice unusually measured.

Harry comes through the front door carrying an enormous

holdall. He drops it to the floor with a thud as soon as he sees her. 'Oh, Jesus! Look at the state of you. What happened?' He runs forward and puts his hands on her shoulders. 'Ruth? What is it? Where's Teri?'

Frank's staring at her and he knows. She can see it in his face. He's almost smiling. His eyes flick to the cellar door and then back to her, and Ruth feels her cheeks heat up.

'Teri!' Harry cries, letting go of Ruth and barging past Frank towards the front room. Frank lets him go, then walks straight to the cellar door. He unlocks it, his eyes still on hers and that half smile on his lips. Then he disappears down the cellar steps.

Harry re-emerges, glancing first at Ruth then at the cellar door before he follows Frank down the steps.

Ruth bolts. She runs up the stairs, Heathcliff bounding after her, aware that something's wrong but also ready for a game. She opens her bedroom door and sees the little girl, Mina, sleeping peacefully in her bed. She walks across and scoops her up in her arms. Mina stirs, opens her eyes a fraction.

'It's okay,' Ruth tells her. 'You can go home now.'

The girl's body is light enough, but it's awkward coming down the stairs with her. As she reaches the bottom, she sees Kamal stumbling out of the front room, still in a daze.

'Go!' she tells him, pushing Mina into his arms.

'I . . .'

'Just go! Now. Quickly, before they come up.' She opens the front door and half-pushes him out.

He hesitates for just a moment, the little girl cradled in his arms. 'Thank you,' he says, before she closes the door on them.

III

The curious thing, the thing that has her thinking so hard about everything, weighing it all up in her mind for days to come, is the fact that Frank never even tells her off.

They find her there, when they come back up, standing with her back to the front door as if she can physically stop them going after Kamal. But Frank says nothing, just dips his eyes once to the floor, making sure the holdall is still where Harry had dropped it. Then he turns and heads into the front room. Harry follows, his face ashen after what he's seen in the cellar. Ruth tiptoes after them both.

'Where's Teri?' Harry asks. But the way he says it reveals he already knows the answer.

'Gone,' she tells him anyway.

'Allergic reaction,' Frank says. 'Could have happened at any time.'

'Sure,' Harry says, but not a one of them believes it.

'We just need to get rid of her now. We'll shove her in the foundations before we finish off that room under the stage. Then we go on. As though nothing's happened.' Her father's eyes never leave Ruth. 'Only five hundred grand richer and with two less people to share it with.'

'The Picture House?' Harry's voice is strangled. 'But . . . it's his bloody building!'

'All the better. If she's ever found, they'll figure it was him.'

'Oh, sure,' Harry says again. 'And you think he'll keep quiet about your little arrangement?'

'He will if he knows what's good for him.'

Harry says nothing to that.

'Rabbani's not gonna say nothing,' Frank goes on. 'And that bird of yours has flown the coop.' His gaze leaves Ruth for a moment. 'Shame about that, but she wouldn't have stuck around long anyway. Probably for the best.' His eyes find her again. 'The thing is, we're all part of this now, but only one of us is a murderer. No one needs to know she was here. No one will even know she's dead. And if anyone finds out, I'll know who to come for, you get me?'

Ruth can feel her body trembling. She and Harry say nothing.

'Good,' Frank adds. He turns to Harry. 'Clean this place up while I deal with downstairs.' Then it's Ruth's turn – his lip curls as he speaks. 'Don't just stand there, you useless bitch. You can take the rubbish out.'

She does as she's told, of course. She's not even slightly surprised when she finds the half-empty packet of prawns on the top of the bag.

friday evening

1

'He killed him in the end.'

They're standing in the run-down auditorium, looking down at the hole in the stage that Tyler had created when he'd fallen.

'Heathcliff,' Ruth clarifies. 'He got sick, and Frank didn't want to pay any vet bills. So he took him out back and hit him with a spade. He made me watch.'

Mina had driven while Ruth told her story. She'd only agreed on this trip on the proviso that Ruth let her ring for backup first. Even then she wouldn't have let the other woman come in here, but something in her gut had told her to go along. It's probably what Tyler would have done.

'Ruth, I ...' She has no idea what to say, so she watches instead as Ruth shuffles ahead in the light of the torch on Mina's phone, listening as she talks on, as though to herself.

'That's how I planned to do it to him. With a spade. If I thought I could have managed it, I would have.' Ruth stops, staring down into the darkness, and Mina realises with a lurch in her chest that this is the spot. The place where Alison Beech lies buried in cement. They've found her. *Tyler found her! He literally fell on top of her.* The thought almost makes Mina laugh, and she wonders if she's hysterical. Whatever happens to him, she thinks he would be happy about that.

'I hoped you'd put it down to a mercy killing, because he was sick and in pain. But it wasn't, and I wouldn't have lied about that either, if he'd asked me about it. Tyler. But he didn't.'

It takes Mina a moment to work out what Ruth's saying. She must have misheard or . . .

'Ruth. Are you talking about your father?'

'It wasn't mercy,' she says. 'I looked him in the eye and made sure he knew what I was doing. It was the opposite of mercy. I wanted him to suffer.'

Mina's suddenly very aware of her surroundings. She's alone in a dark, crumbling building, with a woman who has just confessed to murder. She should just get out of here until the others arrive. As her heart hammers, Doggett's voice invades her head. *You have to be better than the rest of us.*

She keeps her voice steady. 'Ruth, I need to read you something now, okay? I need you to listen. Ruth, I'm arresting you on suspicion of murder. You do not have to say anything, but it may harm your defence if you do not mention when questioned something which you later rely on in court. Anything you do say may be given in evidence. Ruth, do you understand what I've just told you?'

'Yes, I understand.'

Mina's not sure if she really does, but right now all she wants to do is get the woman out of here.

'Okay, let's get you back to the station then, eh? You can tell me about it there after we've found you a solicitor.'

'What about her?' Ruth asks, pointing. 'What about Alison?'

Mina swallows down a wave of equal parts revulsion and sadness. 'She'll be okay a bit longer.'

If Ruth hears her, she shows no sign of it. 'He made me do it. He turned me into a murderer.'

She's close to the edge, and Mina rushes to take hold of her hand, stopping her with her arm outstretched. For a moment she hadn't been sure whether Ruth had been about to jump in the hole after Alison. She gently folds Ruth's hand back to her side and guides her down off the stage.

'*No!*'

The scream takes them both by surprise as a man comes hurtling down the aisle towards them out of the dark. Mina flinches, adopting a defensive stance, but Ruth steps forward to meet him.

'I'm sorry, Drew—' Her words are cut off as the man – Drew – lashes out at her, hitting her hard in the face with the back of his fist. Mina lunges for him, the urge to protect hard-wired into her, but he pulls something from his pocket and, almost in the same movement, seizes hold of Ruth as well. Still startled from the punch, she puts up no resistance, and before Mina can move more than a foot or so the man has Ruth pinned in front of him, a screwdriver pushed tight against her neck.

'Don't!' he warns, but Mina has already stopped, her hands raised in front of her in that universal if useless attempt to stall.

'Okay . . . okay.'

'She's there, isn't she? I heard it. I heard what you said.' He's crying, the tears thick and wet on his cheeks. 'Why didn't you fucking tell me?'

'Drew, I did. I—' Ruth tries to talk, but he pushes the screw-driver further into the folds of her neck.

'Don't call me that! My name is Lucas!'

'Hey!' Mina calls. She needs to distract him. 'Lucas, you said? Lucas, look at me. My name's Mina. Mina Rabbani. I'm a police officer.'

'I know who you are!'

Ruth has her hands clutched around Lucas's arm. Her eyes are bulging and she's struggling to breathe. If Mina could just reach her radio . . . but as her hand starts to move, Lucas tightens his hold on Ruth's neck.

'Okay, well, I don't know you yet, Lucas, but I know you don't want to hurt anyone, do you? Please. Let Ruth go. You're hurting her.'

He seems to think about this. 'I do want to hurt her,' he hisses, but Mina notices he loosens his arm slightly. She takes that as a good sign.

His face creases up in real anguish as he directs his attention back to Ruth. 'She . . . She's been here this whole time? All these years . . .' His voice tails off into a wail and the screwdriver pushes further into her neck. 'You knew! You knew!'

'No, I . . . I didn't know she was your mother. If you'd told me . . .' Ruth's voice is raspy, cut off by the pressure on her neck.

His mother. Lucas Andrew Beech. The boy who wasn't kidnapped.

'Lucas!' Mina shouts, grabbing his attention again. 'Look at me.' She waits until she's sure he's focused on her before she goes on. 'You don't want to do this. You don't want to kill anyone.'

'It's too late,' he wails. There are tears coursing down his cheeks. 'All these years I wanted to know what happened to her and nobody else cared! If I ever asked Dad about it he'd just fob me off. Then he got married again and it was like she never even existed. But she did! I was there when they took her. I remember!'

As he's talking, the screwdriver wavers. A thin trail of red seeps down Ruth's neck.

'What do you remember about that day, Lucas?' Mina can feel her heart still thudding hard in her chest. Where the hell is the backup she asked for?

'They . . . They said afterwards it was me they'd wanted. But they took her instead.'

'They took me, too,' Mina tells him, forcing the words out. 'I was the same age as you, and they took me and locked me in a room, just like your mum. I was terrified.' Mina sees his arm tense at that, and wonders if she's misjudged. She pushes on quickly. 'But Ruth was the one who let me go. She helped me, Lucas.'

'She didn't help my mum.'

'None of this was Ruth's fault, Lucas. It wasn't yours either.'

'I know it wasn't my fault.' But his voice betrays him. He's been living with this for more than two decades. 'They didn't even touch me. No one would listen at the time, but they didn't even try to grab me. That bitch lied. They knew what they were doing. They went straight for her. She shouted for me to run but I didn't. I just stood there. I told them again and again. My father, the police. They all said I was traumatised, remembering things wrong. But I wasn't.'

'She loved you,' Ruth says, suddenly. She chokes slightly as Lucas tightens his grip again.

'Let her speak,' Mina commands, and he responds to the authoritative tone.

'I know she did,' Ruth says, meeting Mina's eye. Mina warily nods for her to go on. 'All she ever cared about was whether you were safe. She kept a photo of you in her bag. I . . . I was going to bring it to her when . . .' Ruth trails off, overwhelmed by emotion. Mina silently urges her not to mention the sandwich. She doesn't know how much Lucas heard, but if he discovers Ruth gave his mother the food that ended her life, she's not sure what he might do.

'Ruth was telling me about what happened,' Mina says, carefully. She hopes the woman picks up on her words. 'It might have been Frank who killed Alison, but it was your father who planned it, Lucas. That's right, isn't it, Ruth?'

'I—'

'Think about it, Lucas. That's why they took her and not you. They'd only ever kidnapped children before that but, like you said, they made no attempt to kidnap you. They went straight for your mum. She was never supposed to survive. Your father paid Frank to make sure she never came back.'

Lucas is shaking his head, but Mina can see she's reaching him. It's a risky strategy. She's not even sure she's got it all right. She's piecing it together from what Kamal told her, but she has no proof. If she's wrong about this, she might be doing more harm than good, but at least what Lucas has said fits her theory. She goes on.

'All those times he tried to tell you that you'd misremembered. He was trying to deflect. He wanted to avoid a costly divorce, so he got rid of her. You said it yourself: "like she never even existed". It's him you should be mad at, not Ruth. She was only a kid herself. Her father treated her even worse than yours did you. *He's* the one who should pay. He's the real killer here. Don't let him turn you into a killer too.'

'It's too late,' Lucas whispers, and there's an emptiness to his voice that chills Mina to her core. She tenses, ready to counter any sudden move.

'The only thing I ever wanted was to find out where she was.' Lucas's voice is hoarse and shaky. 'Foster wrote to him, said he was sorry, that he knew who'd done it. But the dementia . . .'

Foster. *That was Lucas?* If he's capable of killing an old man, he's more than capable of driving a screwdriver into Ruth's neck. Mina treads lightly, saying, 'You were angry, Lucas. There was a struggle, and he fell. I'm sure a good solicitor will be able to make a case for it being accidental. But this would be different. Killing a woman in cold blood in front of a police officer is very, very different.'

But Lucas shakes his head.

'I had to hit him. He found me. Here, at the cinema. She must have told him where I was.' The screwdriver pushes forward into Ruth's neck, and she flinches, letting out a whimper.

Mina feels the hair rise on her arms. She wants to take this man down for what he did, but she has to stay calm.

'DS Tyler isn't dead, Lucas. Do you hear me? He's still alive. You can still come back from this.'

He shakes his head again. 'It's too late,' he whispers.

'Lucas, drop the screwdriver. Now!'

He won't meet her eye.

'Lucas!'

'I'm sorry,' Ruth gasps, her hands still clutching at his arm around her neck. 'I'm so sorry for everything.' Before Mina can do anything, Ruth reaches up and grabs Lucas's hand, driving the screwdriver into her own flesh.

'No!' Mina screams as she dives forward.

Afterwards, she figures out that Lucas must have resisted. When Ruth grabbed his hand, he must have instinctively pulled away, because otherwise Mina never could have made it in time.

Her own hands clamp around both of theirs. She twists her body, pushing back against Ruth, against Lucas, pinning him against the row of seating behind them. She hears Ruth's rasping breath, then Lucas's own gasp. She thrusts her full weight against the two of them, digging her fingers into the veins and muscles of his wrist. When she sees the screwdriver drop, relief floods through her in a wave. She immediately pivots, twisting Lucas's hand and using it to turn his whole body. Ruth stumbles away from them and falls to her knees, crying. Mina uses Lucas's momentum to force him in front of her, twisting his arm up behind his back, but he makes no attempt to resist now. She pulls out her handcuffs and places them around his wrists.

'Lucas Andrew Beech, I'm arresting you on suspicion of the murder of Harry Foster and the attempted murder of DS Adam

Tyler. You do not have to say anything, but it may harm your defence if you do not mention when questioned something which you later rely on in court. Anything you do say may be given in evidence.'

Only then does she take a moment to relax and catch her breath, adrenaline coursing through her bloodstream and threatening to floor her. She can feel every muscle in her body trembling.

Ruth is still on her hands and knees, sobbing into the floor. Mina has the strange thought that Emma's going to kill her for contaminating her crime scene. As if that matters after all these years. She bends down carefully and picks up the screwdriver, slipping it into her pocket in case Ruth has any further thoughts of self-harm.

'Ruth,' she says gently. 'You need to get up, love. Come on, now.'

But it's as though a floodgate has opened, and Ruth can't stop her tears now they've started. Still, Mina helps her to her feet and guides her up the aisle, under the crime scene tape and back towards the entrance they'd come in through. Lucas doesn't put up a fight as Mina leads him along behind her, marching the two of them out of the dilapidated cinema and over to her car. Only then does she realise that she can hardly put them both in the back together and re-thinks, sitting them down a couple of metres apart on the kerb with her standing in between.

She pulls out her radio, but the promised backup finally arrives before she can make the call. She's only mildly surprised to see it's Danny, but shocks herself utterly when she throws her arms around him.

'You okay, Min?' he asks.

She exhales loudly and then pushes him away again. 'Fine. It's . . . been a long day.'

He grins. 'It's not over yet.'

She frowns at him. 'What?' she asks.

'He's awake, Mina. Tyler's awake.'

2

The first thing he registers is sound – hazy snatches of conversation that invade his consciousness like insects buzzing around a streetlamp. Then, and far too quickly, he becomes aware of the pain. It's this that brings him back to the world. It stabs at him, refusing to be ignored. His back, his head, his leg ... it travels through his body, pummelling him without mercy, demanding his full attention.

Tyler opens his eyes and winces at the bright light.

He spends the next few hours piecing himself together. He meets new people – nurses, doctors, the teenager who comes in to replace the water jugs. He learns about his injuries, and is relieved to find out the worst is his leg, which is trussed up in front of him like a work of art, pinned with metal and coated in plaster. The outcome is good; he'll almost certainly walk again. A number of people spend a great deal of time asking him questions, shining torches in his face, testing his brain and his memory. But for his part, he's less worried about these abstract injuries than he is the one he can see in front of him. His toes are black and unrecognisable.

He dozes, slips in and out of consciousness. As if he needs any more sleep! He knows somehow, without having to ask, that he's been out for a while. At one point Diane is there when he wakes up. She talks to him, but he doesn't remember much of that conversation, just her wide smile and the obvious relief on her face.

The next time he wakes he is more himself. There is less shock this time, and the pain feels reduced. Perhaps they've given him something. Scott's sitting in the chair next to the bed. He's asleep. Behind him there's a curtain, and behind that a wracking cough that makes Tyler aware for the first time that he's in a room with other people.

He watches Scott for a while and it dawns on him how glad he is that he's there. He looks peaceful. And beautiful. Tyler can't believe he almost threw this away. Scott has on one of his trademark tight shirts – the ones he wears to the office – and Tyler wonders if he's had to cancel work because of him. He feels a wave of guilt for allowing himself to end up in this position, for worrying everyone when he could have made different choices, though he can't, for the life of him, imagine what those choices might have been.

Scott opens his eyes. 'Hi,' he says.

'Hi.' Tyler's voice is disturbingly small, but he clears his throat and forces out the words he knows he needs to say. 'I'm sorry.'

Scott smiles. 'I know.'

He takes hold of Tyler's hand, and they sit that way for a while. They don't say very much, but it doesn't matter. There doesn't seem to be much that needs saying right now.

Mina and Doggett arrive together, and Scott stands up.

'Wait,' Tyler says, and is surprised to have said it.

Again, Scott smiles. 'I think the police have some questions for you.' He leans down and kisses Tyler's forehead.

'I'll be back,' he says, in a lazy Schwarzenegger drawl, and even Tyler understands this reference. He laughs, and then grimaces at the pain that ripples through his body.

'Well,' Doggett says, after Scott has left and Tyler has brought the pain back under control. 'You've managed to get yourself in a right bloody mess this time, haven't you?'

Mina thumps the DI on the arm, and he mimes an exaggerated pain response.

'How are you feeling?' she asks Tyler.

'It only hurts when I breathe.' He grins at her to show it's meant to be a joke.

'How much do you remember?' Doggett asks.

'Lucas Beech.'

Mina fills him in. 'Under arrest for the murder of Harry Foster and the attempted murder of . . . well, you.'

The relief is palpable. Strangely, the case and what had happened to him had been the furthest thing from his thoughts when he'd woken up. Only when these two walked in the door had he begun to process all that had happened over the past few months.

'Your protégée here has been busy in your absence,' Doggett says, and Mina rolls her eyes at the gibe.

Even so, when she speaks, she can't keep her pride from showing. 'We found Alison Beech too. Buried in the cement under the room you fell into at the Picture House. It's going to take a while to get her out, but the imaging scanners definitely indicate someone's down there.'

'And Ruth?' he asks.

'Also under arrest, but I guess it depends on whether whatever forensic evidence we find backs her story.'

As Tyler listens to Mina outline what Ruth had told her, he tries to imagine what it must have been like to grow up in a house like that. As dysfunctional as his own childhood had been, at least he'd had a father who cared.

'Do you believe her?' he asks as Mina finishes.

She nods. 'Every word. I don't think the CPS will consider it worth pursuing but . . .' She trails off with a 'who knows' shrug. 'She admitted to killing Frank as well.'

'Ah, diminished responsibility,' Doggett says. 'She'll get off.'

'Good,' Tyler says. Somehow, he can only see her as another victim. He can't bring himself to blame her for not telling him everything months ago and saving him a lot of pain and aggro.

But then another memory comes flooding back. 'Mina,' he says, 'there's something else you need to know.'

'Kamal,' she says. 'Yes, I know all about it. I've even remembered some of what happened.'

He tries to work out what she thinks about it all, but he can't. 'I should have told you,' he says.

'Yes,' she says, 'you should have.' But then she manages a lopsided grin that tells him he's forgiven. For now, anyway.

'How are things with your mum and dad?'

'Tense,' she says. 'But we'll get there.'

'And Dominic Beech?' he asks.

'We're pretty sure he paid to have his wife murdered.'

He shouldn't be surprised they've come as far as they have, but it rankles that they've managed to get there in a week when it had taken him months.

'The cash drop for the ransom,' Tyler tells them. 'It was the payment for the hit. It was Kamal's job to handle the money. He's an accountant at heart: I'd be willing to bet he's kept a record of the financial trail somewhere, and that he'll turn it over if you offer him some kind of deal.'

Mina's frowning. 'He never said that.'

'Why would he?' Tyler replies. 'If I'd died his problems would have gone away. He was probably hoping for a different outcome.'

The frown deepens, and Tyler feels the need to offer her something, as a consolation of sorts.

'I think he would have told me more if he could have,' he tells her. 'He told me that *family was everything,* and I don't think he was just talking about you. I think he was giving me a nod towards Dominic.' Sort of. 'I just didn't work it out.'

Neither had he worked out the nod Harry Foster had given him at the start of all of this. *It was beach wh—,* Harry had written. But he hadn't meant 'It was Beech who we killed' any more than 'It was beach where we buried her'. No, the most likely interpretation in light of what they'd found out was 'It was Beech who paid for the hit', or something like that. Tyler just hadn't seen it.

'We'll put some pressure on Kamal,' Doggett chips in, 'but it's hardly in his interest to tell us. Unless you've got evidence we can use?'

Tyler shrugs, and instantly regrets it, the pain shooting

through every part of him. 'Everything I've got is in a storage unit. If you can find Teri Greene, I think she'll co-operate and implicate Kamal. Then you'll have the leverage you need to get him talking. Between them you'll get enough to at least make it worthwhile questioning Beech.'

'There's Ruth's testimony as well?' Mina suggests. 'And Lucas's.'

'It won't be easy.' Doggett shakes his head. 'I doubt we'll get enough to make anything stick to *Lord* Beech.' He looks thoughtful for a moment. 'Still, we might be able to make his life a misery. For a while at least.'

One of the hardest lessons Tyler's had to learn over the years is that you don't always get the result you want. 'We found her,' he says. 'That's the main thing.' It had to be enough.

'I guess Franklin's not going to be too thrilled about all this,' he says, after a moment. 'How much trouble am I in this time?'

Mina and Doggett exchange a look. It's a very slight movement, but to Tyler it might as well be a giant, waving red flag.

'What?' he asks.

'Why don't you just concentrate on getting better?' Mina tells him.

'You leave us to worry about the Beak,' Doggett adds.

'Just tell me.'

This time the exchange lasts longer, and it's Mina who finally answers. 'I'm being transferred.'

'*What?*'

'She's using it as an excuse,' Doggett says. 'All this business about Mina's uncle. But the truth is she's been looking to split you both up since she came in.'

Tyler's not really all that surprised. He's suspected for a while that Franklin had an ulterior motive – he just couldn't work out what. Or why.

'Cost-saving exercise,' Doggett supplies. 'Civvies are a damn sight cheaper than detectives. Or maybe she just thinks Mina's wasted mopping up your messes.'

'I'm sorry, Mina.'

'Oh, stop apologising. Not everything's your fault. Anyway, we knew we wouldn't be working together forever. Maybe a change will be a good thing.' She doesn't sound all that sure though.

'Where's she putting you?' Tyler asks.

'That I haven't found out yet.'

'Maybe it'll be the dog-handlers,' he suggests, and she laughs, loudly.

'What about CCRU?' he asks.

Doggett repeats himself. 'You just get better. Diane will take care of things for now.'

He has a feeling Doggett's not telling him everything, but abruptly he feels a wave of tiredness wash over him, and all of a sudden he's really not sure he cares enough to follow it up.

As he slips back into sleep, his last thought is that maybe Mina's right.

Maybe it is time for a change.

Acknowledgements

In 2022, it was my pleasure to appear at the first-ever Bay Tales Festival in Whitley Bay, where a woman named Ruth Weatherstone won the opportunity to have a character named after her in one of my books. Poor Ruth has had to wait more than two years to see her prize realised and I thank her for being patient. Ruth, I hope you enjoy finally seeing your name on the page and thank you for helping to raise money for the RNLI. It goes without saying, but I'll say it anyway, that the character portrayed in this book is fictitious and bears no resemblance to her real-life namesake.

I wanted this book to be a bit different to the previous ones. Firstly, having been eclipsed by her somewhat challenging boss for the past three books, I wanted to give Mina a chance to shine, but for that to happen I needed Tyler out of the way. It was Phillip Nixon, during a particularly boozy evening down the local, who gave me the idea for the structure of this book, telling Tyler's story in the past while Mina investigates what happened to him in the present. Thank goodness my phone notes were readable the next day (they aren't always).

Secondly, all the previous books in the series start with the unearthing of a body. In real life, and you could be forgiven for believing otherwise, this is a very rare occurrence. Cold case teams are not constantly called to grisly crime scenes where they find decaying corpses covered in clues. Most of the work they do is routine police work: re-examining evidence, retracing witnesses etc. Of course, that isn't enormously entertaining, but I wondered if it would be possible to write something that more accurately reflected this process. I'm hugely grateful, as usual, to former DCI Dave Stopford, manager of South Yorkshire Police's Major Incident Review Team, who offered up (among many others) the idea of an anonymous letter landing on Adam Tyler's desk.

I try to find interesting Sheffield locations to appear in the books, and it was a chance encounter with Jessie Scutts (on another drunken night out) that led me to the wonder that is the Abbeydale Picture House. A huge thank you to Jessie and her manager, Mark Riddington, who showed me around one of Sheffield's great architectural gems. To my knowledge there were no bodies or killers lurking in its labyrinthine depths, but it certainly is a crime that we're allowing incredible buildings like these to fall into disrepair.

I know I often say this, but the book you're holding in your hands wouldn't exist if not for an entire team of dedicated people who, for the most part, go entirely unacknowledged. I've tried to rectify this with the post-film-credits-style section below. I am enormously grateful to you all. Thank you. And I really, really hope I haven't missed anyone off (crosses fingers).

A special mention however to Paul Simpson, who has

copyedited every one of my novels. Most people have no idea how important a copyeditor is. Paul makes me look like I'm a better writer than I am. He knows how many hairpin turns there are on the Snake Pass (FYI – none), what time football matches are shown on TV, what year *Ghostbusters* was released at the cinema, how long it takes to get from Broomhill to the Botanical Gardens, how old Tyler was when his dad died . . . The list is endless. There is nothing he does not know. So I am gutted that this will be the last Tyler book he will copyedit, as he is retiring. Paul, I am truly grateful for all the hard work you've put into this series and I wish you the very best for your retirement.

Once again I'm indebted to multiple editors for whipping this book into shape. From the thoughtful, insightful comments I received from Bethan Jones (at yet another crime festival back in the very early stages of this book), to the highly detailed and nuanced edits I received from Georgie Leighton. Thanks, Georgie! You've put so much into this book and have made it a far better story than I could have managed alone.

Thanks, once again, to my incredibly talented agent, gamekeeper-turned-poacher, Sarah Hornsley, as well as the wider team at PFD who have supported me over the past couple of years, in particular Kate Evans and Rosie Gurtovoy.

Thank you, thank you, thank you to Susan Elliot Wright and Marion Dillon. Without these two, my books wouldn't be worth reading. And special thanks to my good friends Dave and Kirsten Barry, who came up with the name Teresa Greene (yes, we were out on a drunken night out on that occasion, as well).

Finally, thank you, reader, most of all.

485

Thank you to everyone at Simon & Schuster UK who helped to publish *Sleeping Dogs*:

Editorial
Georgie Leighton
Katherine Armstrong
Gail Hallett
Aneesha Angris

Art
Katie Forrest

Production and Operations
Karin Seifried
Mike Messam

Copyeditor
Paul Simpson

Proofreader
Amanda Rutter

Authenticity reader
Hamza Jahanzeb

Audio narrator
Jamie Parker

Marketing and Publicity
Sarah Jeffcoate
Jess Barratt
Hayley McMullan
Harriett Collins

Sales
Mathew Watterson
Maddie Allan
Heather Hogan
Katie Sormaz
Jonny Kennedy
Dom Brendon
Rachel Bazan
Robyn Ware
Rich Hawton
Andrew Wright
Naomi Burt
Rhys Thomas
Nicola Mitchell

Rights
Amy Fletcher
Ben Phillips
Namrata Mistry

Finance and Contracts
Keely Day
Meschach Yeboah
Maria Mamouna
Isabel Ireland